W9-BHN-734

THE GUN KETCH

THE GUN KETCH

Dewey Lambdin

DONALD I. FINE, INC.
New York

Library of Congress Cataloging-in-Publication Data
Lambdin, Dewey.
   The gun ketch / Dewey Lambdin.
      p.   cm.
   ISBN 1-55611-356-0
   I. Title.
PS3562.A435G86   1993
813'.54—dc20   92-54471
CIP

Manufactured in the United States of America

10 9 8 7 6 5 4 3 2 1

Designed by Irving Perkins Associates

F LAMBDIN

To my mother,
Edda Alvada Ellison Lambdin.

Her generous support and unflagging
encouragement never wavers, even if she
does think that Alan Lewrie is a trifle
"lewd" sometimes.

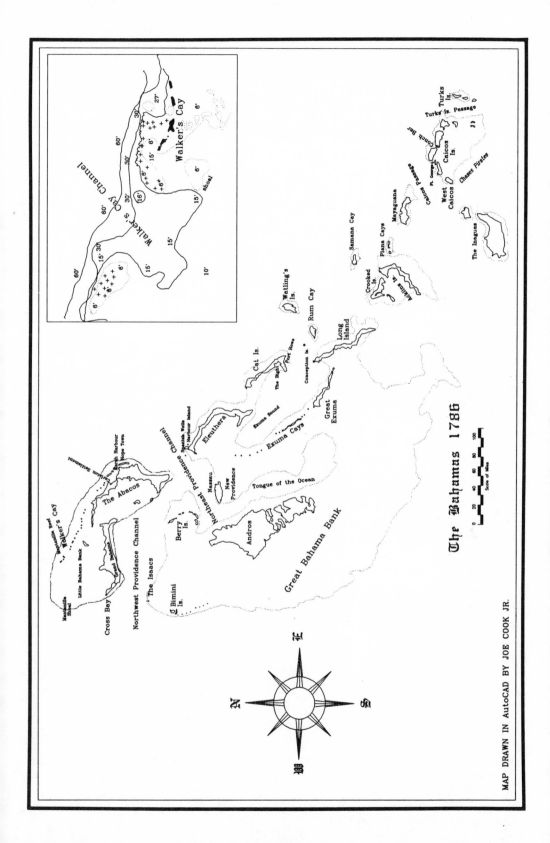

The Bahamas 1786

MAP DRAWN IN AutoCAD BY JOE COOK JR.

Foreword

For those readers unfamiliar with the preceding installments in the adventurous (some would say "reprehensible, nefarious, venal, Just Like a Man, rakehellish squanderings of a ruling-class pig" . . . and, mind you, this chronicler has heard it all at one time or another—but they're all Politically Correct or smugly moral carpers, so who the bloody hell cares what they think?) life of our heroic, if somewhat lazy Alan Lewrie, Royal Navy, allow me to fill you in on some of the highlights of his *curriculum vitae*.

Epiphany Sunday, 1763: Born a bastard. (Now *there's* auspicious onset for you!) St. Martin-in-the-Fields Parish, London, of Elisabeth Lewrie, son of Sir Hugo St. George Willoughby, Captain of the 4th Regiment of Foot, The King's Own. Mother died soon after, and the infant was raised in the Poor House, employed as an oakum-picker and flax-pounder, which showed his nautical bent before he was out of "nappies" in support of H.M. Dockyards.

1766: Rescued by his father (since he had discovered that the last viable Lewrie heir to a positive flood of guineas was none other than our lad Alan) and raised as a gentleman in St. James's Square.

There followed the usual hellish childhood, and a disappointing *series* of schools in which Alan Lewrie excelled at both his studies, and the inventive (some would say inspired) creation of mayhem, one example of which in 1779 resulted in the total demolition, by use of explosives, of the faculty stables and coach house at Harrow.

1780: Arranged to be caught in bed with his half sister Belinda Willoughby so he could be exiled, and never know that he was on the verge of being the last male Lewrie, due that aforementioned golden shower of 'yellowboys,' and shoved into the Royal Navy as a midshipman before he could even learn to say "Jack Ketch."

1780–1781: In 3rd Rate line of battleship *Ariadne*, sloop of war *Parrot*, and the *Desperate* frigate, in the West Indies, where he was thrashed and beaten into a passable midshipman, though of the sort to keep a captain nervous o' nights. Rather a lot of conquests on land and sea, and the theft of a trifling sum of 2,000 guineas off a French prize of war. Devilishly well detailed in *The King's Coat*.

1

1781–82: In the *Desperate* frigate. Participated in the Battle of the Chesapeake, the Siege of Yorktown, escaped, thence to the evacuation of Wilmington, North Carolina, by Crown forces in November of 1781, where he made the acquaintance of the Chiswick family, and the lovely Caroline Chiswick, who figures prominently in this adventure. See *The French Admiral.*

1782–83: Still in *Desperate* serving as midshipman and master's mate, participated in Adm. Sir Samuel Hood's Battle of St. Kitts. In English Harbour, Antigua, rated Passed Midshipman by an examining board, February, '82. Promoted Lieutenant and sent aboard the *Shrike* brig o'war as first officer by clerical error. Commerce warfare on the Cuban coasts, took part in an expedition to swing Muskogean and Seminole Indians into war on England's side, which effort failed (and it was *not* his fault), participated in Capt. Horatio Nelson's abortive attempt to retake Turks Island from the French in the spring of '83, and ended up in temporary command of *Shrike* two weeks before the Revolutionary War ended, and sailed her back to England to pay off at Deptford Hard. See *The King's Commission.*

1784–86: Fleeing an irate, titled, husband who'd caught him *in flagrante delicto* (which seems to be his way of life) *and* an allegedly pregnant housemaid, Lewrie takes service in the Far East in the eighty-gun 3rd Rate ship of the line *Telesto,* now disguised as an independent trader, or "country ship." Voyage to Cape Town, Calcutta and Canton, China, as 4th Officer, where *Telesto* hunts down and eventually destroys the French privateer captain Guillaume Choundas (a right bastard if ever there was one!) and his Mindanao pirate allies the Lanun Rovers. Whilst in India, he remade the acquaintance of his father Sir Hugo, now on service with the land forces of The Honourable East India Company to avoid creditors at home. They reconcile as much as they are able, and participate in the final battles together. Ends up with some pirate loot as his personal pelf and sails for England, the secret task complete, in February of 1786. See *The King's Privateer.*

Lieutenant Lewrie, RN, is now looking forward to the prospect of a peaceful three-year commission in command of a small vessel with the Bahamas Squadron, at least as much as an unwilling Navy officer may "look forward" to continued active service.

But then, with Alan Lewrie's singular inability to keep his breeches buttoned, his hands out of the honey pot, his smarmy wit to himself, or his mouth properly shut, there is the distinct possibility that he's going to come a cropper. Again. And, judging from his own catastrophic past, we may rest assured that somewhere along the line, he simply cannot help getting into both peril and mischief!

Now that we have all this out of the way, then, let us proceed with the continuing chronicle of our ne'er-do-well rakehell.

Book I

"*Sed tamen, nymphae, cavete, quod Cupido pulcher est:*
totus est in armis idem, quando nudus est Amor.
Cras amet qui numquam amavit,

                      quique amavit cras amet!"

"Yet take heed, nymphs, for Cupid is wondrous fair:
when Love is naked, he is fully armed.
Let him love tomorrow who has never loved,

                and let him who has tomorrow love!"

                      Pervigilium Veneris
                      ALBIUS TIBULLUS

Prologue

". . . is not to be entered into unadvisedly, nor lightly; but reverently, deliberately . . ." the vicar intoned, his voice ringing in stony, rebuking echoes from the transept of St. George's of the village of Anglesgreen.

Now they bloody tell me, Lt. Alan Lewrie thought in anguish!

". . . and in accordance with the purposes for which it was instituted by God," the vicar continued, casting a chary eye upon the couple before him, which made Alan almost wilt. He directed his gaze to his right, where Caroline stood flushed and trembling, ready to faint with joy, and the smile she bestowed upon him at that moment was so radiant, so shudderingly glorious, that he found himself quaking as well, not *completely* in terror of his bachelorhood's demise.

"Into this Holy Union, Alan Lewrie, gentleman, and Caroline Chiswick, spinster, now come to be joined. If any of you assembled may show cause why they may not be lawfully married, speak now; or else for ever after hold your peace," the vicar warned, wincing at the words, as if he expected the Hon. Harry Embleton to charge through the doors at the back of the nave on horseback with sword in hand. The crowd . . . a devilish *thin* crowd, Alan noted . . . fairly bristled and stirred, and a sigh or two, a grumbly cough could be heard.

"I require and charge you both, here in the presence of God, that if either of you know any reason why you may not be united in matrimony lawfully, and in accordance with God's Word, you do now confess it," the reverend rushed on in breathy relief.

The tiniest quirk of a smile touched Alan's lips, in spite of his best intentions, as he mulled over his passionate, albeit brief, "marriage" to a Cherokee/Muskogee Indian girl named Soft Rabbit, and wondered if it counted. No, he sighed, no benefit of proper clergy there, he thought; no way out. Damme, and my enthusiasms for quim!

How *do* I get myself into these predicaments, Alan groaned.

"Caroline, will you have this man to be your lawful husband, to live together in the covenant of marriage?" the vicar inquired, not without what to Alan seemed a cocked brow in amazement. "Will you love him, comfort him, honor and keep him, in sickness and in health, and, forsaking all others, be faithful unto him as long as you both shall live?"

"I will," Caroline declared without a pause with a tremulous eagerness and vigor, delivering upon Lewrie once more a visage of pure adoration.

"Alan," the vicar intoned, rounding upon him, and to Alan's already fevered senses seeming to frown the *slightest* bit, "will you have this woman to be your lawful wife . . . ?"

Forsake *all* others? Lewrie shivered. Bloody, bloody hell! Be faithful as long as we *both* . . . I say, hold on, there! Mine arse on a bandbox! The solemnity crushed in upon him then, and *he* like as not would have torn out the doors, if his legs would have shown any sign of strength beyond holding him shudderingly upright.

Yet found himself declaring for all time, "I will," with a force born on a quarter-deck that echoed off the ancient stones like a pronouncement of doom.

There was a tentative Giving In Marriage by Uncle Phineas, in his role of *paterfamilias* for the Chiswicks, before the vicar ordered "Let us pray" and they could thump to their weak knees upon the pad before the altar. And as the vicar recited the short prayer of blessing before the Lesson and Epistle, and the vows proper, Caroline insinuated a slim, cool and soft hand into his and their fingers entwined to squeeze reassurance and strength.

There was no backing out now, Alan thought; in for the penny, in for the pound, ain't I? Ye Gods, it may not be that bad—I do care for her, well as a rogue like me may care for anyone. I might even call it love. Much as I know what *that's* all about!

He returned her squeeze, and they secretly leaned their shoulders against each other, and he became enveloped in the light, citrony scent of her Hungary Water perfume again.

Chapter 1

It was springtime in England! Springtime in Surrey, and the High Road south from Guildford to Anglesgreen was aflutter with the stirrings of butterflies. Young birds flitted and swooped, or sat and chirped at their good fortune to be young, alive, and English. Bees buzzed, and if one listened hard enough, one could hear green buds and tender shoots sigh with delight in the somewhat warm wind.

Two young men rode along the verge of the roadway to avoid the muddy spatters and deep ruts carved by winter traffic, and the creaking wagons and wains of the local farmers, the occasional flock of sheep being moved from one grazing to another.

One young fellow was a countryman, towheaded and sinewy on a middling hired mare, leading a pack horse upon which were strapped a few traveling bags of cylindrical leather, or pouchlike carpet material. He was dressed in a sailor's slop-trousers, shirt and neckkerchief, with a low-crowned, flat-brimmed hat of black-tarred straw on the back of his head, and he gazed with a rustic's fondness on the verdant green countryside, recognizing merit and worth in well-tended flocks and fields, of trimmed hedgerows and woods.

The other was revealed a gentleman by his better horse, by the fineness of his buff-colored breeches and waistcoat, the newness of his plum-colored coat and dark beaver cocked hat, and the sheen of his top boots. This young gentleman snared the attention of passing travelers, and the interest of the farm-girls, whose sap was stirring after a long, miserable winter. There *he* found merit and worth!

He was three inches shy of six feet tall, trim and lean. Hair of middle, almost light brown, crowned his head, and fell in a short queue at the back of his collar, bound with a bow of black satin, and the hair was not drawn back severely, but allowed to curl slightly and naturally at his temples, over his ears, like the bust of a Roman or Greek warrior. The face was tanned much darker than most fashionable young gentlemen would care to display, providing a background for eyes that would occasionally crinkle in delightful greetings to young farm-girls, eyes that were sometimes gray, sometimes blue. And upon one cheek, there was a slight white pucker of a scar, which gave him the dashing, rakehell air of past, and present, danger. Soldier, or sailor, most judged him. A young man who held the King's Commission from his clothing, and the way he bore himself, from his fine manners when he lifted his military-cut hat in greeting, from the effortless way he rode as if born to a house of means, with stables and the license of the hunt which did not come to the son of a crofter or tenant.

Lt. Alan Lewrie, Royal Navy, was feeling pleased as punch with himself, and with life in general, at that moment. The spirited roan gelding he rode was a sound mount, and there was nothing better to his way of thinking than to be in the saddle in the middle of a spring morning. Had his father not practically press-ganged him into the Sea Service, he might have considered a career (a short one until he inherited, he re-minded himself) in a cavalry regiment. What else was there for a younger son that befitted one raised the way he had been? Trade? A clerking job? Certainly not the clergy, he shuddered!

Much as he had at first despised the life he had discovered in the Fleet (and still looked upon with a chary eye as one of continual deprivation and bleakness), he had in his luggage orders that would put him in command of a ship of war, would transport him a quarter of the way around the world to the Bahamas and the West Indies, for three years of steady pay, at five shillings *per diem*, to augment his prize money, his "French" guineas, and his Mindanao pirate's booty, all now safely en-sconced in London at Coutts & Co., bankers and each drawing a tidy sum of its own *per annum*.

And the world, for once, was at peace. Ninety percent of the Fleet was laid up in-ordinary and there would be no round-shot round his ears for a change. He did, good as he felt, admittedly suffer a tiny twinge of feyness from past experience whenever life tasted so succulently sweet. But it was a *very* tiny twinge, and it passed.

He had been far to the west country, to Wheddon Cross in Devon-shire to visit his grandmother Lewrie, now a Nuttbush, which stratagem by the old lady had saved the estate from his father's clutches, though to his cost. She had faded since his last visit in 1784, but was still among the living; though that, mercifully, could not be said of the dour old squint-a-pipes she'd wed to transfer coverture, and the inheritance, out of Sir Hugo's reach.

And now he was due at the Chiswick estate, there to languish in a lotus-eater's paradise of sleeping late, riding to hounds, and splendid country dinners and dances, until he was due to report to Portsmouth to take command of a vessel named *Alacrity*. And on that Chiswick estate would be the lovely and charming Caroline Chiswick, who by her evi-dent fondness in her letters, was positively pawing the ground to see him once more.

"What could be more perfect, Cony!" Alan laughed out loud as he turned to look over his shoulder at his "man" Will Cony, who had shared his adventures (and his misadventures) since Yorktown.

" 'Deed i'tis a fair mornin', sir!" Cony enthused back, beaming a farm lad's pleasure to be in such fair country on such a fine morning. "An' there's the squire's house, round the bend, sir. Not a league from the public house at Anglesgreen."

"We'll stop for a pint, how's that suit you, Cony?" Lewrie promised. "Then on to the Chiswicks."

"Pint'd suit me right down t'me toes, i't'would, sir," Will Cony agreed, kneeing his mare to match his master's quicker pace.

Anglesgreen was a quiet community, sited in a small, winding dell along the banks of a sluggish but clear-watered stream, with banks and bed flowing with rushes and grass. The village was surmounted to north and south, and at the far western end, with low and gently rolling hills, some forested, some asweep with velvety swaths of rippling, growing grain. And those hills from the summit of the nearest seemed to topple, to roll on forever like a delightful verdant sea—north toward Glandon Park and the Thames, south all the way to the Channel at Portsmouth.

There were three curving streets to Anglesgreen, two on the north bank, and one on the south bank, with two narrow stone bridges, one at either end of the village. There were shops on the High Street, Georgian-bricked fronts and bay windows for display, spreading to either side of a much older Tudor-timbered public house called The Ploughman. Behind the High Street, the homes were cottages with thatched roofs, while on the opposite bank the houses were newer, some Georgian or semi-Palladian, roofed with slate, and looked upon with some suspicion as being a bit too grand and uppity.

All three streets curved to match the bend in the stream. At the east end, by the oldest bridge, there was St. George's Church, a high and narrow stone pile dating to the Norman Conquest with a topsy-turvy cemetery nearby that sheltered headstones and monuments green with moss, some from the ancient Anglo-Saxon clan which had erected the now-fallen castle and bailey which brooded half a mile to the north of the first bridge, now lost in scrubby woods and brambles, that marked the edge of the local squire's lands. To the western end, by the second bridge, was a New Green, a parklike expanse of tall oaks that fronted another public house and inn, replete with stables and a budding row of new cottages around it—the upstart Red Swan Inn—it had only been there since Henry V's times, and in tiny Anglesgreen, one could ascertain a body's station in life by whether a person frequented the older, darker (and cheaper) old Ploughman, or rubbed elbows with the magistrate and squire's crowd at the Red Swan. Lewrie, knowing strangers were more welcome with the elite, headed for the Red Swan, and as they rode at a sedate walk up the High Street, villagers wagered, correctly, they'd not tie reins at The Ploughman.

Anglesgreen could be thoroughly boresome, Alan knew—he'd been there briefly once before in '84. But it was homey, a village so typically

English with its stone buildings and fences, its hedgerows and garden plots, that anyone six months at sea would crave its peaceful boredom. The trees were tall, giving acres of shade. Ducks and swans swam the lazy stream in slow glides. Stocky fellows in homespun or a great house's castoffs fished from the bridges and banks, gamboled on the greens, strode about in boots and straw hats, or sat sipping their ales in front of the Ploughman, a solid and dependable yeomanry who paid their rents on time, worked their acres with diligence, both prayed and played with vigor, and formed the backbone of the nation.

There were smells of new thatch, of cooking and baking, of a load of wash being boiled, and the scorch of ironing and starch. Of new-brewed ale mellowing in barrels, and of cartloads of manure and animal fodder. Most especially, ale, Lewrie smiled to himself as he drew rein at last in front of the Red Swan.

There was a "daisy-kicker" there in a twinkling to take reins and lead the horses off for a drink and a rubdown, with the older ostler waiting hopefully by the stable doors to see if he might make money by putting them up for the night, or rent them a coach.

There were quite a few horses tied at the rails, splendid and shiny blooded mounts, all sound "hundred guinea" horses, with bright saddle leather and clean pads. A backgammon game was proceeding at a table without the welcoming double doors, in the shade of the trees, and a lively sound of merrymaking coming from inside.

Alan and Cony entered, handing their hats to a bobbing "Abigail" in homespun and a pure white apron and mobcap. The public room was crowded with gentlemen gathered around a large table, all standing and laughing. One of them Alan recognized, and went to his side.

"Governour Chiswick!" he called. "The very fellow I was looking for!"

"Good God, here already?" Governour said, spinning to take his hand and thump him on the back. "We didn't expect you until the end of the week at the earliest! By Christ, but you're looking fit an' full of cream! The Chinee and the Hindoos couldn't put you off your feed, hey?"

"And I see that married life agrees with your digestion," Alan joshed him, giving him a slight poke in the breadbasket. Governour Chiswick, the whip-lean and dour eldest Chiswick he had met at Yorktown was now becoming a stout, apple-cheeked fellow, a settled and extremely well-married junior squire. Quite a change from the officer of a North Carolina volunteer regiment, and deadly with a Ferguson rifle or sword. Or a pistol, Alan remembered; this was the bloodthirsty, blackhearted devil who'd gut-shot the informer that had gotten half his surviving company killed just before they'd escaped, so he could linger in agony for days. To look at him now, you'd never catch an inkling of that.

"It does, indeed," Governour grinned wryly. "Come here, Alan, and meet the lads. And Will Cony, still tailing along with this rogue of ours? Well, step forward and take a stoup of ale with us. Good to see you, Alan. And you, as well, Cony."

"Thankee, sir," Cony replied, as someone shoved a stone tankard into his paws. He stayed long enough for introductions, then faded off to the counter, apart from "the quality," to have a jaw with the publican, and his pretty serving wench.

"Alan, this is my father-in-law, and you couldn't wish a finer," Governour boasted, and the gray-haired man in question pretended to blush with mock embarrassment. "Sir Romney Embleton; the fellow who saved my bacon at Yorktown, Lieutenant Alan Lewrie."

"Your servant, sir," Alan replied. "So pleased to make your acquaintance."

"My brother-in-law, Harry Embleton . . ." Governour babbled on.

Sir Romney Embleton, Baronet, was about Alan's height, though heavier, dressed rich and fine in dark brown velvet coat, gray breeches and a white, floral-figured satin waistcoat, with the prerequisite black and brown-topped riding boots on his thin shanks. Sir Romney favored an older man's short white tie-wig. He looked to have been in his youth a most handsome and well-setup fellow, with clear blue eyes and a fairly smooth complexion free of smallpox scars and such. The nose was a trifle beaky, and the upper lip long as a horse's.

The same could not be said for the son, the Hon. Harry Embleton, who, though he was dressed richly as his father the baronet in red coat, blue waistcoat and breeches, could not aspire to the easy style and dignity of the father. Harry had the same extremely long upper lip, the narrow horsy face of his father, and, to his misfortune, the same overhanging beak of a nose. But the eyes were set rather close together, and were pouched as though by dissipation or too many late hours. And where Sir Romney's hair might at one time have been blond, Harry's was almost black and lank, tied back in a severe style. And finally and most unfortunately, where the elegant Sir Romney Embleton was blessed with a square jaw, young Harry had a pronounced slope from weak chin to the point where his throat dived into his neck-stock. In profile, he resembled an otter.

"Now were you with the Army, or with the Navy, Lieutenant Lewrie?" Sir Romney inquired as Alan dipped his phiz into his ale.

"Navy, milord," Alan answered, wondering if he was teasing.

"Lock up the maids and yer daughters!" Harry Embleton guffawed. "Or yer footmen! The Navy's here!"

Damn the bastard, Alan winced as several of the rowdies had a laugh at his expense! *I think I could dislike this piss-proud young fool.* Alan stiffened and cut his eyes to Governour, who had winced a little himself.

"I can assure you, Mr. Embleton, *your* virginity is safe with me," Alan stated calmly as the laughter died away. "Damme, but this is a good ale! Haven't tasted its like in weeks."

"Just ashore, are you, Mister Lewrie?" Sir Romney asked quick as a wink to cover the nervous laughter that reerupted, this time at his son's expense. Out of the corner of his eye, Alan could see that Governour had gotten a glum expression, and that Harry Embleton was glaring daggers at him, his face gone paler.

"Since February, milord, but I was visiting in the west country with my grandmother. I don't believe Devon has the soil for grains and hops that Surrey has. Certainly not to make such a splendid ale as this," Alan stated. "Now the Chinese have good ale, surprisingly."

"You were with Burgess Chiswick in the Far East," Sir Romney nodded, dominating the conversation. "A *trading* expedition?"

"An attempt to *increase* British trade, milord," Alan said in reply. He could never discuss what occurred in the past two years until England was once more at war with France. The activities of English warships disguised as merchantmen, had they been known, would be a violation of the treaty terms ending the recent war. "To . . . uhm . . . open new markets and trading stations, in cooperation with the East India Company."

Trade was not a gentlemanly calling, though profit from an investment in trade was quite acceptable, as long as a proper gentleman did not soil his hands with the sordid details of buying and selling.

This facile explanation, breezed off with a languid wave of a hand, sounded semiofficial, requiring the presence of a naval officer, and Alan had gotten quite good at trotting it out since his return.

"Calcutta, Canton . . ." Governour said with a wistful look. "I believe you saw both, did you not, Alan?"

" 'Deed we did, Governour," Alan turned a thankful grin on his compatriot. "And a host of trading posts you wouldn't believe for horrid heat and rain, too. Took me a month to squeeze the last water out of my hats. But tell me, how does the Chiswick family fare? Is Caroline well?"

"Quite well," Governour almost snapped. "Father, though . . . well, there was bad snow last winter, and his horse fell with him. Laid out for an hour or so before anyone missed him, and . . . the surgeon had to take his leg where it had been broken by the weight of the horse."

"Governour, how truly awful, I had no word of it!"

"He recovered at long last, thanks be to God, but . . . if you do recall how he was in Wilmington when you first saw him . . ."

"Ah," Alan nodded. Sewallis Chiswick had been half out of his mind back then, brought on by the death of his youngest son George, of being burned out and impoverished by Rebel irregulars led by his own relations because he was a Tory, a Loyalist, and had equipped the regiment in which Governour and Burgess served. "A heavy burden on you, Governour, which I am sure you managed well," Alan concluded, laying a supportive hand on Governour's broad shoulder.

"Thank you for that, Alan, 'twas well said. And well meant, to be certain. So, how long can you stay with us?" Governour brightened.

"Three or four weeks, if you can tolerate me that long," Alan laughed. "Then it's off to Portsmouth and a new ship, *Alacrity*. To be with the Bahamas Squadron. I'll need a good last dose of country life to do me."

"That we can, that we can," Governour promised. "We'll have you aching for the sea by the time we're done carousing."

"Sounds as if you gentlemen were doing a bit of carousing of your own as I rode up." Alan smiled. "Did you race those fine horses I saw outside?"

"Court day, Mister Lewrie," Sir Romney beamed. "We dealt with a couple of ruffians, and were just recalling their appearance."

"Two poachers," Harry Embleton explained. "We've been missing a rabbit or two from the warren, a deer's carcass was found stripped of meat. Well, last night . . ." Harry had to wheeze in fond remembrance for a moment. "Last night, Douglas here, our gamekeeper, sets a man-trap or two, and bang on midnight, 'blam' goes the trap! We run out to see what we caught, and no sign of 'em. But this morning, bold as brass, they turn up at Mister Gallworthy's the surgeon's, *rattling* with buckshot, and he sent his man to fetch us. Caught 'em with the pelts, the meat, an' all in their larders, and had 'em into court!"

"One fellow's bloody eye was gone!" chortled Sir Romney. "Took the blast right in the face, I suppose, as he crawled up the path in the woods to lay a snare. And will you believe, sir, that he claimed . . . hee hee . . . he *claimed* he knocked his own eye out!"

" 'Cause the Good Lord told him to, haw haw!" another stalwart chimed in. "Said he'd looked at a dirty book o' pictures . . ."

"With only the one eye, mind," Sir Romney snickered.

"An' th' good book says, sir, it says . . ." Harry continued, trembling with pent-up laughter, "iffen yer eye offends ye, then yer s'posed t' pluck it out, ain't ye now, sir? Right, yer honor, sir?"

"As if that offending eye wasn't holed dead center with shot," Sir Romney frowned. "Shot from my spring gun, damme if it wasn't."

"And the other could do no better than to say he'd pelted himself whilst taking a loaded fowling piece down to show it off," Harry grumbled, as though the second victim had been no amusement at all.

"So what was the punishment?" Alan asked, appalled by them all. He'd seen men quilled with splinters, limbs ripped off with grape-shot, or puking blood from stomach wounds suffered in battle. He'd been hit enough to know what agony those men must have endured already.

"Transportation," Sir Romney said. "And the families to be put out of the parish. I'll have no poaching on my lands, and by Jesus, they know it."

"And those two tenancies'll be enclosed. Last of the common lands this side of the stream, anyway," Governour stated calmly. "And they were always behind on their rents. Well, Alan. I have to get back home. Finish up your ale and ride with me."

"Only if you promise you have some more waiting," Alan managed to smile. "Good morning to you, gentlemen, milord. I trust I'll be seeing you again in the next few weeks. We'll hopefully have merry times?"

Chapter 2

"Bloody squires," Cony grumbled as they were fetched their horses. "A spring gun. A man-trap! Jesus, sir."

"And transportation to where, I wonder, with America lost," Lewrie speculated in a soft voice, "the Fever Islands? That new Van Diemen's Land? They'll rot in the hulks for months. Years."

"And the fam'lies turned out, sir, just 'cause they ain't freeholdin'. Damn the bloody Enclosure Acts, too."

"Easy now, Cony," Lewrie warned.

"Oh, I knows, sir," Cony huffed, swiping his hair back from his forehead and putting on his hat. "Might o' been practiced sinners'n layabouts. But they might o' been poor folk what needed the meat t' keep their young'uns fed, too, sir, an' not able t' graze but one cow on the commons. Rabbits eatin' up what little garden they got, an' them not able t' lift a finger, 'cause they's the *squire*'s rabbits. Life c'n be hard fer poor crofters, sir."

"And a damn sight harder now they broke the law poaching," Alan declaimed with a nod of understanding. "But, they knew the risks. And they lost."

"Aye, sir. Makes a man sad, even so, sir."

"That it does, Cony. Let's get mounted, then, and go see nicer people than Sir Romney bloody Embleton."

"Aye, aye, sir."

"That's Embleton land yonder," Governour pointed out as they rode west out of the village and crested one of those rolling hills. "Our land starts at that creek that feeds the stream. Up and over two hills west, about a mile. Then down south to the Chiddingfold Road, and another stream. There were two estates in the beginning, from our grandfathers on down. Two manors, two families. Father was due his parcel in '46, but he wanted to stay in North Carolina, so he sold it freehold to Uncle Phineas to work as one farm. Paid a good price to us, he did, and brought it up to snuff. Altogether, we've about 900 acres in freehold or copyhold. And when we came back to England, Uncle Phineas rented 120 acres back for a token guinea a year."

"The copyhold recorded at which manor?" Alan asked, seeing that only the thin silver line of the small creek and its brushy bottoms separated Embleton land from Chiswick land. "Glandon Park?"

"With the Embletons," Governour said. "Once it was all part of the Goodyers . . . Norman Guidiers, I think . . . but the last of 'em died out, Lord, four hundred years ago? 'Twas then the Embletons were made baronets and awarded the land."

"And the old castle and bailey?" Alan pressed. "Theirs? I've a mind to look it over whilst I'm here. Think you I could?"

"The Embletons should allow it," Governour smiled. "It was the Eadmers, vassals to King Harold, built it. I'll ask for you. 'Twas where I did most of my courting with Millicent. Have to have a care, though. There may be man-traps. That's where the rabbit warren is, below the rise there."

"I haven't offered you my congratulations on your marriage!" Alan exclaimed, hitting him on the shoulder once more. "Slipped my mind completely! A lovely bride, hey?"

"The most felicitous of women, Alan, I cannot find words to say how charming, how utterly . . ." Governour enthused, reddening with embarrassment. Love, which had him half-seas-over, was not an easy topic for English gentlemen. "Wait until you meet her!"

"I look forward to it eagerly," Alan assured him.

They reached a fork in the road and another bridge, this one of stout oak timbers. The fork led off to the right, across the bridge, over which they clattered onto Chiswick lands at last.

"Damn fine lands, Mister Chiswick, sir," Cony volunteered as he beheld the lushness of the growing grain fields to either side, the thickness of the wood lots, and the pastures snowy with young sheep. "Makes old Gloucestershire look like a stone quarry, so it does."

"Two hundred acres in corn and wheat, an hundred in barley and hops. And the rest rotated with sheep for manuring, or hay for fodder," Governour boasted. "Second-best in the county, next to my father-in-law's. Uncle Phineas has made it a paradise. Sheep are the coming thing in the South Counties. Now we've orchards that make the best cider around. And we rent out about eighty or so in sheep."

"Cattle, sir?" Cony asked with relish.

"Not so many as we may sell, Cony, but enough for the use of the home farms. We've pigs and chickens, and ducks, and all. And a small herd of fine horses. You take your pick, Alan, you'll see we have the beginnings of a good stud here."

The road forked again about a quarter-mile on. The right fork went to the thatch-roofed two-story cottage that Alan had visited the last time, and he began to turn his horse's head in that direction.

"No, we're all up at the main house now, Alan," Governour said. "That's leased out. Thought it would be better if Father was under a better regimen of care under Uncle Phineas's roof."

"And the honeymooners have to share a house?" Alan teased.

"Well, no, I've a new place of my own down near the Chiddingfold Road. It was a rough tenantry, after all, that house. A man name of Byford has it now. He's the sheeper I mentioned."

Around another turn, across a pasture, stood the Chiswick manor house. It was of homey red brick, with a Palladian entrance hall added on in front, with two humbler wings of two stories each forking off at angles to enfold a lawn and flower beds around a curving drive.

"Race you to the door!" Governour shouted, putting spurs to his mount, and was off like a shot. Alan howled like a red Indian and got going in pursuit, and his gelding snorted with alarm, checked and rose on its hind legs for a moment, then caught the spirit of the game and plunged into a mile-eating gallop, stretching its strong neck out even with the docked tail of Governour's thoroughbred.

They ran on, Alan's horse gaining until its nose was even with the other horse's shoulder, both riders hallooing and yelling to draw the attention of the house to their antics. Out came an older man in breeches and waistcoat, with a green eyeshade still over his brows, an older woman Alan recognized as mother Charlotte Chiswick, a dark-haired beauty he took for the Amazing Millicent . . . and there was Caroline!

"Beat you, ha ha!" Governour bragged as they drew rein so hard they set their mounts back on their haunches. "Look who's here!"

Alan's horse couldn't help but paddle on across a flower bed and back in a circle, shaking his head and snuffling rage at being bested, curvet-ting as Alan patted his neck and realizing that Caroline had never seen him ride before, which made him sit up straighter and extend his booted feet in the stirrups as he calmed the horse.

He sprang down from the saddle as a groom appeared to take the reins, and strode to her side, arms open in greetings.

"How good it is to see you!" he cried. "It's been a long two years and more!"

"Alan Lewrie, oh, welcome, welcome!" Caroline replied. They met, embraced for a second, then held hands at arm's length to gaze at each other and twirl around in a small circle. "At last!"

She had become *more* lovely! Still too tall at two inches below Alan's height to be thought fashionable, still willow-slim, and what London blades would call "gawky." But filled out rounder and fuller in the most interesting places! Her light brown hair shone like spun gold, her hazel eyes twinkled with joy, and the slight folds below her eyes crinkled in such a merry manner that he thought he could go on gazing at her slim, high-cheeked face for all time.

"We didn't expect you 'til Friday, or the weekend," she said.

"I had good roads," he replied. "I was inspired! I rode like John Gilpin!"

Caroline inclined her head to one side and winked with one eye, forcing Alan to notice that her mother was standing there. He let go of her hands and fell to one knee before the old woman.

"I was inspired by your ginger snaps, Mistress Chiswick," he cried, "I could not wait another instant to taste your ginger snaps!"

"Alan Lewrie, you are such a wag, sir!" Mother Charlotte said with a simpering laugh, tapping him on the head with her fan. "Come here and let me kiss you! Oh, 'tis grand to see you well, after all the adventures you've been up to among the heathens! We've gotten a letter from Burgess telling us all about it. Pirates and such, and a battle! He's well, when last you saw our little Burge?"

"Well, and *full* of ginger, Mother Chiswick," Alan told her with a droll roll of his head. "It's the Hindoo cooking, ya know, full of ginger and chilies. Well, and in command of his own light company in my father's regiment, so he'll continue in good hands."

If you may call that good hands, Alan qualified to himself. The last time he'd seen him, Burgess was up to his teats in tawny Hindoo maidens that he and a fellow officer shared in the quarters as their private *bibikhana*. And his father had been going "brrr!" into a set of dugs himself! Well, he thought, pirate loot and satisfied creditors in London'd keep his father on the straight and narrow. And now that he was confirmed as Lieutenant Colonel of the 19th Native Infantry, he was happy enough. For awhile.

"Uncle Phineas, allow me to name you Lieutenant Alan Lewrie, one who has done so much to restore the fortunes of the Chiswick family, sir."

"Your servant, sir," Alan offered, extending a hand. "I'm delighted to meet you at last."

"And I you, Mister Lewrie," Uncle Phineas replied, not looking one whit delighted at anything in the last thirty years. He was a lean old stick, dressed in rough homespun breeches, wool stockings and old shoes that appeared to have been restitched, but well blackened. The waist-coat he wore was a very old style, as was the linsey-woolsey cut of his shirt and neck-stock. Rich the man might be, but he looked as dowdy as one of his poorer tenants. He must have been in his sixties, wrinkled as last winter's apples, with stray wisps of white hair peeking from under the green eyeshade.

"Can't thank ye enough, Mister Lewrie," Uncle Phineas said as he dropped Alan's hand after one quick, dry, shake, and stuck thumbs into his waistcoat watch pockets. "Gettin' little Burgess employed with the East India Company. Wasn't sure he'd find a situation, not with times so hard. Wasn't cut out fer farmin', that's God's truth! And fer seein' Sewallis an' his family safe to Charleston so they'd be able to come home where they belong."

"And for saving Burge and Governour after Lord Cornwallis surren-dered at Yorktown, Uncle," Caroline reminded him, and he looked as if he'd been reminded of that act of desperation perhaps once too often, for he screwed his wrinkled lips together and merely nodded. "I welcome ye to me home, Mister Lewrie. Stayin' long, is it?"

"A few weeks, if I may be allowed, sir. Better that than kicking my heels in London, or down in Portsmouth waiting for my new ship to be turned over," Alan replied, wondering just what sort of welcome he'd come to. "Ah, Caroline, Mother Chiswick, look who's here, too? You remember my man, Will Cony?"

Cony had arrived with the pack horse, and slid off his own to come to them, hat in hand.

"God bless you, young Will," Mother Charlotte exclaimed. "I remember you well from Wilmington, and all you did to get us aboard that ship! Ah, you're filling out like a yearling colt, you are! And does our Mister Lewrie treat you decent?"

"That 'e does, ma'am," Cony nodded, shy in front of company.

"Well, if he doesn't, I know a snug niche for a good farm lad like you, right here with us, my word on it!" the older lady cackled.

"Missus Chiswick, Miss Caroline," Cony nodded again, blushing.

"More important, have you been taking good care of Al . . . of our Mister Lewrie, Cony?" Caroline asked.

"Saved my life time and again," Alan supplied, for the ears of the comely housemaids who had gathered in the yard. "And did his King's enemies into fillets."

"Then 'tis more than welcome you are in this house, Will Cony," Caroline said, stepping forward to give him a sisterly peck on the cheek, which made Cony turn even darker red with embarrassment. "Home you are, for awhile with us."

"Thankee, Miss Caroline . . . ma'am," Cony bobbed.

"And this is Millicent, Alan," Governour said, turning boyish as he introduced his young wife. She was a lovely girl, smooth and milky of skin, with dark curling hair and startlingly gray eyes, and a merry expression of her own. It seemed as if Millicent had gotten all the Embleton elegance and neatness, leaving her brother Harry with none.

"My best wishes to you, ma'am, on your marriage. You've a fine man in Governour, as well I may attest. Your servant, ma'am."

"Oh, do call me Millicent, Mister Lewrie," she chided with the regal dignity of her father the baronet. "Such old friends of my dear Governour should not stand on ceremony."

"You do me great honor, Millicent, thankee," Alan replied with a short bow, prepared to like her if Governour did.

"Well, let's go into the house and have something to drink," Uncle Phineas suggested.

"Yes, I promised Alan one of our ales, even if he did lose the race," Governour laughed. "Sorry about that, but blood will tell, you know. I told you we had the start of a fine stud. 'Ribbons' was one of our first colts, and he's a treasure."

"Oh, I don't know," Alan japed. "I almost had you neck-or-nothing. Not bad for a fifty guinea New Market gelding."

"He's strong," Caroline said, brushing Alan's horse on flank and neck before he was led away by a waiting groom. "Short but a goer, he looks like. Good build, for the long stretch, not the burst."

"Canter by the hour, he can," Alan agreed. "And worth an ale, no matter his pedigree, hey?"

"Caroline made our ale last autumn," Millicent boasted.

"Oh, just a few barrels," Caroline replied. "To try my hand at it."

"Then I must have some. I'm sure anything she turns her hand to comes out superbly," Alan fawned, and she blushed with pleasure at his words.

"Mmm, yes," Uncle Phineas frowned, wrinkling his nose as if at a peculiar odor. He surveyed the ruin of one of his flower beds, and contemplated, with very little joy of the doing, just how long this ignorant arse was going to plague him!

Chapter 3

Sewallis Chiswick was a lot worse than Alan remembered him. Whereas in Wilmington, the old man had been strong but vague, he was now both reduced to pale ashes of a man, in a wheeled chair, and at times almost incoherent in his ramblings. At least Caroline was now spared the onerous duties of tending to him. After a last few odd pronouncements, a stout matron had announced that Mr. Chiswick would retire, and he was wheeled off to a ground floor chamber, his bib still tied around his neck and spotted with attempts at dining.

It had put a definite chill on supper, though they all tried to find other, more amusing and lighthearted conversation to cover their embarrassment, sometimes laughing too long and loud at hopeless japes, then falling into an uneasy silence.

The supper, though, had been excellent; somewhat plain, but all hearty country fare. There had been a salad (Caroline's own apple vinegar and spices for the dressing), fish from their own stream along with a plate of oysters up from Portsmouth (Caroline's own horseradish to spice them, what the French would call a *rémoulade*), a cured ham baked in a golden honey sauce, snap beans from the garden, tiny new potatoes and shallots, completed, of course, with roast mutton, and followed by a peach "jumble," which Caroline's mother informed Alan was "cobbler" in the Carolinas, her very own recipe, though done personally by the talented young lady with the light brown hair.

"Aye, proper victuals," Uncle Phineas allowed, grudgingly as he wiped his mouth with the back of his hand and untucked the napkin from below his chin. "Our little Caroline'll make a young man a 'goody'," he said, using the old country term for a proper wife (and the first name, or gained nickname, of a third of the poor women of Britain).

Are they at it *again*, Alan sighed, sharing a smile with Caroline as she ducked her head in what he thought was shyness? I'm not under their roof four hours, and they're buttock-brokering her like a brood mare! Just like Burgess did to me back in India.

"Economical, she is." Uncle Phineas went on as he leaned forward to top his glass up with the last of a rather good claret, "Good in the still-room, the garden, the stables. Present the *right* young feller with a goin' concern. Well-setup house, a household run in style, and economy."

Is that his favorite word, Alan wondered? He certainly takes 'economy' to extremes with his own furnishings. No, let's say 'cheap'!

"I am ever amazed at how accomplished you are, Caroline," Millicent chimed in from the other side of the table. "You sew the neatest, finest stitches, play and sing wonderfully well. Why, I believe you could spin straw into gold! Makes me seem such a wastrel drudge in comparison. I'm simply useless at practical things!"

"I assure you you're not!" Governour guffawed. "I know I have the best-run household in the county . . . *two* counties! And a most felicitous one, as well, m'dear. And you to thank for it."

The sight of the bloody-handed Governour Chiswick "pissing down his wife's back" and fawning so gape-jawed foolish over *anyone* was not the sort of thing Alan Lewrie had ever expected to see on this earth! Still, it was interesting to see Millicent deliver a fond gaze at the oaf and lower her lashes in a very intimate, but significant manner, and Alan, being a keen observer of "country-house games" among those circles of rakehells and Corinthians he had known before the Navy, knew in an instant that they'd be at each other before their coach got into their own drive!

"Oh, but you are so clever and accomplished, Millicent!" Caroline assured her. "It is I envy you, while I merely learned country things in the Carolinas."

"And all the better for it when the time comes to wed," Phineas Chiswick pronounced. "Ye'r, both o' ye, the finest young ladies o' me acquaintance, an' here ye'll be livin' side by side, sittin' in the same pew, an' more than just neighbors all yer lives, God willin'. Like the way ye play yer music . . . Millicent to the harpsichord, an' Caroline, yer flute. A fine duet ye'll play in the North Downs in future!"

"Uncle . . ." Caroline attempted to protest, wringing her napery into a ball. Alan perked up a bit; this was more than shyness on her part. It sounded more like an old topic which had been done to death, and still dragged up for tasting often as communion wine.

And what does he mean, Alan asked himself, all this 'side by side in the same pew,' by God? Just who *are* they buttock-brokering her to?

She looked out of the corner of her eye to Alan and he lifted one eyebrow to quiz her; and for a hopeless, unguarded moment, there was almost panic on her face, and a silent plea.

What the hell is going on, he mused? Caroline Chiswick is one woman I never expected to look so lost and helpless. Why, she's the most capable young woman I ever did see!

"Speaking of a duet," Mother Chiswick intervened, "Mister Lewrie has never heard Caroline play her flute. She is most talented, I assure you, sir. And dear Millicent fairly makes the harpsichord sing with the angels! What was that piece we heard in London that you both do, my dears? By that German fellow. The dead one."

"Handel, momma," Caroline replied, looking in a bit of a sulk.

"Public music-hall antics," Uncle Phineas groused, ringing his tiny china bell for port, cheese and biscuit. "Trash. Germans, hah!"

"I fear most of the great composers *are* German," Alan chuckled. "There's that fellow in Vienna who's making quite a splash, another of 'em . . . that Mozart. I heard some of his stuff in London before I went to Devon. And Bach, of course. Now you can hardly call 'Jesu, Joy of Man's Desiring' music-hall trash, Mister Chiswick."

"Oh, we know that!" Millicent enthused. "Caroline, Mother Chiswick, let us leave these fine gentlemen to their port, whilst we set up the parlor for music and *écarté*. Mother Chiswick is correct, Mister Lewrie . . . Caroline is divine on the flute!"

She was indeed divine, for an amateur. While Governour turned pages for them from behind the harpsichord, they played several duets together. And Millicent proved to be a most accomplished young lady as well, playing with feeling and passion, instead of the clumsy, almost monotonous clumping pace and never-varying strength of tinkling one usually heard in someone's salon.

They did assay a Handel piece, a short sonata originally for flute and continuo, intermixing a program of country airs and sober Bach cantatas. Alan watched Caroline, a cup of tea cooling on his knee; he was impressed by the solemnity and deep concentration she showed, but disturbed by the too-bright glitter of her eyes when at the sadder pieces.

Millicent noticed, too, and began to play rounds for them to sing, Governour bellowing out hunting songs and things he'd learned in North Carolina. Alan had to rise and try to sing "pulley-hauley" chanties for them, rollicking verses each more improbable, and more scandalous than the last, until Uncle Phineas announced that he was tired of all the folderol and was off for bed. And no one seemed the slightest bit interested in écarté, so Alan could only peck Caroline on the cheek and be lit up to his room for the night, there to ponder what could make a girl of such a gay and stalwart nature so sad.

"Mrroww!" Then again, louder and more plaintive. "Mrrrowww!"

Howls of torture, of black-hearted denial! Lewrie sprang awake in his bed and tore back the curtains. There came another "Mrroww?" from the door, softer and more pleading this time. "Oww?"

"Bloody, bloody hell," he muttered, swiping his hair out of his eyes and staggering to the door. He opened it and beheld a very ragged yellow ram-cat of his acquaintance seated on the parquet flooring, one William Pitt. If anything, he had gotten uglier since he'd last seen him in 1784. One ear was tatters, one eye squinted, and the tail was missing a patch or two. But it was the same huge, one-stone in weight monster that had ruled the *Shrike* brig with claw and fang.

"Pitt, you bastard!" Alan said, stooping down to touch him.

But William Pitt was having none of that. He shied away and ran into the bedchamber to leap for the bed, making the mattress bounce on its rope supports, and lashed his tail as he stood there, bristled up.

"Well, you wanted to come in, so what is it you want from me, hey?" Alan went back to the bed and sat at one end, wary that the cat had not remembered their brief, grudging, alliance, and would rip into him as was the animal's wont when he first reported aboard, a barely "wetted down" commission officer.

He wiggled his fingers and Pitt flicked the good ear, shook his head, then ambled over to sling his considerable bulk against Alan's hip and begin to purr loud as a bilge-pump chain. In stupefied amazement, Alan discovered that William Pitt would allow him to scrub under his chin, on the top of his head, and on his chest!

"By God, but you've mellowed," Alan whispered in awe. "Like as not, you'd of had my fingers in shreds by now. Killed any livestock this week, have you? The odd pig?"

There was a rap on the door and Cony entered with a small tray which bore a china cup, a lidded silver pot, and a sugar and creamer.

"Mornin', Mister Lewrie, sir." Cony bubbled over with bonhomie. "Well, if 'tisn't yer ole cat, William Pitt. Got ya up afore I did. 'Tis a fine, fine, mornin', perfect for a canter on the downs. Hot chocolate t' perk ya up, sir. 'Ere ya go. Push ya into clothes, an' there's a country breakfast a'waitin' below-stairs, sir. Now, a maid I made h'*acquain*tance of, she tole me that this cat 'ere, 'e's *yews*'lly a'cryin' at Mistress Caroline's door o' the mornin's, but I s'pose 'e got yer scent an' come t' see iffen ya'd remember 'im, sir. 'Nother sugar in that, sir?"

"Thankee kindly, Cony. Have you eat yet?"

"Oh, aye, sir!" Cony beamed as he fetched duds from traveling bags. "Why, this house is a grand feeder, an' the scullery'n all bung t' the deckheads with fine folk. Some of 'em right pretty, they is, so I'm set from now 'til th' 'Piphany. You'll be needin' me on yer ride this morning, sir?" Cony asked with an askance glance.

"Ah, no, I don't believe so, Cony," Alan replied after one sip of the perfectly wonderful chocolate, recognizing when his man was so cheerful that he was practicing his own form of coyness. "We're both here to enjoy ourselves. Ow!"

He had ignored William Pitt, who had rolled over on his right side and was pushing *hard* against Alan's nightshirt with all four of his paws, claws out and huffing for more attention!

"Now there's a bloody wonder," Alan sighed, mystified once more and turning one hand back to ruffling the cat's throat and jaws. "Why don't you just fart about today, have a yarn or two with your new, ah . . . compatriots. Even go down to the village for a pint or two. I'll not need anything more 'til, oh . . . supper, say?"

"Er, thankee, sir!" Cony showed quick gratitude, then feigned con-triteness at abandoning his master, and his responsibilities. "Iffen ya think there's no service I could be a'doin' for ya, that is . . ."

"There's two shillings on the dresser there," Alan said as he finished the cocoa and set the cup down for Pitt to peer and sniff at. "I trust the girl is pretty? Aha, so that's it, you rogue! Maybe you could practice some of your Hindi on her. *Hamare ghali ana, achcha din?'* "†

"*Larkee bahut sundar hai, jeehan, El-looee Sahib.*" Cony blushed a bit, though still more fluent than Lewrie would ever be. "*Bazaari-rahndi naheen hai. Makaan naukari-larkee.*"*

"*Namasté*, Cony-*ji*," Lewrie snickered, putting his palms together and bowing his head, "May God protect you, Cony."

"Got me a cundum, sir," Cony whispered, darting out the door as Lewrie shucked his nightshirt and reached for his stockings.

"God damme, I've corrupted him, swear if I haven't, hey, Pitt? Do they let you take breakfast? Hungry?"

Alan finished dressing and headed for the stairs, and William Pitt leaped off the bed and made a tawny streak ahead of him.

God, there was leftover ham! Salted kippers, hard peppery sausages, crisp bacon strips, boiled, fried, or scrambled eggs on the sideboard, warming in candle-heated covered servers! Racks of thick, chewy home-baked bread toasted on forks over the kitchen fire and fetched out by the half-loaf! The remains of the peach "jumble" sat on a raised pie plate, and stone jugs of preserves, jams and marmalades paraded down the length of the breakfast table, along with huge, sweaty globs of home-churned butter between every two place settings.

And for the *serious* feeders, there were pork chops sizzling on black-iron pans, heaping bowls of gruel, and three different kinds of cheeses. As for beverages, there was ale, a lighter, gassier beer, tea, coffee, more chocolate, or a heavy, almost-black berry wine made on the property. More of Caroline's doing, he discovered, though he could not assay a taste after heaping a plate and taking three cups of strong tea.

There was a mob at table; Caroline, looking a bit perkier this morning, dressed in a middle-green wool dress with a short jacket for riding on over it, Governour in rustic and worn boots, breeches and waistcoat so he could tour the properties. Millicent was there in a white sack gown, shawl and mobcap. Mother Chiswick was turned out in gray wool. There was the head groom, the gamekeeper, the assistant estate manager, who was trying to keep track of a two-sided conversation between Governour and Uncle Phineas, who was gnawing his way through a

† "Hello, won't you come into our street?" A whore's greeting.
* "The girl is very pretty, yes, Lewrie master. Not a bazaar-whore . . . a house serving-girl."

stack of pancakes, pork chops and ale, both eager to be out and doing, and a continual parade of underlings there to take orders and turn to with a will.

Alan picked at his food, trying to carry on a conversation with Caroline, who was seated by his side this morning, with William Pitt in either his or her lap, peeking over the top of the table and singling out particularly dainty delicacies from their plates with one sly paw, when not being offered fatty bacon fast enough to suit him.

"Christ, is it always like this?" Alan managed to ask in one of the lulls, broken only by the sounds of somewhat sedate chewing. "I've seen quieter twopenny ordinaries on Boxing Day!"

"I'm afraid so, Alan." She smiled. "The work of a farm starts early, and never stops."

"Then thank God I was never cut out to be a farmer," Alan said in reply. "The Navy's Bedlam enough. Cony mentioned something about riding this morning?"

"If you would wish it, Alan," she assured him. "If you would rather loll about for the morning, we could go later. That is, if you could tolerate my being your guide."

"Anywhere, as long as it's not here," he chuckled, patting her hand. "And anywhere with you, Caroline."

"Then let's be on our way, right now!" she urged, half-rising. "If you have eat sufficient?"

"Point me to a horse!"

Chapter 4

She rode as if the Hounds of Hell were at her heels, astride the older-style saddle and bent over low, her light brown hair touched with gold streaming from beneath her straw bonnet like flame. Her mare was a good'un, making it hard for Alan's gelding to keep up for at least half a mile, until they thundered up a rising down towards a patch of wood lot, their mounts sucking and blowing like bellows.

At last they slowed to a walk as they neared the summit, and Alan could draw alongside her to see what had vexed her so.

"Good little mare you have there," he complimented her. "And you ride prettily. But what was all the hurry?"

"I just wanted to get out from under foot," she replied, just a touch wan, though flushed with the exertion and the excitement of a hard ride. "I liked our little house near the road better, instead of all the coming and going around Uncle's. At least down there, we felt . . . settled and at peace. Snug in our own house, at last."

"I don't see why you had to move, really," Alan said as their mounts cropped grass after getting their wind back. "Surely the maid that cares for your father could have come there instead."

"Uncle insisted on it," Caroline replied with a wry grin, which flitted away quickly. "He insists on rather a lot of things, I fear."

"Caroline, is there something the matter here?" Alan asked. "Far be it from me to presume to intrude in your family's affairs, but . . ."

"Oh, Alan, you who've done so much for this family already," she warmed to him, leaning over to lay a gloved hand on his sleeve. "As if we don't consider you kin by now . . . of sorts! You do not intrude to ask me anything."

"Then what's going on?" he shrugged.

"When father lost his leg and fell ill, he was months in bed," Caroline sighed, looking away down the toppling downs toward the sea to the south. "Governour was head of the family, then. But he was still estate manager to Uncle Phineas. And just married to Millicent Embleton. So, by rights, Uncle Phineas is the master of the land. And of our lives. What did the Romans call it . . . *paterfamilias?*"

"And the booty that Burgess sent home from India did not help?"

"Only in improving our finances," Caroline said with a frown. "But not in our station, you see. We are still tenants. Relatives, yes, but mostly tenants when it comes to Uncle Phineas. We had hoped for a warmer reception from blood kin."

"I remember in London, when we were finding Burge his situation, your uncle did not sound wholly . . . solicitous and charitable to you."

"It was his obligation, nothing more," Caroline told him. "A chore of blood. He was eldest, responsible for his younger brother's folly. That's what our plantation was in the Carolinas . . . folly. Their father united the two estates after my granduncle died without issue. I've always felt Uncle Phineas feared that father would split it again, even after getting a fair price for it when he sailed for the Colonies. He didn't have to pay him a shilling for it, after all. He was the eldest, due to inherit everything."

"Yet he gave back 120 acres, for a guinea a year," Alan pointed out.

"Oh, yes, he *rented* back 120 acres. But that ended last year!" Caroline almost hissed in anger. "Father too ill to work it, Gove up on the larger tract, or pining for the Embleton land . . . who else could do it? Mother? My mother is a dear woman, Alan, but she depended on my poor father for everything! It could have settled on Burgess, but you know what he thinks of farming."

"And Governour makes no objections?" Alan asked, unable to see the (used-to-be) fiery young hawk-face accede to losing land.

"Dearest Alan, Governour will inherit all when the time comes," Caroline barked in sour amusement. "The last, eldest Chiswick male. Then Uncle Phineas will have what he's always wanted."

"And what is that?" Alan asked.

"An heir to hold the land. If he's said it the once, he's said it an hundred times." She frowned. "The land is forever. Men and women rise up and die, but the land is always. And he doesn't want to see it in a stranger's hands. The Embletons get what they want as well," she almost spat in conclusion.

"And that is?"

"That the two biggest estates are united." Caroline shivered. "After all these years, with Governour and Millicent wed, they are linked."

"Now I see why Governour would not object," Alan laughed in understanding. "There's always the off-chance he'd outlive Harry and end up with it all."

"Oh, yes!" Caroline nodded. "And to ensure his complaisance, Sir Romney's putting Governour up for Commons next by-election, as his pet member from a rotten borough he controls up north. Harry already sits for Anglesgreen. There're not twenty men with the hundred pounds in rents or income to vote here, and even less in Teverly New Town." Caroline shrugged, then smiled ruefully. "Forgive me, Alan, a woman is not to know such, or involve herself in men's doings, but that's the way things stand here."

"As if that ever stopped you!" Alan hooted, trying to cosset her out of her bleak mood. "I've seen you before, remember, so eager to talk about any subject, then fade back into the woodwork when you think you've overstepped yourself. What a bloody waste!"

"Thank you, Alan, I do appreciate your understanding." Caroline truly smiled for the first time that morning. "Yes, I find it hard to be so . . . subservient! In North Carolina, so much more was expected of a woman, so much more was she allowed, as a helpmeet to her man and her family! Here, one *sews* neatly," she complained. "One plays an instrument. One reads, and distills, and orders servants, and cannot dirty one's own dresses at gardening, but must tell others what to do. Here in England, I feel so like an ill-bred . . . *lout!*"

"Out of place?" he muttered, laying a hand on hers this time, and she seized his hand like a drowning victim and linked their fingers. "Not a pink-cheeked, rude Colonial, surely."

"Out of place, yes," she sighed, almost on the point of tears. "Truly, I wonder if I have a place! Or a life I may call mine own."

"And what sort of a life do you desire, Caroline?"

"I wish to be happy, Alan. I wish to . . . to wed someone I love so deeply, and if I do indeed have the . . . the *economy* to present that man with a well-run home, then that is what I want. I want children, and perhaps one maid-of-all-work to help a little. But I want to be useful, not only around the house, but on the land. And to myself and those I love. I know I may not aspire to a man's role in this life. I have no wish to enter Parliament, or fight wars. But I do wish to be able to use those talents God gave me as a woman, and the mind I believe He gave me for something more useful than . . . *baking!*"

"To be able to talk about any subject without restrictions," Alan suggested.

"Oh, God, yes!" Caroline beamed, laughing at her immodesty, or what most in Society would have called an unnatural, desexing immodesty. "To be included when men talk about important matters and not be run off to the parlor to drink tea and get the card table ready. To be *listened* to, if I feel I have an idea they haven't. Not patted on the head and told 'tut-tut, there, there, little girl'! Even if it's but the one man who would listen to me, that would be enough, I think."

"And no one is listening to you now?" Alan said, letting go her hand and dismounting. He held her mare's head while she got down, revealing a dizzying vision of a slim white leg above the tops of her riding boots for an instant as her gown and petticoats raked down the saddle.

"Burgess used to," she said, taking his hand once more as they strolled to the south edge of the rolling, wooded hill to look at the splendid morning view. It was a little cloudy and gloomy yet, before the sun broke through, and the tiny dells among the downs were clotted with wisps of mist. "And when I was with you, I felt that you did, or at least attempted to, Alan. But very few people now. Now, *I* listen, and I am told what I feel, what I should think."

"Whom you should wed, perhaps?" Alan said, stopping them so she would turn to face him. "Is that why you are so sad? I came down, expecting to see the pert lass I remembered, and I find you troubled and melancholy. Who is the right young man of whom your uncle speaks?"

"I have two wonderful choices in life." Caroline gloomed again. "Three, really. The last may be the most acceptable; it does not demand me living a lie. I may take service as governess to a widower's children. Mr. Byford, who rents the land and house *we* once had."

"And the other two?"

"Between Embleton and Glandon Park, there is a family with more than one thousand fine acres," she said with an impatient shake of her head. "George Tudsbury, another widower, is in need of a wife. He's in his forties, with three children to raise, most fortunately all of them girls, who may not inherit the land if a younger wife is living. He's a very good friend of my Uncle Phineas. Of much the same tastes."

"Ugh!" Alan exclaimed. "And again, ugh!"

"He, at least, is a decent man, Alan, with no vices. And no hard edges, such as Uncle Phineas. In that, at least, they differ."

"May I assume that he is your uncle's preference?"

"No, you may not. There is also Harry Embleton." She tensed.

"Mine arse on a bandbox!" Alan cried. "Why, I met the bastard!"

"And what did you think of him, Alan?" Caroline teased, enjoying Alan's use of what she had come to know as his favorite phrase.

"Caroline, were I a London pimp, I'd have him wash first, and then charge him double for the insult to me whores!" Alan shouted.

"Oh, God, Alan, I do so enjoy talking with you!" Caroline laughed out loud, taking hold of his upper arms. "You're just the breath of air that I've been needing! You're right, he is a . . . a bastard!" She took a deep breath, astounded by her own boldness. "He's a cruel, cruel . . . a . . . God, if he were in the Carolinas, he'd be a Low Country slaver, no matter the quality of his birth. He's dull, he's . . . they have a library at Embleton Hall, hundreds of books, and I doubt he's read more than three in his entire life. It's all horses and hounds, politics and sport, who he insulted last, how he put someone in their place . . ."

"And you've expressed your lack of interest to your uncle, I take it?" Alan asked. "Yet he still allows these gentlemen to call?"

"Insists upon it." Caroline sobered once more. "It matters not which I end up choosing, as long as I choose. He gains more land on either side. Or I may remain a spinster, earning my own keep, should I spite him."

"Governour won't back you?"

"Oh, Governour is all for Harry, they hunt and fish and ride together, God knows what all," Caroline said with a wave of her hand, as though to drive away a pesky wasp. "Thank God Millicent is for me. She has not pressured me in any way, much as she might care to have me as sister-in-law. I cherish her for deflecting some of Governour's insistences. He thinks that I am of an age to marry, and that beyond the two men, I have few other choices for a suitable match. Therefore, I must marry, and if I must, then Harry is the better, the richer, and the younger, and not as plodding as Mister Tudsbury, who merely wants a married governess for his living children. He points out that if I marry Harry, then either he or I end up with the two estates in time."

"What a marvelous bloody bargain," Alan glowered. "And you the prize mare to seal it. Christ!"

"Now you see why I have been so downcast," Caroline sighed. "And why I was so looking forward to your visit! When you wrote to say that you had first to visit in Devon, I was almost beside myself. But now you're here, and for a few weeks, at least, I shall feel more at ease. The dashing Alan Lewrie could cheer up the dead!"

"I'll do all in my power for you," Alan vowed. "I'll sing songs, I'll play the merry-andrew and be your court fool, if that's what it takes! Shall I do a handstand?" He laughed, trying to balance on his palms, and ended up rolling flat on his back. "I know," he suggested, getting to his feet quickly, "what if I climb this damned oak and fetch you an acorn or two?"

She was almost shrieking with laughter as he tried to scale the stout trunk to the lowest boughs. "Come down here, at once! Oh, Alan, not an acorn, I beg you!"

"Bloody squirrel, then!" he huffed, springing at the tree once more and clawing his way up about six feet off the ground.

"William Pitt fetches me quite enough squirrels, thank you! Do come down, Alan! I'll settle for a leaf! Just a leaf!" she cried, in stitches at his antics. "I'll take one that's fallen. My kingdom for a fallen oak leaf! God, but you do look foolish! Is that the way you scale the rigging on your ship?"

"I'm graceful as a bloody monkey!" Alan crowed, and began singing a suggestive chantey called "The Holy Ground." He finally dropped to the ground and scooped up an entire pile of oak leaves and brought them to her, dribbling a trail behind him. He knelt at her feet and heaped them round her boots. "For you, my lady, queen of the hill! Oak leaves for your kingdom!"

"Arise, Sir Knight! I dub thee knight of my realm!" She giggled, touching him on both shoulders. He stood, and there was not a handspan between them, and they stopped laughing. She looked up at his face, uttered a tiny, hitching little sound that sounded like a sob, and threw her arms around his neck. Her cool lips pressed upon his, her breath warm and clean on his mouth, and he put his arms around her, lifting her off her feet to drape against him. She felt so light, so slim and completely encirclable in his arms, and Alan's head spun with the scent of clean hair and soap, of the light, citrony and balsamed tinge of the Hungary Water she had dabbed on.

Burgess, forgive me, but I think I want to tup your sister! he thought. And what your family thinks of me after that, bedamned!

The sound of hooves interrupted them, two sets of hooves at the least, of horses being urged up the hill to them, and he set her down and stood a little back from her, full of regret that the moment had passed. His groin was on fire, and his heart was pounding such as he had never experienced with common lust, or the fine edge of expectation before consummation. Caroline Chiswick made him dizzier and woozier to hold and kiss than anyone he had ever known!

And I've had my share now, haven't I, so I ought to know, Alan told himself. Damme to hell, but I think I'm in love with her, not . . . not just afire to *have* her! Damme if I ain't been toyin' with the thought of her since '81!

Caroline brushed his cheek with her gloved hands, and stepped forward for one last, too-brief, open-mouthed kiss, then took a few steps away, composing herself to see who was coming.

"Have they sent someone after us?" he asked softly.

"I don't know . . . Heavens, it might be something wrong with father! I can think of no other reason. Dear God, no! Alan, pray for him, a short prayer to spare him, now!" she commanded in a fret.

Two riders topped the rise, and Alan, turning to look at her, could see the tension still in her pose, for it yet might be bad news of Mr. Sewallis Chiswick. But the light in her eyes, and the joy on her face that *he* had put there a minute before fell away like an extinguished sunset when she beheld who led the pair of horsemen.

"My dearest Caroline!" the Hon. Harry Embleton exclaimed as he drew rein to lord over them from horseback. "Your uncle said he thought you might have come this way. Had you forgotten that he had given us permission to take a morning ride together this day?"

"Good morrow, Mister Embleton," Caroline nodded coolly. "And good morrow to you, Mister Lane. You have met Mister Lewrie, I think."

"Mister Embleton, sir," Alan grinned, touching the right side of his cocked hat in greeting like a casual salute to a deck-officer. "And I believe I met Mister Lane, Douglas Lane, is it, yesterday, at the Red Swan? Your gamekeeper, is he not, sir? Joy of the morning, sir."

"Mister Lewrie," Harry Embleton replied, sounding a bit arch as he squinted his close-set eyes at him, then just as quickly lost interest and turned his gaze to Caroline. "Well, shall we have our ride, my dear?" he asked, turning almost cloyingly mild.

"Mister Embleton, I do recall that my uncle did give us his permission, but I considered that was dependent upon whether I gave *my* consent to it," Caroline replied. "In fact, in the excitement of Mister Lewrie's arrival, I quite forgot it. Perhaps you should talk with Uncle Phineas, and *me*, for another time."

God, the girl has steel in her backbone, Alan exulted!

"Well, since we are all here, that is . . ." Harry suggested, looking extremely miffed and hunching down into his coat collar.

Since there was no way to turn him down without being rude, she heaved a small sigh to show the slightest bit of exasperation at his intrusion, and allowed as how they *might* ride for a piece together.

"If you would assist me, Alan?" she asked after he brought her mare to her. Embleton sprang down from his saddle to come to her side but Caroline was already taking Alan's offered hand to steady her as she put a booted foot in the stirrup and got aboard. "My thanks to you, Alan." Leaving Harry flicking reins on his boots foolishly.

"Any time, Caroline." Lewrie smiled, looking up at her. And it mattered to him to see how she would handle this; most women he'd known would have exulted in having two men snarling over them, and would have gotten a certain joy out of the heightening of a bad situation.

Alan crossed to his gelding and mounted, then walked up to her side. "Well, where to, now? Down towards that middle stream you told me of? After clawing up this hill, I'm sure the horses could use some water."

"Yes, that sounds pleasant," she replied, and led off without a backward glance. Harry and Alan caught her up and rode to either side of her.

"A lovely morning," Harry Embleton said. "D'ye know that we put up a fox on the way over. Be good sport. Wish we had the hounds with us. Do you hunt, Lewrie?"

"Not for a long time, in Kent. Cruel, it is," Alan replied.

"Blood sport not t'yer taste, then? My word, you've come to the wrong place, hey, Caroline?" Harry guffawed.

"I was speaking of the horses, sir," Alan smiled evenly. "Too much neck-or-nothing, like a steeplechase these days. Now a proper hunt, you have to stop and let the dogs have their scent, take care of your animals. I've seen too many fine horses put down to some fool's carelessness to suit me."

"I do think it cruel as well to kill a blooded horse for the momentary joy of chasing a fox, whose pelt price would not buy a new saddle-pad,

Mister Embleton," Caroline added. "Much as I love riding and going hard 'cross-country, I'd never lash little Sabina here to her death." She patted the neck of her mare lovingly. "And the hunt does result in a lot of damage to crops and such. Surely, snares are to be preferred to keep down the fox population."

"Foxes be too clever t'snare, Miss Chiswick," Lane said from behind. " 'E takes too many rabbits'n hens. An' it's good sport!"

"Caroline has ridden on our hunt, haven't you, my dear? I had no idea you disliked it so," Harry pouted.

"I did not say I disliked it, Mister Embleton. I merely said that *some* are too heedless of their horses." She replied without turning to look at him. "Now, last fall, you lost that fine gray taking a fence, when the gate was open not a furlong farther down to let the dogs through. And think of the colts you could have had from that black that fell going down the steep bank. A thousand guineas lost!"

"Don't trouble your head about profit or loss, Caroline," the Honourable Harry stated with a little titter of amusement. "They gave good sport in their lives, and that's what horses are for. And we own enough of them. Mister Lewrie, I say, you ride well, I see. Perhaps you might be interested in taking a look at Douglas's mount there. I think you could appreciate his formation. Douglas, here, you ride with Mister Lewrie for a span, whilst I and Caroline go ahead."

"I see he's a good'un," Alan said, turning in the saddle to eye the horse in question, then turning back. "I'm more taken with Sabina here. Is she from Governour's stud, Caroline?"

"Indeed she is, Alan. Isn't she beautiful?" Caroline waxed almost rhapsodic about her mare, who perked her ears up and arched her neck as she was praised. "She's such a big hearted old baby, I cannot tell you how often she's gone the limit, when she knows she should quit. Good-gaited, too! And on a canter, you'd think you were in an armchair!"

They discussed the finer points of the mare to exhaustion, and to the total disregard for the earnest Harry Embleton, who sulked on the far side, his ears burning and his breakfast congealing into some stony lump in his stomach.

"And what are the horses like in India, Alan? Did you get to ride while you were there?" Caroline demanded to know. "Heavens, more to the point, what is *India* like! Your letters told me some, but not in such detail as I would have liked."

"Well, picture . . ." Alan began, happy to monopolize another topic which might be good for the rest of the morning.

"You exchanged *letters?*" Harry sniffed. That did not sound very prom-

ising, and he felt another spasm of jealousy and hatred for this interloper. He hadn't known that they wrote each other! Such was for people
already plighted or betrothed, or those who would be when circumstances allowed, dammit all!

"Oh, yes. Father gave his permission in Charleston, long ago, Mister
Embleton," Caroline told him, looking in his direction for the first time
in half an hour.

"But he's . . . I mean, your uncle . . . *he* is aware . . ." Embleton
flustered, almost drawing rein to pull away.

"That my father is no longer able to direct the affairs of his children,
Mister Embleton?" Caroline huffed, not liking to be reminded of that
fact. "And, at twenty two, I am hardly a minor to have to ask with
whom I am able to correspond."

"As a friend of the family," Embleton sighed, finding a cause for relief.
"I see."

"As a friend of our family, certainly," Caroline said, turning to smile
at Lewrie. "As one of my dearest acquaintances, as well."

"A lovely spot, this," Alan said, pointing to the grove of willows by
the little freshet toward which they'd been riding. "God, wish we'd
thought to pack a lunch. Have what the Frogs call a *pique-nique.*"

"We could do that tomorrow!" Caroline exclaimed. "Oh, let's do!"

"Or we could ride back to the house and put one together now!" Alan
suggested. "It's what, mile and a half out and back?" He took his watch
from his pocket and studied it. "Just in time for dinner."

"Will you ride with us back to the house, Mister Embleton?" Caroline
asked him. "Perhaps you could dine with Uncle Phineas and Governour.
And I know Millicent hasn't seen you since last Sunday church. You
owe your good sister a visit, you know," she concluded with mock sever-
ity, then turned back to Lewrie. "Should I bring my flute, do you think?
If you do not find my playing tedious."

"I insist on the flute," Alan laughed. "I was quite taken with your
playing last night. It was only then I learned you were so musical. And
talented. A French-style *pique-nique,* a bottle of wine, and music! What
could be grander!"

"Give my regards t'my sister," Harry Embleton glowered, turning tur-
key-wattle red at not being invited to join them. "I've things to see to at
home, then. For today, at any rate. My dearest Caroline, allow me to call
upon you for another ride, soon? I shall speak to yer uncle, then, for his
permission?"

"You *may* speak with my uncle, Mister Embleton," Caroline said with a touch of ice, sidling her mare round in a small circle to end up with Alan almost between them. "We shall see."

"G . . . good day to you, Caroline," Harry grumped, sweeping off his hat and making a bow. "And to you, Lewrie."

"Good day, Mister Embleton," Caroline nodded.

"Joy o' the mornin', Mister Embleton," Alan said with a grin, raising his own hat in parting.

Harry sawed the reins about and put spurs to his stallion, off in a cloud of dust and high dudgeon, lashing with the reins to goad the poor beast into a furious gallop. Lane touched the brim of his hat and took off in pursuit, hoping young Harry didn't kill another animal in his rage.

Chapter 5

For perhaps a week longer, Lewrie and Caroline were inseparable. There were more daily rides, *pique-niques*, strolls through the village to shop together, with Alan allowed the signal honor of carrying her basket for her, of opening doors for her, of offering her his arm upon which she would from time to time rest her soft hand and forearm.

There was Divine Services at St. George's with Alan ensconced by Caroline's side in the Chiswick pew-boxes, holding the prayer book and hymnal for the two of them, which perforce required them to come together, demurely, at hip or shoulder. And in the yard afterwards, it was Alan who was by her side as introductions were made to other young people of her acquaintance, especially the other young ladies of Angles-green and its environs; introductions at which Alan Lewrie strove to shine, to be singularly pleasing and courteous, though never more than mildly interested in anyone else, as he appeared so attentive to Caroline and her mother. The other girls tittered behind their fans and prayer books, casting sly, meaningful glances at the pair. Or peeked from beneath their bonnets or over their shoulders at the Hon. Harry Embleton, who ground his teeth and cursed under his breath at being shut out so completely, left to stand in foolish neglect when he insinuated himself into their company.

Alan had always considered Caroline Chiswick the most delightful young woman of his acquaintance, the most skilled, the easiest to talk to, and one of the most intelligent. Beyond her fair, willowy beauty, which any young girl could for a time boast, there was an intellect, a depth beneath the frippery and japery which had always intrigued him. She was not a snickerer or titterer, much; and though it was the nature of young women to be enthusiastic and at times giddy (or so Lewrie thought from past experience of young women who could be styled "ladies") there was beneath Caroline's merry nature a placidity, a centered calm not unlike the eye of an Indies' hurricane, where one might discover a safe lee, abounding common sense, and natural grace and warmth far more alluring than the most exciting young "chick-a-biddy," which would be there when all else failed or withered.

What had he really known of her before, he wondered? A brief encounter in Wilmington during the evacuation in '81, a day and night aboard the *Desperate* frigate on the way to Charleston, and one soul-shattering midnight kiss on that freezing quarter-deck. Letters on rare occasions when mail caught up with his ship. And then three weeks of closely chaperoned, and too-brief, meetings in London whilst he finagled an appointment for her brother Burgess through his patron Adm. Sir Onsley Matthews, a whole three years later!

All of which had led him to say that "now there's a sensible and lovely young lady who'd make me a fine wife . . . someday." Assuming he lived long enough to wed, he qualified; assuming he ever had an urge to do something so completely stupid, and alien, to his rakehell, Corinthian nature!

Now, in a positive orgy of constantly keeping company with her, and, given the heady rush of randiness she aroused in him, her wholehearted approbation of him, and her merriest, most affectionate and warmest encouragements, Alan Lewrie gave up *thinking* and dove in to wallow in that affection, consideration and encouragement.

His heart, too, went out to her, when he contemplated which of her gloomy choices for her future she might have to accept once he was gone. He had met the Tudsbury fellow her Uncle Phineas liked, and the tenant Byford, and it made him ill to think of either of the elderly farts sharing table with her, much less bed. Worse than Harry Embleton, damme if they weren't, he gagged!

There was, too, at last, Lewrie's perverse streak to consider. He doubted he'd ever warm to the Hon. Harry Embleton, who struck him as the sort of complete fool who, were it raining claret, would have but a flour-sieve to catch it in—and he'd drop that! Lewrie knew his constant, and seemingly affectionate attentions to Caroline made Harry's liver fry.

He knew Harry detested him more than cold, boiled mutton, and made no bones about it. One could toast bread on his overt scorn, his hostility.

And, being Alan Lewrie, Lewrie cheerfully, and with much mirth, enjoyed every cutty-eyed glare, and schemed to see what new devilment he might invent to vex him.

"I haven't the lip for it, I fear, Caroline," Alan admitted to her after a paltry assay at playing her flute. He laid it aside on the blanket and lay back on an elbow to poke into the commodious food basket to see if there was anything left of their rustic repast.

"Perhaps a flageolet would serve better," Caroline told him, a wry smile still on her lips from the horrible sounds he had produced. "One blows into the end, not across, and how one's lips are pursed is of no matter."

"Pursed lips are unsuitable for other amusements, as well," he chuckled, trying not to sound (too much, anyway) as if he were leering.

"We were discussing music, sir." She reddened, eyes demurely downcast, but with a smile on her face.

"I enjoy music immensely, but I've never seemed to have had a talent for the playing of it," Alan shrugged. "I admire your gift as a musician. Almost envious, in truth."

"Ah, but have you ever really applied yourself, Alan?" she said, teasing, inclining her head to one side and making her long, glittery light brown hair swish most fetchingly. "I cannot imagine anyone so capable as you not mastering anything he attempted."

"God bless you for your high regard of me, Caroline!" He sighed in pleasure, taking her hand to bestow a brief kiss upon it, "I hate to disabuse you of the notion, but I ain't perfect, not good at everything. Thankee kindly for it, though."

He lay back on the blanket to stare up at the sky, his coat and waistcoat for a pillow. She reclined as well, on the other side, with two decorous feet of blanket a gulf between them, though she still held his hand across that space.

"Lord, what a perfectly lovely day it is!" He chuckled happily.

"It is indeed," she agreed, eyes shut and lips curved in a secret smile. "And a ruined castle of our very own, not that Norman pile!" she concluded with a little laugh.

Days before, they had ridden with Governour and Millicent to the Guidier castle and bailey to tour it, escorted most unctuously by Harry and his constant minion Douglas Lane, the gamekeeper, who was there to disarm the man-traps and spring guns. What joy there may have been in the excursion had been ruined by Harry's black looks, alternated with his feeble attempts at gallantry and possessiveness.

"This may be just as old," Caroline boasted. "Older, perhaps. Not as grand, certainly. But ours."

On Chiswick land, far by the northwestern bounds, there stood a tiny ruin atop a bare hill. Norman keep, Angle or Saxon hill fort, ancient Roman camp, or Celtic *oppidum* reared before Caesar's times, no one could tell, for it had lain empty and barren time out of mind.

There was a spring and a wellshaft full of stones and trash on the western side, inside a fosse now filled with weeds and bushes, behind a raised earthen parapet and man-high wall of dry-laid stones, now mostly tumbled down to lower than one's knees in most places. A watchtower reared from the center on a higher platform of stone and earth like a broken tusk, the narrow doorway gouged into a shallow Vee-shaped opening one could now drive a cart through, and its circle of walls no more than waist height, the whole green with moss and the hardiest grasses.

The spring now trickled down a grassy slough through a rent in the wall and the moat, down a slight slope littered with remnants of the walls' stones, to the musically trickling creek which marked the boundary. Inside the parapet and fosse the horses grazed and sipped water, while within the circumference of the fallen tower, they lay at their ease. They had ridden to it that morning, partly for Caroline to show off what Chiswick land could boast against Embleton, and partly for the deliciously daring separation it afforded them from the great house and its doings. They could quite easily imagine that not a single human being stirred within two miles of their aerie.

Alan was blissfully content—and most pleasantly stuffed. They had dined on cold sliced tongue and mustard, served gaming-house style, *à la* Lord Sandwich, between crusty new bread slices, on fried chicken, cheese and sweet pickles, and had washed it down with a cool bottle of Rhenish. Another sat waiting to open in the chill waters of the spring, an expertly tied 'round turn and two half hitches' on its neck made from a length of small-stuff to draw it up with, which Caroline had thought most clever of him to bring along, and also most knacky of him to know how to tie.

She let go of his hand, and he put both of his palms beneath his head, as he gazed up at the fleecy clouds that sailed overhead, framed in the circle of the watchtower's ruin as if seen through a spyglass. Birds flitted and warbled through his squinted vision, a pair of rooks sailed along from one tree to another, and a falcon circled lazily above them.

He heard music, as Caroline sat up, legs tucked to one side, and began to play a very old country song he'd heard before but never knew the name to. He gave her an encouraging smile before turning his face back to the sky and closing his eyes, more than ready for a short nap of satiation and peace.

Almost at the verge of sleep, he did not notice when her music ceased. Almost adrift, he barely sensed her shadow over his sun-shut eyes, no more than he might have noticed a cloud occluding the light for a second or two. He grinned slightly as something soft tickled his cheeks, as a sweet, fruity perfume insinuated its way into his snoozing awareness of grass, wool and fried chicken.

What woke him was the soft, moist pressure of her lips.

His eyes flew open, and there Caroline was, kneeling over him, bending down with one hand supporting her, the other holding her hair back, a most fond look on her face and in her eyes; grinning at waking him, grinning with delight at the way she had done so, and grinning with excitement of being, for a fleeting moment, just a bit wanton.

Chaperoned as they had been, as in public as they had been in the last week, they had not had opportunity to kiss beyond that one enthusiastic, but interrupted, moment the first day they'd ridden.

Alan smiled back at her, and she leaned forward once more to bend down to him. Then, being Alan Lewrie, his baser instincts took over, and he raised a hand to caress her cheek as their lips met, to stroke under her thick hair to the base of her neck and hold her from escaping, his arm encircling her upper back; the other to explore the length of her, down to her waist from her shoulder. To draw her down to recline against him. His nether regions sprang awake as well as their lips parted, as their tongues met and circled—his with long practice, hers in a shivery experimental response.

To his immense surprise, she did sink down beside him, atop him, sliding her feet down toward his, as he began to kiss her cheeks, her eyelids, her nose, and her brow, to nuzzle deep under her hair to her ears, below and behind them into the secret hollows of her throat, and under her chin, down past her collarbones to her exposed chest.

With a shuddery impatience, she put her arms about his neck and sought his mouth with hers once more. With a swishing of cloth, in ancient instinct, one thigh crept up across his outstretched legs and near his groin. Mewing with her first heady experience of passion, she returned his attentions measure for measure, her breath coming ragged and sweetening cow-and-clover musky as it mingled with his, as his free hand stroked down her flung-across thigh to discover the last hem of her skirts, the smoothness of a stocking tied above her knee, and the exquisitely maddening softness and smooth-as-talc texture of her thigh. She shivered and wriggled against him as he made his way, soft as butterflies and caressing with his fingertips, all the way up the back of her leg to the fold where slim thigh ended, and soft-but-firm buttock began. Until she began to weep against his neck, her tears and breath hot as a forge.

"Oh, God, Alan, but I love you so much!" she cried, trembling with her passion. "I've always loved you!"

He froze. After a moment, his insistent hand came back up to her back to hold her close and stroke her hair. She kissed him once, twice, thrice more, chastely soft then rolling with enticement each time, before she leaned back the slightest space.

"I have loved you ever since you first came to our door, in those rented rooms in Wilmington, Alan," she told him, her lovely face alive with fleeting emotions, first joy and pleasure, then hesitancy at her revelation. "Five years I've dreamt of this. Five whole years I've wondered how you'd feel. I know *proper* young girls ain't to own to such. I *know* young English ladies oughtn't say such things, but . . . at last, you're here where I may at last tell you face to face . . ."

"And other things," Alan shuddered, trying to be light.

"And other things," she echoed, nodding slowly and resting her body a little more atop him again. "Our too few letters, they'd never serve to tell you, Alan. You were half a world away, at sea, and you could have dismissed me as a foolish young chit, had I ever dared record my feelings towards you on paper. But now, we have so little time before you're off again . . . I could no longer keep it to myself, do you see, Alan? Before you sail out of my life again, you *have* to know how much . . . God save me! . . . how *deep* in love I am with you!"

"Oh, Caroline!" he whispered into her hair, folding her into his arms tighter and closer, for want of something else to say, as his mind rattled about like a startled sparrow in a cage. And, like a sparrow, seeking an exit! "You darling, darling girl!"

Damme, what do ye do now, ye poxy clown, he wondered? What do ye say to the poor little mort?

It was not as if he *hadn't* been half-seas-over about her those past five years! Every one of her letters that had survived the post and the voyage of delivery had been a veritable feast for his soul, every sight and scent and sound of her in their too-short *rencontres* had made him woozy with both delight and lust.

But then, so had a *platoon* of delectable young mutton!

"Have I been a fool all this time, Alan dearest?" she asked in a small, slightly scared voice against his cheek. "I do confess I love you, have loved you such a long, long time! I've dreamt about you, thought about you . . . made up silly fantasies . . . !" She rushed on, frightened by his silence and unwilling to give him pause in which to answer, fearing an answer which would break her heart.

He could not hurt her feelings . . . could never even consider hurting her feelings! Of that he was sure. She was indeed dear to him. But by replying with the truth, or nearly the truth, he would step over the bounds of flattering but playful gallantry and "cream-pot" courtship into another, infinitely restrictive world.

Of course, he speculated quickly as she prated on, her family might not approve, after all, and would deny them. Or, he could vow his love for her, but plead his new commission in the Bahamas, requiring a long betrothal, for what that was worth to her, sparing her Tudsbury's, Byford's, and most especially Embleton's advances; then, what he might do with his own life overseas would be his own, still, setting anything permanent far off into the future.

Could he spurn her affection and break her heart? No. Could he be callous enough to sail off and leave her to a cruel fate? No. Could he rescue her? Yes, he could. And still remain mostly free.

"I love *you*, Caroline!" he muttered in reply at last, stopping her lips first with a fingertip, then once more with a kiss, and she yelped aloud in shivery relief, in pleasure, and in sudden, springing joy. And when she drew back once more to gaze upon him, her visage crumpled somewhere between tears and heavenly elation, the look she bestowed upon him, so full of love and promise, was all the reward that any lover could ever hope to see.

"Truly, I do love you!" he grinned back at her, jolting himself with the horrifying thought that, for once in his miserable "damme-boy" life, he was telling the truth when he said that to a young lady.

"Oh, Alan! God, you've made me so *happy!*" she exulted with a trembly laugh of victory. "My Alan! Wonderful, marvelous Alan, my own love!"

There ensued a few feverish minutes during which neither of them had need for speech as they swooned with the wonder of kisses and caresses, of rolling about on the blanket, limbs twining as they took the measure of each other, heated nearly to a forge's glow, or the blue white heat of steel. Experimenting with how two alien bodies would mesh together in the years to come, first clumsy and with no clue where hands and arms would be most comfortable or exciting, but learning quickly.

Though still gowned, Caroline was explored with gentleness, and nowhere Alan caressed or kissed her did she flinch from, though she started now and again as she experienced sensations she had not in her limited knowledge ever even imagined. And she chuckled and sighed and groaned with delight; laughing once out loud in reverie of a neighbor boy in North Carolina who had dared to kiss her on the shoulder and lips one night when she was sixteen—purse-lipped—and how she had at that time thought that the heady sensation she had experienced then was the height of human passion!

Alan reclined atop her. Her sack gown and underskirts were rucked up near her hips, her thighs parted, by his weight and ancient instinct on her part, their groins pressed close and shifting slowly—again in instinct on her part, as Alan tenderly undid the buttons of the back of her gown, rained kisses and endearments muffled by her flesh upon her shoulders, her chest, and the tops of her breasts.

"Alan," she groaned. "We . . ."

"Yes," he muttered hoarsely.

"We should stop. For now, dearest." She concluded, "Please?"

Jesus bloody Christ on a cross, he groaned to himself! Damme, not *now!*

But he, with the utmost regret of his life, suffered himself to slide to his left, to recline beside her, though with one arm behind her, still. There was no way he would be able to ride back to the great house in his raging, aching tumescence; he thought he would be fortunate, indeed, if he might manage to walk!

But she was right, he thought, miserably, as he enfolded her once more and confined his attentions to kisses and close hugs, with no more attempts at removing her gown. I'll not make her think she was tumbled in a hayrick like a goose-girl, he told himself! What if she became pregnant—I haven't my sheep-gut condom with me. A pristine betrothal could become a sword-point wedding in the blink of an eye, and *then* where'd we be, I ask you?

"You'll make me yours, soon, dearest Alan," she comforted. "I must own to ignorance about . . ." Caroline blushed and fumbled a tentative hand against his shirt buttons. "I'm told by older ladies it *may* be pleasureable, after the . . . after the first . . ."

"I'll not cause you pain, Caroline," he vowed. "I love you!"

"I know you would not!" she asserted strongly. "Please be a little patient with me, dearest. I know you love me. I've seen it in your eyes,

I've heard it in your voice, every time we've been so fortunate as to be together. I would not have bided my time a whole five years if I had *not!* I believe that . . . with you, it will be a complete pleasure. If this is anything by which I may judge! Do remember, I'm a country girl, after all, with two older brothers."

"Eh?" he asked, puzzled by her seeming *non sequitur.*

"The barnyards." She flushed again, lowering her gaze. "And our studpens. And their boasting, when they thought no one heard."

"Oh!" he fathomed with a furtive smile.

"Once we're wed, then, I know my introduction to the pleasure of marriage will be gentle and tender, and so full of joy," she said.

Marriage, he gasped? Sweet Lord Jesus, what have I . . . ?

"You are so smart and knowledgeable, Alan," she sighed happily. "And you are a man grown, after all, and . . . a sailor. One might hope . . . somewhat experienced . . ." She beamed, stroking his cheek fondly.

"Uhm," he allowed with a sage nod, squirming inside, thinking it wouldn't do if she knew he'd rattled half of London. "I will own to . . . ermm . . . previous encounters, infrequent though they were, being so much at sea. And only when . . . well, when the need was hellish."

"Then you must teach me, sweetest Alan," she said, smiling an enigmatic smile which he was not sure signified that she knew he was lying like a butcher's dog. "I will be a most willing pupil," she ended with a most fetching shyness, and a heart-stopping promise.

"Ah . . . hmm," he mused nonplussed, with his erotic fantasies at a furious gallop. Right, then; could it be *that* bad?

"You *do* wish to marry me, do you not, Alan?" she asked.

"Of course I do!" he heard himself say, "I love you!"

"Oh, Alan!" she cried, hugging him. "The first banns could be read this Sunday. We could be wed three weeks from now! Let us go ask of my family right now, so there's no possible delay! Mother may be half-expecting our wonderful news . . . though the others will be all amort over it!"

"Most likely," Alan agreed wholeheartedly. And damme if I ain't amort meself over it! Christ shit on a biscuit—*marriage!*

"Not only have you saved me from any number of cruel, cold destinies, Alan," she enthused as he got her to her feet and they embraced close together once more, "but you've given me every last measure of happiness I ever imagined I could know! I was so fearful you'd want to make a higher rank in the Fleet before you'd wed. I was fearful you'd have found someone else, all the years you were gone. That I was only spinning daydreams. We *are* awfully young. Most wait until their late twenties, when they're solidly established and all . . ." A hint of doubt swept over her face. "Are you as sure as I, Alan my love?"

"I love you, Caroline," he swore. "We love each other. Now, why would I risk losing you after all this time, and run the risk of never finding your like again?" There was truth in that, as well.

"Then let's hurry home!" she beamed.

Chapter 6

"Goddamn my eyes, sir!" Uncle Phineas screeched loud as some goosed panther once they bearded him in his study. "Goddamn my *eyes!* I'll not have it! And Goddamn yer blood, too, sir! Never! Never, do ye hear, Mister Lewrie?"

"What possible objections could you have, Uncle?" Caroline inquired quite reasonably, having had an inkling or two as to what the man's reactions would be beforehand.

"Phineas, Alan Lewrie saved my sons at Yorktown, evacuated us from the wrath of those ignorant Rebels," Mother Charlotte hissed. "Why, without his continuing good offices, Governour and Burgess like as not'd be dead these five years past, and us, your own kin, lynched for Tories and buried under some crossroads in Wilmington!"

"This is man's business, Charlotte, and I'll thankee to remember that!" Uncle Phineas shot back. "Aye, ye may feel grateful to the pup, aye, he's done ye service. But, he's a swaggerin' rogue of a fortune hunter."

"I beg your pardon!" Alan snapped.

"Ye'll not coozen one acre o' land outa me, Mister Lewrie. Not one farthin' o' Chiswick rents'll ye have!"

The fight had been going on for a good five minutes, with Alan and Caroline, Governour and Mother Charlotte present, and the top was still on the decanter of brandy, nothing having been settled.

"My dear sir," Alan replied coldly, "for one of your farthings, I'd call you out for those slanderous allegations."

"Alan!" Caroline wailed, sure he'd blown the gaff. "Don't . . ."

"I've my Navy pay, sir," Alan said, getting to his feet. "Aye, I've no lands of my own. My father and his elder brother squandered the last blade of Kentish grass I'll ever *hope* to see. But there's two hundred pounds *per annum* from my grandmother Lewrie in Devon, and roughly six thousand pounds with Coutts & Co. I stand to inherit from her. No land, though; that's spoken for by her late husband's kin, the Nuttbushes of Wheddon Cross. But there's another five thousand pounds of my own . . . prize money from the War, and from my last service in the East Indies. D'you think I need one whit of yours?"

The idea of posting banns, of publicly stating his love for Caroline, of being wed—much less betrothed—gave him the squirting fits so bad he'd not trust his own arse with a fart. But he had had just about enough abuse poured upon him, and upon Caroline as a foolish chit of a girl too stupid to know her own mind, or recognize a scoundrel when she met one.

"My stars!" Governour exclaimed, and gave a whistle at those sums. "Like to purchase freehold land, Alan? With that much, you could have your pick around here, hey?"

"Oh, do shut up, Governour!" Uncle Phineas snarled. "No, as head of this family . . ."

"My *father* is the head of *my* family, Uncle Phineas," Caroline pointed out.

"Bah! And a precious lot of good his wits'll do for ye, girl!"

"Phineas!" Charlotte gasped. "How dare you!" She put a handkerchief to her eyes, not for the first time during this battle, at that latest cruelty. "How dare you impugn my dear husband. Your own brother!"

"Any court in the land'd recognize my rights as elder in matters such as this, Charlotte. Forgive me me outburst, but this fella's driven me beyond all temperance." Phineas calmed. "In Sewallis's stead, it falls t'me t' decide what's best fer our dear Caroline, and I don't judge this best."

"Uncle, I will not be sold to Harry Embleton," Caroline told him. "I am old enough to know my own mind. Old enough to wed whom I will."

"Who said anythin' 'bout *sellin'* anybody to anybody?" Phineas Chiswick snapped, irritated beyond measure by her calm demeanor.

"Uncle, Alan has substance," Governour commented. "Not merely wherewithal to establish a household, or obtain lands. I've found him to be a most talented and capable young man. He's a fine future in the Navy. End up an admiral, like as not."

God spare me, Alan thought of *that* idea!

"Governour . . . !" Phineas harrumphed, as though Brutus had just slipped the dagger into his Julius Caesar.

"Yes, he does," Mother Charlotte echoed.

"And she loves him, Uncle Phineas." Governour reddened.

"Good God, what's fleetin' heat got t'do with anythin'?" the old man groused. "Marriages'r fer-bloody-ever in our class. Let the young'uns run off with just *any* sparkin' rogue'r round-heeled lass, and where's sense, logic, and bottom t'be, I ask ye? Then where's a parent's wishes come inta play, a parent's better sense? And cream-pot, stableboy love don't last beyond the first swaddlin' clothes, and then, where's the girl? Miserable, I tell ye, bound to a bully-buck scoundrel and half-way t'the poor's house!"

"I suppose that is why you never married, Phineas," Charlotte Chiswick muttered loud enough for all to hear.

"Charlotte, ye . . . !" the old man gaped, strangling on curses and turning red as roses in near-apoplexy.

"I approve," Charlotte stated, mouse-timorous of stating any opinion. "And, I am certain Sewallis would as well, were he . . ."

"Oh, mother, thank you!" Caroline squealed, going to her.

"I don't!" Phineas barked.

"I do," Governour said, once the echoes had died away. "After all, I wed for love. Mother's told me long ago, before the war, she did. Were Alan Lewrie truly a black-hearted schemer, were he truly worthless, I would not approve. I had hoped, of course, that she and Harry might . . ."

"Gove, believe me," Caroline assured him, sharing his sadness, if only because her brother was sad for what was not to be, "I could never feel the slightest affection for Harry. For anyone but Alan."

"Ye throw away a future baronet, a Member of Commons, and the finest estate in Surrey," Uncle Phineas griped. "And if not Harry, a man of worth and bottom, like . . . like . . ."

"A man old enough to be my father, Uncle Phineas," Caroline said. "There could be no pleasant converse with Mr. Tudsbury for me. I cannot find contentment in contemplating acres, with nothing more in common with him."

"Not one shillin' o' Chiswick worth'll ye have," Phineas vowed, deflated and confounded at last, but willing to go game though he was blocked at both ends. "No dowry, no 'dot,' no annuity."

"I would find that acceptable," Caroline stated, going from her mother's side to take Alan's hand as she sensed he would relent.

"We have more than enough, sir," Alan added.

"She will not!" Governour insisted, slamming a fist onto the arm of his chair. "My sister'll *not* slink away like a midnight eloper. She will *not* go unblessed nor unencumbered with proper due!"

"Amen, my boy," Mother Charlotte agreed, though softly.

"And just what, beyond her paraphernalia and household goods, d'ye think there is t'spare, lad?" Phineas rejoined nastily. "Summat from *yer* revenues? Recollect, the girl herself swears I've no rights over her. That Sewallis is head o' her family. Well, let him dower her, then! Hunnert pound'r so *per annum*, hey? That sum about right? Oh, let's make it hunnert'n eighty pound t'keep her while her husband is gallivantin' about the Bahamas fer three years."

"I know how constrained our finances are, Governour," Caroline told her brother. "I will not demand anything that would deprive you or Millicent of a single morsel."

"Burgess sent home nigh on three thousand pounds, Caroline," Governour stated. "I could . . ."

"No," she insisted, hitching a deep breath. "And a simple wedding. So no one will be begrudging, or beholden, later."

"Just as long as we have even a semblance of a blessing," Alan said, left out of the conversation, and the long-running dispute among the Chiswicks, gladly up until that moment. And even more impressed with Caroline's level-headed sensibility. "We'll not coach to Gretna Green. We'll not elope to Portsmouth, and some sailor's chapel in a warehouse stew. I have enough to rent or purchase a decent cottage for us, and enough to provide for her proper comfort and station in life while I'm away. Should you demand a long engagement . . ."

"Alan!" Caroline protested, thinking still of a quick match.

"Should you demand we wait until I've returned from my active commission, I would provide for her, gladly," he concluded. Damme, but they're hitching the cart to this horse a tad *rapid* for my likes, he thought! It was one thing to win approval and blessing, but he'd thought the altar could wait awhile longer, surely!

"Alan!" Caroline frowned, trying to sound fond, though vexed.

"Forgive me, Caroline, but I'll not abduct you without your family's blessings," he said. "Much as I adore you, I'll not have you starting life with me under any sort of cloud. I'll not have anyone in this world ever suggest we did not begin on the right footing."

"Oh, Alan, you're such a dear." Caroline relented, a little.

Then why do I feel like I'm declaiming like a posturing clown, like one of the actors in *The Beggar's Opera*, he wondered (not for the first time) whenever he'd assayed sounding noble, decent, and upright? *Most* sensible people throw fruit at such players!

Damme, I could damn near give *me* hives!

"She is not due to inherit anything, unless absolute disaster strikes this family, Uncle," Governour sighed, rapping his knuckles on the side table for caution, "Pray God it don't." He added for extra measure, "You disclaim responsibility for her, then?"

"I do," Phineas smouldered.

"Then as eldest, in our father's stead, I'll pledge that when our finances are sufficient to spare an annuity, Caroline'll have an hundred and twenty pounds. Alan, dear little sister Caroline, devil if I know just when that'll *be*, God bless me, but I'll swear you that on paper!"

"Governour, you don't have to." Caroline teared up, rushing to embrace her elder brother. "But thank you, and God bless you for it."

"Thankee, Governour," Alan added, going to take his hand and give it a vigorous pumping.

"Ah, I should have read the signs, you know, Alan," Governour chuckled, shaking his head at his blindness. " 'Twas all we ever heard from her . . . Alan this, Alan that. And nary a swain no matter how he tried could sway her. You *will* be a good husband to her. You'll be good and true to her, and make her happy."

Lewrie didn't think that sounded much like a question. And for a fleeting moment, he conjured up the scarifying image of Governour's ruddy phiz framed over the yawning barrel of a dragoon pistol, big as a twenty-four-pounder, pointed right between his eyes.

"I swear I will, Governour," he smiled.

"He will be," Caroline agreed happily, an arm linked with his.

"Swear you will, *indeed*, you will!" Governour barked with wry amusement. "We'll have a coach brought 'round. Mother, I do believe you'd do well to accompany them to the vicar's, hey?"

"Just let me go and change, son."

Chapter 7

Hounds yelped, handlers cursed, and riders jollied themselves in mounting and boasts, as servants of Embleton Hall made their way between the fidgety horses with trays of stirrup cups to hand up to eager hunters. And tried to avoid the stalings on the drive and the grass, the fresh puddles of urine as fine horses tittupped and farted prior to a morning's run across country.

Harry Embleton reined his overeager stallion in roughly as he attempted to join the Chiswick party. At the dinner and dance the night before, he'd suspected there was something different about Caroline. She'd danced with him three times; a bloody wonder, that. And she'd been pleasant, for once, though distant, as was her usual wont, but he'd sensed it was for a different reason. For awhile he'd imagined that she was finally coming 'round, that Governour had worked on her long enough to incline her affections toward him. But then, she had danced *five* times with that interloping Lieutenant Lewrie, and had evinced such a rosy-cheeked elation towards him that it had taken all of his self-control not to have rushed onto the chalked dance floor to pull the smarmy devil away and thrust him from the house! The common, jumped-up . . . son of a whore!

That Lieutenant Lewrie danced extremely well, with such liquid grace and style to any music, and set every eligible girl to twittering like so many brainless hens, was infuriating as well.

And what did all those curious stares and giggles, those sly looks from the girls mean, he wondered? They had been directed at him as much as Caroline . . . surely that meant something wondrous was about to occur! But, they giggled and leered at Lewrie, too!

He had thought to ask of Governour, Millicent, or her uncle, but could not stoop so low as to garner gossip. A young man in his class and position could not; would not!

"A fine morning for the fox, reverend," he said, tipping his hat to the vicar as he passed him and his daughter Emily. Emily had once been spooned by Governour Chiswick, had "set her cap" for him, in fact; now she'd lost Governour, it was not much of a secret she pined for Harry.

There were few suitable bachelors left in the parish. Surprisingly, she did not gush over him so blatantly as would be her custom, and only looked away, reddening a trifle.

"Aye, 'twill be, young sir," the vicar agreed, though shying.

Devil take the lot of 'em, what *was* the matter this morning? Harry wondered. Do I look like I have leprosy?

"Harry, me lad!" Roger Oakes bellowed, waving to him to come see him. "A wager? Twenty guineas, first to the hitching rail?"

Harry turned his horse's head to join him, distracted.

"Twenty's an insult, Roger," Harry sneered. "Make it fifty."

"Done!" Oakes replied heartily. "Mind you, you kill that fine animal, no matter you're first, and the wager's off."

"If he goes under as your poor prad may, then I've lost both race *and* guineas. Good enough for you, you scapegrace?"

"Aye, fair enough. Hoy, lad. Brandy here for two," Oakes ordered a scurrying footman. "Been down to the church, Harry?" he asked as two more of their fellows joined them.

"Not since Sunday last," Harry shrugged, looking over his shoulder at Caroline, who was beaming and laughing with Governour, Millicent and the dashing Lieutenant Lewrie, missing the wink Oakes tipped the others.

"What's posted makes interesting reading," Oakes sniggered.

"Damn yer blood, Oakes," Harry snapped, having just about all he could take of leering, winking, and tittering, of odd reactions to his presence. "What's got into everyone today? And what's so bloody important posted at church?"

"Banns," Oakes smiled maliciously. "To be read o'Sunday, and read last night, I'm told. That makes two, I'm thinking. But, then, there may be a need of haste, aye lads?" And the rest chuckled over the rims of their stirrup cups.

"And who's the unfortunate young drab?" Harry smiled, sensing a wry jape or two over some yokel's slut. Or a juicy scandal.

"Caroline Chiswick, of all people," Roger informed him with a wink. "Damme, when we met Lewrie, he told you *your* virginity was secure. Didn't say anything about the lovely Caroline, though, did he? Ha ha! Damned fast workers, the Navy!"

"Goddamn you . . ." Harry shouted, striking the cup from Oakes's amazed hand. "Devil take you, you . . . !"

The Master of the Hunt was summoning riders, and the Master of Hounds, his own father, was pacing away, blowing his shrill horn to get things started. There was a good scent laid down with a brush to spur the hounds into the countryside, where they'd be sure to get a true spoor, and they were off in a brindle, speckled flood, yelping and baying as if they'd treed or denned something already.

"Apologize or owe me satisfaction, damn you, Harry!" Oakes demanded, face white with umbrage. He took Harry's wrist in his hand to hold him. "I'll not take that, even from a friend!"

"You'll have to stand in line, you bastard!" Harry screeched, tears in his eyes. "Someone else owes *me* satisfaction first!" He twisted free and put spurs to his stallion, making it rear and whicker with anger at his treatment.

"Now you've done it, Roger," one of the stalwarts commented as they got under way, "that lunatic is going to kill somebody!"

"If he doesn't kill himself first," Oakes shrugged, unfazed.

Off her own land, in public, Caroline was required by Society to ride a sidesaddle, so they made slower going in the middle of the pack of riders. Sometimes at a trot, sometimes at a sedate walk, as the hounds cast back and forth near the edge of Embleton lands.

They milled about for awhile before the hounds at last had a scent, and then they were off once more, this time at a lope behind the Masters and the hounds.

The first jump, once the pack increased speed, they took side by side, and Alan whooped in joy, sharing a brief grin of pleasure with Caroline. It had been years since he'd hunted down in Kent, in the times his father Sir Hugo still had acreage and the privilege of the hunt; 1779 since Alan had gone down for a summer after his last expulsion, just before his unwilling entry into the Navy. He had to admit he was rusty as a rider, but it was coming back to him, as was the heady exaltation of galloping cross-country and Devil take the hindmost.

There was a second jump over a narrow but high-banked stream, and a third not two musket shots later, this time over a hedge, onto Chiswick land. And then the pack veered left toward the great house.

Moments later, the hounds were circling and leaping around an oak tree, baying and yelping loud as the Hound of Cerberus, and they reined in behind the Master in confusion.

"Oh, bloody hell!" Sir Romney chortled. "Damned dogs've treed a cat, damn my eyes! Heel, sirs! Come away, damn you all, heel!"

"Good God, it's William Pitt!" Caroline gasped as the ragged ram-cat lay hunkered on a high-enough limb, bottled up and spitting, and raking the air with one paw, claws extended, at any hound's nose that came within scratching distance.

"Your pardons, milord?" Alan asked of Sir Romney as he rode up to him. "Might I pass you for just a moment? He's my cat, d'you see. And Caroline has been . . ."

Harry rode up as well, having gotten a later start off the mark from his house, but galloping all the way. He sawed his reins, setting the stallion back on its quarters and skidding dirt with its hooves beside them, jostling both men's mounts.

"Harry, we've treed Mister Lewrie's beast, yonder!" Sir Romney laughed as handlers began to drive the dogs off, beating at them with switches. "Think his tail'd make a good brush on my walls, hey?"

Harry gave Lewrie a black glower and spurred past him to ride under the tree, reaching up with his riding crop to slash at the cat, making Pitt howl with each lashlike blow, forcing the cat to slink backwards on the limb and climb higher.

"Feed the bastard to the dogs!" Harry almost screamed.

Lewrie spurred forward as well. Harry's actions had awakened the hounds to return to the tree and redouble their yelps, howls and blood lust. They were now almost uncontrollable.

"Damn you, sir!" Alan barked in his quarter-deck voice. "You hurt that cat, and you'll answer to me!"

"Goddamn you!" Harry shouted back. Alan took hold of his whip hand and pulled it down to waist level. Harry struck out with a left, letting go of the reins, striking Alan in the cheek and knocking his hat off. And, as Alan rocked back upright, Harry slashed him across his face with the riding crop as the excited horses circled and bit at each other. Lewrie's gelding shied away from Harry's stallion to the right, and Lewrie yanked reins to circle him small and return to what was now a fight.

"Damn you, Harry, what's got into you?" Sir Romney demanded in a hoarse shout above the gasps and cries of the other riders at this outrageous conduct. "Stop, I say, boy! Hear me?"

Lewrie spurred his mount forward to rush him, like a joust. The horses met right shoulder to right shoulder, and Lewrie swept out an arm to drag Harry from his saddle to sprawl heavily on the ground, then leapt down to finish him.

Harry twisted 'round and almost got to his feet, though he'd landed hard and lost half his wind. He slashed once more with the crop, grunting "You bastard!" with the effort. Alan ducked the blow to his right, letting the leather crack on the back of his coat, and then brought both fists upwards and to his left, right into Harry's startled face! Harry Embleton was almost lifted off his feet and did a half-turn, yelping in sudden pain, to go down hard and stay down, rolling on his back with both hands to his nose, too hurt and out of wind to rise.

"Damn you, sir!" Sir Romney snarled, "If you've hurt my boy, I'll . . ." He threatened, his own crop raised as if to strike Lewrie to protect his son.

"He *struck* me, milord," Alan snapped, whirling to face him, his eyes aflame. "With fist and crop. *Not* the actions of a gentleman, milord! I'm within my rights as an English gentleman to demand satisfaction from him for that. Is that your desire, milord?"

Sir Romney looked into those eyes. Odd; he'd recalled them as being light, genial blue. But in anger, Lewrie's eyes glinted as bright and steely gray, and as hard, as a drawn sword. And in them, he saw implacable rage . . . and murder!

What Harry had done, for whatever mystifying reason, smacked of lunacy, Sir Romney shivered. And truly, totally unforgivable; and so public! The best of local Society, the cream of the landed gentry and superior classes the parish and county could boast had seen it!

"No," Sir Romney grunted unwillingly, the surrender wrenched out of him. Slowly, he lowered his fist to the pommel of the saddle. And he lowered his eyes, unable to match glares with the young man.

"See to your son, milord," Lewrie ordered. "And call off your hounds." Ordered, to a man whose every whim, whose every pronouncement was nearly sacred writ to parish, village, and county. Without waiting to see if that order would be obeyed, sublimely confident that it would be, Lewrie turned to see to his horse, to gentle him and stroke him over for possible injury.

"Mr. Lane, Toby . . . get the pack away and home," Sir Romney sighed, dismounting to go to Harry and help him to his feet, to pry his hands away from his face to look upon his smashed nose.

Caroline rode forward to join Alan as he remounted, sure his gelding had suffered no hurt. "Good God, Alan, are you alright?"

She put out a gloved hand to his cheek and turned his face to look at it. "He welted you with his crop," she huffed, by turns solicitous to him, and outraged at Harry. "And bruised your cheek!"

"Nothing a cold cloth and a measure of brandy won't heal." He smiled, reaching up to take her hand in fondness for a moment. "Now, how to get Pitt out of this tree?"

Alan rode under the limb and drew rein. He stood high as he might in his stirrups and reached up, wiggling enticing fingers.

"Come to me, Pitt," he cooed. "Come on down, you silly fart. Don't hiss at *me* . . . 'twasn't me treed your silly arse! Pitt, these dogs'll tear you apart if you don't come down to me. Come on, now."

The cat slunk backwards toward the trunk, reached the fork and mewed uncertainly as it turned tail-downward, and inch by wary inch, began to crab down the trunk towards Alan's outstretched hands.

"There's a brave little man," Alan encouraged. "Now come to me, that's the lad." He stretched upward and put a hand under Pitt's tail, another 'round his middle. It was like trying to peel off barnacles. "Let go the tree, you stupid little . . ."

Pitt at last turned his head and leaped, curling up in a ball of angry fur as Alan fumbled him onto the saddle and his lap. Once there, William Pitt lay still, suffering for once the indignity of being enclosed and held, though he trilled deep in his throat, moaned and hissed, licking his chops at the affront.

Sir Romney had walked Harry back to his horse, away from the softly gossiping onlookers. Suddenly, he broke away from his father and advanced on Alan and Caroline, to end standing by her stirrup.

"Is it true, Caroline?" Harry demanded in a broken voice. "Is is true you're to wed this . . . ?"

"It is, Harry," Caroline nodded somberly.

"And all we've been to each other means nothing to you?" He fumed, gaining strength from what to him felt like betrayal.

"We have been neighbors, Mister Embleton," Caroline continued. "I have never encouraged your attentions. Had you misunderstood my *cordiality* for something more, for that I offer my apologies, Harry."

"He's a nobody!" Harry groused, a little muffled from the hurt to his nose, which was now oozing blood and mucus, and swelling large as an angry turnip. "Not landed, not . . ."

"I love him with all my heart," Caroline replied, turning to Alan as she said it, rewarding her choice of mate with an expression that left no doubts, even among the onlookers out of ear-shot.

"Be-damned to you, then!" Harry raged, pink-tinged tears trickling past his nose. "You cheap, bloody whore! You silly, misguided . . . brainless . . . faithless . . . *bitch!*"

Alan, encumbered with Pitt in his lap, began to spur forward, but Caroline acted for herself. She leaned forward and lashed Harry with her reins, with which she had been nervously toying, across his ruined beak! Harry yelped in redoubled agony and sprang away, hands up to protect his face once more, hunching over as Caroline rode forward, herding him like a steer and lashing at him.

"*That* for your slurs, Harry Embleton!" she cried. "*That* for your cruelty! Slander me, will you? Put your dogs on our cat, will you? *That* for a purse-proud . . . Tom-Noddy! You vile wretch!"

"Caroline, for God's sake!" Alan shouted, riding up even with her and taking her hands, taking her reins to stop her and lead her away before even more lasting harm was done. "Drop it! Dead'un!"

"Damn him!" She spat, her color up and her hazel eyes ablaze.

"I *think* he got your point, m'dear," Alan told her. And he could not help himself from betraying his feelings with an approving smile. Caroline blew out a deep breath and looked at him, then she began to smile, too; lowered her head and bit her lip to keep from laughing out loud at the sight of Harry scuttling away, though no more blows struck him.

"By God, you're a Tartar, no error!" Alan told her. "I hope you have not deceived me with amiability. Am I to wed a termagant?" he cajoled, leading her towards the Chiswick house.

"Oh, Alan, no!" Caroline softened at last. "You must never think that of me! It's simply his . . . I am sorry I usurped your place as my defender, darling. But the fool rowed me beyond . . . he *struck* you, Alan! He'd have killed Pitt to spite us. And what he called me! Had I a gun, I'd have soon shot him as looked at him. Had I a sword, I'd have run him through, God help me!"

"Sounds termagant to me," Alan said, tongue in cheek.

"I promise I shall be a proper wife to you, Alan." She calmed. "Properly demure and so very affectionate and complaisant. Surely, I trust to your affectionate and gentle nature. There will be nothing but the sweetest tranquility and joy between us. I know that, sure as I know anything in this life!"

"A 'goody'," Alan japed. "Your uncle's favorite word."

"Oh, aye, a 'goody'!" Caroline replied, throwing her head back to chuckle with wry amusement. "Though I fear he favors 'economical' the more! Your 'goody', at last, my dearest love."

They took hands between, riding knee to knee and gazed into each other's eyes.

Damme, Alan thought, but she's got more bottom than any woman ever I did see! With her wits, and her fire, I'm in for a lively old time with her. Might be more interesting than I thought. Who said a marriage *had* to be drab as ditchwater?

"Your uncle won't care for this much," he sobered.

"Dearest Alan, I don't know anyone in Anglesgreen who will," she rejoined. "This is the stuff Welsh feuds are made of. Will you duel him?" she asked suddenly, realizing the ramifications. "I beg of you, do not!"

"He's a hen-hearted buffle-head." Alan sneered. "And he got a lot worse than he gave, after all. I doubt Sir Romney wants his boy carved up any more than he already is. He'll be a lifetime living this shame down, and I doubt he's the nutmegs to do more than slink away to London or Guildford. Away from all his friends and neighbors who saw his beastly behavior."

"He looked and sounded completely daft, Alan," Caroline said with a frown. "Oh, Lord, what if he found the bottom to challenge you? Crossed in love, bested before his contemporaries . . ."

"By you, as well, Caroline," Alan laughed heartily. "If indeed he does summon up the stones, I'll be *your* second!"

Book II

Chapter 1

There was no challenge, though it had been deemed prudent for Lewrie to ride back to London to gather what household furnishings he possessed from storage with the Matthewses at his old lodgings, to make himself scarce for a week or so, whilst Caroline gathered her own *trousseau* and goods, bought what was lacking, and ordered a new gown from the dressmaker's.

There had been a lot of sighing, mooning and handwringing in the Chiswick house. Uncle Phineas, bemoaning his now-confounded schemes, praying only for icy civility at best from the Embletons for the rest of his life; Mother Charlotte sunk deep in the moping Blue Devils which required an hourly change of handkerchiefs and lots of sad "alases"; Governour and Millicent squint-a-pipes, split two ways by fondness for Alan and Caroline, and regrets for connections which were now effectively severed, removing Millicent Chiswick *née* Embleton from familial converse, and Governour from hope of support for Parliament, or the conjoining of the lands.

It had been a rather grim wedding party, with half the guests either secretly armed to prevent further scandal, in support of the Chiswicks; or present to gawk and gossip as if their nuptials were a raree show or dramatick which would end in high-flown and safely vicarious violence. Well represented though the gentry were, there had been few representatives solidly partisan, or beholden, to the baronet and his son. And, of course, no Embletons at all, save wan, but game to the last, Millicent.

The wedding supper had been held at the Ploughman instead of the Red Swan Inn, and Alan suspected that whenever he had cause to return to Anglesgreen (God help him on those rare occasions) he would do his tippling and socializing there for the rest of his natural life, odious as that thought was to him once he had inspected the dim, sooty, slightly rank gloominess of that shoddily delapidated establishment.

And, finally and most unhappily, it had been deemed, again, prudent, for the "happy couple" to depart instanter for Portsmouth, rather than consummate the vows in any local bed.

They had had to coach as far as Petersfield to feel safely out of range of any residual rancor. Once there, in a homey, low-ceilinged set of

63

rooms at a rambling old coaching inn, the happy couple celebrated the especial bliss of newly begun married life in proper style, which left Caroline purring, and Alan so ecstatically spent, and so delighted by her physical charms and her ardor that he wondered just how he was going to deal with being separated from her once his new ship was ready for sea.

Charms or no, there was a thrill of expectation that morning. Following a teasing, tickling, mirthful and infinitely pleasing bout after the "abigail" at the George Inn had brought their tea, breakfast in the public rooms, and a lingering goodbye kiss, Alan still felt an impatient urge to tear away from her.

Dressed in his best, brand-new uniform, white waistcoat and breeches gleaming, and buttons and metal appointments shining fit to blind the unwary, Lt. Alan Lewrie, Royal Navy, made his presence known at the shore offices of the Port Admiral before going out to his new command.

"And you are?" A punctilious silver-buttoned naval clerk said with a traplike opening and shutting of a severe little mouth.

"Lewrie, sir," Alan replied. "I'm come to take command of *Alacrity*."

The clerk looked him over carefully, one bored eyebrow cocked in cynical appraisal. Silver-Buttons had sometimes been appalled by the turnout of some holders of the King's Commission, by how shabbily and "pinchbeck" salty stalwarts could dress themselves, as if their slightest attempt at neatness was a civilian crime.

Silver-Buttons also made a rough estimate of Lieutenant Lewrie's value during his appraisal. Real gold coat buttons, not gilded; a new cocked hat, and by the officer's London accent, probably from James Lock. Real silver buckles on his shoes; good watch and impressive fob, and a damned good sword, even if it was a hanger and not a slim, straight smallsword. A Gill's, and they didn't come cheap! Hmm!

Silver-Buttons rang a tiny handbell on his desk to summon his compatriot, the regulating captain of the Portsmouth Impress Service. Aye, this Lieutenant Lewrie had the wherewithal, unlike so many others, and could *pay* to get his ship commissioned and manned when the pettifogging frustrations of the Dockyards (and Silver-Buttons knew just how to invent said frustrations) became insurmountable for an aspiring young captain. Not *too* much, though, Silver-Buttons decided; that scar upon the cheek, that restless look in those genial eyes (were they gray or were they blue, he dithered) spoke caution, and a limit to what Lewrie might abide before making loud complaints to Silver-Buttons's superior.

"Might I see your orders, Mister Lewrie?" The clerk smiled, deciding upon a larger measure of civility than was his wont

Alan surrendered his documents from the Admiralty.

"You'd be amazed how many Sea Officers positively *lurk* around this anteroom," Silver-Buttons "tsk-tsked" as he read those precious papers. "Or attempt to bluff their way aboard a ship, bold as a dog-in-a-doublet. One must be certain of the bona fides in these times. Aye, yours are quite in order, sir," he concluded with a smirk.

"Quite, sir," Alan nodded, itching to get his documents back, and safely into a deep side pocket of his coat. "Would it be proper for me to make my courtesy call to the Port Admiral at once, sir, or might I perform that chore after reading myself in?"

"I regret to inform you, Lieutenant Lewrie, that that worthy is not here. Nor will he be for the rest of the week," Silver-Buttons sighed with an audible sniff. "Matters of state in London, with the Board of Admiralty, do you see? Ah, Captain Palmer! Captain Palmer, allow me to name to you Lt. Alan Lewrie, come down to assume a new command. Lieutenant Lewrie, our Regulating Captain."

"Your servant, sir," Lewrie said, extending a hand to the oily older man who had appeared with breakfast grease on his chin.

"Nay, I be yours, sir, And that, soon, I'm thinking. And what ship?"

"The *Alacrity*, sir."

"*Alacrity, Alacrity*, hmm . . ." Silver-Buttons mused, searching his files stacked in untidy piles on a sideboard.

"A ketch-rigged sloop, sir. To turn over, then fit out for the Bahamas Squadron," Lewrie prodded impatiently.

"Ah, here we are!" Silver-Buttons brightened. "Ten-gunned, once a bomb ketch. Should have been in port over a month ago, but she found nasty gales returning from Gibraltar and broke her passage, hmm . . . once in Lisbon. And a second time in Nantes. Odd."

"Odd, sir? What's odd?" Lewrie fretted. "Was she damaged? How badly? To dock in Frogland . . . she is *here*, is she not, sir?"

"Well, of course she's here, Lieutenant Lewrie!" Silver-Buttons snapped. "Else how would I have this paperwork, hey? Came in Tuesday last. As to her material condition, I haven't a clue, though. I can not be expected to keep track of everything! Aha. Docked and breamed last week, her coppering redone, and is now lying at anchor, awaiting turnover."

"And does that say how many hands stayed aboard, sir?" Lewrie continued. "Any Discharged I must recruit to replace, or will the men turn over entire?"

"Portsmouth's full o' willin' hands, sir," Captain Palmer said after masticating a last, fetching bite of bacon. "I'll be that able to fulfill yer ev'ry desire. Bahamers, is it to be, did y'say? Then y'd rest easy to know there's Cuffy sailors aplenty, awishin' the hot o' their tropics. Mr. Powlett's Marine Society o' London's sent down a draft o' their very best, and were ya able to deem 'em Ordinary Seamen, seein' as how they know their knots an' can box the compass good as a hand a year at sea, then half yer problem's solved, I say!"

"I see, sir," Alan nodded. West Indies sailors were as good as any he'd seen in his limited experience, though most English captains would not take them. They were better behaved, more religious, and a lot less likely to cause trouble as long as they were treated fairly. He didn't know squit about any Mr. Powlett's Marine Society of London, but it sounded very much like some Poor Relief for street urchins. If they'd gotten any instructions at all, they'd stand head and shoulders higher than truculent, ignorant landsmen from a debtor's prison.

"I must confess ignorance as to my needs for personnel, Captain Palmer," Lewrie said, finally getting his documents slid back to him, and into his pocket once more. "I shall go aboard *Alacrity* and read myself in at once, determine my lacks, and get in touch with you, sir."

"Afore the Admiralty changes its mind, hey?" Palmer cajoled.

"Quite, sir," Lewrie smiled bashfully. Captain Palmer had hit the nail directly on its head.

"God, she's lovely," Alan breathed as he beheld the gun ketch which lay at anchor before him as he was rowed out by a bargee.

"Ever' ship be, sir," the bargee grunted over his oars.

Alacrity was a saucy thing. Seen side-on, which view disguised her wide beam, she possessed a lovely, curving sheer-line to bulwarks and gunwale, and the jaunty, upward thrust of her jib boom and sprit yard made her appear eager and lively. She was about seventy-five feet on the range of the deck, and ninety feet overall from taffrail to the tip of her bowsprit. She was rigged as a two-masted ketch, a bomb ketch of the older style with equally spaced masts, the after mast by the break of the quarter-deck railings shorter than the mainmast forward. Her principal motive power would be those two courses rigged fore-and-aft on the lower masts, hoisted like batwings from gaff yards atop and long booms below. She sported crossed square-sail yards for tops'ls on both masts, and stays forrud for outer-flying jib, inner jib and fore-topmast stays'l.

Her hull below the black chainwale was linseeded or oiled a dark brown with a glossy new sheen, while her gunwale and bulwarks, all her upper hull was a spritely blue several shades lighter than royal blue, and her rails, transom carvings, quarter-galleries, beakhead and projecting strips above and below the gunwale were done in a yellow deep enough to at first be mistaken for giltwork. Her crowned-lion figurehead at the tip of the beakhead, below the thrusting jib boom, was the only place true gilt appeared.

"Boat ahoy!" one of the harbor watch shouted in query.

"*Alacrity!*" the bargee bellowed, and raising several fingers in the air to indicate the number of side-boys due their visitor; and with his shout telling them that their new lord and master had arrived. He stilled his oars and let the rowboat coast to give them time to sort out a proper welcome.

The boat at last thudded against the hull by the boarding battens and dangling man-ropes. Alan hitched his hanger out of the way, set his hat firmly on his head, and stood. He reached out, took hold of the man-ropes and heaved himself onto the wide and deep shelf-like battens to ascend to the entry port cut into the bulwarks above. He heard the sweet trills of bosun's pipes squealing his first salute as a captain of a man of war, and once through the entry port and standing on the starboard sail-handling gangway (*his* gangway, he relished!) he doffed his hat in reply. Surprised as they were to see him, he was as much surprised to see a Commission Officer standing before him with a sword drawn and presented in salute.

"Welcome aboard, sir," the young man said once the ceremony was done, and he had sheathed his sword.

"Lewrie," Alan announced. "Alan Lewrie. And you are?"

"Ballard, sir," the trim little officer replied. "Arthur Ballard." He pronounced it Bal'-*ahhrd*, emphasizing the last syllable.

"Are you temporary, or . . . ?" Alan quizzed.

"First officer, sir," Ballard informed him with a slight raise of his eyebrows. "A bomb would normally rate but one Commission Officer as master and commander, sir, but rerated as a sloop, sir . . ."

"Ah, I see!" Alan nodded with a smile. He would have someone else to help with the navigation, and the watch-standing, which suited his indolent nature perfectly! "Did you turn over with her, sir, from her previous commission?"

"Came aboard to join four days ago, sir, just after she left the careenage," Ballard rejoined.

"Right, then," Lewrie said, digging into that side pocket for his precious orders. "Assemble ship's company, Mister Ballard."

"Aye, aye, sir," Ballard intoned with a sober mien.

It was thin audience Lewrie had to witness his reading-in. Two gangly midshipmen of fourteen or so, hopefully salty enough from being at sea since the usual joining age of ten or twelve; eight or nine boys dressed the usual "Beau-Nasty" he took for servants and powder monkeys; twenty or so hands from fifteen to forty dressed in blue and gray check calico and slop trousers, plus the older men who affected cocked hats and longer frock coats with brass buttons who would be her holders of Admiralty warrants; the bosun, carpenter, cooper, sailmaker and gunner, and their immediate mates who were the ship's career professionals.

Alan read them his orders, savoring every mellifluous, ringing phrase which directed him "to take charge and command" of His Majesty's Sloop *Alacrity*. Finished at last, he rolled up the document and retied the ribbons, wondering if he should say else.

"I am certain," he began, looking down at their hopeful faces peering back up at him from the waist amidships, "that many of you came up on blood and thunder in the recent war, as did I. Service in a ship in peacetime may not hold the everpresent threat of battle. We may have more time for 'make-and-mend,' more 'Rope-yarn Sundays.' But that is only after we've drilled and trained to be ready to fight, and I am satisfied. And our old friend the sea is still a demanding mistress. I deem peacetime service no less rigorous than war. Mind you, I'm no Tartar nor a slavedriver. But I am a taut hand, and a taut ship where every man jack works chearly for me, our ship, his mates, and our Fleet is a happy ship, I've found. And that is what will satisfy me, and that is what will bring us safely home from the fiercest gales or the hottest fight, should they come to us. Fair enough?" he asked, expecting no answer. "That'll be all for now. Dismiss the hands, Mister Ballard."

"Aye, aye, captain," Ballard replied, using that honorific for the first time now that Lewrie's assumption of command was official. "Ship's company, on hats and dismiss! What next, sir?"

"Introduce me to the warrants and mates, Mister Ballard."

Once more, Lewrie felt he was standing outside himself like some theatregoer, judging his own performance on the Navy's stage. He had almost reddened with embarrassment as he uttered those trite-but-true phrases he'd borrowed from other, and whom he considered, better, men.

I've six years in the Navy; why do I still feel like such a low fraud? he asked himself.

He knew his own preferences for peacetime service would be to cruise like a hired yacht, sip claret and dine well, perhaps carry some doxy in his cabins for sport. Yet he wore the King's Coat, and perforce had to live what felt like a great sham; a sham which he was sure others would someday recognize.

"Mister Fellows the sailing master, sir," Ballard said as Alan's senior mates gathered round. Fellows was short, wiry, ginger-haired, and seemed like a timorous store clerk. "Mister Harkin the bosun, sir." Harkin was built like a salt-beef barrel with arms as thick as hawsers, and a round hard face. "Mister MacIntyre the surgeon's mate. This is Mister Taft, the sailmaker, Mister Fowles the master gunner . . ."

"Fowles?" Lewrie interrupted. "*Ariadne*, winter of '80. You were but an able seaman then. My first ship as a newly."

"Aye, sir, I were. Thankee fer 'membrin' me, cap'n, sir," the clumsy older salt bobbed happily. "An' that 'appy I be t' be a'servin' unner 'Ram-Cat' Lewrie, sir."

The introductions finished, Lewrie plucked at his uniform.

"I meant to pay my respects to the Port Admiral, else I'd have dressed more suitable for a first-day's inspection, men," he said with a small jape at himself. "Something less *grand!* So, I'll delay going over the ship from bilges to mast trucks until tomorrow at eight bells of the morning watch. At which time I will wear slop clothing and put my nose into everything. So put right what you will, and have a list ready concerning any deficiencies you want corrected in your departments, or items still wanting, hey?" He gave them a warning, and time enough to present a going concern, sure there were glaring faults hereabouts in a ship fresh from the graving dock and careenage, with most of her furniture and fittings recently reloaded. "Mister Ballard, let us go aft. I assume the ship's books are in the great-cabins?"

"They are, sir. This way, sir," Ballard replied gravely.

"How many hands have turned over, Mister Ballard?" Alan asked as they descended to the waist from the quarter-deck for the hatch to the aft cabins.

"At present, sir, there are thirty-six hands aboard, ordinary, able or landsmen. All but eleven may be rated seaman. The purser Mr. Keyhoe has nine men away from the ship at present, to row him over to the dockyards. *Alacrity* came into port with fifty-five, ten short of her rated complement. Five were discharged, sprung or ruptured, three retired. But, there's a new frigate fitting out here, sir, and we lost eleven hands into her. The port admiral sent an officer aboard and got them to . . . ahem . . . volunteer for her," Ballard said with a wry pout.

"Well, damn my eyes," Lewrie said with a weary disgust. There was no getting around the problem of manning the King's Ships. Seamen were always the rarity. One could bedazzle calf-heads at a rendezvous tavern to take the Joining Bounty with tales of far-off ports of call, and there were young lads aplenty who'd shun their farms to run off to the sea, boys enough with stars in their eyes to sign aboard as servants or powder monkeys. But, seamen . . . !

In peacetime, the Impress Service could not press by force ashore, even if the regulating officers could find a bribable magistrate who would sign a permission. Even in wartime, the press could not take a man outside the ports, could not (in theory) press-gang civilian landsmen— only recognizable sailors. *Alacrity* could, should the need be direful, board arriving merchant vessels in the Channel, or in legal "soundings" of the British Isles and press seamen. But such men were resentful and mutinous, and Alan didn't much care for that solution. Neither did he care for the scrapings from debtors' prisons, those who knew nothing of the sea and only took tops'l payment to get out of gaol for their debts of less than twenty pounds.

"We need twenty-nine more hands to make our rated sixty-five," Alan figured. "At least ten or twelve of those have to be able seamen. Let's be pessimistic and say ten. A dozen landsmen for waisters, and make what we may of them. Captain Palmer suggested a Mr. Powlett's Marine Society of London. Know much of it, Mister Ballard?"

"Aye, sir," Ballard nodded. "They take poor's rate tykes off the streets, scrub them up and teach them some knots and pulley-hauley. I do believe they teach them letters and figures, after a fashion, too, sir. Some practical boat work on the Thames . . ."

"If they can read and write a little, they're miles better than most, then," Lewrie snorted. "He offered them in lieu of ordinary seamen. What think you of that idea?"

"If they're not too young, they may make topmen, sir. And God knows, we may lash and drive anyone to knowledge, given even a slight spark of common sense to begin with, sir."

"Damned right!" Lewrie chortled, having been driven and lashed himself to his lore. "Good Christ, what a brothel!"

His great-cabins were empty of furnishings except for a double bed (a hanging cot for *two*) and a few partitions, and the chart room desk and shelves. The black and white checkered sailcloth deck cover yawned vast. But the cabins were painted a showy French blue, picked out with gold-leaf trim, with borders, overhead deck beams, transom settee and window frames all painted a gaudy pinkish red!

"Quite elegant, sir," Lieutenant Ballard said with a tiny smirk; just the slightest quirky lift of his mouth, and a crinkle to his eyes. "I am informed your predecessor Lieutenant Riggs adored his comforts more than most officers. You'll be wishing to repaint, of course, sir."

"Damned right I do," Alan growled. He knew what the Navy thought of "elegant"! Any officer, unless he was so senior he no longer had to cater to anyone's opinion, was thought unmanly should he aspire to any degree of comfort or sophistication beyond bare-bones Spartan, living as hand-to-mouth as a lone gypsy on the Scottish border. "In the meantime, I would admire if you would arrange for my personal furniture to be fetched offshore. I'll sleep ashore for the nonce, at The George, until we put this right. And the painter will have to work around my things."

"Aye, aye, sir."

"The books, Mister Ballard?"

"On the chart table, sir. I'll leave you to them, then."

"Thankee, Mister Ballard, that'll be all for now."

"Shall I have some coffee sent aft, sir? From the wardroom stores for now. As a welcome-aboard gesture, as it were, sir."

"Thankee, again, Mister Ballard, aye."

"Oh, whom should I ask for at The George, sir?" Ballard asked, pausing in his leave-taking.

"Uhm . . . with Mrs. Lewrie, Mister Ballard," Alan blushed, making the removal of his hat, taking a seat on the one stool remaining, and opening one of the ledgers a suddenly all-engrossing activity.

"Aye aye, sir!" Ballard replied, lifting his brows in wonder.

Damme, what have we here? Arthur Ballard asked himself after he gained the weather-decks. Mr. Fowles called him "Ram-Cat" Lewrie? Rare for an officer young as me to have a nickname already. Must be a holy terror! And married? Unless Mistress Lewrie is his mother . . . God no, who'd have his mother come to see him off! God in Heaven, a married officer, then?

"Whew!" he whistled softly. "Mister Harkin, boat party! Take the cutter!"

Chapter 2

"How long before you're ready to sail, Alan?" Caroline asked, once they were tucked companionably into the high bedstead, and the last candle had been snuffed for the night.

"Four days, I should think." He yawned. "She had at least a half-hearted refit before I got her. Coppering's good, hull's sound, and the bosun has most everything set to rights again. Once we're done loading stores. And our passengers."

"Oh, God, your . . . what did you call them . . . live-lumber?" She snickered in the dark as she snuggled to him, as he put out an arm to receive her head on his shoulder.

"More," he complained, putting his face to her sweet hair.

"More? How?" she asked.

"God knows, darling. There's that Trinity House master, Gatacre and his mapmaker. They're to swing hammocks in the wardroom. Six midshipmen in a draft for the Bahamas Squadron, and never one of them ever aboard a ship, hanging like bats from the overhead on the orlop right aft by the fishrooms. And this morning, the Port Admiral tells me I'm to transport a chaplain and his wife and servants to Nassau, in my cabins. That means I'll have to feed and water them, out of my own purse, damme. I'll end up in a hammock in the chart-space if they keep shoving bodies at me! Least they could do is put plate aboard."

"What's that?"

"If you carry coin for the treasury, or solid pay out to a foreign station, you get a small percentage. No hope of that, though." He sighed. "Some Reverend Townsley and his lawful blanket."

"Why, I met them, Alan!" Caroline exclaimed. "They're staying here at the George. Stiff company."

"Must be a poor sort of hedge-priest if he has to take chaplain pay," Alan chuckled. "You never see reverends in wartime. Too busy at saving civilian souls of a sudden, don't ya know! What were they like?"

"Snooty as earls." She shivered against him. "They're related to some captain . . . no, some comm-something . . ."

"Commodore?" Alan asked suspiciously.

"That was it. A Commodore Garvey, out in the West Indies."

"Oh, stap me, he's commanding the Bahamas Station!" Alan cried. "They could ruin me if I treat 'em less than royal. Gawddd!"

"We took tea together this afternoon," Caroline said. "He said your commodore already had his wife, son and daughter out there. The son's in the Navy, too. A midshipman, I think he told me. Or maybe he'd just made lieutenant. I forget. They're a formidable pair. And with two wagonloads of goods. So they couldn't have left a poor parish," she decided. "Unless they looted it on their way out."

"Two wagonloads, lord," Alan groaned. "Where'll I stow it all? Maybe I should just give 'em my cabins for the entire voyage. And I'll leave 'em blue and rose, too. That ought to be grand enough for 'em."

"I think they're lovely."

"The Navy wouldn't. I should have painted earlier. Let them describe their quarters to Commodore Garvey once they get to Nassau, he'll think me a primping dancing-master."

"I still say they looked elegant," Caroline decided aloud.

"Found lodgings yet?" he inquired. "There's little time left."

"I know, my love!" She sighed as she burrowed deeper into him with sudden ardor. "I've seen several. I'll take care of it, never fear. Oh, God, this is going to be so hard, to watch you sail away, and here I am, in Portsmouth, where I don't know a soul! Four days?" She wailed softly.

"Four days we should make the most of," Alan muttered, running a hand over her hip and thigh, delighting in her shivers of expectation. That night in Petersfield, they'd left a candle burning in their eagerness, and she'd come to him with a robe on, not a bedgown. A robe which slid down her shoulders and parted to reveal a girlish slimness, a veritable feast of creamy skin and proud young, close-set breasts, a taut, flat belly trimmed by riding, and long, incredibly fine and tapering smooth legs. He still had not gotten over the wonder of being with anyone so delectable, of her being his to caress and stroke into passion at a whim.

Like Venus on the half-shell, he exulted silently, like Aphrodite rising from the waves . . . but even better!

"You don't think me gawky and spindle-shanked?" she teased him as he nuzzled her graceful neck. "You don't prefer more roundness?"

"God, Caroline, you're the loveliest woman ever I did see!" he told her truthfully. She rolled on top of him to kiss him, to receive his kisses as his hands slid down to her firm little buttocks to draw the bedgown higher. She uttered a thrilling little laugh as he found her hips, as his fingertips brushed her bare flesh.

She sat up astride of him to lift the bedgown over her head, raising her arms high and inclining her head with her hair loose and long like a silvery shimmer in the almost-dark. His hands rose to take possession of her firm breasts and she leaned into his palms for support, and excitement.

"Rough hands," she whispered, taking one so she could kiss it. "A sailor's hands. Rough from all those ropes and things."

"Too rough on you?" he grunted in rising ardor.

"Never a bit of it, my love," she chuckled again, softer. "I know it's not seemly, but I want you to teach me something new, Alan."

"Wanton jade!" he teased, sitting up a little to nuzzle at her nipples, which had gone puckery-hard from his caresses.

"Your wanton jade!" she promised, going goose-pimply with rising delight. "Only yours, darling. Make me yours again."

He drew her down to him, enfolding her in his arms so they were drawn against each other, her knees up by his chest, and one hand of his stroking the softest, most intimate of her flesh.

"Oh, God, but making love is so . . ." she moaned, near to transport. Her hips were moving now against his hand, her upper body rocking slowly left and right. She began to slide off to draw him over, but he stopped her. "Come to me, now," she implored.

"Right where you are, love," he grinned.

"Oh, yes!" she sighed, gasping as she felt his member brushing her. She slid down just a trifle, rose up on her palms as he fitted himself to her and thrust upwards with gentle but insistent pressure.

Down a little more she slid, then gave out with an inarticulate groan of surprise and pleasure as he slid deep.

"Riding St. George," he exulted as she made more happy groaning sounds, each ending on a rising note.

"The dragon spitted from his lance below . . . ohh!" she laughed.

"Sit up, darling," he coaxed. "Sit up, Caroline!"

"Oh, it's so . . . oh, yes!" She bit her lip, rolled her head to either side. He took her hands and held them tight, their fingers entwined fiercely. Hips rocking, upper body swaying, her head far back and her throat bared to the ceiling in her ecstacy, she met his movements, anticipated and amplified them. "Oh, so completely . . . so deeply! Jesus, I'll surely *die* of more! Ahh-hahhh!"

"Then I think we'll die together," Alan panted, swooning, with the entire world reduced to the friction of moist flesh, and his own release building like the pressure from a powder charge in gun's barrel. Time slowed down, time had no meaning, the planet and its tawdry doings ended beyond what they could touch, feel, or hear. And then she broke, weeping with release, crying out as if given a tiny glimpse of paradise, and he took hold of her slim hips and firm little bottom, and drove upwards, reveling in the creaking of ropes that supported their mattress, the pump-washer sound of their two bodies fused, her astonished further cries as she collapsed on top of him with her breasts brushing his chest, and then the far-away groan he shouted to the night as his groin and his brain exploded into royal fireworks.

Neither of them had an ear for the irritated thumping of the lodgers next door. Not the first time that night, nor the second.

"It's *so* unfair," she whispered much later, after their third congress of the night, just before well-earned sleep.

"What is?" Alan mumbled, his mind reeling.

"That we, at last, know joy of each other for such a short time before we must part," she sighed, snuggling down inside his embrace, one thigh across his exhausted lap and her long hair draped over his chest. "I wish you could smuggle me aboard your ship and take me wherever you go. To know so much pleasure from your dear hands, Alan. And then to be deprived for three whole *years!*"

"It's a hellish wrench for me, too, darling girl," he admitted, eyes shut and almost glued together for want of sleep.

"If only we had longer, a year or more, so I might have grown accustomed," she wished. "Or does it ever cease to be such a wonder? Will making love with each other be forever this new and daring, dear?"

"With our enthusiasm, I'd wager deep on forever," he chuckled as he stroked her long, smooth back.

"Spinsters succumb to the green sickness," Caroline muttered.

"Now what would you know of that?" he chid her gently.

"Fall ill and die for lack of it!" she laughed. "And their only cure is . . . this. Now I know how marvelous it is, I'll be taken to my bed for want of more! We both will. You'll sail back from the West Indies and find me wasted away to nothing, from want of you, and nought a cure for me but your rapt . . . attentions! None but your kisses and caresses will save me."

"Then I wish us a very long recovery," he rejoined.

Several long minutes passed as Lewrie began to breathe deep on the verge of slumber, then:

"Alan?"

"Ahmm," he uttered.

"I can't go home to Anglesgreen."

"Uhmm, I know."

"And I don't know a soul in Portsmouth," she went on softly.

"Uhmmhmm."

"Reverend Townsley is taking his wife out there. And your superior thinggummy in Nassau . . . he has his wife and daughter with him already. There're so many Loyalist families settling in the Bahamas. With their wives and children. We once considered Eleuthera, ourselves."

"Hmm?"

"Why could you *not* take me with you?" she queried hopefully.

"Oh, Caroline, it's heat and flies, bad as India," he grumbled, wakened enough to counter her. "Mosquitoes, roaches big as . . ."

"As if in North Carolina I'd never seen a palmetto bug," she scoffed. "That was a polite way of saying a 'cockroach' big as your thumb!"

"There's fever, Caroline. Yellow jack and malaria. Cholera now and again. Poxes that no one even knows what to call by name!" he objected. "No, dear, dear as I desire you with me, I cannot. I love you too much to subject you to such risk!"

"I've been inoculated against smallpox. We had physicians good as London," she pressed, though in a soft, almost wheedling tone as she stirred her body against his. "I've seen yellow jack before. I might have had it when I was little. I can't remember."

"You don't know what you ask, Caroline," he groused, sitting up in bed, now arguably awake, though the hour was late and he had to rise at first light. "Caroline, believe me when I tell you that I love you to distraction. Frightened as I was of marriage, more than most bachelors, believe that, too . . . life with you is a joy beyond all imagining. And it will be in future. But if we're to have that future, you must be here for me to come home to. If I lost you out there, I'd . . . were I selfish enough to take you with me and something happened to you, I'd wish to die, too!"

And damme if I don't mean every word of it, he realized; she's become as dear to me as . . . Christ, who'd have thought!

"I stand just as much chance losing *you* in the islands, Alan," she fretted, squeezing him tight. "What life do you think I'd care to live, with you gone in a shipwreck, or carried off by some fever! And I'd never have been a real wife to you but this single fortnight! Oh, Alan, take me with you, do! At least, when *Alacrity* puts into Nassau, we could have a week or two here and there together, in a snug little home of our own! Is Nassau such a terrible place, then?"

"Pirates, footpads, cutpurses," he described to her. "There're drunken sailors and their whores, reprobates and discourteous rabble; carousing and caterwauling 'til all hours . . ."

"Like Portsmouth, is it?" she asked, and even in the dark, Alan could almost espy her puckish grin. "Yet you entrust me to this town, half the world away from you. What would be worse about Nassau?"

"Caroline, it's so . . ." he sighed, his desire for her, and the lust for unknown adventures crossing swords with each other, just as they had before he'd become so quickly engaged.

"I know, I'm being so foolish and missish, Alan," she weakened. "Do but consider it, though, darling? Please, love?"

Her kisses stopped any further objections he could muster.

"Let's sleep on it," she urged sweetly, fluffing up his pillows and guiding him to recline again, so they could snuggle even closer to each other. "I do love you more than life itself, Alan. Goodnight, my dearest love. Goodnight, my darling."

Chapter 3

"We're making good progress, even so, sir," Lt. Arthur Ballard told him a few days later as they sat in Alan's now-furnished cabins, sharing their morning tea.

"Still four hands short, even with the West Indians, the debtor landsmen, and the volunteers," Alan sighed over the rim of his mug. "I s'pose it can't be helped. And damme if I'll make the Impress Service any richer than I already have. How are the Marine Society lads?"

"Quite pleasing, considering, sir," Ballard smiled. "They taught them knots, boat-handling, mast drills . . . they'll work out, sir," he said. "They're eager to please. More than one may say about the men from the debtors' prisons."

Lewrie was pleased with Ballard as well. Arthur Ballard was an inch shorter than he, just a few months younger, but had joined as a cabin servant at nine. He'd served as an Ordinary Seaman and a topman since his fourteenth year, had made midshipman at sixteen, so he was thoroughly seasoned. He'd been third officer in a frigate, rising to second officer before she paid off in late 1785.

He was a neat little fellow, though of a more serious bent than Alan was used to in officers so close to his own age. Ballard was regular and square; squarish head and regular features. His hair was wiry and wavy, set close to his head. His brows were a trifle heavy, thick and dark, shading intelligent brown eyes which regarded the world so soberly and adjudging. His nose was short, straight, and a bit broad. His face ended in a square chin, with a pronounced cleft.

But even at his young age, his mouth bore frown lines to either corner. Betraying his sobriety, though, evincing a passionate nature he wished to contain, were lips full and sensual in a broad mouth, the lower lip quite plump and slightly protruding.

Ballard dressed neatly, but in slightly worn uniforms, like an officer who actually lived on his pay and little else, pulling it off with his sobriety and great care for his person. Those uniforms draped a body neither very broad nor very slim, which gave him stolid solidity without true bulk. Yet within that body was a powerful set of lungs, a deep baritone voice which could carry forward without the use of a speaking trumpet, and a surprise to the unsuspecting person who might meet him and at first dismiss him.

Caged, Alan thought of his first lieutenant. He's like a beast in a cage. Not the pacing kind. He's the sort who sits and waits for his keeper to drop his caution someday before he flees.

"Sail drill in the forenoon," Alan announced at last. "Working parties after the midday meal. Livestock for the manger. And household goods for the Townsleys to be stowed."

"Their goods first, then, sir. No shite on their furniture."

"Aha, very good, Mister Ballard," Alan laughed. "Once loaded, one more day in port for last-minute items and then . . ." He sobered.

"Off for the Bahamas, sir," Ballard said with a trace of glee.

"All for now, Mister Ballard," Lewrie said, rising carefully so he did not smash his skull on the low overhead, which allowed him only three inches more than his full height, and only between the deck beams. "Oh, there's goods of mine as well to be stowed. Make them first in, last out. And I'll see the ship's carpenter, Mister Stock."

"Aye, aye, sir," Ballard said, mystified.

Alan put his hands in the small of his back and paced aft, ducking each threatening rosy-painted beam, to the sash windows for a view of the harbor as he pondered his most recent decision.

He had put this one off quite late; how to make room for both himself, the Townsleys and their servants, in his great-cabins, which would not make a decent set of rooms at The George.

Great, hah! He mused. Only to a mate in a dogbox below!

And make room for Caroline.

She hadn't nagged or harped upon it; yet she had kept the idea of going with him ever in his mind. Daily, she'd worn a little more of his resolve down. First with affection and passion, then with her clear-eyed discussions of Bahamian weather, living conditions, which winds blew all feverish miasmas to leeward to the real Fever Isles . . .

She'd marshaled support from other senior naval officers and wives staying at The George or other establishments nearby, never at all giving them the slightest hint that she was more than curious as to what her dear husband might face in that particular clime. Slowly, she'd changed his mind. As she had excited his tenderest affections for her that were only half-formed and ill conceived weeks before back in Anglesgreen. Had made herself dearer to him than he had ever hoped to imagine, until he could not picture himself without her for three whole years.

There were, too, his rising fears.

Being loved at all was, to put it mildly, just a *tad* outside his past experiences. And to be loved and adored so openly, so deeply and enthusiastically was such a blossoming wonder that he found himself waking in the middle of the nights to marvel at the stunning creature who shared his bed, and slept so trustingly and vulnerably in his arms. To watch her dress, brush her hair, enter the public rooms when he sat waiting for her, was a heart-lurching joy. And their converse over a weighty matter or a jest was an absolute delight.

What had he known as love before? Pretty much a spectral semblance —flattery and *entendres* which passed for wit and talk, followed by ogling, grappling, and frantic coupling on whatever fell to hand.

Never regard, never esteem, fellowship, never . . . some affection, of course, but nothing of a lasting nature.

On, off, and where the devil'd I drop me shoes, he scoffed!

Granted, it would be bad for his career. But had he not already blighted that by marrying at all so junior an officer? And, once this commission was ended in 1789, would he really shed a tear to spend his life ashore on half pay, no matter how much pride he had at last derived from his growing skill as a Sea Officer?

He could spend that life with Caroline, with enough money to buy land, to live off interest with Coutts & Co., some investments in funds.

"Two weeks ago, the idea scared me witless, and now . . ." Lewrie puzzled, bemused by his eagerness to admit that he was married, and married most damnably well, too, to an absolute gem of a young woman!

Even if it had come about like an unintentional dismasting.

Yet . . .

Lewrie knew people; admittedly some thoroughly despicable ones. He knew the enthusiasms of "grass widows", and the sort of men who went baying like a pack of hounds in pursuit of abandoned and lonely women; God knows *he'd* prospered on them. He could see how other officers and Portsmouth gentlemen regarded her so hungrily when he and Caroline were out and about the town already. Might she . . . even Caroline . . . succumb at last, missing lovemaking so much after a brief, glorious introduction, with him away for three years, might she . . . ?

"Christ, I've rattled too many wives and widows," he muttered in gloom. "Ironic justice, that'd be. Maybe innocence and ignorance would be a blessing! God, surely not her!"

So when, the night preceding, Caroline had shyly confessed that she had not actively sought decent lodgings, and begged his forgiveness for scheming to go with him, he had been more than relieved of all his worries, and had surrendered to her will most ecstatically.

There was a rap on the cabin hatchway.

"Ship's carpenter Mister Stock, sir!" the lone seaman on guard called out, filling in for the Marine sentry *Alacrity* did not have.

"Enter!" Lewrie replied.

"Yew wanted t'see me, captain, sir?" the youngish Mr. Stock said as he ducked his head to enter and removed his stocking cap.

"Aye, Mister Stock," Lewrie brightened. "I need your expertise to rearrange my cabins to accomodate our passengers. I'd thought you might be able to turn the starboard quarter-gallery into a second 'necessary closet', give our passengers some canvas and deal partitions to provide privacy . . . oh, about here, say. And their maid needs sleeping space. The manservant will berth below in the stores room."

"Uhm . . ." Stock pondered. "Foldup pilot-berth here, sir, over the sideboard in the dinin' coach f'r the maid. Double berth f'r the married folks." Here Stock actually blushed! "We've partitions enough, sir. And yon double hanging-cot a'ready. Not a day's work, sir."

"Best build a double hanging-cot for them," Lewrie said. "Leave me equidistant room down the starboard side, and a passageway t'other side. I'm . . . ahumphh . . . partial to the existing double."

"Oh, aye, aye, sir," Stock agreed with a sad expression.

Chapter 4

"God, what a bloody pot-mess," Alan fumed on sailing day as he beheld his little command turn from a trig gun ketch to a bloody Ark, from a sane and rational construct to a barking shambles!

"Heave, and in sight!" Parham, one of his fourteen-year-old midshipmen howled from up forward.

"Jib halyards, gaff halyards, peak halyards, Mister Ballard!" Alan snapped. The inexperienced landsmen and volunteers were being trampled by the ordinary and able seamen; the draft of midshipmen flitted about trying to appear useful, or to avoid a mob of hands who suddenly stampeded in their general direction. A yearling steer gave out a mournful bellow of annoyance, the pigs and sheep squealed or baa-ed in sudden terror, and ducks and geese in the fo'c's'le manger squawked and fluttered, so that *Alacrity's* foredecks were nigh awash in feathers. There was a deal of cursing from professionals, too.

The ship's boys served as nippermen, seizing the lighter line to the heavier anchor hawser, whilst inexperienced landsmen under the direction of the bosun's mate, a Portugese named Odrado, tried to deal the stinking coils of salt-stiffened cable into manageable heaps, then down to the cable tiers to drape over the bitts to dry. And it was a truism that had *Alacrity* been a 1st Rate 100–gunned flagship, they would still not have had enough deck space for the nippers, the men on the cable, the hands heaving on the capstan, the sailhandlers or the sheetmen on the gangways ready to brace the jibs and gaff sails.

Blocks squealed, *lignum vitae* sheaves hummed, and gaffs cried as the sails were hoisted aloft.

"Payin' off t'larboard, no helm, sir," Neill said from the long tiller sweep with his fellow Burke standing by, ready to lend strength for when the wind gave enough way through the water to make the rudder function.

"Forrud!" Lewrie bawled. "Walk your jib sheets to larboard and haul away! Brace up the after course, there, lads! A luff, no more, foredeck!"

Alan spun to walk to larboard to peer over the side to see if there was even the slightest hint of a wake, and to gauge distances to other anchored ships. He almost collided with the Rev. Townsley and his wife who were gawking about like farts in a trance, cackling with amusement and treating the spectacle like a raree show.

"Your pardons," he said, not sounding much like he meant it as he brushed past them. He had advised Caroline to stay below and out of the way until he sent Cony for her, once the ship had gotten under way and things were a bit less disorganized.

"Brace on the capstan, well the cable!" Ballard called, tending to his chores. "Ready on the cat!"

Thank God for a first lieutenant, Lewrie thought. And thank God for a competent one. There, a wake, he exulted! He tossed a chip of scrap wood over and watched it bob astern, foot at a time.

"Bite t'the helm, sir," Neill cried.

"Larboard your helm, Mister Neill. Bring her up to weather on a soldier's wind for now. Forrud!" Alan called, once more stumbling over the Townsleys, who had moved to the forward left corner of the quarter-deck nettings. "Haul away on your larboard sheets!"

"Silly bugger!" Burke yelped as his way with the tiller sweep was impeded. Alan didn't have to turn around to see who it was that had gotten in the way.

"You might do better all the way aft by the taffrails, reverend," Alan said, then shouted, "'Vast hauling! Luff enough! Now belay!"

Alacrity was free of the land, free of the bottom, and moving faster. The wind was from the west, with a touch of northing, giving them a clear shot down the western passage past the Isle of Wight, with enough strength to it to let them harden up to weather to keep off the coast to their lee, to go close-hauled if they had to without a tack. With luck, and no traffic, they could get to sea in the Channel on one long board.

Lewrie heaved a slight sigh of relief. Comical as they might have looked to ships longer in commission and practice, *Alacrity* was on her way. He walked back up to starboard, along the narrow space inside the quarter-deck railings and the after capstan-head to starboard, the windward side, which was his by right as captain.

"Anchor's fished, catted and rung up, sir," Ballard told him, touching his hat with a finger. Those studious brown eyes held the slightest hint of glee. "Cable's below, hawse-bucklers fitted."

"Thank you, Mister Ballard," Lewrie smiled. "Not *too* awful, considering. Two rehearsals seemed to have turned the trick. Thank you again, for your suggestion."

"My pleasure, captain," Ballard said, inclining his head, his long upper lip curving just a trifle.

"I'd admire should you attend to the gun salute to the flag," Lewrie instructed. "The experienced hands, mind."

"Aye, aye, sir," Ballard said, turning away.

Lewrie looked down on his gun deck and gangways. What had been total disorder was now flaked down and lashed, hung on the pinrails in neat loops; halyards and sheets, braces and lifts, were stowed for instant use. Senior seamen were explaining things to their rawer compatriots, beginning to play the role of "sea daddies."

William Pitt sprang up atop the quarter-deck railings, his tail lashing with excitement. Alan reached out and ruffled the fur behind his ears. "How does it feel to have a ship of your own to terrorize again, hey, Pitt? Good?" Pitt tucked his paws in and lay still.

For an English day, it was remarkably lovely. There was some bite to the breeze, of course, but the sun was out, peeking between thin scud, making the waters of the Solent gleam, giving them color for once beyond steely gray, brightening the vista of ships and sea.

"Cony?" Alan called, flinching as he remembered Caroline.

"Aye, sir."

"My respects to Mrs. Lewrie, and inform her the deck is quiet enough for her to come up," he told him, unable to control a blush at using the unfamiliar title "Mrs. Lewrie."

"There's the pretty!" Caroline said, stroking Pitt as she came to the quarter-deck by one of the short ladders from the gun deck, and Pitt stood to get his petting. "Oh, how marvelous!" she exclaimed in delight, coming to his side to link arms with him. "A perfectly gorgeous morning. Good morning, Mister Ballard."

"Good morning to you, ma'am," Ballard replied, doffing his hat to her. "Your pardons, ma'am, but 'twill be a little noisy in a few moments. Aft, there! Prepare to dip the colours! Mister Fowles, be ready!"

"Aye, aye, sir!"

Abeam of the principal fort, Alacrity began to thunder out a gun salute. She dipped her colours briefly as the equally-spaced shots rang out, with Fowles pacing aft from one gun to the next, muttering the ancient litany of timing, ". . . if I weren't a gunner, I wouldn't be here. Number three gun . . . fire! I've left my wife, my home, and all that's dear. Number four gun . . . fire!"

"Thank you, Alan dearest," Caroline whispered to him between shots. "I'll never give you cause to regret your decision. I love you so completely!"

"And I love you, Caroline," he whispered back, bending from his rigid pose of lord and master for a second, grinning foolishly.

BOOM!

"At least on passage, I shall learn what sort of life you lead aboard your ships," Caroline went on. "So I may understand you better and picture you more clearly when you're away."

BOOM!

"Oh, Alan, we're setting out on a grand adventure!" She laughed. "Such a honeymoon, no one has ever had!"

"There, there, my dear," Lewrie comforted, almost gagging himself as his bride "cast her accounts." She knelt in the starboard quarter-gallery, the "necessary" converted from a wardrobe little larger than a small closet. "It passes. It will."

She looked up at him, dull-eyed and wan, her lively face now devoid of expression. "Dear Jesus, could I but . . . Harrackkk!"

Back her face went over the hole as her body rebelled at such infernal motion, at the stomach-churning odors of ship and food. He knelt with her to hold her head, to apply a towel below her chin as solicitously as he could, for one whose cast-iron craw had withstood the fiercest gales since his first hours in the Navy. But he had to dwell on the smells of fresh-sawn wood and new paint *most* closely!

There was a rap on the flimsy louvred door to their share of the great-cabins. "Mister Ballard's respects, sir, and I am to tell you he is desirous of tacking ship," a thin voice called out.

"Mister Mayhew, is it?" Alan asked, trying to differentiate between two soprano midshipmen.

"Aye, aye, sir," the fourteen-year-old said, voice cracking.

"My compliments to the first lieutenant and I shall be on deck directly," he instructed. "Caroline. Dearest . . . I must go on deck to oversee a change of course. I'll be back soon, I swear. Do you think you might be alright until then, love?"

All she could do was nod, dazed by illness, her face twisted in misery as it was poised over the slop chute. He kissed her on the top of her head, rose, and made his escape, feeling pangs of guilt.

The Reverend Townsley collided with him in the narrow larboardside passageway, hands to his mouth and sprinting for the "jakes." But *Alacrity* was loping like a deerhound over the sea, stern rising high then settling like a dog's haunches as it dug in for a thrust with its back legs, dropping with a giddy swoosh. One moment, running aft was hastened by the slant of the deck; the next moment one churned in place or lost ground as the bows plunged. At least, laid hard over on her starboard side by the wind she did not roll. The good reverend danced in place like Punch pursuing Judy, then was almost hurled the last few feet to crash into the transom settee and the stern timbers. His feet went flying over his head and he landed like a pile of dominie's washing—black "ditto" coat, breeches, stockings and waistcoat all of a piece. He regarded Lewrie for a mournful moment like a hound being put down would stare at the gun, then spewed the last contents of his body over his lap and chest.

So much for serving fresh pork roast, Lewrie gagged as he turned away to stumble forward; there's four shillings wasted!

The door to the Townsley's cabin was swaying open, left gaping in the reverend's haste, and Lewrie caught a peek of Mrs. Reverend Townsley and her prunish maid fighting to share a bucket.

"Oh, land us *ashore*, Captain Lewrie!" she wailed, giving him such a glare as said that it was all his fault. "No more, I beseech you! We shall all drown for sure. Gracious Jesus, to be on solid ground . . . !"

"Approaching a lee shore in the dark in these seas, ma'am, would be drowning for certain," Lewrie explained. "Sorry. Excuse me."

Bad weather might be best, he thought as he gained the quarter-deck; save me money feedin' 'em broth an' gruel for a few days!

"Wind's dead on the bows, and blowing right up the Channel, sir!" Ballard had to shout at him. "And now the tide's turned, we're set too much northerly on the larboard tack, headed for a lee shore!"

The English Channel was a nasty piece of water, with tidal flows as strong as spring rivers in spate. Those, combined with the current and wind, could waft a ship along quick as a "diligence-coach" on the high road. Or nail her in place for twelve hours, no matter how much wind or sail area to beat against them.

And *Alacrity* was like all shoal-drafted converted bombs, tending to slip to leeward like a sot sliding off a chair. Closehauled into that stiff wind, she would require four or five times the mileage to make good a direct course with a more favorable beam or stern wind.

"On the starboard tack, we have sea room 'til dawn, when this tide turns!" Lewrie declared in return. "Aye, make it so, Mister Ballard! Before you tack, though, take in the outer-flying jib. She's too much pressure on her bows, and I'll not have her broach beam-on to wind and sea if she tacks too sharp!"

"Aye, aye, sir!" Ballard agreed with a firm nod, and the first, slight smile Lewrie had seen him attempt. "Mister Harkin, 'All Hands!' Stations for stays! Fo'c's'le captain? Take in the outer jib!"

Getting her head 'round was no problem, with no need to pay off a point free on the helm to gather speed for a successful tack. They drove her up with her helm alee and *Alacrity* tracked about quick as a wink, deck leveling as she approached "stays," sails luffing and thundering, blocks rattling and tinkling, hull and masts crying.

"Meet her!" Alan warned the helmsmen. "Nothing to loo'rd!"

"Let go and haul!" Ballard screamed over the howling wind. Her bows crossed the wind and in a moment, she was laid hard over on a new tack, sails cracking like cannon shots as they filled and bellied out hard as iron, some luffing still as inexperienced men tailed on sheets too slowly. But paying off a bit too far and pressed hard over.

"Helm down, helm down! Keep her hard up aweather!" Lewrie said, throwing his own strength to aid Neill and Burke on the long tiller. "Thus! Steer west-sou'west, half west."

"Better, sir," Ballard stated after the deck was back in order.

"Smartly done, Mister Ballard, for such an inexperienced crew," Lewrie complimented him. "Thank God we have enough skilled hands, or we'd have rolled her masts right out of her."

"Thank you, sir."

"This may blow out by morning, sir," Fellows the sailing master opined after recovering his hat from the scuppers. "Damme, though, she swims even this lumpy sea devilish nice, don't she?"

"Aye, she does, Mister Fellows," Lewrie agreed. "Mister Ballard, before you dismiss the hands, take a second reef in the gaff courses, now we've unbalanced her by taking in the flying jib. Trim her until you're satisfied. Hank on a storm trys'l and bare the tack corner for a balance on her head. Able seamen only out on the sprit tonight, mind."

"Aye, aye, sir," Ballard said, going forward.

"On starboard tack all day tomorrow, most like, sir," Fellows decided. "Once the tide turns, with the current . . . tack again, I fear, as we fetch Alderney in the Channel Isles."

"I'd admire were it Guernsey, but we make too much leeway," Lewrie agreed, picturing a chart in the mind's eye. "Then larboard tack all the way toward Torquay and Tor Bay, and hope the winds back north."

An hour later, *Alacrity* rode much easier, with her large gaff sails reduced in area, and their centers of effort lower to the deck, and the center of gravity. Eased as she was, Lewrie had the galley fires lit so hot beverages could be served to ease suffering.

"Clear broth and biscuit," Ballard mused. "Just the thing for touchy stomachs. Though my other ships ran more to hot rum and water."

"Royal Navy's panacea for all ills," Lewrie chuckled as he had a cup of steaming black coffee and rum.

"I think it . . . uhm . . ." Ballard began to say, then had a second thought. For a fleeting moment, he showed indecision.

"What, Mister Ballard?"

"Oh, just that I thought it most considerate of you, sir. To be solicitous to the hands, their first night at sea. Easing the ship as we have. The galley . . ."

Of course, Lewrie thought! We're feeling each other out!

For the next three years, they were stuck with each other, for good or ill; two total strangers thrown together at the whim of the Admiralty, an Admiralty which would not, or could not, take into account the personalities of officers when handing out active commissions. It could be a good relationship, or a horror; it could be friendly, or it could be cold and aloof as charity!

"Well, half of 'em're cropsick as dogs at the moment," Lewrie shrugged. "They need something hot they may keep down. Or won't claw on the way back up! And what's the sense of thrashing to windward as if we were pursuing a prize? The tide'll turn, after all. Best those new 'uns make an easy adjustment to the sea. Don't make 'em hate the life they signed on for so eagerly."

"Most captains would not consider such, sir."

"I had a few good teachers," Lewrie allowed. "As I'm sure you did."

"Aye, sir," Ballard grinned. "And how fares our live-lumber?"

"Wailing and spewing," Lewrie snickered uncharitably. "Praying for dry land, last I saw of 'em."

"And . . . and your good lady, sir?" Lieutenant Ballard asked carefully.

"Good Christ!" Lewrie cried. "I told her I'd be right back, and here it's been two hours at the least! Uhm, when I left her, she was suffering bad as the Townsleys, Mister Ballard."

"My tenderest respects to Mrs. Lewrie, sir, and I pray that her seasickness will soon abate," Ballard offered.

"I'm certain she will be heartened by your kind concern, sir," Lewrie replied. "Stap me, two whole hours! She'll scalp me! But, I must confess, being on deck, being active, relieved some of my pangs, too."

"Uhm . . . and will Mrs. Lewrie be . . . ah . . . ?" Ballard squirmed.

"Oh," Alan snorted, "do I intend to cruise the West Indies with my wife aboard? Was that your question, Mister Ballard?"

"Your pardons, captain, I mean no disrespect. It's just that the warrants, some of the turned-over hands were talking, and . . ."

"Do they disapprove?" Lewrie demanded.

"Your predecessor, Lieutenant Riggs, had no storm damage, sir," Ballard admitted. "He shammed it, and used Admiralty promissory notes in Lisbon and Nantes to stock his wine cellars. He was never without female companionship aft. A veritable parade of foreign morts, I'm told, sir. I gather that the people resented it, and feared you might be . . ."

"I'm no Augustus Hervey, Mister Ballard," Lewrie said, thinking even so that he'd made a fair beginning on that worthy's estimable record of over 200 women in a single three-year commission.

"Hardly a man may be, sir, and may still walk," Ballard found courage to jape with a droll, dry expression.

"Much as I might *care* for it, mind . . ." Lewrie laughed. "But, as you say, the hands would grow surly and insubordinate were I to parade what they want and can't have in their faces. I may not be an experienced captain yet. But I do know better than that, sir!"

"I'm sorry if I discomfited you, sir. And I am of the same opinion as you, sir, and understand completely," Ballard said, even if he didn't yet understand what would compel a man to wed so early in a career, risk the loss of it. It had taken so much for him to even get to sea, and progress as far as he had, son of a Kentish innkeeper, a private school letter boy. Had it not been for a Navy captain who kept lodgings with them when he was ashore doing his father a favor to take young Arthur on as a cabin servant, he might still be forrud garbed in slop-clothing, still a topman and Able Seaman, a mate at best!

"If you will allow me the deck, sir, you may see to your wife," Ballard extended as a peace-offering. "For this evening at the least, unless there's an emergency, you might . . ."

"No, Mister Ballard," Lewrie decided, finishing the last dregs of his coffee. "I'm no Augustus Hervey. Nor am I a Lieutenant Riggs. Call me, as stated in my Order Book, should circumstances merit. But I will take advantage of your kind offer and go below for awhile. God, over two hours! She'll have my liver! Good evening, Mister Ballard."

"And good evening to you, sir," Ballard replied, relieved. "And do convey my sympathies to Mrs. Lewrie."

"I will and thankee."

He's a raw 'un, no error, Ballard thought as Lewrie stumped down to the weather decks. Means well. But not too well. Ain't playing a 'Robin Goodfellow' to be popular with the hands, just taut but caring. So far.

Ballard should have envied Lewrie bitterly. He was taller and fairer, boyishly handsome, and came with an indolent courtier's repute; he'd not gained the sobriquet of "Ram-Cat" Lewrie for his choice of pet alone, Ballard grimaced! Womanizer, a brothel-dandy, he'd heard, with the confidence around women that Ballard lacked, the *panache* the Frogs called it to spoon them just shy of scandalous, and the devil-take-ye glint in his eyes to seem dangerous and desirable.

Yet he was a good sailor, and a married one!

Ballard should have resented Lewrie's rapid rise in the Service. Six years from gentleman volunteer to not only Commission Officer, but a captaincy in foreign waters! While it had taken young Arthur Ballard long nights of study, years of quiet observation to develop his skills with a stubbornly silent will to equal or best his contemporaries, and gain this first coveted slot as a first officer. Eleven years to his commission, to Lewrie's six! Why, he should have despised him for a whip-jack sham, a well-connected idler!

Oddly, he did not. Lewrie was too much of a puzzle to envy or despise. Trust? Ah, that might come as they progressed together. He already felt he might come to trust him. But it was early days.

The one thing that genuinely irked was the lovely Caroline who adored the fellow so enthusiastically, the sort of young woman Ballard had always most desired, but never seemed to find. And Lewrie had found her so effortlessly!

"Caroline," he whispered, testing her name on his lips.

"Say somethin', Mister Ballard, sir?" Neill the quartermaster inquired.

"Steady as you go, Mister Neill," Ballard said, shrugging deep into his soggy grogram boat-cloak.

Caroline was asleep on the transom settee's pad, curled up hard against the stern timbers by an open sash window overlooking the wake, hugging her knees. Alan took the painted coverlet from the hanging-cot and folded it about her to ward off the chill of the stiff winds.

"Oh, you're back!" she groaned, weary as death, spent from all her wracking heavings. She reached out for him, weak as a kitten, as he got a damp cloth to wipe her face. She didn't sound accusatory, he noted with relief!

"I'm so sorry, Caroline, but that's a ship for you," Alan lied. "It took forever. A tug here, a pull there. Are you feeling perhaps the tiniest bit better, darling?"

"A bit," she allowed. "Now you're here. Just hold me, Alan."

"Miss me?" he teased, easing down on the edge of the settee by her side as she rolled to him and embraced him.

"My love, I was much too . . . *busy,* to miss you," Caroline sighed, amazingly able to jest even then. "The fresh air helped best. Once I got the window open, and made my *final* offering to Neptune, I was dead to the world."

"You should get into bed. Sleep's the thing for you now. The bedbox doesn't pitch or roll. Would you care for some brandy?"

"I do not trust myself," she said after one quick peek at their hanging-cot, which swayed impressively. She rinsed her mouth with the brandy, but spit it out over the stern, not trusting her stomach with any fresh contents, either.

"You are so good to me," she crooned sleepily, stroking his face as he came back to her side. "I'm so sorry to be a burden, when I promised just this morning I'd not be."

"You're no burden, love," Alan smiled. "Every sailor has to find his sea legs. You sleep, now. And you'll feel better in the morning."

He reclined with her, stroking her hair until her breathing went slow and regular. Only then did he close his own eyes and nod off, his head pressed against hard oak, lulled and hobbyhorsed to sleep by the ship's motion.

There was a rapping on the door.

"Unnh?" he groaned, starting awake from treacly sleep.

"Midshipman Parham, sir. The sailing master's respects, and he wishes to shake out the second reef in the main course and inner jib, captain, sir."

"Very well, Mister Parham," Alan replied, reeling with weariness. "I'll be on deck directly."

Chapter 5

Once out of the Channel and around Ushant, *Alacrity* became a much happier, and tauter, ship. Seasickness abated, and the hands, back on their feet, were then brought to competence with drills and hard work.

Fire drills, boat launchings and recoveries, procedures for man-overboard rescues and working the ship became the day's chores. They tacked, they wore ship, spread or brailed up the tops'ls and royals, struck or hoisted the topmasts; they replaced entire suits of canvas. Cables for towing were laid out, then recovered, boarding nets were strung along the sides and hoisted from the yardarms, then lowered and stowed away. For the complete neophytes, and the newest midshipmen, the bosun and his mate conducted classes in knots and in long- and short-splicing, with the next day's exercises applying those newly won skills in practical uses. There was practice at musketry, at pistol shooting at towed targets, cutlass and pike drill under the first officer or the ship's corporal, a heavily scarred bruiser named Warwick. They learned to serve the great guns, the ship's ten iron six-pounders, two-pounder boat-guns, and swivels.

Discipline was brought to full naval standards gradually, once the hands gained some knowledge. Defaulters were allowed a chance to make honest mistakes with light punishment; stoppage of tobacco or the precious rum issue. Stiffened rope "starters" used as horsewhips on the slow and clumsy were at first discouraged—Lewrie did not feel the sting of a starter in the hands of a mate on some poor inexperienced landsman much of a goad to learning.

Later, the starters could be plied more freely, if a man was truly shirking. Later, insubordination and the usual sins—drunk or asleep on watch —were awarded days of bread and water, along with a touch of the "cat"; one-dozen lashes for a first penalty, two dozen for the second. Back-talkers, mostly the landsmen who insisted on their God-given right as Englishmen to complain at brusque usage, were "marlinspiked" into silence, with a heavy iron marlinspike bound between their teeth for a day. And the midshipmen suffered being bent over a gun barrel to "kiss the gunner's daughter," to be whipped on boyish bottoms rather than fully male backs, or suffered to be "masfor to be "masar to be "masarheaded," consigned to the cross-trees aloft without food or water in all weathers and told to remain there, shivering and puking at the exaggerated motion of the ship, until Lewrie saw fit to relent. In a harsh age, Ballard and the warrants at first thought their new captain a little too mild, until they saw him administer captain's justice fair-handedly, and issue lashes with the cat-o'-nine-tails in the forenoon watches on those few truly recalcitrant or shifty.

They were fortunate in *Alacrity*—and Lewrie and Ballard thanked God for that good fortune—to have at least half the crew made up of seasoned people, to have had the men "pressed" for them reasonably intelligent and healthy, that a fair portion of those pressed were volunteers. Times were hard ashore, what with Enclosure Acts, unemployment and low wages, so Navy pay was steadier and surer than day-laboring. And the £ 14 12s. 6d. net pay for a raw landsman was half again as much as he could make as a civilian. Even figured at a parsimonious lunar month instead of the calendar month, with deductions of sixpence for Greenwich Hospital and one shilling for the Chatham Chest monthly, plus the purser's subtractions for tobacco, shoes, slop clothing, plates, scarves, hats and sundries, it was a decent annual living.

Alacrity settled down to being a somewhat happy ship. Most of her people were young and full of energy, even after a full day's work or drill. In the short dogwatches of late afternoon, when the weather permitted, there were sports and competitions, watch against watch.

And there was music and dancing, with fiddles, fifes and drums, stacks of spoons slapped upon knees if nothing else for meter, English morris dancing, Irish jigs and Scots reels, along with hornpipes or West Indian dancing.

Sometimes, midshipman Parham on fiddle, bosun's mate Odrado on a beribboned guitar of which he was especially proud, the carpenter's mate, a Swede named Bjornsen, on fife, and Caroline with her flute, would play concerts by the quarter-deck rails. The Reverend Townsley made hymn books available for those seamen who could read, and the crewmen would gather aft for a singalong, or stare rapt at drawing-room compositions they'd never heard before, their eyes alight to Bach, Purcell, Handel or other great composers. But then Caroline would insist on rollicking airs familiar from an hundred village greens or taverns, or plaintive ballads, sometimes tunes she'd grown up with among her North Carolina neighbors, and the hands would sing along lustily, all over the scales, but enjoying themselves greatly.

The Townsleys disapproved of some songs—but then, they disapproved of a lot of things. Divine Services could not be conducted on a daily basis, but only on Sundays after Divisions, and after the first one,

Lewrie had suggested shorter sermons and more hymns. And when the second droned on long as the first, he'd ordered the bosun to pipe "Clear Decks and Up-Spirits" to issue rum, ending services quite effectively!

The Townsleys sniffed prudishly at breakfasts, when Alan and Caroline emerged from their tiny cabins, flushed with excitement from making love. Once over her sea sickness, Caroline began to enjoy voyaging, and both hanging-cot and transom settee provided ecstatic pleasures. The Townsleys, far past their own first remembrances of passion, coyly hinted that too much laughing, giggling and "odd noises" in the night had disturbed their slumbers. Which hints only served to spur Lewrie and his enthusiastic young bride to even greater feats of passion, of an even noisier nature.

And the Townsleys were upset that Lewrie did not wish to break his passage in Vigo, Lisbon, or the Madeiras, but, with Gatacre and his own sailing master John Fellows to assist, determined upon taking a faster route for the Bahamas, edging more westing to each day's run so that *Alacrity* was well out to sea and beyond the normal "corner" at which most ships would turn west for the Indies off Cape St. Vincent.

He did it admittedly to save his fast-dwindling supply of wine and brandy, for the good reverend made more than free with the bottle at meals, and raided the wine cabinet in the narrow passageway every night. At least he did until Cony placed a bottle of undiluted Navy rum mixed with sea water in the brandy's squat decanter, and beyond a startled splutter or two, and a fit of retching, no more was heard of Reverend Townsley after Lights Out for the rest of the voyage.

And so the weeks passed, from brisk Westerlies in the Bay of Biscay to tops'l breezes standing into spectacular tropic sunsets on the Atlantic crossing. From the gray green of the Channel to cobalt blue of Biscay, to bright blue waters of the Americas. From shivering with cold to the need for a hand fan in the daylight hours as *Alacrity* reeled off 200 miles from one noon to the next, until she rode a river of air, the Nor'east Trades, into the Providence Channel.

Their last sunset together was a beauty, beginning just at the end of the second dogwatch. From the deepest rose to palest saffron, it flamed across the whole of the western horizon, heightened by the darker clouds. The sea glittered on the glade of sunset, turned gold and amber ahead of *Alacrity*'s course, fading to a deep blue gray to either beam, and almost black astern. The first stars were out, and a gibbous moon, brushed more gold than silver, rode low on the evening's horizon. The wind was steady but gentle, pressing *Alacrity* forward with a starboard quarter-wind that filled her winged out gaff courses, and the reduced tops'ls. The heat of the day, which had not been particularly fierce that early in the year, had faded, and the evening air was fresh, clean, and most temperate.

"Well, gentlemen, it is about time for Mister Gatacre to give you one last lesson in taking the height of the evening stars," Alan told the crowd of midshipmen. "And time for me to dine. Show heel-taps on your glasses, and be about your duties."

With his cabins crowded so, it had been impossible to dine any of his officers and warrants in on the voyage, as a captain usually did to get to know them better, so he had been reduced to a nightly "court" on deck once the weather had moderated as they neared their tropical destination, with wine served out to be sociable.

"Ahem," Midshipman Mayhew coughed, rising. "Uhm, sir . . . and Mrs. Lewrie? We . . . uhm . . . we should like to propose a toast to your lady, sir. I think I speak for all of us, for all the ship's people forrud as well . . ."

"You'd better, Mayhew, we deputed you, remember?" Midshipman Parham teased and the boys laughed nervously.

"Well, sir, and Mrs. Lewrie . . ." Mayhew began again, turning somewhat sunset-hued himself. "For those whose first voyage this is among us, and for those of us who've sailed before, I have to state that we shall remember forever how pleasant this passage has been, because of our captain's lady. For her kind words, for her musical accomplishments. For her grace, and niceness of condescension to all hands. And for moderating a taut-handed captain's wrath upon us," he concluded with a jape. "To Mrs. Lewrie, might it be possible for her to sail with *Alacrity* forever!"

"Hear, hear!" the others chimed in, "To Mrs. Lewrie!"

"I thank you all, young gentlemen," Caroline blushed prettily. "May you have joy of your future careers. And my affection and gratitude for an exceedingly pleasant voyage to you, as well."

"Thankee, ma'am," they shambled, "thankee," as they set down their empty glasses and wandered off forward to the sailing master.

"That was so sweet of them!" Caroline sighed, touching an eye to control tears.

"There's no one like you in their experience," Alan said as he took her hand. "Nor in mine." They sat down together on the signal-flag lockers by the taffrail in the very stern. "Nor any voyage like this for them again, most like. It ain't the usual Navy experience. The lads in the draft, God knows what sort of captain they'll have next, if they get a ship at all."

"It was sweet, all the same," she insisted, dreaming on the horizon. "And a heavenly voyage for me. Our honeymoon. A lovely month at sea."

"Seasickness notwithstanding?" he japed.

"The Townsleys notwithstanding," Caroline whispered, leaning close to laugh with him. The cabin skylight was open to catch air, and their words could be heard below-decks by their "passengers" as they dressed for supper. "You will go easy on Parham and Mayhew, I trust, dearest? I know they're incorrigible imps, bad as my brothers when they were that age, but they're good lads at bottom."

"When they deserve it, I assure you I will, love."

"So much to do on the morrow," Caroline sighed, leaning close to him again, shoulder to shoulder. "Get ashore. Find lodgings and furnish them . . . I shall miss this. God, to sleep without you will be dreadful!"

"And I you, Caroline."

"How long do you stay in port, do you think?"

"A day to unload, another to replace firewood and water, some more rations . . . three days at the least, ten at the most, I suspect." He scowled, putting an arm about her shoulders. "Small ships spend less time at sea than most, and *Alacrity*'s about as small as one may get in the Fleet. And it's not as if I have to perform war patrols, cruising until the salt meat runs out. Half a month could be spent swinging at anchor in Nassau Harbor."

"I'd care very much for that," she said, snuggling into him. "Oh, look. The last of the sunset. Let's watch, do! My last with you, for awhile." She sniffed a little.

"But many more to come for us," he promised. "Many, many more!"

They waited until the last spark had dropped into the sea before rising, and the world turned quickly dark, as the night usually fell in the tropics.

"I love you, Alan!" she whispered, turning her face to him in the companionable, and secluding darkness aft.

"I love you, Caroline!"

"A quick supper, and an early night," Caroline vowed.

"As that Pepys fellow said, my love," Alan joshed, " 'And so to bed!' "

"Oh, then, let us hurry!"

Book III

"Look from your door, and tell me now
the colour of the sea.
Where can I buy that wondrous dye
And take it home with me?"

BLISS CARMAN

Chapter 1

Nassau, and its snug protected harbor, had changed drastically since Alan Lewrie had last seen it in 1781. Where there had swum tall frigates, there were now only brigs, sloops and cutters to represent the might of the Crown. But the commercial shipping had increased an hundredfold, and the town itself now boasted attractive stone public buildings where once there had been only wood biscuit boxes with palmetto thatched rooves, and the once-sleepy streets were humming with commercial endeavor. There were hundreds more homes to be seen, and, of course, since Nassau had been a shoddy pirates' haven since the 1600s no matter the strenuous efforts of a string of royal governors since Woodes Rogers's days, it boasted more taverns, more ordinaries, more public inns of dubious repute, and more out-and-out brothels.

But the transformation was stunning. With the arrival of thousands of dispossessed or disgruntled American Loyalists who had fled their spiteful Republican "cousins," the population had doubled and tripled. Humble Bay Street was now a good road and was fashioned "The Strand," while Shirley Street, named for a former governor, had become more sophisticated than a sandy lane lined with ramshackle, and could boast many fine residences, stores and shops. Though the official area of town was still bounded by Bay Street on the harbor, on the east by East Street, the west by West Street, and on the south by West Hill and East Hill Streets, more modest lanes had been laid out east and west of Government House. And "Over-The-Hill," the slumlike "stew" behind Bennett's Hill where the free blacks, poor whites and the criminal elements made their homes, had mushroomed.

The morning was not particularly warm for the Bahamas, in Alan Lewrie's experience, no warmer than high summer in rural England, and the trade winds did much to moderate it, though late summer in these islands could be at times oppressively hot and humid. Alan was grateful to note that, despite the hundreds of draft animals on the streets, the swarms of flies and mosquitoes had diminished greatly, due perhaps to the marshy areas he could recall from previous visits, which were now drained and filled and claimed for small farm plots and houses. Even in his best blue wool broadcloth uniform coat, and kerseymere waistcoat and breeches, he was not unduly uncomfortable, even inside the local shore offices for the Royal Navy squadron.

"Commodore Garvey will see you now, Captain Lewrie," the clerk at last announced and Alan rose, shot his cuffs and tugged his uniform into order to enter his new commanding officer's presence.

"Lieutenant Alan Lewrie, sir," the clerk said for their master's benefit. "Just come in from England in H.M. Sloop *Alacrity*, sir."

"Saw you come to anchor," Garvey grunted from the tall windows where he stood in shadow, hands behind his back and head bowed by what seemed all the world's troubles. "No more than adequate work, that."

"A new crew, sir, in commission two months," Alan checked, wary at once and hedging defensively. There had been little wrong with the approach down Hog Island, their reach across the wind between there and Silver Cay south and east, or their rounding up to windward and coming to anchor amid the disorderly swarm of shipping just in line with Frederick Street. With tops'ls already brailed up, harbor gaskets on, and yards squared, they'd cruised in neatly with the after course and two jibs standing, fired their salute, and coasted to a stop without a flaw, and the best bower anchor was let slip the instant they lost way. Alan was away in his gig before the stern kedge anchor could be rowed out and set, but he'd seen that go well, too!

"I'll brook no lame excuses from a newly wetted down junior, Lieutenant Lewrie," Garvey barked, though it was more an old dog's jowl-flapping petulance. "You may be one of those who deem a peacetime Fleet all 'claret and cruising', but you'll find to your dismay I demand the utmost of my captains. Should you persist in whip-jack seamanship and slovenly navigation, our waters here in the Bahamas will lay you all-aback quick enough."

Garvey made his way from the tall double windows to his desk, out of the shadows into proximity enough so Lewrie could see his lord and master, no longer silhouetted against the glare.

"I . . ." Lewrie began to rejoin.

"Muddle through at your peril, sir," Garvey threatened. "Either you'll wreck that fine little armed ketch of yours, or you will answer to my exceeding wrath. Do I speak plain enough for you, Lieutenant Lewrie?"

"Indeed, sir," Lewrie said, fighting to hide his resentment. As he once had as a midshipman when dealing with ship's officers, he gave Garvey a sweet smile of complete agreement, one which had always turned away wrath, as the Bible promised; or masked ironic amusement.

"I have despatches and the latest post, sir," Lewrie offered, bringing a thick canvas-wrapped packet forward. "These are the official correspondence. These are your personal letters. Your clerk already has the squadron's mail, sir."

"Sit," Garvey commanded, pointing in the general direction of a wing chair as he leaned forward and dragged the personal bundle toward his side of the desk. "Brandy, Lieutenant Lewrie? Claret, perhaps?" The man had turned uncommonly civil and benign in an instant.

"I would admire coffee or tea, sir," Lewrie stated, settling on the front edge of the chair. "Bit early in the forenoon for me, sir."

"Hmmph," Garvey frowned as if disappointed.

And Lewrie was left to stew and fidget for many long minutes as Garvey sorted through his *personal* mail, breaking the wax seal on the more interesting to read a snatch or two, then set them aside for closer perusal later. It was quite outside Lewrie's experience for a serving officer to ignore the official despatches so blithely. He'd "kissed the gunner's daughter" for being late in delivering orders aboard his first ship in favor of sorting through the personal missives for something from home first!

Horace Garvey—another bloody "Horry"!, Lewrie thought with wry humor—was slightly stoop-shouldered, and fond of his table, too, if the gotch-gutted appliance that bulged his waistcoat near to bursting was any clue. His face and hands were burned dark by tropic sun, finely wrinkled and splotched here and there from ancient searing. Or by drink. His forehead was high and narrow, the nose a prominent narrow beak, and his eyes were downward-turned at the outer corners, and slightly watery and gooseberry. At one time, Garvey had probably been a rather striking specimen, about Lewrie's height, and fashionably slim, but that heroic (and gentlemanly) frame had put on poundage in the trunk and face, though his limbs were still long and spare.

"You departed which port, sir?" Garvey asked at last.

"Portsmouth, sir," Lewrie piped up. "On the 16th last."

"A fast passage," Garvey nodded.

"We had good westerlies in the Bay of Biscay, and a favorable slant of wind off Lisbon, sir, allowing us to 'cut the corner' without dropping as far south as Cape St. Vincent," Lewrie boasted just a trifle. "My sailing master, and my supercargo master James Gatacre assured me I'd find leading winds around thirty-eight degrees north and sixteen west, so we might reach to make enough sou'westing to pick up the Trades, sir."

In Lewrie's last ship, *Telesto*, Captain Ayscough had sneered at the old way of navigating, where ships would fall far south to run across the Atlantic on a line of latitude for Dominica in the Leewards, even were they headed for the Bahamas, even were they bound for New York!

"Did you, indeed," Garvey sniffed, sounding unimpressed. "And whilst in Portsmouth, did you by happenstance come to hear of passengers who were to be given government passage to the Bahamas, sir?"

"Oh, do you mean the Reverend and Mrs. Townsley, your brother-in-law and your sister, sir?" Lewrie smiled as Garvey sat up with a show of interest at last. "They are arrived in my *Alacrity*, sir!"

"With you!" Garvey barked. "In that cockleshell of a ketch?"

"Aye, sir," Lewrie nodded.

Damme, just what *does* please the bastard? he wondered.

"Damme, I'll lay into the officials who entrusted them into a frail vessel such as yours!" Garvey ranted. "Was there no other ship available, no West Indiaman? Callous hounds! Mark my words, I will *blister* Whitehall with a letter expressing my displeasure. One does *not* treat relations of a senior officer so . . . so . . . !"

"She is a converted bomb, sir. Quite sturdy," Lewrie offered.

"Foul, miserable, cramped, bucketing about like a dory in all weathers. And you did not break your passage to ease the misery your passengers surely experienced, sir?" Garvey accused.

"Sir, my orders said to 'make the best of my way,' " Alan replied evenly. "From long usage that is to say, just short of 'with all despatch,' as I am sure you are aware, sir."

"Then you're a fool, a heartless fool, sir!" Garvey snarled.

"My other passengers, sir . . ." Alan winced as he carried on.

"What? More to be crammed in any-old-how?" Garvey sneered.

"Mister Gatacre and his assistant, sir. Seconded from Trinity House to the Admiralty to conduct a hydrographic survey. And a draft of six midshipmen, sir. I assume they are mentioned in the official despatches, sir," he concluded with what he hoped was a suitably subtle reminder about the Navy correspondence.

"As if I need more midshipmen!" Garvey scowled. "Newlies?"

"Two rather young, sir, two middling . . . twelvish. And, uhm . . . the last two from the Royal Naval Academy at Portsmouth, sir."

"Worse than King's Letter Boys!" Garvey sneered. "Sots and mountebanks! Latin, math, and not a single block in any of their rigging! Hah! Top-lofty cunny-thumbs and cack-hands, not an iota of wits in the lot! Foist 'em off on me, will they? *Wellll* . . . I'll put a flea in the Admiralty's ear about that, too! Boys cannot learn the sea in a bloody classroom, can't make the connections in the Fleet necessary for patronage and advancement. Chasing and caterwauling is all they pick up at that damn fool . . . Academy!"

"They did learn sea skills on passage, sir."

"A plow horse leaping two stacked boards ain't a blooded hunter, Lewrie, nor never will be."

"They are indeed a scurvy pair of Tom-Noddys, sir," Lewrie agreed, assaying a small witticism to ease the tension of this vitally important first interview with the man who could make or break him in the next three years, which had so far been tantamount to a disaster. "At present, they're no better than fresh-caught landsmen. Confused they may be, but neither of them is backward. They learn fast, sir."

"What is your armament, sir?" Garvey inquired suddenly, changing tack abruptly. "Your draught?"

"*Alacrity* mounts ten six-pounders, four dismountable two-pounder boat-guns, and the usual swivels, sir," Lewrie answered crisply, glad to be back on safe professional matters. "Properly laden and ballasted, she draws just shy of nine feet. Say a half less than nine, sir."

"Hmmmm," Garvey mused, idly toying with the lid of his silver ink-well, opening it and closing it again and again, as if something other than ink would magically appear for once. "Anything needful?"

"Firewood and water, the usual plaint, sir," Lewrie smiled in reply. "Restock our biscuit and salt-meats from the dockyard . . . she is in all other respects ready for sea, sir."

"A touch too weak for deep-water patrolling," Garvey surmised. "We've more than our fair share of pirates and buccaneers, still, and ships voyage past the Bahamas at their peril. Too many privateersmen from the late-lamented war, spoiled by easy pickings. You're not well armed enough to cow merchantmen violating the Navigation Acts, either."

"Aye, sir," Lewrie responded automatically whenever some senior officer paused to gather his thoughts, as he did in this case.

"Shoal-depth enough, though, to be useful inshore, in most instances, where the opposition would be even smaller and weaker-armed than your ketch. This fellow Gatacre, d'you say . . . I was to supply him with a suitable vessel?"

"I could not presume to know his complete orders, sir," Lewrie wavered, "nor the contents of whatsoever directives from the Admiralty accompany him. I may only suppose. He did, however, express a desire for two local-built luggers, in addition to ship's boats from the vessel supporting him, sir."

"And what do you possess for ship's boats, sir?" Garvey smiled.

"A twenty-foot launch, a cutter of similar size, and my gig, sir."

"Since he is already aboard your vessel, Lewrie, and you have *room* enough aboard, after all, I do believe I'll let him stay there," Garvey smirked. "The other cutters and such of this squadron would cramp him unmercifully. But *Alacrity,* now used to extra 'lumber' aft, will cope, I am certain. And those two Naval Academy midshipmen?"

"Aye, sir?" Lewrie felt his buttocks puckering in dread. He'd been charitable at best as to their prospects and abilities, but would be glad to see the back of them. He'd not have them if they came with a post-captain's rank!

"Good at mathematics, to the exclusion of all else useful," Garvey said, leaning back in his cool leather chair. "And who could be more helpful to the exacting work of hydrography than superior students of mathematics and surveying, hmm?"

"What a splendid idea, sir!" Lewrie beamed, pissing down his back as if the bastard had done him a signal honor, though he seethed at the very idea! "What *eminent* good sense it is, sir. I should be delighted! May I suggest to Mr. Gatacre that he may feel free to call upon you to discuss his other requirements, then, sir? Once you have had time to peruse what the Admiralty wrote you concerning his duties, that is. A day, perhaps, at your convenience, sir."

"Uhm, of course, he may," Garvey replied, taken aback by Alan's reaction. "You may." He'd thought to punish this upstart for treating his kin so badly, to be the whipping boy for the Admiralty's callous uncon-cern for their comforts. To put this "newly" in his place, right from the start!

"And may I be allowed to inquire, sir, as to whether I may give leave tickets to my hands, too, sir?" Lewrie fairly oozed unctuous oils of socia-bility, sounding as though butter would not melt in his mouth. "Once *Alacrity* is reprovisioned and suitable luggers found, before we begin our surveying, sir?"

"I might allow it," Garvey almost sulked, put out that Alan was not "put out." "Within reason, mind."

"Further, sir, might I inquire as to your Standing Orders for the Baha-mas Squadron?" Lewrie pressed, bestowing blissful smiles upon his sta-tion commander. "Do you require captains to sleep aboard, as I do be-lieve the Channel Squadron is wont to do in wartime? Or may I consider shore lodgings for myself between voyages, sir?"

"Like to stretch your legs on solid ground, do you?" Garvey asked, lifting an eyebrow, which evident suspicion as to his motives almost made Lewrie cringe with worry it might be disallowed.

"A run ashore now and again would be welcome, sir," Lewrie replied with bright-eyed innocence. "Within limits, of course, sir."

"I do not begrudge my officers their pleasures, Lewrie," Garvey informed him. "What's good for Jack is good for his betters aft. So long as you conduct yourself with the proper decorum expected of a Sea Officer, a Christian, and an English gentleman."

And just when did you last see *decorous* Sea Officers, Lewrie asked himself in wonder at such a ludicrous statement? Leaping rantipole and playing balum-rancum in church? Hymn-singing in brothels?

"So I would have time to seek out an establishment, sir?" Alan said, cocking a brow of his own to nail the agreement shut without having to mention the necessity of such lodgings, or the fact that he had brought Caroline with him. He didn't think Garvey would care for that.

"I suppose," Garvey sighed. "Yes, you may."

"Thank you, sir. Quite grateful. Quite."

"Before you sail, I will send specific orders aboard, Lewrie," Garvey went on, pulling the packet of official documents to him for an excuse to dismiss him. "As to the survey, what needs doing against our piracy problem, the enforcement of the Navigation Acts, and how I expect ships of the Bahamas Station to conduct themselves. Use your hydrographic work to familiarize yourself with what perils our waters hold. And remember, I warn you now, to handle your vessel with due care and sober rectitude, or I'll dismiss you from her command and replace you with an officer who does things my way. Hear me?"

"I understand you completely, sir," Lewrie told him with such a sober and abashed countenance that even Garvey thought he'd gotten his message rammed home sufficiently.

"What with all this correspondence, and the cares of this squadron, I have no more time for you, Lewrie. You may dismiss."

"Thank you for receiving me so promptly, sir."

Chapter 2

"Fubsy, crusty, dilberry," Lewrie seethed at supper ashore that evening, "combed like a louse from the hairy, dirty black fundament of all Creation!"

Caroline put her napkin to her mouth to hide her snickering.

"Pompous, posturing, pus-gutted, hymn-singing . . . barnacle!" He ranted on, though in a low voice, as he wrangled knife and fork over a stringy cut of beef tougher than old anchor cables which would end up costing him half a crown when the reckoning was fetched.

"Alan, dearest," Caroline suggested once she trusted herself to lower the napkin and not cackle out loud at his frustrated antics, "I am so sorry this Garvey was so uncharitable towards you, truly. But he is your superior, after all. Do compose yourself. Or, at the least, wait until we're in our set of rooms. Who knows who might be listening?" She waved one hand at the many officers at table nearby.

"Sorry, Caroline, but the man rowed me beyond all temperance," Alan sighed, giving up on the "choice cut of English beef-steak" and leaning back in his chair. At least the wine was more than palatable, and he topped up their glasses. Bloody shilling the bottle, he noted chalked on the neck. Nassau had grown no less expensive than it had been during the war. "I don't believe anything could please the man."

"Out of sight, out of mind, then," she replied. "On this survey of yours. Which I am certain you shall complete most successfully, if I know the slightest bit about you. And when you return, he may by then have more regard for your abilities."

Alan reached across the table to take her hand and give her a thankful squeeze. "You're right, of course." He calmed, and rewarded her with a fond smile. "Thank you for having good sense enough for both of us, darling. And for *your* regard for my abilities. Truly, I am coming to realize that I am the most blessed of men."

"When you go on a rant, you are so almighty amusing, though," she confided with a quiet laugh. "Thank you, Alan."

"For what, my dear?"

"For taking me into your confidence," she said. "For sharing with me your worries, and your hopes. For listening to my thoughts."

"Always, my dearest," he vowed happily.

"Ahem." The black waiter coughed as he came to the table.

"You may clear mine," Alan said. "The dogs may now break their teeth on it."

"Uhm, yassuh. Uhm, dese notes be fo' you, sah. Dot gen'mun in de cornah, Cap'um Finney, like ya an' de missus t'join him ot his table. Un' dot Navy officah ovah dere, sah, he does, too, sah. De missus done with her groupah, mo'om? He's a sweet fish, mo'om. He kin eat good, sweet as de lobstah, any day." Alan opened the first note to find an almost illegible scrawl, and looked up to gaze upon the man who had sent it. Captain Finney was a civilian in overdone finery, handsome, blond and darkly tanned. He peered at Alan with an almost hopelessly naive expression of longing, and ducked him a smile. He was surrounded by a brace of shoddy types, though, with a trio of obvious trulls for companions. Alan wanted no part of them. He opened the second note.

"Got de Stilton un' ex'ra fine biscuit, got de fine port, got de key-lime puddin', un' got de Brazil cawfy, black un' hot," the waiter enticed. "Sah, mo'om? Raisin duff? Sherry trifle? Key-lime puddin'?"

"Let's have the key-lime pudding!" Caroline suggested eagerly. "It sounds marvelous, and I've never had it before!"

"Let's do," Alan agreed. "For two, with coffee. And please give Captain Finney our regrets, but I do not know him, nor wish to join him. Do, however, deliver my compliments to Commander Rodgers and we will be delighted to join him and his companion. We will take our dessert and coffee with them."

"Ah tell 'em, sah."

Lewrie smiled at the Navy officer, then turned and gave the man Finney a short, dismissive shake of his head. He turned back to look at Caroline, and winced as he saw her single arched eyebrow.

"If that suits you, Caroline?" He grimaced. "Forgive me, dear, for not asking your preference, but I'm so new at being married, I . . ."

"Oh, Alan, we both are!" she whispered, forgiving him instantly, and tilting her head to one side fondly. "Two invitations?"

"One from the Navy officer yonder. A Commander Rodgers. And one from the thatch-haired fellow and his crew. Some fellow named Finney."

"Heavens," Caroline muttered as she eyed the other party. "Too seedy a lot for me. Alan, I could swear those women with them . . . Dear Lord, darling. So that's what prostitutes look like?" She grinned.

She shivered and turned her gaze back to Alan.

"Finney is the one in the center, dear?" she asked. "The man just leered at me! Of course, we'll accept Commander Rodgers's kind request. He's senior to you? And kindly disposed to you, there's a wonder, after your horrid morning. Let us, do."

Thank bloody Christ, Lewrie thought, relieved to have escaped a thoughtless deed; damme, but this marriage business is a terror!

He knew himself well enough as a selfish rogue, and he was used to giving orders and having them obeyed, so having to take counsel with someone else, not having *his* wishes treated as Holy Writ, was a wrench.

They crossed to the other table and the introductions were made. Commander Benjamin Rodgers was about thirty, a trifle stocky, and dark as a Welshman. His companion was a young lady in her middle twenties named Elizabeth Mustin, a saucy brown-haired piece with sparkling blue eyes, and a most impressive, top-lofty figure.

"Off that ketch-rig come in this morning?" Commander Rodgers asked, then answered his own question. "'Course you are, ya had to be, a new officer I never clapped top-lights on before. Knew it! Welcome to the Bahamas Station, Captain Lewrie. Take joy o' your posting!"

"Thank you, sir. And your ship is . . . ?"

"*Whippet*, twenty guns. 6th Rate Sloop o' War," Rodgers answered.

Lord, yes, he was senior! Sloop was a loose catchall term for any vessel larger than a bomb, revenue cutter or armed yacht below the standardized Rates; *Alacrity* was technically a sloop, no matter how she was rigged aloft. But a Sloop of War was a miniature frigate, smallest of the three-masted, ship-rigged vessels in the Fleet, and her captain was Post-Captain in all but name, sure to be "made post" soon.

Rodgers already wore a post-captain's "iron-bound" coat, but for three cuff buttons instead of four, and profuse with gold lace. It was a rarely awarded brevet rank he held (commander was not made substantive until the 1850s), but it was one dripping with promise, the mark of a man rising to the top of the seniority list like a signal rocket.

"Are there many on station, sir?" Alan asked.

"Only one more, *Ariel*," Rodgers informed him. "You know how reduced the Fleet is, as I'm certain our lord and master told you when you reported to him this morning. Saw you being rowed ashore like Hell's Fire was licking your gig's transom, hey?"

"Aye, sir," Lewrie grinned as their coffee and pudding arrived.

"We're a sorry lot these days," Rodgers babbled on happily. "A single 4th Rate fifty-gunner, *Royal Arthur*, our flag. We possess but one frigate, Captain Childs's *Guardian*, and she's only a twenty-eight, at the best. We've half a dozen others, from revenue cutter-sized, two-masted lugers or schooners, or brig-rigged or ketch-rigged sloops, like yours. Too few, too slow, too weak, and too bloody lost from where troubles occur. Oh, pardons Mistress Lewrie, for my language."

"I have heard worse, from my husband, Commander Rodgers," Caroline informed him with a chuckle, "and that, recently."

"Mean to say you two really *are* married?" Rodgers marveled. "I thought . . . pardons again, but my experience o' Navy marriages is that most of 'em're but a convenient sham, and for a man t'risk his future 'fore makin' post . . . ouch!"

"Pay him no mind, Ben's a conceited arse," Elizabeth Mustin said after poking her *innamorato* in the ribs, but with no real sign of anger. "Yes, dear . . . some officers *do* wed those they love."

"You set a hellish-bad example for all of us, Captain Lewrie," Rodgers admitted, not the slightest bit abashed. "Once the word gets out, every girl in port'll be having your good lady over, to fathom how she got you to go for the high jump! My dear Mrs. Lewrie, this is the sort o' fame you could dine out on for years, don't ya know. What say ye to a toast to the happy couple? Champagne, hey?"

"Yes!" Elizabeth enthused. "Champagne. His favorite tipple!"

"A brace o' bottles, hang the cost, and my treat, sir!"

"Most gallant, sir," Caroline said before Lewrie could answer. "We would be delighted, thank you."

"Waiter?" Rodgers hallooed. "Bloody *love* the stuff, dearer'n a babby craves his mother's milk. Might a'been nursed on good vintages, far's I know, an' bawled fit t'bust t'be weaned, hey? Thank God we've peace with France just long enough to stock up for our next set-to, or pray our smugglers're bold enough to dodge the King's Customs. So, I s'pose Commodore Garvey gave you your marchin' orders already, sir?"

"Hydrographic surveying, sir," Alan replied, sketching in what Garvey's interview had been like. "God knows where, though."

"Best thing," Rodgers announced. "Outa sight, outa mind. And this Trinity House fellow Gatacre'll be just the thing. Bahamas are bad-charted, if charted at all below the populous islands."

"Caroline thought it a blessing, too, sir," Alan agreed.

"And what did you think of our lord and master, sir?" Rodgers asked, sounding offhand, but looking cutty-eyed at him.

"Ah, sir," Lewrie opined, on his guard. But he didn't believe Rodgers's ebullient personality would sit well with Garvey, either, so he could not be a favorite. "Hmm, sir!" he added, rolling his eyes.

"Did he offer drink, Captain Lewrie? And, did you accept?"

"He did, sir, but I did not. I didn't get my requested coffee."

"Then thank your lucky stars ya didn't!" Rodgers muttered as he leaned a little closer. "It all has to do with his son. Shipped out as a midshipman in *Royal Arthur*, and soon's they dropped the hook, he was commissioned, and a good man turned out to make room for him. He's fourth lieutenant into her now. If Garvey had a budget that'd purchase more patrol craft, he'd be on his own bottom, even as we speak! Garvey rewards his favorites, and chastises those that cross him. What he is lookin' for is any excuse to promote people up an' outa *Royal Arthur*, so the squadron is captained by his protégés, and young Virgil Garvey prospers. Any slip on your part'd give him an excuse for Virgil t'be third lieutenant. Oh, we all walk small about our Horace, we do!"

"God, sir," Alan chilled, "my passengers, they'll tell him I'm married, that I brought Caroline here. He's already criticized me for my ship-handling!"

"Ah, rot! Ya brought her in sweet as pie. He tried that on me, first I sailed in. Let's just say you're never t'be one o' his 'elect,' sir. As if he's Noah himself!" Rodgers sneered, warming to his screed. *"Royal Arthur* doesn't stir from her moorin's but once every six weeks, and that for a short run to Harbour Island or Spanish Wells over on Eleuthera and back. He's wedded t'his *palacio* ashore. I would be, too; 'tis a damned impressive pile. No, 'tis best you're far away for now. There's other unfortunates not among the 'saved' for him t'cull through so his syco-phants can advance. More'n a few as *need* replacin', had I my way, sir!"

"Sounds positively Manichaean, sir," Lewrie quipped. "All of this talk of the saved, the elect."

"Well, stap me!" Rodgers hooted in surprise. "What the devil are you doin', wearin' our good King's Coat, an' makin' noises like a man's read a real book! Don't ya know English tarpaulins're supposed t'sound so sim-ple-minded, even the others notice, sir? Stump about the quarter-deck yellin' 'Luff!' and cursin' 'damn my eyes,' ha ha!"

"Damn . . . my . . . eyes," Lewrie pronounced tongue in cheek, slowly as if trying it on for the first time. "And is that best uttered with one hand on the hip, sir? Perhaps . . . gazing aloft and wondering what the devil all that laundry's drying up there for, sir?"

"Goddamme, but you'll do, Captain Lewrie! You're a jolly young dog, and blessed with the second-handsomest lady in the islands. I do avow you'll do right well for me! My irreverent sort of fellow."

"I will endeavor to please, sir," Lewrie smiled back, lifting a glass of champagne to his lips. This Rodgers was a merry wag himself, of the sort Lewrie would feel most comfortable and sportive, and found himself liking Commander Benjamin Rodgers a great deal, wishing he was the commander of the Bahamas Squadron instead of Garvey.

"And do you lodge in town, Miss Mustin?" he heard Caroline ask, conducting their own conversation apart from Navy gossip.

"God, no! Nassau's fearsome noisy and rowdy, Caroline. May I call you Caroline? And you must call me Elizabeth. If only to escape the stenches, I have a small house east of town, out toward Fort Montagu. One gets first shot at the Trade Winds out there, blowing all manner of nastiness alee, as Benjamin puts it. A Loyalist family of my acquaintance bought a plantation there, but the soil is awfully thin . . . played out . . . so they're running up houses."

"Thank God for the Loyalists, or Nassau'd still be dull as a dead dog," Rodgers commented. "They've braced this colony up good as a soldier's wind and got it moving. God help the American Republic, after running the best of 'em out. And God be thanked they lit here."

"Caroline is of a Loyalist family," Alan bragged.

"Never you mean it!" Elizabeth gushed. "Truly? Why, so am I, my dear! New York."

"North Carolina!" Caroline rejoined, and they both fell into a swoon of comradeship at once. "God, how wonderful, I can't . . . !"

"We've a funny society here in the Bahamas, Lewrie," Rodgers told him as he topped up the champagne glasses. "Ain't this grand stuff, though? There's us on top. Government, military and naval officials from home. Right under us are the old-time families from Nassau, Eleuthera, Long Island or the Exumas, the rich traders and planters who've been here for years. Third-best, but greater in numbers are the emigré Loyalists. Under them you have the poor whites, the artisans and tinkers and such. Ex-pirates, deserters, freebooters and buccaneers, who small-hold or fish, ply their poor trades or loaf about. Then come the Cuffys, and it's the same story chapter and verse as it is for the whites."

"How so, sir?"

"Free blacks first, o'course, then slaves at the bottom. But they have a caste system bad as any I've read of among the Hindoos. Octoroons, quadroons, mulattoes, brown to coal black'uns. So a free black but a blueskin is rated lower than a free black who's almost white, d'you see. Straight or woolly hair, pale or dark skin. Now the blueskin may be a home owner and educated, with a shop of his own, makin' enough money to bloody *vote* in England, but his fellow with the straight hair and talk of Portugese sailors in the family tree is the better man, even were he dirt-poor, illiterate and ignorant as so many sheep. Damned funny world, ain't it?"

"I've heard that said, sir," Lewrie japed, raising his glass in a mock toast. "Though I've never heard much laughter about it."

"Hah, you're a sharp 'un, sir! A glass with you, my lad."

"Uhm, about losing my ship, sir . . . ?" Alan inquired urgently as they lowered their glasses to refill.

"Who are your patrons?" Rodgers asked unashamedly. In the Navy, family connections, petticoat influence, and favors given and gotten mattered almost as much as merit and seniority, or competence and wits. Young officers aspired to a circle of "sea daddies" who looked after their careers; senior officers culled their wardrooms and lower decks looking for protégés with connections, too, or talents and abilities. A man was judged by the quality of his protégés, by his wisdom in the choices he sponsored so the nation and fleet were better served, and success by a junior shone just as brightly on his "sea daddy."

"Retired Admiral Sir Onsley Matthews, sir," Alan stated. "And I received this commission from Admiral Sir Samuel Hood."

"Ah, didn't we all, though," Rodgers grunted, since Hood had sat in charge of the Admiralty's professional side for several years.

"From his hands personally, sir," Alan boasted. "First in '83 off Cape François, then this February along with Admiral Howe, at the Admiralty. Face to face, as it were, sir."

"Don't come any better than that!" Rodgers said with brows up in appreciation. "I know for certain neither o' those worthies suffer fools gladly. Damme, what wicked fun! I do believe I'll have a chat with our lord and master Commodore Garvey tomorrow. Put a word or two in his ear about your . . . dare I say . . . august connections to shiver his tops'ls! Make him wonder what you're doin' here in his command. If you're here to keep an eye on him."

"Even more reason for me to sail as far off as possible," Alan sighed. "And stay there until I rot, sir."

"Aye, but with a rovin' commission, an independent ship, free of all his guff," Rodgers chuckled. "Can't ask for better duty, nor better chances for mischief, I'm thinkin'. No, once I drop the word on Garvey, your command'll be safe as houses. He'll fear to displace you so his son may prosper."

"That is a relief, sir."

"Damme, I may have to start bein' sickeningly patronizin' to you m'self, Lewrie," Rodgers laughed. "If I mean to aspire."

"If you do not fear Captain Garvey, sir," Lewrie responded, tongue in cheek, "perhaps I should begin to patronize *you?*"

"One never knows, does one?" Rodgers snickered, eyes alight.

The waiter came to open the second bottle of champagne, and Alan leaned back in his chair to see the civilian Captain Finney and his party leave the room. Finney's jaw was tight and working fretful flexings. He swiveled his head to look back once, and gave Lewrie a petulant glare.

And fuck you, too, Alan thought smugly, whoever you are.

Chapter 3

"Hmmm," Lewrie had opined when Caroline had shown him which house she wished. It had once been a gatehouse stables, then some overseer's cottage for the Boudreau plantation, a Bermudian "saltbox" done in stone, little better than a country croft. It had one large parlor and dining room in one half, and two bedrooms for the other, with deep covered porches front and back. A breezeway had been added on the right-hand side opposite the sitting rooms, what Caroline termed a Carolina "dog-run," to make a covered terrace and separate the house proper from the added-on kitchen and pantries, and their great heat. Off the back porch was a detached bathhouse and 'jakes.' It had clearly seen better days, and needed work.

"Bit . . . dowdy, ain't it?" he'd suggested dubiously.

"The Boudreaus want an hundred guineas a year for their row houses, Alan," Caroline had told him. "Wood, with barely a scrap of land in back. Sure to be eaten to the ground by termites in a year! Here, we have stone walls, and stone floors, and stone will be cool in high summer. The Boudreaus will replaster, replace the shakes, and allow me to retar against the rains. I know it looks a fright, but with some paint, our furniture, draperies . . . and just look out at this view! All this for only sixty guineas the year, Alan!"

The house faced nor'east, fronted by Bay Street, across the sound from the eastern end of Potter's Cay, turned cater-corner to face the Trades so the porches and "dog-run" would be cool even in midafternoon heat. And from the porch, Potter's Cay and Hog Island were dark green and pale dun, swimming in waters that ranged from as clear as gin or well-water to aquamarine, turquoise, emerald and jade, and there was an inviting beach just across the road on the East Bay.

"Here, we'll have half an acre for a small vegetable garden, and flower beds, Alan," she'd praised on. "Should I wish a coach or saddle horse, I may day-rent from them, 'stead of us having to buy mounts or an equipage and paying to stable them. And they'll allow me all the manure I wish for the garden and all. The Boudreaus are Charleston Loyalists. Low Country Huguenots, Alan. Wonderful people, and when Betty

Mustin introduced us and they found I was from North Carolina, well
. . . 'tis a marvelous bargain, dearest!"

"Well . . ." he'd waffled, not seeing the possibilites.

"So close to them, I'll need but one maid of all work at a day, Alan,
saving us even more on servants' wages. With their land played out, and
a glut of slaves now, they're servant-poor. Oh, do but indulge me in this,
love! And when you return, I'll have us a home to do an admiral proud!"

"What the devil's a fellow to do?" he sighed to himself, wondering again
at his easy surrender to her will, at how quim-struck he had become so
quickly. So like a—by God—so like a *husband!* He shivered at the image. Why, next would come children, sure as fate! Nappies and fouled
swaddlings! Conversations centered upon a host of domestic dullities—
teething, potty training, breeching, and all! No, he thought grimly,
surely not with spritely Caroline, please God?

And though the house was a bargain at sixty guineas, there was more
to consider; those drapes, those painters and plasterers, those improvements. His purse was nicely full, but not bottomless. Yet to move them
in, stock the larder, purchase implements for the gardens, equip the
kitchen and outfit those porches with some needed furnishings had set
him back an additional sixty guineas already, so there had gone most of
his grandmother's remittance, and the £500 he had brought out had to
be left with a local banker for her to draw upon for "improvements," the
bulk of it, and her household allowance doled out to her with his shore
agent at what he prayed was a liberal eight pounds the month. Suddenly,
marriage was becoming more a "pinchbeck," coin-counting drudgery
than a terror, he decided.

"Pray God Phineas was right," he muttered aloud. "She'd better be
'economical' as Christ feeding the five thousand."

"Sir?" Lieutenant Ballard asked, interrupting his pacing to leeward.

"Eh?" Lewrie jerked, wakened from his pecuniary musings.

"I swore you said something, sir."

"Just maundering to myself over the high cost of domestic life, Mister
Ballard," Lewrie said with a shy grin, waving one hand idly. "Pay me no
mind. Now we've what seems a constant three-and-a-half fathoms to
work with in this Exuma Sound, I was indulging myself."

"Aye, aye, sir," Ballard said, going back to his duties.

Alacrity stood sou-sou'east with a touch of easting, driven by the
trades large on her larboard quarter. The day before they'd gone closehauled up the chain of cays and shoals east from Nassau toward

Eleuthera, threaded the Fleeming Channel near Six Shilling Cays, and now loped across the Exuma Sound for their first survey area.

Well, perhaps "loped" was too strong a word, since they towed a pair of local-built, two-masted luggers of thirty-foot length, with their own ship's boats atrail of them on long towing bridles, so their forward speed was much impaired.

Lewrie wasn't sure he wanted too much speed, anyway, given the clarity of the sea around them. He could look over the side and see the bottom quite easily in the midmorning light, could espy the occasional coral head to the west as the Sound shoaled, and observe *Alacrity's* shadow rising and falling away as it passed over stray startling batwinged rays and sharks below, or shimmering clouds of bright-hued fish.

James Gatacre and his assistant came aft from the bows, trailing the four midshipmen. He ascended to the quarter-deck and peeked into the compass bowl. He laid a thick-fingered hand on the traverse board, which made John Fellows the naval sailing master sniff suspiciously. Gatacre turned his heavy, craggy head aloft and eyed the set of the sun. He peered down at the issue chart and paced off progress along their course from the Fleeming Channel entrance.

"Ahum," he said, folding up his dividers and shoving them into a pocket. "Captain Lewrie, my compliments to you this morning, sir."

"Mister Gatacre," Lewrie nodded pleasantly.

"Might I humbly suggest to you, sir, that we get the way off her and come to anchor in the next ten minutes or so?" Gatacre said. "There are rumors of a sandshoal, and sand bores . . . ahum, just about here, to be plumbed, sir."

Lewrie peered at the chart himself. Where the dead reckoning of their course ended, assuming the chip log was right and they were doing six knots and a bit, where Gatacre's thick thumb rested, given four miles to the inch, they were . . .

"God's teeth!" Lewrie spat. "Mister Ballard, all hands! Take in tops'ls, pay out a cable to the best bower, hand the forecourse and the inner jibs."

"Nought to dread, Captain Lewrie," Gatacre smiled confidently. "We've a good two miles before we fetch it. Assuming the position of the wreck was taken correctly, o'course. Nought to dread."

"The wreck!" Lewrie goggled. "Christ on a bloody cross! Quartermaster, put yer helm down. Two points to weather. Mister Ballard? Loose sheets and let her luff!"

"Did I not mention it last night in your cabins, sir?" Gatacre frowned.

"You mentioned shoals, sir. But said nothing about a wreck."

"Bless my soul, I was sure I had, sir," Gatacre chuckled at his failure, bemused by a faulty memory. He stuck a forefinger into his ear and waggled it about vigorously, as though that action restored thoughts.

"A shipwreck." Lewrie muttered to himself. "Mine arse on a band-box!"

Book IV

Chapter 1

It was just as well that "Dread-Nought" Gatacre was armed with a host of assorted charts from France, England, Holland and Spain that spanned centuries of sailing in the Bahamas. He also possessed tomes of Sailing Directions from ancient to modern, gathered by the Admiralty over the years and pored over closely for the slightest variations in cartography, or acceptable agreement over soundings, bearings, and channels among the coral reefs, the sand shoals and sand bores.

Else we'd be at this 'til the Last Trumpet, Lewrie thought.

Had they been forced to dismiss all preceding data, he doubted if they would have finished mapping the chain of cays that led from New Providence to Eleuthera in *Alacrity*'s three-year commission, and would still have been hard at their task when the last ship's boy had become a doddering white-haired pensioner.

Fortunately, many of the foreign charts proved truthful, so it was mainly a list of unsurveyed waters they had to explore, or those areas where no consensus could be agreed to, shortening their task considerably.

Mid-spring became high summer as *Alacrity* felt her way south, three months' labor that passed in fits and starts. There were fast, exhilirating passages in brisk winds and balmy weathers, followed by long days at anchor, with the boats and luggers dragging and sounding with short lead lines, oars dipping across glassy-calm bays.

They scouted all down the length of Exuma Sound's western side, past all the shoals and cays. They plumbed the waters around Conception Island and Rum Cay, peeked into Crooked Island Passage, along the windward shores of Acklins, then beat to windward for Samana Cay, the Plana Cays, then sou-east once again to explore the jagged reefs of Mayaguana Island.

As settlers flocked into the Bahamas, as plantations and towns grew on the islands south from New Providence onto virgin territory, the need for safe Sailing Directions for the lower Bahamas became a crucial matter. As civilization invaded those cays that had before only been watering anchorages (or pirates' lairs), the Fleet had a vital need for potential bases from which to protect trade.

119

It was vital, yes, and a sober responsibility; but it was fun! Hot as it became as they proceeded southerly, the winds were bracing and cool. And when a blow came up, a safe anchorage could always be found in which to ride it out.

With four boats to be worked, most of the hands had to be away from the ship during the days, free of onerous, repetitive labor, and the hands enjoyed that. The midshipmen were each assigned a boat of their own, separated from their officers' exasperations, and they enjoyed that, too. And when the hydrographic work became boring, there was always a passage to somewhere new to break the monotony, and then arms drills, fire drills, gun drills and such were a welcome break in routine, to which all hands fell to with a will.

They took midday meals away from the ship for the most part, and the cays and islets provided good sport for hunting or fishing, with wild pigs or goats fetched back to supplant salt rations in the messes. And those islands which were populated provided welcome entertainment. After a good day's labor, a signal gun would summon the boats back alongside for a later-scheduled rum issue, supper, and "easy discipline" period of music and song before Lights Out and sleep.

And it was lovely, for the Bahamas were a sailor's paradise for startlingly beautiful waters and islands, for high-piled banks of cloud scudded along by bright, clean winds. Instead of being far out to sea, deprived for months of the sight of anything green, of anything fresh to eat, they partook of fruits and vegetables daily like so many Lotus-Eaters, and feasted their eyes on trees and grass, walked beaches unmarked by human feet, and sometimes rested in the shade of Madeira mahoganies, sea grapes or pines and palmettos, amid lush and fragrant flowering shrubs, listening to the ocean's breeze stir fronds above their heads, or the sea raling gently on the sands.

"Some do say there's routes 'cross the Caicos Banks," Gatacre told them at supper one evening. As usual, he had a folded-up chart near his plate at which he jabbed now and then with an inky finger, or a mustard-smeared knife. "And rumored entrances on the loo'rd so a ship o' moderate draught might pass through the breakers."

"We could spend the rest of summer 'til hurricane season seeking them," Lewrie commented between bites of their supper.

"A real boon to settlement of the Turks and Caicos, were they to exist, though, sir," Lieutenant Ballard suggested, neatly delivering some iguana to his mouth. They were anchored off Fort George Cay, by the isles on the nor'west side of the Caicos, where a palmetto-log, sand and "tabby" coral-block fort guarded the approaches to the Salt Isles. Will Cony had gone ashore with Lewrie's light-caliber fusil earlier, and had bagged a couple with neat head shots, and the ship's cook had skinned and roasted them, pronouncing them good as chicken, any day.

"Aye, Mister Ballard, lookee here," James Gatacre went on. "A bigger sort o' islands here in the Caicos. Blue Hills just a little way below us t'the sou'west. Some name it Providenciales. Fourteen mile long, fairly wide. North Caicos a few miles nor'east, then ya have Middle Caicos, East Caicos t'east an' south. All of 'em huge, by Bahamian standards, well-watered inland, and fertile fr any sorta agriculture. Like an atoll, they are, strung 'round this shallow bank, though. To find good anchorages, ya have t'sail all the way 'round, outside the Caicos Banks. But, with navigable passes, commerce could flow with little dread o' piracy or enemy ships in time o' war."

"The local garrison commander knows nought of 'em," Lewrie said with a shrug. "Fort George depends on a monthly packet, long way about."

"Bloody soldiers, what'd they know?" Gatacre sneered. "I've my doubts they'd know how to bait a hook were they starvin', an' that from the beach!"

"And in wartime, Fort George, and any number of outposts would be cut off from Turks Island or South Caicos, and would fall without a way to resupply," Lewrie added. "And it's not just protecting the salt trade. Look wider afield. Mouchoir Passage, Turks Passage, the Silver Bank Passage, Caicos . . . even Mayaguana and Crooked Island Passages up north of here. Any ship leaving the Caribbean through the Windward Passage *has* to thread one of those to get to the open sea. A British base in the Caicos could guard them all. Or deny them all."

"Salt's important, too, sir," Ballard stated.

Since the late 1600s, Bermudian ships had been coming to the Turks to evaporate sea salt in shallow salinas, then rake "white gold" in the summers. There were few settled islands so far, but displaced Loyalists and other opportunists were beginning to flood in, so a Crown presence was now necessary.

"What about this pass here between Water Cay and Blue Hill's eastern tip, sir?" Lewrie asked. "This quaintly named Leeward-Going-Through?"

"Narrow an' shallow fr deep-draught merchantmen, or men o' war, sir," Gatacre frowned. "An' coral reefs which block access west toward

Discovery, Proggin, or Sapodilla Bays. Our best hopes are o' findin' a pass outa Caicos Creek'r Malcolm Road on the western coast, maybe from Clear Sand Road south o' West Caicos. What lies beyond 'em is a myst'ry so far, though. South o' West Caicos, there's reefs an' shoals aplenty. Passes, even so, but where they lead? Been a graveyard o' ships down there. Ye have deep water, God, fathomless deeps t'leeward. Then, in less'n three cables, half a nautical mile, it shoals so fast, and the breakers're so rough, that you're smashed like an egg on rock an' coral 'fore ya could put yer helm over! There's said t'be millions in pound sterlin' o' gold an' silver litterin' the ocean floor. Might ya dredge along the inner reefs, past the breakers, I 'spect there's untold fortune, an' that but a fraction o' what these shoals have claimed, since the days o' Cortez!"

"My word," Lewrie started. "And in shallow water, d'ya say!"

"Shall we haul up a bucket of doubloons before or after breakfast, captain?" Ballard japed.

"Now you've done it, Mister Gatacre," Lewrie sighed. "Talk from the wardroom always gets forrud quick as lightning. We'll be lucky to get a decent hour's work from the hands tomorrow!"

"Ah, don't ya think such talk'll make 'em pay *real* close attention t'the bottom, though, sir?" Gatacre snickered.

Chapter 2

Malcolm Road led nowhere but to high bluffs and jagged coral heads. Caicos Creek had been promising; twenty-four feet of water at the narrow entrance, and led east to South Bluff on Blue Hills, thence to Proggin Bay and Sapodilla Bay, then Discovery Bay, which was a good anchorage. But a reef with exposed coral heads blocked progress to the east, and the Caicos Bank shallowed to six feet not very far offshore to the south, and continued like a clear-water lake all the way to the horizon and the tempting sight of other islands.

And there was not twelve feet of water from South Bluff across the direct course to West Caicos inside the Banks to Clear Sand Road, so they had to thread their way back out Caicos Creek to reach the sea, then proceed south along the leeward coast of West Caicos, which was the situation for which they sought a solution in a nutshell.

"At least we know there's 100 fathoms depth within a mile of shore," Lewrie announced as they loafed along under reduced sail in West Caicos's lee. Hands in the forechains were swinging the deep-sea lead, while the luggers prowled much closer inshore of *Alacrity*. "A touch rocky for good holding-ground, but one could come to anchor quite close up to the beach yonder."

"Aye, sir, though if the winds veer westerly, I'd not trust it for a storm . . . good Christ!" Gatacre snapped suddenly.

William Pitt had dined on iguana the night before, too, but had salvaged himself a few choice morsels of offal before it had been cooked, and had appeared on deck towing a taloned paw in his mouth nearly the size of his head. He brought it to Lewrie's feet and dropped it, sat back on his haunches and looked up, evidently quite proud of himself, expecting a pet or two.

"Stole it from the cook, did you, Pitt?" Lewrie chuckled as he bent down to rub the ram-cat between the ears. "I suppose that qualifies as 'hunting.' Good cat. Good lad, you are."

"Gawd, what a stench!" Gatacre complained softly.

"One should not complain about stench until one has discovered a bread-room rat half his size in one's shoes o' the morning, sir," Lewrie told him.

"At least he is useful in that regard, captain."

"Profitable, too, Mister Gatacre," Lewrie joshed with a droll expression as he rose. "The midshipmen's mess pays dear for "miller" fattened on ship's biscuit."

"Dear God, ye . . ." Gatacre winced, looking a touch queasy.

"I suspect the purser Mr. Keyhoe breeds 'em, as a sideline to tobacco and slop goods. Fresh meat's always been . . ."

"No bottom!" The larboard leadsman sang out. "No bottom to this line!"

"Quartermaster, ease your helm alee. Pinch us up shoreward a point," Lewrie ordered. "We'll rediscover the 100-fathom line."

"Sail ho!" the masthead lookout called as well. "One point forrud o' the starboard beam! Three-master, runnin' sou'east!"

"Busy morning," Gatacre mused. "Must be on passage for South Caicos or Turks Island, if she'd dare run down these breakers heading sou'east, sir. Anyone else'd give 'em a wide berth."

"May she have joy of it," Lewrie nodded. "Cony, do you discard this little 'offering' of Pitt's for me, would you."

"Aye, aye, sir."

And for another hour, they loafed south, with the merchantman looming hull-up over the horizon, coming within a league to seaward, then passing ahead as she cleared Southwest Point on West Caicos Island, and gradually began to subside below the horizon.

"Deck, there!" the lookout called again, urgently. "There be luggers clearin' the point, fine on the larboard bows!"

"Mister Ballard, recall the ship's boats at once," Lewrie said. "Do not use the signal gun. Make a hoist, instead. I'll thankee for the loan of your glass, sir."

"Aye, aye, sir," Ballard nodded, taken unawares.

Lewrie slung the telescope over his shoulder by its rope strap and trotted forward to the taller foremast. He stepped up onto the bulwarks and swung outboard onto the ratlines of the shrouds and began to scale the mast as high as the fighting top.

From there he could see four, possibly five shallow-draft local-built luggers, some with one mast, some with two, all bunched together like a sailing race. They had low freeboards, appeared scrofulous as badly maintained fishing craft, but would be fast. But there were, to his eyes, far too many men aboard the nearest ones to be fishermen.

"Pirates, by God!" he exclaimed, turning to the lookout. "We're going to see some action, damme if we ain't!"

Without pausing to gather the breath he'd lost in climbing the mast, he took hold of a tarred backstay and let himself down hand over hand, half-sliding with his legs wrapped around it, to the deck.

"Mister Ballard, the boats!" he panted.

"Coming now, sir."

"Coming? So is bloody Christmas! Stir 'em up!" Lewrie paced, eager to get sail on his little ship and clear for action. "Tell off a midshipman, and two hands per boat to tend them. None of the gunners, mind. Mister Harkin, prepare to crack on sail! Mister Fowles, ready your guns now with what hands you may gather! It's pirates after yon merchantman, Mister Ballard, standing out under the point, and so far, they won't know we're here until we clear it. Mister Gatacre, Mister Fellows, what do your charts tell you about shoal-water south of here? I wish to press up to windward, inshore of them, so they cannot escape back over the Banks."

"Uhm . . ." John Fellows spoke up quickly, more attuned to haste than the civilian Gatacre. "There's reputed to be ten fathoms close-to along the reefs, captain. Once 'round the point, it runs east-sou'east across the mouth of Clear Sand Road. There's passes through the reefs after Southeast Reef, one after Molasses Reef . . . ah, here . . . and *maybe* a pass below French Cay, here . . . another here before West Sand Spit?"

"Do we keep the wind gauge, we deny them those passes, and keep them seaward," Lewrie nodded with a grim smile. "Good, Mister Fellows. Thankee. Damn my eyes, where're those bloody boat crews?"

"Alongside now, sir," Ballard replied, sounding a touch eager himself now.

"Leave Mr. Shipley with 'em," Lewrie decided, relegating the more useful of the Royal Naval Academy midshipmen to their command. "He's to put into Clear Sand Road and anchor to await our return."

"Aye, aye, sir."

"Mister Harkin, pipe 'All Hands!' Get sail on her!"

Alacrity began to fly as the tops'ls were freed by men aloft on the footropes. Clews were drawn down to spread them to the wind and they bellied light-air full, rustling and drumming. Outer-flying jib and fore-topmast stays'l soared up the stays up forward, filled with air, and were manhandled over to the starboard side by the fo'c's'le crew. Though still in West Caicos's lee and robbed of the full power of the Trades, there was a rivulet of wind close inshore that swept almost due south along the coast, a wind she took full advantage of.

"Mister Ballard, beat to quarters," Lewrie snapped. "Before we meet the stronger winds below Southwest Point."

"Aye, aye, sir."

The gun lashings came off, the tackle and blocks were laid out on deck clear of recoil, and the guns were run in to the full extent of the breeching ropes. Ship's boys came up from below with the first leather or wooden cylinders which contained premeasured bags of powder from the magazines. Gun captains under the direction of the quarter-gunner Buckinger fetched rammers, wormers and slow match, while the train-tackle men appeared with handspikes and crow-levers to be used to shift aim right or left quickly with brute force. Gun captains went to the arm-thick shot garlands made of salvaged towing cable to select the roundest, truest iron round-shot stored within, rolling them and turning them over and over to look for imperfections or dents which could send them off-aim.

"Charge yer guns!" Buckinger snarled. "Uncover yer vents!"

Alacrity trembled to the slamming noises of flimsy partitions and furniture being slung below on the orlop stores deck, out of the way so her crew would not be decimated by clouds of flying splinters.

"Shot yer guns! Tamp 'em down snug, now, lads. Wads!"

"Open the gun ports and run out, Mister Ballard."

"Aye, aye, captain."

The six-pounders' wooden trucks squealed as the heavy carriages were hauled up to butt against either bulwark, with the black iron muzzles now protruding through the swung-up gun port lids.

"Overhaul yer breechin' ropes, overhaul yer runout tackles!" Buckinger roared. "No man steps in a bight, right? Lose a foot, an' ya got none t'blame but y'rself. And answer t'me later!"

"And here's the wind, please God, sir," Ballard said with his excitement tightly repressed. *Alacrity* had cleared Southwest Point, skating across the open waters of Clear Sand Road, and found the ever-present Trades, which laid her over fifteen or more degrees onto her starboard side. "Hands to the braces, hands to the course sheets!"

She heeled harder still until the angle of her sails were set, then rose up almost level and set her shoulder to the sea, her bluff bows snuffling foam as tops'ls rustled and cracked with the new-found power. One could *feel* her leap forward, one could exult in the way she sprang to life, hot-blooded and eager as a racehorse.

"Hoist the colours," Lewrie said, as Cony fetched him his coat and hat, and his sword to buckle on.

The three-masted merchantman had turned south once she had seen the suspicious luggers pursuing her, to open the distance and turn the hunt into a long stern chase. But the luggers were fast off the wind, sails winged out like bat's wings and skimming the shallow-draughted boats across the bright blue waters quick as pilot boats. Two of them had gybed and were a little west of the trading ship, while the other three were boring in for her larboard side. As *Alacrity* plunged along, they could see tiny puffs of smoke on the merchantman's high stern from a pair of light chase guns, and white feathers of spray leap aloft near the luggers. The luggers opened fire in reply, and near-misses splashed close alongside the trader. One hit twirled lumber into the air from her poop rails. What seemed like minutes later, the flat sounds of the artillery reached them like far-off thunder.

"They *still* don't see us!" Lewrie exulted. "Quartermaster, a point more aweather. Steer us just inshore of that trio to larboard of the chase. We'll trap them between our guns and theirs."

To leeward there was a clear, sharp horizon, the sea dark blue and winking in the morning sun. Ahead and to windward, the shallower waters were a palette of greens and pale blues, the white breakers of the reefs curling and spuming like artillery shots, and beyond toward morning the Caicos Bank lay still and calm, the palest aquamarine with the clouds mirrored upon it like some desert mirage.

At last, though, someone aboard the luggers looked aft in the act of reloading a boat-gun and gave a great shout of alarm, and Lewrie saw fifty heads swivel about, and fifty mouths gape open in the round iris of his telescope.

Alacrity ran down on them, commissioning pendant streaming long as a tops'l yard, the red ensigns of the Bahamas Squadron flaming huge and menacing to leeward from her taffrail and her foremast truck, her gun ports open, and a frothing white mustache of foam growling under her bows.

Fast as the luggers were, *Alacrity* had infinitely more sail area, a longer waterline, and she drew closer to them as they bore off from the merchantman to run south. The pair to leeward gave up their chase and turned to join their comrades, thinking that there was safety in numbers.

"Mister Ballard, I make the range possible for random shot," Lewrie said at last. "Let's try our eye on those two yonder."

"Aye aye, sir!" Ballard replied eagerly, almost running to the quarterdeck nettings to look down into the ship's waist. "Starboard guns, Mister Buckinger! Take them under fire!"

Number One starboard gun barked, its crew shying back from the recoil run as the gun captain jerked the lanyard of the flintlock igniter. The barrel was cold, so even at maximum elevation, the round-shot struck short, but within line of the target. Slowly, the other four cannon of the starboard battery exploded stinking clouds of powder that swirled downwind toward the luggers.

Number One fired again, this time with a warm barrel, and its round-shot scored a hit so close-aboard the leader of the pair that it heeled over almost on its beam ends and rolled back upright, its single mast snapped off and the large lugsail draped over its stern.

The trailing lugger ducked leeward behind its injured consort, which act raised sarcastic jeers and catcalls from the British gunners as they pounded shot around the now-stationary target. Another strike lifted the injured lugger clear of the water, breaking it in two and spilling its crew into the sea. The pirate lugger behind it continued on course, weaving at speed to throw off their aim.

"I'd not like to be swimmin' in these waters," Gatacre shivered. "Sharks and spets a'plenty. Cowardly bastards. Leave their mates to drown or get chomped. Gahh!"

"Mister Ballard, tell the gun crews well done. Cease fire for now," Lewrie ordered. "Quartermaster, put your helm down two points. We'll shift our attention to the trio there. How close may we come to Molasses Reef, Mister Fellows?"

"The charts *infer* there's ten fathoms within a cable, cable and a half, sir," Fellows told him, rolling his eyes and shrugging. "I'd suggest we stand off at least two cables . . . about 400 yards, captain. We'll be fetching Molasses Reef in another mile."

The trio of luggers ahead of them were now bending their course sou'easterly, as though to run down close to Molasses Reef themselves, or make for the reputed deep-water entrance at its north end, trying to dart under *Alacrity*'s bows to escape.

"Quartermaster, helm down another point. Mister Ballard, take the nearest lugger under fire," Lewrie smiled. "Discourage them."

Hot now, the gun barrels had a harsher, more insistent sound, and the low carriages and barrels leapt as they discharged, rearing off their front wheels to crash back to the deck. Hot barrels meant slightly greater range. Five tall feathers of spray erupted as graceful as poplar trees all around the single-masted lugger which trailed the trio. Once the foam and spray had subsided, they could espy her hauling her wind to bear away out of range toward the open sea. The leading pair fitted with two masts turned more southerly to continue to run as well, denied a chance to get to windward.

Alacrity had taken the pass below Southeast Reef from them, the pass above Molasses Reef. Once more the luggers tried to turn up into the wind below Molasses Reef, but *Alacrity* was too close, and, hauled up onto the wind herself, had cannonaded that idea from their minds. The morning wore on as they chased them south, slowly gaining.

A low-lying spit of sand, French Cay, fell astern by noon, and once more, the luggers turned east to seek escape into the Banks, but *Alacrity* peppered them with round-shot so fiercely they turned south again, daunted by the rapidity and closeness of her fire.

"West Sand Spit in sight, sir," Fellows announced. "Fine on our larboard bows. Five miles, about. There's a long reef with breakers and exposed coral below it. Fifteen miles, it runs, sir, all the way to White Cay and Shot Cay."

"And no more passes after this 'un?" Lewrie demanded.

"Two, perhaps, sir, either side of White Cay," Fellows shrugged.

"Deep water east of us now, Captain Lewrie," Gatacre told him. "Seven fathom reported. Five fathom from that thumb o' deep water as runs south to West Sand Spit. Do they wish escape so bad, sir, this'd be their last chance. Ye'll have 'em close-aboard in two more hours."

"Deck there!" Midshipman Parham howled from aloft in a squeaky wail. "Chases go closehauled on the wind, sirs!"

The four surviving luggers had caught up with each other in a loose gaggle, the two-masted ones outdistancing the single-masted. All had turned due east to beat against the Trades as close as they could bear. They were at best three-quarters of a mile ahead, with *Alacrity* able to run down on them to close the range rapidly before she turned up to windward and took them under fire again, this time at about four cables' distance. They were daring the best killing zone for a long-barreled six-pounder, showing their desperation.

"Helm down, quartermaster. Mister Ballard, hands to sheets and braces! Haul taut, closehauled to weather!" Lewrie ordered. "Quoins out on the starboard guns and prepare to open fire!"

The angle was almost right for all but the leading lugger, which had gotten too far to windward for *Alacrity*'s guns to bear.

Fists rose in the air as gun captains signaled their charges ready. Flint-lock striker lanyards were taut as bowstrings.

"Fire!" Lewrie called out.

Alacrity roared out her defiance, thrashing along with wind singing in her rigging, foam flying about her hull, spray leaping high as the clews of her jibs. The guns crashed and bellowed, and a wall of smoke gushed from her to be ragged away astern.

"Fire!" And another broadside howled from her artillery.

A single-masted lugger was torn to splinters, leaping stern-high and pitch-poling, tumbling as if she'd tripped over her own bows! She crashed upside down into the sea in a welter of white water and began to sink at once.

"Reefs ahead to larboard!" a lookout shrilled.

"Helm up, quartermaster! Bear away starboard!" Lewrie shouted.

"Deep water to starboard, sir!" Gatacre counseled from a perch on the starboard bulwark where he could see ahead and below.

"Ten fathom t'this line!" a leadsman shouted back from the foredeck, pointing to his right to indicate blue water and safety.

"The clever bastard!" Lewrie sighed with relief. "He knew what he was about, turning to windward so early."

"To wipe us off him in passing, so to speak, sir," Lieutenant Ballard commented. "The guns cannot bear, sir, unless we turn up to windward again."

"Eight fathom t'larboard! Eight fathom t'this line, sir!" the other leadsman sang out. "Clear water ahead."

"Mister Fellows, Mister Gatacre, do you think there is depth enough for us to continue the chase, sirs?" Lewrie inquired.

"For a space, sir," Fellows allowed.

"Another mile or two, sir, if we're quick about it," Gatacre recommended.

"Quartermaster, put your helm down. Lay us closehauled."

"Aye, aye, sir! Closehauled t'weather!" Neill parroted.

The luggers had gained at least half a mile on *Alacrity* after she was forced off course, and now lay more ahead than abeam of her after she began to beat to windward once more. The gun crews had to pry the guns about to angle them within the ports to point at the foe, grunting and sweating as they put their backs and arms against the metal crow-levers and handspikes.

"Quartermaster, pinch us up and let her luff," Lewrie snapped. "Gun captains, as you bear . . . fire!"

One at a time the guns belched and leapt, rolling back from the gun ports and snubbing on the breeching ropes, slewing a bit due to the acute angle and making the tackle men, swabbers and loaders jump back.

"Tacking!" the foremast lookout wailed.

Lewrie stepped to the left side of his small quarter-deck for a view. The luggers had tacked across the eye of the Trades and were now heading west-nor'west, back the way they had come all during the long morning chase. But this time, they were *inside* the Caicos Bank, sheltered from pursuit beyond the reefs and breakers, skimming along over pale aquamarine waters far too shallow for *Alacrity*.

"'Vast, there!" Lewrie roared. "Mister Buckinger, ready the larboard battery. Quartermaster, ease your helm two points aweather. Mister Ballard?"

"Aye, sir?"

"We'll not have much time, I'm thinking, so be ready to haul our wind and come about to loo'rd."

"Six fathom!" the leadsman warned.

"Guns ready, sir!" Buckinger called out.

"Open fire, Mister Buckinger."

Alacrity rocked with recoil, and spent powder smoke rolled over the decks like a thick fog, only slowly wafting away. Shot moaned in the air, across the shoaling waters, across the sand and coral reefs which separated them from the foe. A second broadside; a third, and one of the two-masted luggers was at last hit. Two shots slammed home, rocking her at the extreme limit of *Alacrity's* range. Powder charges or a cask of powder aboard the lugger must have taken light, for there was a sudden ruddy mushroom cap of flame, followed by a squat, bulging hump of gray-black smoke shot through with whirling wreckage, then a hailstorm of splashing debris and she was gone! The sound of her ruin came to them as a twofold *Crump-*Fhwumph as the smokecloud turned to a sooty mist chased low across the shallow sea, and the white-roiled waters became a series of ripples.

"Out of range, sir," Buckinger informed them from the foot of the ladder to the waist.

"Three fathom!" a leadsman called mournfully. "Three fathom to this line, and shoal waters ahead! Two cable, no more, sir!"

"Mister Ballard, haul our wind. Mister Buckinger, secure your guns for a gybe," Lewrie commanded.

"Run out unloaded! Bowse up to the bulwarks and belay!" the quarter-gunner told his hands. "Put those slow match out."

"Sheetmen, brace-tenders, stations for wearing ship! Off yer belays and haul taut!" Ballard instructed. "Ready about? Helm hard up to weather, quartermaster. Wear-ho!"

Once settled on her new course out toward safer, deeper water, and the guns secured with charges and shot drawn, vents covered and striker pans emptied, ports closed and the guns lashed securely hard up against the hull, Lewrie had all hands summoned. They thundered aft to mill about at the foot of the quarter-deck, grinning with delight and chattering their excitement.

"Lads, we did damned well!" he told them, putting a brave face on his embarrassment. "From powder monkeys to waisters to the guns. We shot like a crew three years in commission, and I'm well pleased with you this day! Mister Keyhoe? We will splice the main-brace!"

They cheered the announcement of a double rum ration, one free of accumulated debts among themselves of "sippers" and "gulpers."

"Then!" he continued, raising his hand to silence them, "then, lads, we pick up survivors and clap 'em in irons. We go back to get our boats and other mates in Clear Sand Road. And hunt the rest of this pack of murderers and cutthroats down and bring 'em to court to hang! Mister Harkin? Pipe 'Clear Decks And Up Spirits'!"

After the clamor died down, Lewrie paced aft to the taffrail on the

windward side. He raised his telescope and glared at the surviving luggers as they receded from view two miles or more away now, hull-down,
with their sails mirrored on the glassy waters inside the Caicos Bank.

He had hurt them. He'd sunk three out of five of them, saved a
merchant ship . . . come to think on it, he gloomed, where *had* that
bugger gone so quickly, without a word of thanks . . . he'd put the fear
of King's Justice in the rest of them. But it wasn't enough.

The fact remained that he had been outmaneuvered . . . fooled!
He'd almost lost his ship on those razor-sharp reefs! Somewhere out
there was a very clever criminal, laughing fit to bust he was certain, at
how he'd bested him! A criminal who had outsmarted him!

Chapter 3

"A 'Brother Johnathon' ship," Lewrie chuckled wryly. "I saved a Yankee's ship. And now here he is, selling bold as brass!"

"That you did," the local magistrate Mr. Lightbourne said as they
strolled past the open-air market of sheds just above the high-tide line.
"I've no way of stopping him. No reliable baillif, no real power to regu-
late for the Governor-General."

"But this is a violation of the Navigation Acts, sir," Lewrie insisted.
"Is there no King's ship in these waters?"

"Nothing against your fellow officer, Captain Lewrie, but there is but
the one tiny single-masted cutter, and she's off at the moment," the
gloomy magistrate said, halting their stroll to make a point. "Sir, were it
not for Yankee ships coming to the Salt Isles, we would *have* no imported
food or goods! Not in the winter months after salt-raking season, to tide
us over, certainly. When British ships put into port, their prices are dear.
Dear, sir! With a half-battalion of troops, a fleet of revenue cutters, the
full force of the King's Customs, I even *then* would have no hopes of
enforcing steep prices, just to benefit fat London merchants, who got
this Order In Council passed."

"So you have to tolerate this?" Alan said, trying not to sound too
accusatory. To Mr. Lightbourne's reluctant nod, he went on. "May I take
it, sir, that some revenue is gathered? Some import duty?"

"Uhm," Lightbourne shrugged eloquently, but meaning "no."

"The Navy cutter," Alan said. "Did she just happen to be away as an interloper is selling here in Cockburn Harbour? Or anchored here when Yankees enter Hawk's Nest Harbour over on Turks Island?"

"Better that than being sued, sir," Lightbourne told him. "Try to arrest a foreign vessel, impound its goods, and one ends up in court months later, with damned little support from the Crown. Try to panel a court, I dare you! They vote for acquittal every time, and then the accusing officer is liable for damages. For slander, false arrest, for restraint of trade . . . lost incomes. For demurrages accrued while the suspect vessel was at anchor, *and* the crew's back wages, by Tophet!" the fellow spluttered. "Now you shew me the Navy officer able to defend himself against that, or the one with a purse fat enough to afford counsel and court costs. Oh, the Navigation Acts are a grand idea, but no thought was given to just *how* Crown officials were to enforce them, sir! 'Twould be better were we to accede to the inevitable, deal with the possible, and levy imposts to gain a little from each shipload. But to *bar* foreign traders and goods, to demand all British trade to and fro is done in British bottoms, well . . ."

"The only way possible would be if the foreign vessel resisted being stopped and inspected," Lewrie surmised aloud as they resumed a leisurely stroll past all the palmetto-roofed sheds, the canvas-topped pavilions heaped with goods of every description. "If they fired on a King's ship."

"Aye, and they're not *that* stupid, sir," the magistrate said with a wry chuckle. "Thumb their noses at you, bare their bums . . ."

"Introduce me, anyway, sir," Lewrie sighed in resignation.

He was led to an open-sided pavilion where several civilians sat in the shade imbibing wine or ale. As Lewrie approached, dressed as a Crown officer, several of them found reason to finish their ales and make off, while the rest shifted uneasily.

"Mister Lightbourne," a gray-haired sea captain nodded to the magistrate. "A splendid good afternoon to ye, sir."

"Captain Grant. Allow me to name you Lieutenant Alan Lewrie, captain of His Majesty's Sloop *Alacrity*, sir."

"Captain Lewrie," Grant beamed, extending a calloused hand.

"Captain Grant, your servant, sir," Lewrie rejoined, taking the hand. "Is that good ale you're enjoying there, sir?"

"Philadelphia beer, Captain Lewrie," Grant allowed. "It travels well, though. Do sit and enjoy a mug, if you've a mind."

"I would, sir," Alan replied, removing his cocked hat and taking a shaky seat in a sprung chair at the rickety table which rested on a shipping pallet over the sandy soil.

"Here on some official business, are ye, Captain Lewrie?" Grant inquired with an innocent expression, and a deal of humor.

"To seek a small measure of gratitude, Captain Grant," Alan said as a wooden mug appeared, foaming and aromatic with hops. "You and I almost met two days ago, off West Caicos, sir."

"Aha! Your *Alacrity* was the brave little bulldog that saved me bacon from those pirates, was she?" Grant boomed. "Well now, 'tis 'deed happy I am to make your acquaintance, Captain Lewrie! Devilish it is, sir, the brass o' those cutthroats. 'Tis getting so an honest trader goes in fear o' his very life, engaged may he be 'pon his 'innocent' occasions! My undying thanks to ye, sir! Should have seen it, lads. Chased them buggers right to the razor's edge o' the reefs off French Cay, he did, within a whisker o' tearing the stout heart o' his fine little vessel out! Oh, ye've bottom, ye have, sir, no error! I saw ye sink one. Rest get away?"

"Sank three, sir," Lewrie replied as the others gave him cynical cheers. "And captured a dozen survivors. We have them in Mister Lightbourne's custody at the moment. Two boats escaped me."

"You'll get 'em," Grant prophesied. "Eager young feller like y'self, they got no chance, sir."

"I will, thankee, sir," Lewrie smiled, getting to the meat of the matter. "As for the ones now in custody, though . . . a case must be laid, sir. Not merely my word they were taken in arms. I need your testimony as the intended victim, Captain Grant. Else they'll be set free instead of swing. To continue their foul activities of preying upon . . . *honest* merchantmen, engaged upon their lawful occasions."

"Well, now, young sir . . ." Grant frowned, ready to strangle on such a preposterous notion. "*Me* testify? Bless me soul, captain! A long voyage to Nassau . . . weeks waiting for the court to convene, sir. Demurrages piling up and all . . . were I to be paid recompense, I might be able to. But, hurricane season's almost upon us, and me poor old *Sarah and Jane* . . ."

"Mister Lightbourne does assure me, Captain Grant, that a deposition would be sufficient," Lewrie interrupted. And was galled by the sarcastic humor from all present his suggestion elicited.

"My, ye are a young'un, ain't ye now?" Grant chuckled. "For me to depose in a British court . . . *American* master and all . . . wheww!"

"You would have to lay yourself open to a charge of violating the Navigation Acts, I know, sir," Lewrie said, reddening with anger at their laughter. "And their lawyer would make Puck's Fair of you. But, were you to state that you were on passage for Hispaniola . . ."

"Ahh!" Grant smiled as he was let off the hook. "And we said that you *forced* me to enter harbor here . . ."

"So your testimony could be written out by a Crown official," Lewrie sketched on. "An unbiased magistrate appointed by the Governor-General of the Bahamas, who could provide additional testimony to the unimpeachable nature of your voyage, sir."

"Why, bless me soul, young, sir, if ye ain't the knacky'un!" Grant hooted and leaned back on his rickety stool. "And whilst I was in port here, not o' me own free will, as it were, I do believe I did trade Hispaniola goods fer salt. Straight across the board, hey?"

Lewrie blushed once more, feeling sullied by what he was being forced to ignore. "Your, uhm . . . commercial endeavors following what testimony you render, sir, are none of my concern, Captain Grant, and surely are not required to be cited in the deposition."

Playing fast and loose with King George's official edicts was an unsettling experience for him, one he knew for certain he did not wish to repeat. Sins of a personal nature were one thing, but . . . the Law! And placing his personal honour in jeopardy, to boot!

"We understand each other, Captain Lewrie," Grant simpered.

"This *once* we do, sir," Lewrie insisted. "Yet I would pray you complete your trading and clear these waters with all haste. I *might* just be possessed of a deep-enough purse to defend myself were I of a mind to inspect your vessel the next time I see her. Do we understand each other now, Captain Grant?"

Grant laughed and gave him an elaborate seated bow. "I do stand admonished, Captain Lewrie," he allowed with a wry expression. "We'll not cross hawses again, more'n like. And if we do, I'll try to outrun ye 'stead o' bribing ye. Ye catch me, though, I just might try the depth o' that purse o' yer'n. Can't expect the fish to be hauled aboard without a fight, ye know."

"I know," Lewrie nodded.

"Still want that deposition, then?" Grant asked.

"I do, sir, if you're still of a mind."

"Then let's be about it," Grant agreed. "Faster I give me testament, the faster I'll be out o' yer hair."

"And out of port," Lewrie prodded.

"And out of yer jurisdiction," Grant beamed. "Fair enough."

*   *   *

"Galling, ain't it?" Mr. Lightbourne said as they walked back to the Commissioner's House together. "Now you begin to know what I face here in the Turks. No support from Nassau. No real authority. Threat of being lynched were I too effective. Or turned out by those bone-lazy worthies on New Providence for being incapable, were they to discover the true circumstances which obtain here. I've turned many a blind eye, long as there's revenues from salt quarterly. Yet I cannot blame the people hereabouts for wanting lumber and luxury. They'd go naked and starving without the illicit trade. There'd not be one decent shack to live in without it."

"Mmmm," Lewrie frowned, pacing into his advancing shadow, eyes downcast.

"I do not sell my office, Captain Lewrie," Lightbourne told him. "Nor do I think you would. Watch yourself, though."

"Sir?"

"There's enough would sell their honor, turn the blind eye, and pray not to be bothered. Some of our exalted, so to speak, superior to you and me. And some so venal they'd even countenance your pirates, long as it was foreign-flagged merchants they plundered. Have a care, Captain Lewrie, whom you arrest. They might turn out to have powerful allies."

"You caution me to ignore the Navigation Acts, sir?" Lewrie demanded, stopping his stroll and looking up sharply at Lightbourne.

"I caution you, do nothing rash, Captain Lewrie," Lightbourne shot back, his own honor touched. "Think deep before you commit yourself. Before you do what honour dictates. But don't trust to a single snare. Lay yourself a web maze-y as a spider's, so there is no way for your prey to wriggle out. And, like me, be thankful for a small victory now and then, 'stead of going crusading."

"I see," Lewrie softened, seeing what sense Lightbourne was endeavoring to give him. "Thankee, Mister Lightbourne, I'll take a round turn and two half hitches. Look before I leap, then. And that's a trial best tested later. For now, I'll be satisfied with running the rest of this gang to earth. No way I suppose those in custody'd talk to us? Tell us where the rest may be found?"

"This lot're practiced sinners, Captain Lewrie," Lightbourne shrugged resignedly. "Honor among thieves . . . some freebooters' code of silence . . . the black spot and all that. They'd rather swing game on the gallows and be infamous for a few days. No hope of that."

"Then it'll take combing these islands," Lewrie vowed. "But comb 'em I will. However long it takes."

Chapter 4

"Make 'Captain Repair On Board,' Mister Mayhew," Lewrie ordered as *Alacrity* ranged up to within half a cable of the wayward Navy cutter *Aemilia*. They had spent a whole day and night seeking her, first in Hawk's Nest Harbour on Turks Island, Long Bay and Balfour Town on Salt Cay, and had finally discovered her cruising south of Big Sand Cay in the Lower Turks Passage.

The young officer who came through *Alacrity*'s starboard entry port came most unwillingly, having dressed hurriedly and still had a blotch or two of shaving soap behind his ears, a fresh tea stain on his shirt front, and acted very put out and sulky.

"Courtney Coltrop," the officer said before Alan could open his mouth, his demeanor on the ragged edge of open insubordination. "I was not informed another ship was in my area, sir."

"Alan Lewrie, Mister Coltrop," Lewrie said, taking an intense dislike to him at once, and spurning the honorific of "captain" which he merited. "You're a hard man to find, sir."

"I do not maintain a set patrol, sir," Coltrop almost sneered, "so I may spread confusion among our King's enemies the better."

"Pirates and smugglers, aye," Lewrie glared. "Such as the Yankee trader in South Caicos harbor yesterday, which you did not find on your irregular patrol. Nor the pirates off West Caicos the other day. Ever patrol as far as that, do you?"

"The bulk of the trade is here in the Turks, sir," Coltrop said, waving an arm about the empty straits. "And I am one small cutter with a huge area to cover. Here now, what's the date of your commission?" he demanded, irked at the preemptory questions.

"February of '82," Lewrie snapped. "Yours? As if it matters."

"March of '83, sir," Coltrop reddened, realizing that he was junior at last, and should begin to show proper courtesy. Though it was a mystery to Lewrie that the lout would not automatically assume the deference due a captain of a warship larger than his tiny sixty-foot cutter. Alan put it down to insufferable, overweening pride, or impeccable connections and patronage; some powerful "sea daddy."

"Mister Coltrop, you were unaware that a substantial band of pirates were active in the Caicos? There was no rumor of an action off West Caicos three days ago, sir? No hint of past depredations?"

"No, sir," Coltrop grunted, considering the consequences.

"If you would be so kind as to join me in my chart-space, sir, I will discover the matter to you," Lewrie smiled benignly, "and use your knowledge of these waters so we may hunt the others."

They repaired below to Alan's quarters; Lewrie, the truculent Coltrop, sailing master Fellows and James Gatacre. Lewrie sketched out the area where the action had occurred with a pair of dividers.

". . . picked up our boats here, and searched the foreshore for them," he said, laying the dividers aside at last. "There was some sort of tempo-rary camp, but no arms or stores. Palmetto lean-tos or shacks. Empty and abandoned. They had nothing to return for. But I believe they have some lair in the Caicos still."

"That don't follow, sir," Coltrop told him, screwing his face into a moue of disagreement. "They're freebooters. Live wild like so many bloody gypsies! More than like, they came up from Tortuga, off Hispan-iola. Maybe over from Spanish Florida or Cuba, with all their goods in their boats. You scared the bejesus out of 'em, so they crossed through one of these passes after dark to scuttle off to safer waters. They're probably drunk as lords in some hurricane hole this very instant. Just came over for the odd raid or two."

"One or two luggers I deem a raid, sir," Lewrie smiled. "But five boats, with about eighty or ninety men between them, would need a shore base where they might store their ill-gotten gains. One or two boatloads could take one ship of the summer trade, at best, but five seems enough to raid all summer, and they had to have a place to cook, to sleep, to keep a lookout for inwardbound ships."

"Well, one would *suppose*, sir," Coltrop sighed as though he was bored. "But, given the hurt you allege you dealt 'em, I'd put my guineas on their being long gone from the Caicos by now."

"A fatal assumption for the next ship taken, if such assumption is wrong," Lewrie snorted. "They've two swift luggers still, and could take at least one more vessel, so they have some profit to repay their pains. And I doubt if determined and ruthless men know when to quit. For revenge, if nothing else."

"Conversely, Lieutenant Coltrop," John Fellows said, raising his gin-gery eyebrows, as was his wont when he got excited, "what if there were ships already taken? They must have stowed that plunder somewhere in the Caicos, and they'd not sail away without it. An even more compelling argument for them remaining. I wonder if you are aware of other ships that may be missing, sir?"

"Lord!" Coltrop gaped in mock wonder. "How would *I* know? With absolutely no method of determining how many ships set sail for the Turks to begin with, the when or the wherefrom?"

"You've heard no talk among the arriving masters? No rumors of 'what happened to Old So-And-So'?" Lewrie pressed.

"It is not within my duties to question arriving masters, or to deal with them except as to whether they abide by the law, sir."

"Yet in pursuing your duties of enforcing the Navigation Acts, in boarding and documenting arriving ships' manifests," Lewrie cooed, trying hard to rein in his growing anger, "in determining whether a vessel is allowed to enter British ports you have absolutely no converse with their captains and mates, sir? Is that what you are telling us, sir?"

"I have heard no gossip, no complaints, no speculations about missing vessels, sir," Coltrop replied stiffly, haughtily.

"Very well, then, Mister Coltrop," Lewrie said after a deep breath and a long sigh of frustration. "Let's proceed along another tack. Mister Fellows my sailing master, and Mister Gatacre, who now directs my ship's activities as her supercargo from the Admiralty," Lewrie said, inflating Gatacre's status without having to tell a baldfaced lie, or be specific, "deem that our pirates need a place where there is a tall headland. They need a reliable well or stream for water. Shelter from seaward to hide their boats, and what prey they take so they may loot 'em at their leisure. Shoal-waters wide enough to prevent pursuit by a warship or gunfire closer than random shot. And easy access to the Caicos Banks so they may flee if their lair is found. Not too close to Fort George Cay up north, nor close to Turks Passage, where you patrol. That means they must be based either to the west of the Bank, or somewhere along the northern side of North, Middle, or East Caicos Island. Now, just where, assuming our suppositions about their needs are correct, in your experience in these waters, would you believe the most likely hideout to be?"

Coltrop leaned over the chart, hat under one arm and elbows tucked in close to his sides as if he wished to avoid touching it, or getting in any way involved. He blew out a breath, puffing his cheeks in perplexity.

"Lord, sir," he said at last with a hopeless smile. "'Fraid I haven't a clue! Sorry. Know the Turks Passage and all, d'you see, but . . ."

"Good Christ!" Gatacre exploded. "You're about as useless as teats on a man! How long you been in these waters, puppy?"

"Year and a bit, sir, I . . ." Coltrop shuddered, too scared of Gatacre's uncertain amount of seniority to continue his smug bluster. Gatacre wore navy blue, but it was a civilian suit, more apt on some merchant master, but for a military cocked hat big as a watermelon. The buttons were plain pewter, though, so what was he if not some civilian official from the Lords Commissioners of the Admiralty, a secretary who'd report back about Lieutenant Coltrop and tell them . . . Lord!

"And you've leashed yourself to the Turks Passage?" Gatacre went on indignantly. "Never explored the Caicos? Or are they too far from your bottle'r your table? The brothels *that* good in the Salt Isles, are they, sir?"

"Sir, I . . . !"

"Ever been down to the Ambergris Cays? As far north as Drum Point on East Caicos? Took a peek into Windward-Going-Through, have you?" Gatacre sneered. "God, I've never heard of a Sea Officer with an active commission so unaspiring, nor so unambitious!"

"I *have* been to Fort George Cay, sir, to deliver supplies as needed, sir," Coltrop quavered out. "I have put into the Ambergris Cays when the whales run, sir. But this is the wrong season. There's no one there now! The whalers won't be back . . ."

"A fine place for pirates, then," Lewrie commented. "An empty whaling station. Deep water for their ships. Huts for shelter, trypots and fuel for cooking in place. Water. A tall headland or two. That's where we'll search first. *Alacrity* to Big Ambergris, and your cutter to Little Ambergris, where the depth is too shoal. What does your cutter draw, Mister Coltrop?"

"Uh . . . seven feet, sir. But, sir, if there *are* pirates, then surely my place is in Turks Passage to defend. To accompany you, I must leave shipping open to God knows what."

"By whom, Mister Coltrop?" Lewrie fumed. "Tripolitan galleys? Levant corsairs? There's one band of pirates we know of, and if we put pressure on them with our search, we halt their activities. Did you not tell me your patrols are irregularly timed, so you may, how did you put it, 'sow confusion and doubt'? Well then, let's go sow some doubt and confusion! And capture ourselves some pirates."

"Sir, I . . ." Coltrop began to protest, then swallowed his outburst. "Of course, sir. I am certain the *Aemilia* will be of inestimable assistance to you, sir." Coltrop turned suddenly sweet, and got his pride of old back a bit too quickly for Lewrie's taste. "Do you know she is named for our commodore's daughter, sir? In her honor?"

So *that's* who his powerful "sea daddy" is, Lewrie thought as he studied Coltrop's regained smugness with distaste!

"Commodore Garvey will be most pleased that she will figure in your . . . uhm, adventure, Captain Lewrie," Coltrop grinned.

"Then you'd better take care she doesn't trip on a shoal and wet herself, musn't you, Mister Coltrop?" Lewrie smiled back at him. "Go board your *Aemilia* and set course for Little Ambergris while we still have some light. And mind your soundings."

"Aye, aye, sir."

"Poxy bastard!" Gatacre grumbled once he was gone. "I've never seen such a worthless, idle . . ."

"A well-connected bastard, though," Lewrie grunted. "I can't wait to read his report on the action. Damme, Mister Gatacre, if we don't find these pirates, if they take a ship under our noses, he'll have my nutmegs on a silver tray!"

"Best do what all the good captains do, then, sir," Gatacre chuckled as they walked forward to go on deck. "Plaster a confident grin on yer phiz an' dare anybody to gainsay ya!"

Chapter 5

Of course, nothing went that easily. There were signs of recent human habitation on Big Ambergris, much like the abandoned camp on West Caicos. Their suppositions the pirates were still around were fulfilled, but just where they had gone remained a mystery.

For another week, *Alacrity* and *Aemilia* prowled in company, back up Turks Passage toward Drum Point on East Caicos, along the spectacular coral reefs by Lorimers Point and Joe Grant's Cay, which sheltered the mouth of the Windward-Going-Through channel between East and Middle Caicos Islands. The bluffs were high enough behind the reefs to provide excellent watchposts. When they went ashore in luggers and ship's boats they found sources of water. There were deeps very close inshore where looted ships could be scuttled to avoid detection. But no pirate band.

Lewrie was getting extremely frustrated. It was not the sneer on Lieutenant Coltrop's face which upset him, though that irked him everytime he had reason to talk with him. He realized he had made the pirates, and their destruction, a personal quest. There was Commodore Garvey to please, to impress with what he could accomplish. And capturing or destroying these buccaneers would be a way to expunge the chagrin he felt about his bargain with the American Captain Grant, turning a blind eye to his violation of the Navigation Acts. And, in that first flush of exultation he'd shown to his crew after sinking those luggers, he'd over-stepped himself and promised they would get the rest. Now, if he did not, he felt the men would lose confidence in his abilities, and his captaincy of *Alacrity* would become a drudgery instead of a delight.

Being someone else's junior officer felt *so* damned good, Alan told himself in the echoing privacy of his cabins aft. Without Caroline aboard, he was severely limited now in whom he could confide. Oh, he could dine in bags of people and share jests with them as the most genial of hosts. But it wasn't the same as being able to unburden his cares and worries on someone else.

But then, that's why they pay me five grand shillings a day!

"Sir!" Lieutenant Ballard said, coming to Alan's seat on the taffrail signal-flag lockers. "*Aemilia* has put about and is bearing down on us."

Lewrie rose and made his way forward. It had just gone five bells of the Second Dogwatch, Evening Quarters had been stood, and the hands had eaten and were now entertaining themselves in the cool afterglow of sunset. Mr. Midshipman Shipley and his mostly hapless colleague, Mr. Midshipman Joyce, were doing hornpipes in the waist for the amuse-ment of the people forrud, part of the larboard watch's price as losers at drills that afternoon.

"Was he not to peek into Highas Cay and Bottle Creek, sir?" Ballard inquired. "Perhaps he's seen something at last."

Lewrie snapped a quick look at Ballard to see if his "at last" was a subtle condemnation, but Ballard had a telescope to his eye and was intent upon the ghostly shape of *Aemilia* as she sailed back east to join them.

"He was, Mister Ballard. As you say, perhaps this hopeless search of ours will be rewarded . . . at last," Lewrie could not help rejoining.

"They're somewhere out here still, sir," Ballard said quickly. "I know you're correct about that. It's just the 'where', or how long they might remain if they fear a new, more active warship is stationed in the Turks and Caicos. I'd hate for them to run before we nab 'em."

"Thankee, Mister Ballard," Lewrie relented with a shy grin. "I was beginning to fear I was the only one who wished to continue this chasing of wild geese. Chasing shadows, more like."

"Most deadly shadows, sir," Ballard intoned with a sober nod, but with a quirky little grin of his own. "Should Lieutenant Coltrop be the bearer of glad tidings, do you wish the taffrail lanterns lit, sir? Or should we proceed darkened?"

"There's a ninety-foot-tall bluff at the extreme west end of Middle Caicos, just by Highas Cay," Lewrie pondered. "Do not give a possible watcher anything to bite on. And alter course to seaward. If *Aemilia* has news for us, he'll come to us out there. I only wish there was a way to signal him without a fuzee to stay dark."

"Here, sir!" Coltrop jabbed exultantly at the chart. "Just under the headland overlooking Highas Cay and the narrow channel between Middle and North Caicos. There were cook fires! I saw the smoke, sir!"

"Did you stand close inshore?" Lewrie asked, unable to hide his mounting excitement. "Did you see a camp?"

"Didn't want to blow the gaff, sir," Coltrop laughed, for once almost pleasant to be around. "I stood north for a time, as if to go to seaward of North Caicos, then doubled back. But as far as I know, there should be no one there. A few farms so far on North Caicos, a fish camp or two . . . but none on Middle Caicos yet."

"What do they call this area, Mister Gatacre?" Lewrie asked.

"Conch Bar, sir," Gatacre replied. "There's rumored to be some caves there that Indians used in Columbus's time. 'Tis a barren place now, though."

"Watered, though," Fellows insisted. "And where you find water, you'll find our pirates. Look, sir, it's perfect! Bluffs to spy from, just as we deduced. Deep water, about an hundred fathoms, close up to the reefs and shoals. An inlet between Highas Cay and Conch Bar Bluff where ships may moor. An escape run down this passage south to the Banks. And their main camp would most likely be about a mile in from the shoal-water line, out of range of random shot."

"Depth, though, Mister Fellows," Lewrie implored.

"Unsurveyed, sir," Fellows had to admit, deflating. "A fathom, maybe less, once inside Highas Cay."

"And it may be a fish camp, after all," Lewrie fretted out loud. "But, then again . . . we must examine it. If their main camp is inland, about a mile or better, that would put them . . . here . . . down by this last point, opposite the second islet past Highas Cay. They see us coming, they run through this passage for the Banks where we cannot follow. To prevent that, we must use all the ship's boats and our surveying luggers, and land a party between them and the escape route. Cross the shoals above Bottle Creek, wend our way under the shoreline into that channel, to . . . here. At dawn, *Alacrity* must be just without the shoals to cover Highas Cay and deliver unaimed fire on this inner point as a diversion. And to flush them out, if they get the wind up. Mister Coltrop, I want *Amelia* inshore even further. Make the best of your way across the shoals with your seven-foot draught nor'west of the inner point of land, to block any possible escape up Bottle Creek and out to sea off North Caicos. And scour the beach under the bluffs with your four-pounders."

"Good God, sir, I'll rip her bottom out, sure!" Coltrop gasped.

"Close as you may, without holing yourself. Make a demonstration. Frighten them into running straight at me," Lewrie decided.

"You, sir?" Fellows goggled. "Sir, it's . . . well, it's been the traditional thing for the first officer to . . ."

"It's the riskiest part of our venture," Lewrie countered. "If they're not pirates, I wish to be the one nearest on the scene to call it off. And if they are, I've more experience with landfighting."

"Should we not keep an eye on them for now, sir?" Coltrop asked. "Send for troops from Fort George Cay? Surely, it's their . . ."

"If they are pirates, Mister Coltrop, they saw you, sure as I'm standing here, and they're considering whether they should stay or run. We cannot take the time to send for troops and let them escape. I'll begrudge not a single wasted hour . . . not a single wasted minute!"

"Aye, aye, sir."

"Sir, it's my place of honor!" Ballard protested as the boats were led around to the entry ports, as the armorer's files and stone rasped to put brutally sharp edges on steel blades and points. "How else are lieutenants to rise, if they go in their captain's shadow?"

"With the shore party away, *Alacrity*'ll be short-handed, Mister Ballard. I need you aboard to run her as Bristol-fashion as a 1st Rate," Lewrie smiled. "And keep her off those shoals."

"Once one makes captain, sir, it's time to let a younger man be one's goat," Ballard rejoined, not backing down an inch. "Let the junior officers make a name for themselves, or a muck of it. Is it that you see me making a muck of it, sir?"

"I have the utmost confidence in *you*, Mister Ballard," Lewrie said.

"'Tis Coltrop I don't put faith in. I scare him. You don't. And if I have to *tow* his damned cutter inshore to get him in place, I'll do it. I'll scout him an anchorage for dawn during the night. And then be there to give him strict orders to take that anchorage or suffer the consequences. You have a copy of my orders to him in yours. If he fails . . . should I fall and this expedition fails, you must see to it that he pays the price for not supporting me. I'd rather be the one to risk my life on such a slender thread as that idle fop, than risk yours . . . Arthur."

"I see . . . I think, sir," Ballard surrendered at last.

"Growl you may, but go you must," Lewrie laughed, clapping him on the shoulder in parting. "Old Navy proverb. Might be the Thirty-Seventh Article of War, hey, right after 'The Captain's Cloak'?"

There were only thirty-six Articles of War; the last gave a blanket power to a captain's lone decision for anything not covered by the specifics of the other thirty-five—the Captain's Cloak.

"The very best of fortune go with you, sir," Ballard said.

"And enjoy your temporary command, sir."

Chapter 6

It was slow going, rowing or poling in the darkness. First to run through the boisterous shoals two miles above Highas Cay, safely hidden by the night. Then to grope about close under the foreshore of the low islet that screened Bottle Creek from the sea. Inshore, the Caicos were rife with mosquitoes and biting flies, and once out of the Trades and into the marshy-smelling mangroves along the beach, they were almost eaten alive.

Aemilia followed, sounding her way through a two-fathom pass. She threaded her way into Bottle Creek, behind that inner, second isle to screen her from view, and Alan found an anchorage for her, sounding with a short lead line and counting the marks in it by feel, until he had her a spot where the bottom was ten feet, or would be at high tide. The cutter's light four-pounders would not make much real impression on the pirate camp from that range, but it might put the fear of God in them.

Then they completed their voyage, snaking out of Bottle Creek south along the shore of North Caicos, staying to the western side of the possible escape channel to avoid detection, and went a mile below the suspected position before turning to cross the narrow strait.

"I kin smell 'em, sir," Cony said, his poacher's senses alert. "Wood smoke. An' cookin'. Goat, more'n like. Mayhap fish stew on the boil, too, sir. Right savory, iff'n ya don't mind my sayin'."

"There, sir!" one of the hands poling up forrud whispered. "I think I see fires. Like they wuz usin' one o' them caves t'cook in."

Once on the eastern shore, they poled back north in water just a bit deeper than their shallow-draught keels, about four feet, until the coast bent back nor'west past the mouth of a tiny inlet.

Half a mile, little more to go, Lewrie decided. And hard sand all the way to the point. We're on foot the rest of the way.

"Put into the inlet, men," Lewrie ordered in a harsh mutter. "Leave the boats. No one is to show a light, no one is to load his musket or pistol until I return and tell you to. Not a sound, now. Mister Parham, Mister Mayhew. You and the bosun's mate are in charge until Cony and I return."

Taking only edged weapons, Lewrie and Cony set out up the hard sand of the beach for a ways, then moved into the deeper, softer sand above the tideline toward the sheltering sea grapes and stunted low bushes. A ledge of rock began to rise at their right hand as they progressed, and climbed higher and higher in irregular slabs as they neared the suspect camp. Soon, they were creeping along its base for concealment as it rose above their heads.

"This'll climb all the way to the sea bluffs," Lewrie muttered. "I don't think there's a way up it."

"Too crumbly, sir," Cony agreed in a whisper. "Limestone an' ole coral. Cut ya t'ribbons iff'n ya tried it in the dark, it would."

"Listen!" Lewrie cautioned, kneeling down lower.

There were sounds of shouting, of laughter. And of music that came to them under the rush of the night winds and the continual sound of foliage stirring. And then there was a womanly scream.

"Wimmen!" Cony hissed close to Lewrie's ear. "Might be a party they's 'avin'. Might they be fishermen after all, sir?"

Lewrie laid a finger to his lips and took a deep breath to make his limbs obey him. He half stood, and placed one tentative foot in front of the other, his grasp sweaty on the hilt of his hanger. With tremulous caution, they gained another long musket-shot, about sixty yards, to an outthrust of rocky ledge. To go around it would mean exposing themselves to the camp. They found a narrow crevice that took them up top, then crawled on their bellies through sharp-edged grasses and coarse bushes until they could see.

It wasn't a fish camp, Lewrie thought, feeling a flush of relief fill him. There were the two luggers that had escaped him, along with another pair, larger and two-masted, anchored very close inshore to the beach. And on the beach below him, were a brace of longboats with their bows jammed snug on the land. The longboats were royal barges compared to the scrofulous condition of the luggers, obviously taken from some earlier prize of theirs; perhaps from two different prizes, since their paint-schemes did not match.

There was cooking smoke coming from the mouth of the nearest cave under the bluff, several more smaller fires burning in a circle beyond the boats. There were crates and chests scattered about for rude furniture, several more piled up and covered with scrap canvas near the mouth of the cave, more still piled on the lower beach.

And just offshore, anchored fore-and-aft parallel to shore was a two-masted schooner of about sixty feet overall, on which lanterns burned at helm and forecastle.

The people on the beach got Alan's attention next. They were a gaudy crew, dressed "Beau-Nasty" in checked shirts, opulent satin waist-coats, sashes around the waists Spanish *hidalgo*-style, in either breeches without stockings, or slop trousers. They wore neckerchiefs bound about their heads like gunners would to protect their hearing, or in tricornes or straw hats; each affecting a highly individualistic and rakehell sense of fashion.

And they went armed.

Swaggering, they were, under the weight of pistols stuck into their waistbands or sashes; cutlasses or swords at their hips. Some muskets stood propped against crates of loot, and there were weapons enough in sight to equip a half-battalion of light troops.

"There's the wimmen, sir," Cony pointed out.

Spanish-looking in the firelights' flickering glows, or black and sheened with sweat. They were swilling rum, wine or brandy with as much gusto as the men, their finery obviously looted goods, too.

They lay there and watched the piratical band roister for half an hour, carefully counting heads, trying to pick out leaders who sat apart more quiet than the others. They watched fights and brawling, among both the men and the women. They watched men take women off to the cave, or up the beach beyond the light.

"Prisoners, sir," Cony mouthed almost silent, tugging at Alan's shirt sleeve. "Them wimmen yonder. Back by them covered crates."

Lewrie pulled out his telescope and brought it forward inch at a time, careful that the lens did not reflect firelight. He studied the party of women by the pile of loot. Slaves, some of them, and some white-skinned and bedraggled—free women and their maids, he speculated? As he lay in the hide, watching, one of the men he thought of as a leader went to the women, staggering drunk, and reached down to pull one to him. She began to scream and plead, only her loudest and most inarticulate cries reaching them. Brutally, he backhanded her into silence, then dragged her back down the beach to the circle of fires to throw her down, peel off his breeches, and fall atop her, to the exultant cheering of his band. And once he had slaked his lust with her, three more sprang forward like inferior wolves to savage her.

"They'll *kill* them wimmen oncet they're done with 'em, Mister Lewrie!" Cony whispered, mortified by the sights he had seen without being able to lift a finger to help. "Jesus, God a'mercy!"

"Might have been saving 'em for tonight," Lewrie nodded, "If they sail on the morrow, they'll want no witnesses left alive. See, those goods piled close to the beach? So they may begin loading the schooner and the biggest luggers. If we'd waited, we'd have lost them. Let's get back to the boats. It lacks two hours 'til dawn."

Cony went, unwillingly. And it was only once they were back on the beach, with the horrifying sights and sounds of pitiless rape put behind them, that he trusted himself to speak.

"Wisht there was ought we could do for 'em, sir, tonight, that is," he whispered plaintively. "Dawn might be too *late* t'save 'em."

"I want you on that ledge at dawn, Cony," Lewrie told him. "I want you and my fusil, and the Ferguson rifle up there, in good hands. Pick your likely country lads. And gut-shoot anyone that lays a hand on 'em, or even glares in their direction. That suit you, Cony?"

"Aye, sir, it sure t'God does!"

Chapter 7

The dawn smelled of crushed foliage and trampled flowers, overlaying mud and mangrove marsh. Of damp sand and beach burrowers, the fish-scale aroma of the coast most landlubbers mistook for sea air. The true sea-air smell came on the whispering Trades, the baked salt and iodine tang of ocean deeps, borne by winds ceaselessly stirring from across thousands of miles of brine. Damp clamminess was stripped away by the breezes, even as they brought the balmy warmth of a humid sunrise, bedewing the steel in his hand.

Lewrie's nostrils drank in the smells, almost quivering like a beast's, much as his limbs trembled in anticipation, stiff with a too-short and troubled nap, as they made their stealthy approach-march.

Damme, but this is a daft business—and a bloody one, Alan thought, keyed up, rumpled and miserable. But don't this morning beat all for handsome!

An hundred sunrises could pass unremarked. But take up arms, and the risk of dying before breakfast, and even a winter rain could be sweet, its bitter, soaking chill savored because one was still alive to suffer it before the madness set in.

He turned to study his men. There were thirty from *Alacrity*, half of her adult crewmen, and twenty hands off *Aemilia*, almost half of her crew, too. They yawned and scratched, flexed their fingers on their weapons nervously, eyes shifting as squint-a-pipes as a bag of nails at every rustle in the bushes, every sea-bird's cry, or soft lap of the inlet's surf on the beach. Armed to the teeth, they were, with cutlasses, clasp knives, long boarding pikes, good Brown Bess .75 caliber muskets, wicked needle-sharp offset bayonets jammed in the waistbands of their slop trousers; as desperate a crew of cutthroats as the pirates, to look at them, laden down with clumsy Sea Pattern pistols for each man in addition, with all the powder flasks, bullet pouches and cartouche boxes hung about them as they plodded and scuffled, strung out in a long single file below the rising ridge of crumbling rock, half buried in the greenery for cover.

"Just 'round this outcrop, seventy yards or so," Lewrie grunted, calling a halt at last. "Mister Parham, your boat-gun at the foot of the shelf. Mister Mayhew, your two-pounder atop the shelf with Cony and his marksmen. Grape, canister or langridge at first, and keep 'em away from their boats as I bade you. Right. The rest of you lads, I want you ready to rush out and form a skirmish line from Mister Parham's gun to the beach."

There was a faint rustle in the air, and Lewrie pulled out his watch to check the time, which made him nod grimly. The rustle became a sizzling swoosh of roiled air, then a quavery moan. *Alacrity's* guns had just opened fire a mile-and-a-half away, shooting almost blind at the bluffs. Fowles's first ranging shot was on the way.

There was a thunderclap so close it seemed it went off in his pocket as the bluff to the north above the sea caves was struck. The iron ball exploded in a bright yellow flash of sparks, metallic shards, and shale, starting a small avalanche of gravel.

And the sunrise echoed with the soft *Fumm-umm* of an unseen gun.

"Now where are you, you silly bastard?" Lewrie fretted, turning to look for *Aemilia* across the channel. Once she found her proper position, even her puny four-pounders could rake the beach, and the anchored vessels, across the quarter-mile strait. He was relieved to see a bowsprit protrude from behind the low foliage, and the first starkly pale tan panels of her jibs stood out against the dark green and dun.

Another round-shot droned in from the reefs, fired at maximum elevation with the quoin block removed from below the barrel's butt, and this struck short of the bluffs to raise a great pillar of foam in the inlet, about half a cable short of the anchored schooner.

The pirates were up, now, stirring and circling in hungover and bleary-eyed confusion. Some lay still, too comatose from rum or their excessive indulgences to be wakened. Women camp followers screamed or cursed in a cacophony of dialects and languages. Orders were shouted that for the moment went unheeded. They mostly dashed to the piles of weapons, drew swords to brandish against just what they did not yet know, stampeded first toward their boats, then back to the shelter of the piles of goods, or the bluff and the dry-cave entrance, as a ball moaned overhead to bury itself in the sand.

"Come on, Coltrop, come on!" Lewrie hissed to speed the cutter as she made her entrance as slow as a one-legged dowager trying to go up a flight of stairs. *Aemilia* was turned bows-on now, rounding the first western tip of the islet, her gaff mains'l winged out alee and her commissioning pendant streaming as long as she was. "Oh, bloody hell!"

Coltrop had run her aground on a sand bar! She canted over a little to leeward and came to a stop, slowly pivoting on her bows to show her starboard side, far short of the near tip of the islet where her guns would be in good range.

"I *warned* him that channel was tighter'n virgin's quim!" Alan raged. The bottom was hard sand, though, so he might yet get her off it, if he tried . . . but no!

Coltrop fired from where he was, the two four-pounders in her starboard battery coughing out round-shot at the schooner. They hit short and ricocheted once, almost rocked her as the ripple patterns expanded, but the range was too great to do any harm to her, or the beach. .

There was no help for him, then. Lewrie and his party of fifty were on their own, with six men tied up in serving the boat-guns. Up against sixty or seventy alert and armed pirates!

"Mister Parham, shift your aim for the thickest throng yonder. Open fire," he ordered, hoping to cut the odds down, niceties bedamned.

"There are women among them, sir!" Parham protested, shocked.

"Cutthroats' whores, Mister Parham, cutthroats themselves, if they get their hands on you. Shift aim and fire! Mister Mayhew? Canister, up there! Volley into the next-biggest batch." Mayhew's face appeared over the lip of the rocky shelf for a moment, turned pale as he gulped, then withdrew.

"Anyone with a weapon, you are to kill," Lewrie told his hands. "And I mean anyone."

The boat-gun gave out a chuffing bark, a *Rrrupp!* of anger that startled a cloud of sea birds which had fled *Aemilia's* rude disturbance of their morning back out into mid-channel. A moment later, Mayhew's gun on the ledge barked as well, both explosions echoing and reechoing along the rocky bluffs.

Two spreading shot-gun blasts of tightly packed canister flayed the sands, creating twin dust clouds. Shrieks of alarm, cries of pain erupted, as pirates and their fell women who had clumped together for mutual comfort in the face of danger were scythed down from behind, too intent on *Aemilia,* or the artillery fire from seaward.

"Skirmish line!" Lewrie shouted, stepping out in front. "Form line! Cock your locks! Level! Fire!"

Trigger mechanisms clacked, flints flew forward to scrape on frissons' filelike rasps, pans ignited with tinny, high cracks, and Brown Bess spat out a sputtering ripple of musketry to raise even more screams, more terror, confusion and agony. And more pirates down.

Lewrie strode out in front as his men hastily reloaded, sword in hand, in the coat, cocked hat with dog's vane and gold lace, of a Sea Officer.

"In the King's name!" he bellowed in a quarter-deck voice. "I order you to lay down your arms, put up your hands, and surrender!"

Even the cries of the wounded ceased for a long, startled moment. Several of the nearest buccaneers did drop their weapons, while others further on ran about like headless chickens seeking an escape.

Then a musket shot sang past his ears like a fat bee, and some desperado shouted with derision. They knew they would hang if taken, and some would rather go game, be slain, than face the noose. "Take 'em, lads! Them or us!"

"Mister Parham, fire!" Lewrie yelled, stepping back as several more shots rang out defiance. "They had their chance!"

The boat-guns lashed out again. Lewrie's muskets came back up, and locks were cocked. The barrels leveled. And fired.

"At 'em, Alacrities!" Lewrie called, waving his sword over his head to spur them on, and drawing his first of four pistols. "Come on! Take the boats!"

They surged forward at a shambling trot in the deep sand, going for the luggers first to deprive the raiders of an escape by water, to the beached longboats where they could kneel and fire.

"Aemilias, take cover and shoot! Alacrities, with me!"

You want to escape, he thought grimly—want your boats, hey? Then come and take 'em from us, you bastards!

The pirates did come, spurred by desperation. Without their boats they were nothing—crippled sailors, no matter how they had besmirched the noble calling of the sea. But they had to come across the bodies of their dead from the boat-guns' lashings, over whimpering and shattered wounded, so it was not a daring, neck-or-nothing charge. Blades clashed as Lewrie and his seamen met them. Some pistols popped, and white-faced men shouted in each others' faces to fan alight their flagging courage. They met and merged, and swirled in melee.

But when bayonets jabbed, when muskets swung or butt-stroked, when boarding pikes lanced wicked points forward, and when Navy hands went into the fearsome full cutlass drill, shoulder to shoulder, there was nothing in the world that could stand before them.

Right foot stamp, downward slash! Left foot, backward slash! Advance and balance motion, stamp and slash . . . slash and advance!

Alan crossed blades with a coppery skinned man with long and greasy hair, bare but for too-tight breeches and a flowered waistcoat and sash. His heavy cutlass rang on Alan's hanger all the way up his arm. He drew back to slash and Alan lunged low, giving him eight inches of steel in the belly! He moved right to face another foe armed with cutlass and dagger. This one Alan shot in the chest. A third came at him, a black armed with an ornate smallsword which he poked with inexpertly like a spear point.

No swordsman, Alan noted—a slavey just out of the fields. He parried, slashed to his right, shying him. Flying cutover to reengage steel against steel, a ringing double parry to force him high to open his guard, so he could raise a foot and kick him in the balls. The man doubled over, dropping the sword, and Alan chopped down into his neck and shoulder, then trampled over him. A seaman following put a pike into the fellow's stomach to finish him off.

"*Madre de Dios!*" a skinny little fellow paled as Alan advanced on him with gore sliming his threatening blade. He turned to run and the pikeman behind sprinted forward, shouldering Alan out of the way and jabbing the fellow through the kidneys.

Lewrie drew a deep breath and pulled out another loaded pistol while he had time, his hands shaking too hard to stuff the empty one into a coat pocket. He let it drop to the sand to retrieve later.

More pirates were throwing down their weapons, those wounded and unable to fight longer, those who had given up all hope of escape. They threw themselves on their knees or curled up in fetal positions, waiting death or capture.

John Canoe trotted past, a huge West Indian seaman who'd taken his name for the manner he'd escaped his former owners years before. He engaged one of the few pirates who still had fight in him, a man as big as himself with a thick beard. John Canoe battered the man's cutlass aside with easy strength, then ran him through to the hilt, and lifted him up off the ground to dangle and wriggle like a piked salmon, keening shrilly in terror around his bloody vomit.

"Watch out, Canoe!" Lewrie shouted. "Ware left!" as a black woman camp follower rose up and ran at him with a carving knife to avenge her man. Lewrie skipped to his left for a clear shot, took careful aim, and bowled the howling harpy over from a dead run with a .69 caliber ball in the chest, to skid bawling and writhing at Canoe's bare feet.

"Ya *silly* wo-man! Ya who'!" Canoe cursed her as he dropped her dying man on top of her. "*Heah* be ya whi' mon lovah, bitch! Wot kine o' fool ya *be*, ya fock de ones dot whipt ya, gahh!" Then he turned to Lewrie and gave him a sudden, radiant smile. "Ah thankee berry moch, cap'um, sah!"

Those freebooters who still hoped for escape had by then retreated into the cave at the top of the beach, and were sniping at the sailors.

"Take cover up here, lads!" Lewrie shouted. "Behind these boxes and chests! Shoot slow and steady to keep 'em busy. Mister Odrado?"

"*Si, sehnor capitan,*" the Portugese bosun's mate panted, coming to his side, weary with the effort expended on killing.

"Round up the whole prisoners and put 'em at the base of that ledge down the beach. Tell off ten of the Aemilias to guard 'em. I want 'em searched close for weapons, mind. Don't let any more of the lads take hurt now this is almost over. The wounded may lie as they are for now. Theirs, that is. Get ours down to the boats."

"I do it, *sehnor capitan.*"

"Early?"

"Aye, aye, sir," the quartermaster's mate answered.

"Take three hands with muskets, just in case, and scale up the goat path yonder to the headland to signal *Alacrity* to cease fire," Lewrie ordered, as a broadside of five rounds warbled in short.

"Canoe."

"Aye, aye, sah."

"Go tell Mister Parham to bring his boat-gun here so he may put shot into the cave. Tell Mister Mayhew to cover the schooner for now with round-shot. Got that?"

"Mistah Par'um ta fetch he gun, Mistah Mayhew ta aim he gun at dot schooner wit' roun'-shot, sah. Aye, aye, I tell'm, sah!"

"Good man! Mister Warwick?"

"Aye, sir," the burly ship's corporal grunted.

"Four men with you to search the luggers. I don't want any surprises at our backs. Then row out to the schooner and take her. Find papers if you can to see who she belonged to."

"Aye, aye, sir," Warwick nodded, then trotted off.

Lewrie wiped his blade clean of gore and sheathed it, then took out his pocket watch. Amazingly, everything had happened in a brutal seven minutes! He turned to look down the beach. It was a horrible litter he beheld; the dead spilled like so many isolated heaps of old clothes; some wounded gasping and choking on blood, writhing or twisting in pain and clawing at their hurts. Thankfully, damned few of 'em were Navy. He could see only three men he considered dead, and perhaps eight being tended by the luggers.

Parham and his gun crew came lumbering along the hard-packed sand where the going was easier for the small but heavy two-pounder on its small-wheeled carriage. They were half dragging it, with help from Cony and his country-lad marksmen, now that they had run out of targets to snipe at.

"Sir! Sir!" a sailor called from the firing line behind the crates of looted goods. "White flag, sir. Think they strikin'!"

A tall man in gaudy but bedraggled finery appeared in the cave mouth, waving a white rag spitted upon his smallsword.

"Cease fire!" Lewrie ordered. He walked forward, up past the crates into plain view, and trudged perhaps ten more yards through the deep sands. "Do you surrender?" he asked.

"Wanna talk, Navy," the filthy rogue in stolen silks and satins rejoined with a maddening calm. "An' who might ye be, I'm askin'?"

"Lieutenant Alan Lewrie, Royal Navy. Captain of His Brittanic Majesty's Sloop *Alacrity*," he snapped.

"Compliments t'ye on a neat bit o' business this fine mornin', from meself, Billy Doyle," he said, taking off his egret-plumed hat and performing a mocking bow. "Billy 'Bones', they names me. *Capt'n* Billy Bones, o' the Ancient Brotherhood, like. Aye, y'er a hellish crafty sprat, ye are, Capt'n Lewrie. Pulled it off sweet as a . . ."

"Damn your blood, Doyle," Lewrie fumed. "Surrender or die."

"Ah, that's the way ye be, hey?" Doyle simpered. "Bloody high-handed as a Protestant squire. Squire's son, are ye? Thought so, I did. Lookee here, now, squire's son. I wanna deal with ye. Ye got buckos o' mine I want back, an' the wimmen yer boys ain't knackered. Ye got me boats. Ye kin keep the bloody schooner, an' the loot, an' bad cess may it bring ye. Lots o' loot yonder, squire's son. Gold an' silver . . . plate an' jools. Lashin's o' wine an' brandy. I do 'spect yer lads're thirsty, hey? They kin use some 'blunt' in the pocket, 'cause they ain't no prize money to share out over pirates, an' damn' little head money per foe, neither. You let me an' me lads go, take our boats an' steal off, an' it be all yer'n, ev'ry shillin'. An' ye sail back t' yer admiral full o' glory. An' wealth. Now, wot ye say t'that, squire's son Lewrie? Ain't that a handsome trade?"

"Doyle, I have two boat-guns with me," Lewrie said, insulted beyond all measure but keeping a sober face. "Have you a timepiece? And just who owned it first, I'm wondering? I give you five minutes to throw down your arms and come out of that cave. Or I open fire upon you with canister and grape. I do not treat with murderers and rapists. I will not let cutthroat scum free for any price."

"Might change yer mind," Doyle snickered. "Niver kin tell, eh? I got somethin' else ye might like better, Navy. Lookit this, now."

He gestured to someone deeper in the cave, and two more of his henchmen came forward, each holding a white woman in his arms, wrists cruelly bound before them. And daggers at their throats!

"Ain't they a handsome pair o' young pieces, squire's son?" the pirate leader scoffed. "Pretty'z yer sisters, I wager. Milky-skinned, they are. Soft young quim, a right set o' squire's daughters! An' I just might have 'nother brace back in the cave, mightn't I? Ye touch off yer cannon an' these're dead, an' so're the others. All that canister an' grape-shot a'splangin' an' whirrin' about in here . . . oh, 'tis a terror wot ye'd inflict on the lasses!"

"Goddamn you!" Lewrie gasped. The women were muffled with a filthy handkerchief over their mouths so they could not contradict Doyle's words. All they could do was implore with their eyes.

"Take yer men back o' that ledge where ye come from s' clever, Navy," Doyle insisted. "Pile yer muskets this side. Leave yer cannon! Ye turn me lads loose yonder an' let 'em aboard the luggers. Then we come out an' sail away. Ye tell that cutter over there not t'fire on us as we go down-channel. I give ye me Bible-oath no harm'll come t'these young tits, an' I'll leave 'em safe an' sound on French Cay'r West Caicos. Mebbe West Sand Spit, 'ccordin' t'me whim o' the moment, so's ye gotta rescue them 'fore ye can hunt me. An' ye still keep the loot. Now how's that for a bargain? Lookee here, I'll give ye five minute t'make up *yer* mind, squire's son."

Lewrie turned on his heel and stalked back to the line of men at the crates. He looked for Cony and locked eyes with him, jerked his chin to draw him over, then turned to the aghast Parham.

"Load with canister and grape, Mister Parham," he muttered in an outraged snarl. "Aim high for the roof of the cave, just inside the entrance, and stand ready."

"But, sir . . . !"

"I gave you an *order*, Midshipman Parham!"

"Aye, aye, sir," Parham replied meekly, ready to spew.

"Goddamme, sir," Cony whispered, looking ready to be sick as well. "Wot're we t' do, Mister Lewrie?"

"How good a shot are you and Norton, Cony? A head shot such as took that iguana t'other day?" Lewrie inquired.

"Well, sir, Norton's Georgia-Loyalist. Use'ta shoot squirrel with a Pennsylvania rifle, 'e did. An' it's thirty, forty yards fer me an' the Ferguson, if we hunker down behind a crate yonder."

"When I signal, shoot the men who hold the women. Can you?"

"Lord, sir!" Cony shivered. "Them a'hidin' b'hint 'em an' all. Small target at forty yards, even with . . ." He patted the Ferguson.

"Their throats are slit, else, Cony, Norton," Lewrie warned.

"We kin try, sir," Norton promised, shifting uneasily.

"We saw three captive women last night, these two and one older. We have to risk losing the third if she's still in that cave," Lewrie almost choked. "Or we let these scum go to *maybe* save all three!"

"Norton's right, sir, we'll give 'er a try," Cony vowed.

"Good! Damn' good, men, and thankee," Lewrie nodded grimly in gratitude. "Mister Odrado? Fetch me a hale prisoner up here. Bound."

"Si, capitan," Odrado replied, puzzled. "Aye, aye."

Lewrie strode back up the beach, farther than before, and just a bit off to one side of the mouth of the cave. He drew one of his dragoon pistols, checked the priming, and pulled it to half-cock.

"'Hoy, Doyle!" he shouted. "Ahoy, the cave!"

"Ah, ye'z made up yer mind, ye have, squire's son?" Doyle japed as he appeared with his lying flag of truce on his sword once more.

"Aye, I have," Lewrie rasped. "Doyle . . . I think you're bluffing. I don't think you have any more hostages in there. And I don't think you're stupid enough to kill them, when they're the only things keeping you and your bully-bucks alive."

"Don't ye, now?" Doyle postured gaily. "Oh, but ye're a hard'un, squire's son. Worse'n a Dublin publican t'deal with. Lookee this, hey?"

Doyle had the women fetched out again, all three of them this time. He seized one of the younger women and put the tip of his blade to her throat, making her huge brown eyes widen in terror.

"Ain't she a handsome wench, Navy?" he tittered, clawing at her gown to rip it away and expose her full young breasts, tear it down to her waist halfway to her bound wrists. Those shapely breasts were now clotted with scabbed cuts, purpling with bruises. "This'n here, she wuz right good sport, once she got me ideer. Pity she had t'learn the hard way. Might be sportin' agin, soon's ye scrub her up, an' put some rum in 'er. Bit dowdy, now, d'ye think?" he teased, turning her from side to side, like a man appraising a used coat. "D'ye think I'm joshin' ye, now, laddy? Wot say I cut this sweet little dug off, jus' t'prove t'ye I'm that seryus." The blade descended to lift one breast on its razor-sharp edge. "Still, I got me five more t'offer ye, so this 'un won't be missed."

"Bring that prisoner up, Mister Odrado," Lewrie called over his shoulder. "So help me, Doyle, you harm the girl in the slightest, and you hang before the sun is down. You show one sign you mean any harm to any of them, and I *will* open fire, devil take the hindmost, and God protect the innocent!"

"Squire's son don't crave ye, girl," Doyle frowned, and spoke in her ear, making her wail with redoubled panic. But in Spanish!

Now I have you, you bastard, Lewrie thought, wolfish with glee!

"That Spanish I heard, Doyle?" Lewrie forced himself to laugh, "Christ, all this hanging back for fear of harm to Spanish bitches?"

"Now, lookee here, squire's son . . ." Doyle began to splutter.

"This scum a friend of yours?" Lewrie asked as Odrado forced a prisoner to kneel in front of him. "Would you be upset it I shot him right here and now? What if I started in shooting all your men I hold, like the curs they are?"

"She dies, damn ye!" Doyle threatened, bringing the sword-tip up below the girl's jaw, and leveling his arm at full-bent extent for a thrust. "Just t'prove I'm not bluffin'!"

"And then you're one hostage less, Doyle. One dago bitch less! No one *I'd* sport charity for. I dislike dagos more than cold, boiled mutton, don't ya know! Fought too many of 'em in the war, hey?" Alan guffawed, putting an icy edge to his sarcastic laughter. He drew out the dragoon pistol and pulled the dog's-jaws back to full cock, then laid it against the kneeling scoundrel's ear.

"I ain't foolin', squire's son!" the pirate leader snarled at him, pressing the sword's point deeper, drawing a trickle of blood, and a muffled, wheedling scream from the tormented girl.

"Neither am I," Lewrie told him. And pulled the trigger on the pistol and shot the kneeling pirate's head apart like a melon!

"Nombre de Dio!" Odrado croaked, crossing himself.

"Fetch up another prisoner, Mister Odrado," Lewrie instructed, trying to keep his bile down as he turned to blow the remaining powder embers from the priming pan. "And reload that for me."

"Jesus and Mary, ye . . . !" Doyle blanched, then recovered his bluster. "I swear t'Christ, this bitch is dead!" He began to stab her through the throat. She fainted dead away.

"Trade lives with me, will you?" Lewrie scoffed. "I kill one, you kill one, and then you run out of dago bitches a lot faster than I run out of pirates, who don't deserve better, anyway, Doyle. Now would you call that a handsome bargain, you son of a bitch?"

"Christ, yer lunatick!" Doyle goggled, trying to hold the girl up, then letting her sag unconscious to the ground. "Ah, d'ye think I care 'bout them yonder? Keep 'em, then! Do wot ye please!"

"I'll keep shooting them down until I run across one of your cutthroats you *do* give a damn about, Doyle. You do what *you* please with your captives. They don't signify to me!" Lewrie taunted. "You *get* no boats, you *don't* go free, and if you don't give up the women, throw down your arms and come out of there, you're dead! Now, damn your eyes!"

The two buccaneers holding their squealing, struggling captives were just as appalled as anyone else on the beach, and peered around their prisoners to gawk at one of their comrades shot to flinders.

God save me, Lewrie prayed! "Now, Cony!"

Two shots rapped out as Lewrie ducked to the side and drew one of his pistols; one light crack from the .54 caliber fusil musket, an accurate weapon for a muzzleloader, and the deeper report of a breech-loading Ferguson which, in an age where Brown Bess couldn't hit a man in the chest at sixty yards, could reach out flat and true to 200!

One pirate gave out a high scream as he was hit in the temple, the other grunted as he was plumbed right between the eyes!

"*Abajo, señoras!*" Lewrie screamed. "Down, ladies, get down!"

The women had the sense to drop to their knees, but began to scramble and claw away from the terror, away from the cave mouth on their knees and bound wrists, scraping over the rocks despite Lewrie's pleas. "Shit! Fire, Mister Parham! Fire!"

The boat-gun chuffed, and there was a howl over his head as the canister spread with enough wind to take off his hat. The roof of the cave sparkled and smoked just inside the entrance shelf profligate as a royal fireworks show, then the cave sang with whinings and keenings as the musket balls caromed and ricocheted inside to a satanic chorus of screams.

Lewrie rose from his protective squat as the pirate Doyle did, took aim at the amazed man, and fired. Doyle grunted with the impact and went over backwards, lifted off his feet by the heavy ball, and dropped out of sight, but for his heels drumming on the shale.

"Come on, lads, up and at 'em!" Lewrie called, drawing his sword. He stepped up the short slope of rock to peer inside as his men came thundering up to join him.

There was no fight left in them, those pirates who had lived through that lead sleeting. Lewrie knelt by Doyle, who was gut-shot and going fast.

"Jesus an' Mary, wot kind o' King's officer they givin' commissions t' now, damn ye?" Doyle panted, wincing with agony. "Yer not supposed t' . . ."

"Do you surrender to me now, you bastard?" Lewrie grinned.

"Devil take ye!" he groaned and sank back.

"No, the Devil take you, Billy Bones," Lewrie spat. "I just wish I'd had the complete pleasure of watching you swing!"

Book V

"Expulsis piratis—Restituta Commercia"

"He expelled the pirates and restored commerce"

former national motto
of the Bahamas

Chapter 1

Alan Lewrie was jealous.

It was a novel experience for him, this gnawing apprehension, instead of the cut-and-thrust, quickly done sort of rivalrous jealousy of his bachelorhood where the prize was discarded once gained, and the only thing that mattered was outwitting one's rivals. But now, with the prize becoming ever dearer to him, and with the evidence clear after his long enforced separation from Caroline, he was fearful that jealousy, and its attendant alarums, would be a permanent way of life, one never even hinted at in those tales of "happily-ever-after" one read of in fiction.

For the characters of the smugly moral Richardson's novels, or even the risqué rogues of a Fielding book, there was *always* a happy ending where two souls, after much bother of course, share a life together of indolent bliss, with nary a cross word, nary a threat once the principal villain has been dispatched. Spooning and bussing from morning 'til night in blessed mutual agreement, and in such sweetly disposed and addlepated disconnection with the rest of the scurvy world that it could go hang, as long as the Happy Couple got their tea water the right temperature, and nothing more distressful than burned toast ever seemed to plague them from that moment on.

Then, of course, Alan Lewrie grumped moodily, there's the real world, and you're bloody welcome to it! All those writers; Fielding, Richardson, even bloody Smollett, were a tribe of debollocked, clueless, hopeful . . . bachelors!

It had begun soon after his return to Nassau Harbour to a hero's welcome as dizzying as a conquering Roman general might have received; the eight-day wonder, with manacled pirates as his captives to parade under the yoke as a spectacle in his triumph.

The Spanish ladies he had freed were greeted and swooned over in the better salons in Nassau society as the epitomes of romantic tales in which the virtuous young maiden is rescued by an English knight from the dragon's very mouth, and Alan had been feted as their champion, much like a modern-day St. George.

Until, of course, the town had learned that those poor, piteous *señoritas* had not done all a plucky *English* girl would have under the circumstances, that they had not gamely spurned their captors' Base Designs, as heroines in fiction seemed to do when taken by Turks and slung into the sultan's harem. Their social stock fell considerably, and with a great sigh of relief, and many muttered imprecations such as ". . . what may one expect; they're only dagos," and "blood will tell," they were hustled off for Cuba to complete their voyage quicker than one could say "knife," so rude fact could not contradict high-flown popular sentiment.

As that fame faded for Alan, the trial which followed restored him to center stage, which trial resulted in a "hanging fair" as gay and cock-a-whoop as any he'd ever seen at Tyburn. And the trial had kept *Alacrity* in harbor for weeks so testimony could be taken, which had coincided with the height of the hurricane season, so *Alacrity* ended up swinging at her anchors even longer. Which enforced idleness was simply "the nuts" to Alan, for he could spend nights ashore with Caroline in their snug little home, and enjoy the fruits of his valiant labors, and a hero's proper welcome.

Deliriously happy as he felt, it was then that he began to see portents which disturbed him.

It rankled him when officers from the garrison or Fort Montagu down the eastern road, halted their rides together to tip their hats to her and converse a tad too gallantly for his liking. When he and Caroline went to town to shop or accept an invitation, gentlemen came up to them to exchange pleasantries and gossip from past social gatherings. Would they go to tea, to *écarté*, a drum, rout or ball, or a cool evening salon, there would be fashionable young sprogs sidling up to her to discuss people and topics of which he was ignorant. At dances, he would end up grinding his teeth by the punch bowl as Caroline was surrounded by hopeful blades who begged *just* the one dance, or come nigh on snapping his neck to keep an eye on her as he performed his social obligations to dance with the stout, clumsy, or frippish matrons and their pimply, runny-nosed daughters.

In his absence, Caroline had developed social relations with many Loyalist families, and a fair number of old-time Bahamians as well. She had also struck up a close friendship with Betty Mustin, Commander Benjamin Rodgers's "kept mutton," who was no shrinking violet when it came to accepting invitations.

She and Caroline went coaching together, riding horseback as an almost inseparable pair, shopped and visited back and forth as dear as cater-cousins, and made the social rounds together, in company with the much older Peyton and Heloise Boudreau, their landlords, along as chaperones. Innocent as it sounded, Lewrie thought Betty Mustin just a bit "fly," and a disturbing influence.

Perhaps it *was* all innocent socializing, he thought, but then he could remember being "cock of the company" and buck-of-the-first-head in such circumstances, too, in his bachelor days, when he had preyed upon the loneliness of abandoned young matrons with an itch to scratch, and shammed being a "Robin Goodfellow" until they'd come around to his way of thinking. It gave him pause, it did.

Giving him pause, too, was his reticence to believe that such deceit had entered *his* married life, or to bring up the ugly subject. What could he say that would not make him look like a foolish cully? Where could he draw a line without shaming her? How was a fellow to order some simpering young toad to sheer off and leave his wife alone in future? He was even fretful to mention it to her in private, if her tempestuous reactions to their first disagreement were anything to go by.

That had occurred about a week after his return, after the dew was off the rose, so to speak.

"Uhm, Caroline," he had asked, having regarded their paintings and sketches on the restfully pale tan walls of their house and found one missing. "Where's that oil o' mine, the large one with the women taking their baths?"

"That nude harem scene?" she'd frowned, though fondly. "Alan, really, whatever could you have been thinking of to purchase it? It was taking up space, and I could not hang it anywhere decent people might see it. I sold it."

"*Sold* it!" he'd goggled. "But I rather fancied . . ."

"Traded it, really," she'd laughed quite matter-of-factly. "I obtained yon *Sunset Over Nassau Harbour* there. A local artist did it, Augustus Hedley. It has such lovely ships in it, and the colors are quite spectacular, do you not think? As near to any as ever I did see on our voyage here. Whenever I gaze upon it, it reminds me of our honeymoon aboard *Alacrity*, and makes me blissful."

"You can look out the door and see sunset over Nassau Harbour, and all the ships you wish anytime you bloody well please," Alan had groused. "Why not a painting of a gash-bucket, then, if you want to be reminded of the voyage? Or the Townsleys at table? Pretty much the same, really. Horrid feeders, they were. And spewers."

"We won't always live in Nassau, Alan," she had responded with a hug and sweet reason. "And then we will wish a memento of our time here. I quite like it. Don't you?"

"Damned ships aren't even rigged proper, damme if they ain't. Who's this Hedley, then?"

"The funny little fellow in the yellow ditto suits. We met him at the dance last week. He's very talented. He does everyone who is *anyone's* portraits. People say he's good as any in the Royal Academy."

"Well, I hope he does noses better than he does masts, or he's overcharging," Alan had laughed.

"Then must art depict reality so closely one could use it as an illustration in your *Falconer's Marine Dictionary?*" she'd asked him rather sharply. Ominously, there was a tiny vertical line of threat between her lovely brows, a line he could not recall seeing before. He'd sensed an argument, and had submitted, *humphing* into silence.

The real explosion had come later after supper, as they sat on their breezeway savoring sundown and a post-prandial brandy. Alan had speculated, to his cost, which particular shade of green the house was now painted.

"And the Boudreau house up the drive," he'd allowed easily, his feet extended, slumped down in an unpadded wooden chair Caroline had had a local carpenter construct. "Pink as cooked salmon. A bit off-putting, I must say. Whatever happened to white, cream, or gray like a London row house? All these pinks and blues and all . . ."

"And pale mint green?" she had inquired. *Very* coolly.

"Looks as if they could get nothing but castoff paints sent here," he'd blathered on, attempting to be amusing, "that pink must be a mix of ship's bottom-paint. White stuff and red stuff stirred up and slathered on, same as *Alacrity'*d get afore recoppering. I would have thought, long as you were painting, and they were, you'd have put your head together with Heloise and come up with a match."

"I chose this mint green to make our house appear different, Alan," she had replied archly. "Not an extension, the gatehouse or coachhouse to theirs any longer, as long as we live in it."

"Well, it was, though, wasn't it, dear? And will be again."

"So that no one would come riding by, see it, and wonder if it is still occupied by the head groom or their slave overseer! Really, Alan, you don't like it?"

"Well, I didn't say that . . ."

"Look at all I've accomplished," she'd demanded. "Look at all I've done to make a home for us! The garden out back, the flowers, the painting and carpentry work, and the . . . is there nought I have done

that *does* meet with your approval, then? Must you cavil or carp and
. . . and *sneer* . . . at every decision I made in your absence?"

"Caroline . . . !" He'd wilted at her first tears.

"I swear, Alan, you use me ill as . . ." she'd wept brokenly, just short
of bawling fit to bust, "as . . . so many b . . . *bears!*"

And he had had to pursue her, beg at their locked bedchamber door.
Then once he'd at last gained entry, had had to cosset her, to dandle,
kiss and spoon her, to calm her and confess what a total ass he was to be
so unappreciative, and what a treasure she was, so clever and resourceful,
and how pleased he was with things, in the main.

Which had ended their first fight, that and the boisterous and healing
lovemaking which had followed. Their first squall had been weathered.
He dreaded a second.

God a'mercy, Alan thought, she *has* done a lot in a little over four
months. With all her endeavors, who'd have *time* for an affair, I ask you?

The house was painted inside and out, and the wood trim shiny with
white enamel against the interior's pale, sandy tan, or the exterior's light
mint green. The roof had been patched with new shakes and tarred
proof against tempestuous wind and rain. Their few carpets were clean,
his dark blue settee and wing chairs were ensconced as a group at one
end of the parlor area; hers had been recovered with yellow and floral
chintz for another conversational grouping. His old table and chairs
made a gaming area, whilst her table, eight chairs and the sideboard and
cupboard were their dining facilities, and their few precious silver or
silver-plate candlesticks, serving trays and tea things gleamed on display
alongside the locking caddy for tea, sugar, coffee and chocolate.

The floors were spotless, the drapes new, and sewn by Caroline's
hands. Their few paintings (minus his harem scene) looked grand as
Government House; his portrait he'd commissioned in '83 in uniform,
some Chiswick forebears, his granny Lewrie, her favorite pastoral or
hunt scenes, and the sea-battle granny Lewrie'd bought him at Ranelagh
Gardens, and his anonymous Grand Tour sketches.

She'd stored away the heavy velvet bed curtains and replaced them
with light, gauzy draperies to ward off insects—those that the ubiquitous
lizards did not eat rather noisily in the night.

On top of that, she'd camphored every upright clothes closet or
drawer, lined everything with paper-thin cedar strips, kept the house in
Bristol-fashion with just one maid-of-all-work housekeeper who came by
the day, a free black woman named Wyonnie.

And, not content with household economies, she had put in a vegetable garden, had tilled it with the help of Wyonnie's husband and her aged father and his equally aged mule, watered it, tended it, weeded it, to the amazement of Nassau's white society who thought her youthfully eccentric; and to the slack-jawed stupefaction of the free blacks, who had never before beheld a white woman of even the least means do a lick of work if a slave could not be put to it first.

Not content with a goodly crop of victuals such as corn, beans, pigeon peas, tomatoes and salad greens, Caroline, Heloise and Betty had ridden all over New Providence seeking *flora* to plant about the house, to screen the back lot from the main house, and to beautify it. The pale green house was now awash in an informal, lush jungle.

There were tamarinds and acacia, torch ginger and jump-up-and-kiss-me, little Tree-Of-Life bushes with indigo flowers, *frangipani* or red jasmine, cascarillas, bright yellow elder, both red and purple bougainvillea vines on trellises framing the porches and the dog-run. There were flamboyants with blooms as big as birdbaths, poinsettias and poincianas, bird of paradise, angel's trumpet and flamingo flowers in gaudy profusion. There were replanted palmettos for a hedge, and young saplings in tubs —key-lime and lemon trees, sapodillas, soursops and guavas, candle-woods and sea grapes.

And, braving the forgelike heat of the kitchen in high summer (a spotless kitchen!), Caroline had put up exotic new fruit preserves in stone crocks, an impressive selection was now ranked row upon row in the pantry. And that was on top of her cider vinegars, her dried and candied preserve slices, her . . .

Considering all she had accomplished in so little time, at so little cost, was daunting!

I've the handsomest, sweetest, cleverest, and (God rot your soul, Uncle Phineas) the most economical young wife on the face of this earth, Alan concluded. So why do I feel like Harry Embleton?

Chapter 2

"So who is this Finney, then?" Alan asked, attempting to sound casual about it as he emerged from the water and sat down on the hard sand just above the lapping wavelets.

"John Finney?" Peyton Boudreau replied, opening one lazy eye from a doze. "Quite the hero hereabouts, don't ye know, haw haw! A damned rich'un, too!"

"Striking fellow," Alan allowed as he toweled down from a dip in waist-deep water, no more. Most sailors could not swim, and Alan was proof of that particular truism.

"Aye, he is," the elder man agreed. "Pity he's so low."

"Is he?" Alan inquired, relishing this "dirt" on the suitor he feared the most. He'd re-met the artist Augustus Hedley and found him to be a simpering, mincing, dandy-prat lap dog to the Nassau ladies, a flagrant "Molly", said to be exiled on remittance by his family so his predilections would not harm their reputation. Most of the others had sheered off once Alan was back. But Finney . . . !

"Dublin bogtrotter," Peyton Boudreau snickered. "A product of the stews. Went for a sailor young, and drifted out here. The Lord be praised, he's a Bay Street merchant now, though. Owns ships. Has the best imported slaves. Doesn't deal with the dagos in Hispaniola, he sends vessels to Africa for 'black ivory'. Brings 'em in in prime condition, too, 'stead of the usual third lost. Fancy goods from all over, the latest fashions. All the delicacies which make life tolerable. Runs packets from the Continent in all seasons, hang the winter gales or hurricanes. Don't see how he manages that, but he does. Ah, think I'll go back in and dip meself."

Lewrie watched the elegant older man rise and pad into the sea to flop on his belly and paddle about, and wondered how he could gain more information about Finney without looking foolish. Or concerned.

They were on a "maroon" on Hog Island, on the white-sand beach on the nor'west shore. It was a popular amusement in the Bahamas to sail out to a deserted cay with food and "guzzle," set up a camp with furniture, cooking utensils and perhaps a pavilion, and go salt-water bathing in total privacy. Some even spent an entire day and a night, though most returned at dusk. The Boudreaus were great devotees of it, and had suggested that Alan and Caroline, with Betty Mustin along, too, might enjoy the excursion.

Caroline, Betty and the older but still impressive Heloise were down the beach a way, cavorting in the water and laughing and giggling gay as so many ducklings. They had gone into the boat in old sack gowns without stays or underpinnings, with only one underskirt. Straw hats and parasols, their oldest cracked shoes, cotton stockings and towels were the thing for the ladies. Those, and a single voluminous shift of light cotton or muslin to drape themselves in between dunkings. At present, from what little Alan could see, they were bathing nude, or with a short chemise at best!

Alan rose and strode back into the water for more information, the December sunshine almost kind for once to his back and shoulders. After hurricane season ended around the first of November, the Bahamas were cooled by northerly or westerly winds, the daytime temperatures never soared much above mild, and the nights got downright coolish if a brisk breeze was blowing off the ocean, but never shivering cold.

He waded out to chest-deep and bobbed about in the gin-clear water slightly tinged pale turquoise, ducking his head now and again.

"You said he was a hero?" Alan asked once Peyton had paddled near enough. The older man stood in the water and swiped his short-cut hair dry.

"Who, Finney?" Peyton asked, wiggling an ear clear of water.

"Yes, what did he do?"

"Privateer, sir," Peyton smiled. "A most successful privateer. Ended up with a flotilla of his own in these waters. Spanish, French, Rebels . . . no vessel was safe from him. 'Tis bruited about he took over two hundred thousand pounds sterling in prize money. But what sealed his repute was when the Spanish took Nassau in '82, just before the Revolution ended. You know of Col. Andrew Deveaux, the Loyalist soldier from, I'm quite proud to say, dear South Carolina of my birth?"

"I've heard of him."

"Well, he determined upon an expedition to retake Nassau, all on his own," Peyton bragged on his former neighbor. "Sailed a scratch militia here, April of '83, with what weapons they could come up with. Tag-rag and-bobtail effort, with no help from the Crown, you see. Well, Finney threw in with him! Brought a brace of his privateers tricked out as ships of war. They rowed their so-called troops ashore and landed them. Then they had those few men lay down in the boats and rowed back out, looking empty, to supposedly embark another batch. Kept it up until the Dons figured they were hopelessly outnumbered, and they threw it up as a bad bargain, d'you see, haw haw! Quite a stunt! And with not 200 men, all told!"

"A clever fellow, too, this Finney," Alan smiled.

"Well, 'twas more Andrew's idea than Finney's, of course. Our 'Calico Jack' is shrewd, and ambitious. But I doubt he'd have thought of it on his own, don't you know. Or cared much one way or t'other if the Spanish held Nassau another year. He'd have made more profit from taking their ships, whilst his store sold them victuals and wine!"

" 'Calico Jack'?" Alan grinned with mirth. "And how did he come by that charming sobriquet? Wasn't there a Calico Jack Rackham, a pirate, in these waters long ago?"

"There was," Peyton sneered aristocratically. "Finney came by his by the tradesman's entrance, so to speak. And more prosaic. More common, haw haw."

Peyton Boudreau and his wife Heloise were splendid people in the main, though given to languid, highly cultured and snobbish, aloof airs of fallen Huguenot and Charleston Low Country nobility. No matter that their estate had fallen since leaving fabled South Carolina, they were still accounted regal pluses to Nassau society. And told damned juicy gossip with such wit and relish!

"Wasn't always rich, y'know," Peyton continued. "Had but the one packet ship, and a used-goods chandlery past East Hill Street, almost in 'Over-Hill.' Inn, chandlery, an 'all-nations' dram shop. Brokered whores out of there, too, by all accounts. Sold slop goods and shoddy not fit for anyone but slaves and the idle poor. Little of this, then a little of that, to show a profit. Had mongers out with drays hawking his castoffs like ragpickers. But he did the best of his business in calico and nankeen cloth for use on the plantings to dress slave gangs. Condemned salt meats, weevily flour, gin, rum and *ratafia* brandy, that sort of hard bargain, hand-to-mouth trade," Peyton dismissed, raising a cultured eyebrow significantly. "Then, in '75, when the Revolution broke out, everything changed for him overnight. The Admiralty Court gave him a Letter of Marque to turn privateer, and the next thing anyone knew, he was tea-trade, nabob-rich."

"A most impressive feat," Alan had to admit, though it galled.

"For a man who started out illiterate in the gutter," Boudreau sniffed top-loftily. "By the time Heloise and I got here in '82 when the Crown abandoned Charleston, he was strutting golden as an Ottoman sultan, with that big ship's chandlery, his fancy-goods shops on Bay Street, and

half a dozen privateers flying his house flag. But, don't y'know . . ."
Peyton snickered, "the brats in the streets still tailed after him chanting
his cant, 'calico, calico, who'll buy my calico! 'Tis Jack, Jack, the Calico
Man', haw haw!"

"Oh, poor bastard!" Lewrie smiled, relishing what chagrin that would
have caused the handsome Finney.

"Then, of course," Peyton sobered, "that was before he killed three
men in duels for ragging him or sneering at him. And after he and
Andrew Deveaux retook Nassau, he became a veritable social lion. For a
time, mind," Peyton chuckled meanly. *"Only* for a time. One may not
turn a sow's ear into a silk purse, after all. For all his fame and his
money, he's still 'Beau-Trap' and too ill mannered for most decent people. No manners at all, though he's said to work hard at gaining *some*
small measure of refinement. Built that fine town house, hired danc-
ingmasters, tutors in elocution, only the best tailors and such. 'Moik me
a foin gennulmun, damn yuz oyes!' he told 'em, hey?" Peyton scoffed,
cruelly imitating a bogtrotter's brogue. "One may gild dried dung, but all
one has to show for it is gold-plated shit, after all. And, he's still tight
with his old chums from 'Over-Hill.' Niggers, scoundrels, shiftless whites
and whores, pickpockets, cutthroats and such. And he *is* Irish, when you
come right down to it."

"He seems welcome in everyone's salon, though," Alan commented.
"And people seem to accept his invitations willingly enough."

"That's the 'fly' nature of Bahamian society," Peyton guffawed. "How
few of them arose from the better classes? In Charleston, in London it
goes without saying, and I suspect even in his native Dublin, in the
better circles, John Finney'd still not be admitted but to the tradesman's
entrance. There's damned few refined folk'd set foot inside his door. *We*
do not. Nor do those who aspire to true civility ever invite him. In like
manner, he has never seen *my* parlor, *our* salon, sir! Nor shall he,"
Peyton declaimed grandly, then cocked his grizzled head to peer closely
at Alan. "And why this sudden interest, young sir?"

"He has irked me by showing an undue interest in Caroline."

"Ah, I *see!*" Peyton drawled out. "Yes, she did once receive an invitation to some affair he was hosting. Thankfully, she told us of it before
she responded, and we were able to discover to her what one may mention in polite company of his background, which discovery dissuaded her
from attending, God be praised."

"Truly," Alan flushed, embarrassed that the truth was out.

"Sir . . . Alan," Peyton said kindly, "Heloise and I are that taken
with your lovely Caroline. She is a most handsome girl, and a most

intelligent and discerning one, in addition to her sweet and modest nature. Since you and she became our tenants, she has been like one of our own daughters to us. She most sensibly inquired of us the usual things. Where best to shop, where best for bargains and such. And, more importantly, which places best avoided. And, which people to avoid, so no breath of scandal ever taints your good name, or soils her, dare I say, immaculate repute. Unlike *some* I could name to you."

"Yet he seems to be everywhere we go, sir," Alan complained. "And he is so gracelessly . . . impertinent. And persistent!"

"You may not avoid him totally, since our society here is so small a circle, even with the influx of Loyalists by the hundreds," Peyton counseled. "Finney rose from the gutter by dint of dogged and slavish persistence, so one would suppose he believes anything will come to him, if he but perserveres. Still, he knows his place, deny it though he will."

"If he does persist, Mister Boudreau, I'll have to call him out for it," Alan frowned.

"Lord, no, Alan, I beg you!" the older man shuddered. "Do not duel him! He's a crack shot, and chopping fair with a sword."

"So am I, sir," Alan insisted, then blurted out his fears in spite of his best intentions. "If not Finney, then one of the other sparks who flock 'round her like so many importunate . . ." he tangled his tongue on his bile.

"Ah, the rest are but amusing themselves, playing the gallant and serving 'Jack-Sauce'," Peyton dismissed with a chuckle. "Lookee here, young sir. Duck your head and cool your blood, and I'll tell you a tale that'll set your unease to rest, damme'f I won't!"

Lewrie ducked and came up blowing and snorting.

"When Heloise and I were first wed," Peyton Boudreau began his tale with a grin of reverie, "I was that jealous of her. That's the curse one takes upon oneself when one weds an incredibly lovely and desirable lady. As you did. I could not abide the attention all of her old beaus showed her, nor begrudge her time or her laughter they took from me. Now, had she been nothing but handsome, with no bottom or sense, filled with frippishness and flirtations . . . or more so than Charleston society permitted young ladies . . . I'd have slain a few of the bastards. Or died because of it. And lost the last twenty years of wedded bliss. Mind you," Peyton cautioned, tapping his nose and winking, "it ain't all custard and cream, no paradise on silver plate. No marriage is. New marriages even less so, before one becomes accustomed. But, women are not the empty-headed, fragile and vulnerable vessels, not as false a tribe, as the 'Mar-Text' reverends tell us.

"You've a level-headed lady, lad. Have some faith in her good judgment, in her sense of propriety. Caroline's not the sort to do anything, or allow anything or anyone to give you pause. 'Tis all in your head. The more one loves, the more intruders seem threatening. And, believe this when I relate it to you, the girl loves you with a single-minded devotion I could toast bread on! Your name, or tales about you, form half her waking conversation! I doubt she could sew a hem in a drape without thinking of how you would approve of it!"

"Thankee, Mister Boudreau, sir," Alan sagged in some measure of relief. " 'Tis gratifying to hear. But what dissuaded you from dueling those former rivals of your wife?"

"A long talk with a sage old uncle of mine, much like this."

"And did it help you, sir?"

"Not immediately, young sir," Peyton allowed with a rueful grin. "That came gradual. As does wisdom. But I did take a long look at it and discovered that Heloise would allow no gallantries or importunate addresses beyond a very firm boundary, and would give the rogues who crossed that boundary the 'cut-direct' the next time she saw them. I learned to trust her. A hard lesson, I'll admit. But, once learned, I became even fonder of her than ever before."

"Fortunately for you, though, sir," Alan sighed, "you had none but gentlemen who could take a hint to deal with. You had no Finney dogging your Heloise."

"Watch and see if your Caroline cannot put even a thick-skull Irish rogue in his place if he persists," Peyton laughed. "And to the galling scorn even of Bahamian society, haw haw! Trust her to handle herself, Alan. And I will give you assurance that Heloise and I will continue to chaperone and advise her, so you will have nought to give you worry when you sail the next time."

I may be dense as bloody marble most of the time, Alan thought, but even I can recognize good sense when I trip over it!

"I will remember that, sir, and be damned grateful to you and your good lady for it," Alan enthused at last, taking Boudreau's hand and pumping it warmly. "I feared to leave her in Portsmouth without someone to count on. I'm happy to have found good friends here that we may both trust."

"You have, indeed, young sir," Peyton smiled, "you have. Well, all this sun has me parched. There's a bottle of ale with my name on't that'd go down nice. Damme'f I ain't a touch peckish, too. You?"

"Your servant and mine have something succulent on the boil to tempt me, I must allow, sir," Alan said, wading ashore in a ragged set of breeches to towel off and don a patched old shirt without sleeves.

"Conch chowder. The very thing!" Peyton exclaimed. "Lobsters thick as your arm! Let us join the ladies. I see they've come ashore like so many fair daughters of Neptune, haw haw! The lovely Heloise, the superbly handsome and lissome Caroline! The bounteous, charming Betty! Poor chick." He sobered.

"Sir?" Alan asked as they trudged along the hard-packed sand.

"Betty's a sweet'un, near as sweet as your Caroline, d'you see. A trifle headlong in her enthusiasms, and her affections, though, to her cost. A bit too much the hearty coquette, but she has bottom," Peyton assayed. "If not the sense God promised a titmouse."

"I find her a bit forward and . . . frippish," Alan said. "Not the best company for Caroline. As a constant companion, that is."

"In point of fact, 'tis your Caroline who's been very good for Betty," Boudreau countered. "Family scattered hell-to-breakfast, one side Rebel, t'other Tory. Her father's over on Great Abaco farming and timbering. She ran away with that irresponsible Rodgers and let him set her up here as his hired doxy. For *love!* Had she a man who would give her a decent promise of marriage, had she some sense of security in his affection, well, she'd be happy as a kitten in the cream pot! But, he's a slender reed, is Benjamin Rodgers, so she's allowed certain young rogues and Corinthians address her and squire her about on rides, at balls and such, to fill his absences. To make him pay more attention to her when he is in port. And we both know that Rodgers's sort of rakehell never responds to such ploys with anything other than scorn. He'd simply find another, and turf her out to fall further."

I do know that sort of rakehell, Alan thought wryly. Damned well, do I know me of old!

"But, with Caroline, and her eminent good sense to guide her, she's mending her ways," Peyton allowed. "Even turned her hands now and again to gardening and household economies, though I fear she'll never be a tenth part the wonder your lady is. No, don't begrudge Caroline her friend, Alan. Heloise and I quite like her. Just wish she had a better man, one she could trust, one who'd show her the sort of real affection and attention she craves. Do you not know some other naval officers who might wish to meet an attractive young lady, Alan? That sobersided lieutenant of yours, Ballard?"

"I doubt he wishes to marry so early in his career, sir."

"Well, if not marriage, she could be mistress to a better fellow than Commander Rodgers," Peyton suggested. "She could have someone decent to pine for when he's away. She has some means to keep herself. Do give it a thought. Heloise and I would appreciate it."

"I shall, sir."

"Act more pleasantly disposed towards Betty, too, will you?"

"Have I not been pleasant, sir?" Alan inquired, a little irked that Peyton Boudreau, once he had gotten the slightest status as his and Caroline's Dutch uncle, was now ready to play "avuncular" to the hilt!

Damme, you wish to adopt us, Alan thought? Play my father's replacement, you'll have to stand me an hundred guineas a year!

"I have seen some snippishness, Alan," the older man shrugged. "After all, she's not Calico Jack, for God's sake. Caroline dotes on her. If you trust Caroline's good sense and discernment, surely you can be accepting. Betty needs good friends worth having."

"Aye, I suppose so, Mister Boudreau," Alan found himself agreeing. "I suppose I may even come to tolerate Calico Jack Finney, if I follow your advice, and allow Caroline to pull him up short."

"Well, you won't see much of him, now the trial's evidence is common knowledge," Peyton assured him as they neared the campsite. "Lying doggo for awhile, I'm certain, now word is out your pirate leader was Billy 'Bones' Doyle. Might be in mourning, far's I know, haw haw!"

"They were compatriots?" Alan started.

"Oh, Billy Doyle was a mate of his, long before the war. And master of one of his privateers," Boudreau replied breezily, as if it was no matter. "After the war, Finney sold off half his ships and got replacements more suited for trade. Paid half his men off, too. *Gave* Doyle title to a schooner, in gratitude, along with ten thousand pounds sterling profit! A splendid gesture. Doyle was along with Finney and Deveaux on the expedition to retake New Providence, don't y'know. He . . ."

"No, sir, I did not know that. It is news to me," Lewrie said. "And no one commented upon the connection? No one even wondered . . ."

"And why should they, after they parted company a year ago?" Boudreau sniffed. "With Bahamian society riddled as it is with former pirates and privateers, with former cutthroats, and merchants greedy as highwaymen, what's one more knave with a scandal?"

"Amazing," Lewrie goggled.

"Oh, Doyle and Finney were thick as thieves at one time. Haw, haw, thick as thieves, do y'see, sir? I would suppose he dropped him once he'd wasted his money, and his chances to better himself. Quite the cock-of-the-company for awhile, was Billy Bones. But he spent it all on drink and whores, on flash clothes and gay amusements. And some disastrous investments whenever he drew a sober breath. Now I ask you, how may a man *lose* his last farthing in a market so brisk as the Bahamas, were he not a total fool, sir? Made a sorry, surly, besotted spectacle of himself in the end, and sailed off to God knew where to escape his creditors. For which respite the good people of Nassau *thanked* God, I tell you!" Boudreau related with glee. "Just goes to prove the lower orders haven't the wherewithal to improve their lot, to emulate their betters, no matter that the opportunity to do so falls from on high like manna, and is beaconed by a burning bush, haw haw!"

"So the schooner I captured at Conch Bar wasn't a recent prize he'd taken," Lewrie realized. "She was the one Finney gave him."

"Very likely, indeed. Bound to come to a bad end, that sort. Illiterate guttersnipes and mongrels! No matter how high they assay to rise, they always revert to their sorry roots when they fall upon hard times. Back to the criminal habits they learned in their stews! And to be rewarded for criminality in wartime, given stamps of approval, letters of marque, and praised for looting enemy ships! Tosh, I say, sir! What else may one expect, I ask you!"

"Or become a royal governor, like Morgan. Or Woodes Rogers," Alan commented with a wry grin. "They both sailed under the 'Jolly Roger,' Mister Boudreau."

"Well, they were *successful* pirates," Boudreau dismissed with a leer. "And turned on their own kind in the end. Ah, ladies, may we join you for our repast, now you're decent, haw haw?"

Chapter 3

Alacrity would be sailing soon, and Lewrie needed to replenish his personal stores for his pantry and wine cabinet. Leaving Caroline after breakfast, he borrowed a horse and cantered to town. And, out of prurient curiosity, he wandered into Finney's.

There was an entire row of shops for clothing, for shoes, for ladies' fashions and fabrics, with the latest miniature gowns on the porcelain dolls sent from Paris and London depicting the height of that season's styles and colors. There were cheese shops, spirits stores awash in wines, brandies, harsh whiskeys, gins, and liqueurs of a dozen nations. Finney had furniture for sale, wallpapers and chintz for drapes or recovering; kitchen wares from America and home, fine china and silver services, glassware from utilitarian to finest crystal pieces. One entire block of Bay Street on the southern side, and around the corner of Market Street for half of another block was his so-called mart, his commercial fiefdom.

Though he rued giving Finney any of his trade, or any of his money, he did find good prices on quality merchandise, and ended up purchasing stationery and ink, various cheeses and meat sauces, and several interesting books to fill his solitary hours, some with the pages already cut by a previous owner, though offered as new.

Alan opened one of the books and found it dogeared on several pages. It was a recent English translation of a French novel he had heard about, *Les Liaisons Dangereuses* by some Frog scribbler named de Laclos. The dogeared pages contained scenes of a most pleasing and salacious nature, which made Alan smile, even as he winced at the chalked-on price of six shillings. Thumbing further through it, he discovered an inscription in the frontispiece.

"From Daniel,

> To his scamp of a brother Nathan.
> May this inspire you aboard *Matilda*
> on your next Voyage! & May her New
> 1st Mate have similar Joy of the
> swarthy Bahamian ladies!"

Wonder if he did, Alan thought with amusement. And did he have to sell it to pay for the Mercury Cure to rid himself of the pox those Bahamian "ladies" gave him?

He decided to buy it, and added it to the pile on the counter.

"That should be all here," Alan said to the young clerk who was following him about, keeping a running total from store to store.

"Might have a peek at this before you leave, captain sir," the young man suggested. "The very latest scientific device to predict the tropic storm. Hang this on your bulkhead below-decks, and you'll have all the warning a sailing man would ever need."

"How does it work?" Alan asked, looking at a bulbous glass flask with a tall, narrow, sealed neck. Inside the flask was a blue liquid of some kind. It was brass-bound to a wooden plaque.

"The better the weather, the more of the liquid will gather at the bulb-end on the bottom, sir," the clerk told him. "But when there is a storm brewing, why 'twill soar up the neck. The worse the storm to be, the higher will it go, sir. 'Tis said, sir," he confided with an air of secrecy, "that the Admiralty will be requiring every one of their ships to be equipped with one soon. We've shown one on display over t'the ships' chandlery all this past year, and 'tis been a wonder to all who've seen it for how accurately it reflected the weather, it has. And only twenty guineas, sir!"

"Should the Admiralty require it, then let them buy it for me," Alan scoffed. "Let's go select some wines."

"Very good, captain sir."

The spirits shop was set up much like a coffeehouse, or an inn's public room, with tables and chairs. The walls were lined with barrels and wooden cases of bottles, with a combination counter and bar at the rear.

"Well, damme!" Alan was forced to exclaim as he espied an oil painting over the counter. It was his harem scene that Caroline had traded off, to the life! There were the same buxom darlings on the same draped couches, with a slender lass featured in the foreground standing to be toweled after her bath, the one who so-much resembled his first whore in Covent Garden, the infamously handsome "'Change Court Betty" in all her bare splendor.

"Inspiring, ain't it, sir?" the clerk simpered. "Here, Davie, the captain would like to sample some wines this day."

"Aye, sir," the vendor smiled, wiping his hands on his apron as he came from behind his counter. "Pray, have a seat, sir, and take yer ease. Tell us yer wants, sir, an' we'll trot 'em out for yer to select those as best suits yer palate."

Lewrie took a seat and removed his cocked hat. "Let's begin on port. I'll need one case."

"Going back t'sea, are we, sir?" the vendor clucked. "Got a fine 'Rain-Water' Madeira just in. Got a lovely nose, ain't it, sir? Try a sip of that, now."

A door in the back that led to the storerooms opened, and Alan paused with a sample glass to his lips as John Finney emerged, intent on a loose sheaf of papers. He looked up, spotted Lewrie, and smiled hesitantly, then put a bold face on it and stepped forward.

"Captain Lewrie, the top o' the mornin' t'ya, sir," he lilted in an Irish brogue. "'Tis delighted I am t'see you again, sir, and in my . . . establishment, at that," Finney stumbled, seeming to be trying to recall a lesson in elocution, to sound more English, though with a hard emphasis on those "break-teeth" words not common to his everyday speech.

"Mister Finney, good morning," Lewrie nodded, willing to sound at least affable in reply. He even threw in a small grin.

"I trust me . . . my clerk David is satisfactory, sir?" Finney continued, laying his papers down on the counter.

"Most satisfactory, sir, thankee," Lewrie rejoined.

God, but he's an imposin' bastard, Lewrie thought as he sipped the Madeira! Finney stood a full six feet tall, broad of shoulder and deep-chested as a yearling steer. He was sailor-dark in complexion, with a full head of bright blond hair drawn back into a queue as low as his shoulder blades. His face was angular and square, and in his chin there was a pronounced cleft. For someone who'd come up from a stew, he had remarkably good white teeth. And penetrating, sometimes mocking blue eyes. With that heft, he could have looked day-labourer common, but he was flat-stomached, lean in the hips and thighs, and showed a very shapely calf in his silk stockings. His hands and his feet betrayed his origins, though; huge, clumping-long feet and hands square and thick as a bricklayer's, roughened by a lifetime of hard work, no matter the heavy and expensive rings he now sported.

"That'd . . . that is the 'Rain-Water' Madeira, David?" Finney inquired, coming to the table to pick up the bottle. "A pleasing and tasty selection, Captain Lewrie. Not as dry as some. Like it?"

"Quite good, yes," Lewrie agreed. "Though a guinea the bottle is a trifle steep, Mister Finney."

"We could arrange split-cases, sir," Finney assured him, pulling out a seat. "Allow me, sir? Thank you. Say, four bottles or so of the Rain-Water, and the rest made up from a lesser vintage, for guests who can't 'preciate the best, ay? Why deprive y'self o' fine port just 'cause ya dine alone aft most o' the time. And is it sailin' soon ya are, Captain Lewrie?" he asked, lapsing into brogue.

There was a craftiness to the set of Finney's eyes, at least to Alan's suspicious imagination. And yet, there was almost a pathetic eagerness, too. The eagerness of a seller, he wondered? The pandering of the outsider towards a better, Lewrie took a moment to sneer? Or that of a basically lonely man risen out of his element and trying to fit in? To make contact with newcomers who didn't spurn him?

"I have no orders at present, but . . ." Lewrie shrugged, giving Finney the same smile he'd bestow upon any acquaintance. "We've been so long at anchor, it's bound to be soon."

"Davie . . ." Finney said, whirling on his chair, "David, bring out last year's Oporto for Captain Lewrie to try. Four shilling the bottle, I'm that sorry t'say, but nigh as tasty, and a grand bargain. Now wot ya say t'that, sir?"

"Mmm, rather nice," Lewrie had to agree. "Let us say eight of this

Oporto, and only four of the better Madeira. And I'll simply have to treat myself less often."

"Done!" Finney exulted, slapping the table top as if he had won a trick at *écarté*. "Now, wot else will ya be desiring?"

Lewrie spent almost an hour in the wine shop with Finney as his eager-to-please host. Away from formal affairs, the salons and dancefloors where he most likely felt strangled and out of place, he proved a likable enough fellow, Alan had to admit, as they compared voyages, ports of call, and past storms, as sailors ever will.

"An' *wuz* ya niver t'India, now!" Finney had exclaimed with joy. "An' Canton, too? Gawd, 'twas a time, a *grand* time, I had 'mongst the heathens meself! Topman, I wuz, then . . . main topmast captain."

Then Finney would catch his accent and affect his more genteel *persona*, striving for more civil speech. Until his next enthusiasm which put the lilt and Gaelic structure to his words again.

"So, your reckoning, sir," Finney said at last, after Alan had made his final selection. "The split case of port, one cask of brandy, two of claret . . . le'ssee, one cask of Bordeaux . . . damn' good St. Emilion, thet is, an' tastes young f'rever. Two cases Rhenish, one of hock, and the odd case of cordials, sherries, Holland gin and such . . ."

Lewrie saw why Finney had such a scrawl for a handwriting—he was a cack-hand, a left-hander! Another unpopular trait to rise above!

"Twenty-four pounds, six shillings, and . . . ah, the divil with it, let's say twenty pound even, an' be square, sir! Ain't that a handsome bargain for ya, now, Captain Lewrie?" Finney loudly decided at last.

That statement, such an eldritch echo of Billy 'Bones' Doyle's own words from the cave at Conch Bar, nearly set Lewrie's nape hairs on end, bringing back his every nagging suspicion.

"Twenty it is, though I fear 'tis at your loss, sir," Lewrie found wit to reply without betraying the cold trill that took him.

"Don't go bruiting it about the town, though, Captain Lewrie," Finney chuckled. "Or the rest'll think they've been cheated. We're to have this delivered aboard *Alacrity* t'day, then?"

"If you could, that would be fine," Lewrie replied.

"A final glass with ya, then, sir," Finney smiled, reaching for a sample bottle of brandy. "Wot yer hunters call a 'stirrup cup'?"

"Topping," Lewrie allowed as Finney filled their glasses.

"Fine little ship you have there, sir," Finney congratulated. "May I be so bold as t'offer a toast, now? To *Alacrity*. Long may she swim in safety on the King's business." They clinked glasses.

"Thankee, Mister Finney."

"Ah, call me John," Finney cajoled. "Or Jack. 'Tis how I'm known best in these islands."

"Jack. Thankee for the thought, then," Lewrie said, restless to leave as Finney became bolder. *Damme, the next I know he'll name me "Alan, old son" and I'll have to be pleasant to him in public, or have him in for a home-cooked supper! Brrr!*

"Before you sail, Captain Lewrie," Finney suggested, "You and your wife must attend one o' my little gatherings. A pleasant meal. Some cards . . . a little dancing, should you be able to stay later."

Aha! Lewrie thought! *So that's your chummy game, is it?*

"I heard you weren't entertaining lately, Jack," Lewrie told him. "Nor do I recall you attending anything in the last week."

"Well, life goes on, don' . . . does it not, sir?" Finney said, eyeing Lewrie sharply, and the geniality leaving those blue eyes.

"I'm told some of the men who were hung once worked with you," Lewrie was emboldened to say, with a sad and sober expression.

"And so they did, sir," Finney told him, speaking slower, and choosing his words and their pronunciation more guardedly. "What my old Gran told me is true, y'know; you can lead a horse to water, but you can't make him drink? There's some in this world will seize an opportunity to better themselves, and some as won't. For privateering, they were a grand crew, all tarry-handed and smart as paint, as willing to dare as any I'd ever seen, sir. When the war ended and I paid 'em off, I told 'em they'd have an honest berth with me whenever they needed it. Some signed on. Some went their own ways."

"Like Doyle," Lewrie needled, sporting a comiserating smile.

"Aye, like William," Finney sighed, looking wistful for what might have been. "Me . . . my bosun at one time. Met him, Lord, thirteen year ago when we were topmen on a Liverpool 'Black-Birder' on the Middle Passage. I made third mate, he made bosun's mate. He was the grandest seaman of all. But not a thinker, God have mercy. You know sailors, Captain Lewrie. They live from shilling to shilling. What would you find of yer fellow men from one of yer old ships, were ya all to get t'gither? Who among 'em'd prospered, and who among 'em'd sunk? The Fleet can't afford t'be picky when it needs seamen, an' I couldn't turn me nose up at the lads as signed aboard with me. And, when ya get right down to it," Finney shrugged with a sad grin, "ya can't be yer brothers' keeper. A man'll go his own way, divil a try ya make t'redeem him."

"Quite so," Lewrie had to agree with the sentiment, and the sense of what Finney said. "Well, I must take my leave, sir. Thank you for a most enjoyable morning, and a most pleasing reckoning."

"Wotiver yer needs, think o' Finney's first," the man insisted as they rose from the table. "There's no finer selection, an' for you and your fine wife, Captain Lewrie, there'll always be some specials held back, at the same pleasin' prices, break me though they might!"

"I shall keep that ever in mind, Mister Finney," Lewrie said.

"You tell yer missus t'try us first, 'stead o' Misick's, or Frith's," Finney rattled on as he walked him toward the door. "Those stores on Shirley Street'd sell 'Ratty' his own hide, charge extra for a good fit, an 'im niver knowin' 'twas skinned soon as he entered their doors!"

"I shall tell her that, sir."

" 'Dobe planters from Santo Domingo, lime fertilizers . . ." Jack Finney rhapsodized about his merchandise. "The latest fashions, just about anything the new homemaker needs for a burgeoning house, for the ball, for . . ."

"Good day, sir," Lewrie beamed, offering his hand, which Jack Finney took and pumped vigorously. "And once again, thankee."

"I've a drum planned for Saturday, sir," Finney announced of a sudden. "I would be honored should you and Mistress Lewrie be able to attend. Late afternoon's cool, stand-up buffet, champagne . . ."

"Ah, I fear not," Lewrie replied, though they had no current plans for the weekend. "Should *Alacrity* still be in port, we will dine some guests in on Saturday," Alan lied easily. "There's a scheme afoot to introduce my first officer Lieutenant Ballard to a young lady of our acquaintance, and see how they progress over cards and music. A fearsome business! But, let a young wife see others unattached, and . . ." he concluded, making a face and faking a shiver. "Some other time would be more convenient, perhaps?"

"Some other time, then, sir," Finney replied with a shrug of his own, finally dropping Alan's hand. "And good day to you, sir, and thank you for your trade. Do come again, mind."

Lewrie stepped out the door which David the wine clerk held for him, doffed his hat in farewell once more, and strode away toward his horse. He undid the reins from the hitch-rail and looked across the saddle towards Finney's store idly as he fumbled with a stirrup.

Finney stood just inside the still-open door. In an unguarded moment, before he realized that Alan had glanced back at him, he was caught glaring at him from beneath blond brows beetled together with hate. And when caught, Finney put a shadowing palm over his eyes, as if the sun's glare had caused it, made his face bland with a smile of seeming sincerity, and used that shadowing hand to wave him goodbye.

Chapter 4

"You shopped at Finney's?" Caroline goggled once he was home. "Whatever possessed you to enter that man's stores, Alan?"

"Call it curiosity, my dear," he allowed, stripping off his coat and waistcoat, undoing his neckstock and taking his ease in a chair on the front porch where it was cool. Caroline had a pitcher of sweetened limewater near at hand. "Damme if he didn't have good prices, too. And a wider selection. You do not?"

"Only with Wyonnie to accompany me," she frowned. "I find good bargains along the docks, directly off the trading ships."

"Uhm, Caroline, those that sell direct off the ships . . ." Alan complained. "Those goods aren't landed or bonded. The imposts aren't paid. Those are Yankee traders!"

"So I noticed," she grinned between sips of limewater.

"They're violating the Navigation Acts, Caroline," he pressed. "Laws I'm sworn to enforce! Damme . . . dash it all, how does it appear, for the wife of an officer holding the King's Commission, to . . . to . . . !"

"Commodore Garvey's wife shops right alongside me, Alan," she told him. "As does the cook from the Governor's mansion, the butlers for every household that've ever invited us, the . . ."

"Well, I'm damned!"

"Would you rather have my eight pounds gone in a twinkling at Bay Street or Shirley Street shops, then, Alan?" she queried without a qualm.

"Do you need more money, then?" he asked.

"Not a farthing!" she chuckled, leaning back into a chair and putting her feet up on a padded footstool. "Darling, I manage quite well, with more than enough left over at the end of each month. But I could not without seeking out bargains. Alan, I will not break you to support me. I am not spendthrift."

"I know that, Caroline," he softened, reaching out to take her free hand. "And I'd not begrudge you our entire savings, were you to need it."

"I know that, too, love," she purred. "And that is why I will never ask of you until it is needful. I am quite content on my house allowance. And too much in love with you to ever wish to lose your regard by being extravagant. I don't think I'm much for extravagance, anyway," she chuckled. "I'm a country girl at heart."

"I love you, too, dear, for so many reasons," he cooed back to her. "Every day I recognize one more."

"I shall send Wyonnie and her husband to shop the docks for me in future, then, love," Caroline promised. "So we do not give the impression that you condone anything illegal. Now it's cooler, I'll bake more at home, 'stead of buying bread from the baker's. Though summers I will have to trade with the bakeshops. And local dishes are tasty and filling. I need no heavy imported dishes when fish, rice and all are just as nourishing, and the open-air markets are much cheaper. I *love* it here in the Bahamas! And Shirley Street stores are closer and just as economical, if one looks carefully at imported goods."

"Misick's and Frith's," Alan nodded in agreement.

"How did you know where I market, Alan? Have their bills at the end of the month bothered you?" she teased.

"I heard they're a little higher than Finney's, but not so dear as to rival Bay Street," Alan stumbled, feeling a flush of color as he wondered just how Jack Finney had known the exact stores she favored.

Damme, has the man been following her? he shuddered.

"I have a surprise for you, dear," Caroline blushed. "Two, to be truthful. Sit right there and close your eyes."

Hope 'tis a better surprise than the ones I've had this morning, Alan thought, going back over his long conversation with Finney.

"I know Christmas is supposed to be a time of sober reflection, and in England, people spend it with their noses in the prayer book," she said as she came back to the front porch. "No, keep your eyes shut for a space longer!"

She bent down to kiss him for a moment, giggling at his temporary helplessness, and mistaking his agitation for impatience.

"But the Klausknitzers, that German couple, have the most wonderful traditions. That carpenter fellow who made these chairs? They exchange gifts such as the Magi brought the infant Jesus, Alan, and I thought it a grand idea. And the perfect season for mine to you."

"May I look now?" he grinned.

"Now."

First he beheld a shiny tube that she held out to him.

"A flageolet," she said proudly. "Made from tin. You always said you wished you could play a musical instrument, and I thought it the perfect one. There's a little chapbook of tunes and instructions in how to read musical notes."

Now *there's* reason for a crew to mutiny, Alan thought, though smiling happily! I'll make a bloody nuisance of myself, bad as some noisome Welsh harpist!

"Darling, it's wonderful, I had no idea . . . !" he said instead.

"And this," she said, sweeping a drop cloth away from something that was leaned on one of the support posts.

"Gawd!" he could but exclaim in awe.

What he beheld was Caroline's portrait, an oval-framed oil of her from the waist up. She was depicted standing in her flower garden by the front gate, dressed in a gauzy white off-shoulder sack gown and flowered straw hat. Potter's Cay and Hog Island were hinted in the background behind overhanging tropical flowers and palmettos in a hazy spring morning.

"Damme, that's *Alacrity* anchored there!" he gasped out first, as he recognized the ketch in the far background which flew the Red Ensign and streamed a red-white-blue commissioning pendant.

Bloody hell, wrong thing to say, he winced within himself!

"My God, Caroline, the artist has captured you to the life, I swear," he added quickly, kneeling down to look closer. "Why, he did you so true I'd expect your eyes here to blink any moment. And he caught your smile perfectly! 'Tis like having you looking at me from your mirror scantwise, as you do of a morning. When you're looking pleased and full of ginger!"

"I told you Augustus Hedley was a wonderful artist."

Alan rose and took her in his arms, lifting her off her feet to swing her about as he kissed her.

"I take back everything I ever said about him, darling," Alan laughed heartily. "You're right, as always. He is damned good!"

Alan had been married long enough to know to forbear mention that the waters east of Potter's Cay were too shallow for anchoring, or that *Alacrity* did not sport t'gallant yards above her tops'ls.

"Darling Alan, do you really like it?" she teased.

"Like it? God yes, what a magnificent gift!" he assured her. "Now, every time I look up from my desk, or dine in my cabins, I'll have you there, so fresh and lovely I'll ache for want of you."

"Mmm, having you ache, and miss me when you're at sea was my main idea, darling," she murmured coyly in his ear. "Do you still begrudge giving up your awful old harem picture, hmm?"

"Not one whit."

"Augustus'd done so many island scenes, he practically gave our *Sunset Over Nassau Harbour* away in trade," she boasted, pleased with herself, and with his enthusiastic reaction to her gift. "And he did my portrait for only five pounds, and a dozen crocks of my pineapple marmalade. Now, am I not economical, my love?"

"Uncle Phineas would be proud of you," Alan snickered as he let her down to her feet again, though still draped against him. "I am, too. There's only one place I know you to be a spendthrift. And thank God for it!"

"You don't have to go aboard ship until after dinner?" Caroline whispered with a suggestive smile. "Then why do we not go and be spendthrift for the rest of the morning?"

"That's my lass!" he beamed, lifting her off her feet again to carry her inside.

"Bring the portrait," she said between long, seductive kisses. "We'll stand it up against my dressing table mirror and see if I look as full of ginger as you think."

Chapter 5

"Oh, poor little fellow," Midshipman Parham said to himself as William Pitt escaped the great-cabins by the quarter-deck ladder and sat on the deck to scratch at his good ear. The sound of their captain practicing the scale on his tin flageolet came stumbling to their ears through the open skylights aft. "Sound like another ram-cat to you, does it, poor puss? Poor afterguard. Poor me!"

"And I thought you would appreciate music, Mister Parham," Lieutenant Ballard said, hands behind his back and rocking back and forth on the balls of his feet as *Alacrity* rolled along.

"Music, aye, sir, but . . ." Parham shrugged as he grimaced his opinion. Below, Lewrie broke off doing scales and started a halting attempt at the chorus from "The Jacobite Lass", which prompted their surgeon's mate Mr. MacIntyre to sing along, equally badly.

I gi'ed ma love, the white white rose,
that's growin' at ma father's wa.
It is the bonniest flow'r that grows
where ilka flow'r is braw.
There's but ae bonnier that I ken,
fae Perth unto the main,
an' that's the flow'r o' Scotland's men
that's fechtin' for his ain.

"Oh, don't encourage him, Mister MacIntyre," Parham tittered. "Lord, Mister Ballard, sir. The captain cannot play, and Mister MacIntyre can neither sing, nor speak the King's English of a sudden. A proper shambles, that is."

"That's enough, that is, Mister Parham," Ballard smirked.

"And a Jacobite tune, too, sir," Parham continued. "Disloyal to King George, is it not, Mister MacIntyre?"

"*Next* time ye hae a boil on yer bum, Mister Parham," MacIntyre warned, "'Twill be ma dullest lancet, an' I'll nae be gentle!"

"Masthead, Mister Parham?" Ballard intoned with a cock of his head and frown enough to let him know his antics had best stop.

There was another verse, without vocal accompaniment this time, before the music ended with an embarassed cough. Lewrie emerged on deck moments later in breeches and shirt, and looked around as the afterguard and watch-standers suddenly found something vital to do, or something fascinating to see over the side.

"Sea's getting up," Lewrie stated, scanning the horizon about them. "She swims a mite more boisterous than in the forenoon."

"Aye, sir," Lieutenant Ballard replied primly. "Winds are yet steady from the nor'east. Some backing in the gusts to east. Might be half a gale, no more, sir. The weather horizon's clear, for now, though we are getting whitecaps now and again."

The rigging whined with a sudden gust of wind that came more from the east, with perhaps a touch of southing. *Alacrity* rolled a bit more as the winds picked up from astern, and the normally lumpy waters of the Northwest Providence Channel were now long sets of rollers, windward faces rippled like hides by the gusts, and capped with white spume where a borning chop collided with itself.

"Smell rain, Mister Fellows?" Lewrie asked, twitching his nose aweather as the gust faded and the winds clocked back to the expected nor'east of the Trades.

"Sweet water somewhere, captain," Fellows agreed. "Just a hint now and again. I'd wager squalls by seven bells."

"Have the hands eat?" Lewrie inquired.

"Aye, sir," Ballard reported.

"Topmen aloft, then. Take in the tops'ls and brail up secure. Then we'll have gun drill as we planned. But no more than one hour." Lewrie ordered, face wrinkled wary. "We'll practice wearing ship to either beam and firing broadsides at a chase."

"Aye, aye, sir," Ballard agreed. "Bosun, pipe 'All Hands!' Do you send topmen aloft! Trice up, lay out and brail up tops'ls!"

"If this is a late cyclone, Mister Fellows, could we shelter in a hurricane hole on Grand Bahama north of us?" Lewrie asked as the men thundered up from the mess deck. "What about Hawk's Bill Creek?"

"Hmm," Fellows squinted, taking off his cocked hat to scratch at his gingery scalp. "Do we stand on west-nor'west the rest of the day, sir, we'd be too far to loo'rd of Hawk's Bill Creek, and would have to beat back to it, with Grand Bahama a lee shore to larboard. And Grand Bahama's a graveyard for an hundred ships caught such. Nasty coast in a southerly wind. But . . . Cross Bay on the western tip should be abeam by late afternoon, sir. 'Round behind Settlement Point in Cross Bay, there's good holding ground. Low-lying land, with nothing to break a gale, but much calmer waters behind the breakers and mangrove swamps."

"Keep that in mind, if this isn't your regular gale. We could ride a gale out, reaching south. After gun drill, we'll lay out four anchor cables, just to be safe," Lewrie decided.

"Very well, sir," Fellows agreed.

By six bells of the day watch, three in the afternoon, it was clear that this was no average tropic squall line. The horizon astern had darkened to a deep slate gray, shot through with ragged sizzles of distant lightning at the base. The high-piled white clouds of morning had turned gray and lowering, and raced themselves overhead to loo'rd. They took in the outer jibs, reefed the gaff courses once, then for a second time, before wearing ship north for shelter, with *Alacrity* laid over on her larboard side, the wake creaming within arm's reach of the deck as she swooped and bounded fast as a Cambridge Coach, darting for safety like a low-flying tern. It was one thing to trust their stout little vessel in deep water in a full gale, but this had the smell of a bad 'un . . . an out-of-season hurricane.

The first sprinkles of rain hit them as they beat into harbour around Settlement Point, short-tacking easterly, and the wind gusted from the east-sou'east hard enough to make it difficult to breathe.

"About here, sir!" Fellows had to shout in Lewrie's ear. "Best bower, then second bower out there, to south'rd of the first!"

"Ready, forrud!" Lewrie yelled through a speaking trumpet. "Mister Neill, be ready to tack her. Ready, Mister Harkin? Helm up and meet her 'midships! Jesus, let go forrud!"

Alacrity rounded up, everything lashing and flogging, and came to a stop in her own length against the winds as the best bower anchor splashed into the harbour.

"Larboard your helm! Let go main course halyards! Back forrud sheets!" Lewrie called. *Alacrity* almost spun like a fallen leaf over to the opposite tack, and began to sail away to starboard, driven by a triple-reefed after-course and an inner jib reduced to little more than a storm trys'l, the best bower hawser paying off abeam, howling through the hawsehole! "Round up, Mister Neill! Meet her! Let go second bower!"

And pray both the bitches bite, Lewrie thought, as *Alacrity* paid off the wind, with both anchors out, each placed forty-five degrees off her bows!

"Hand the courses, hand the jibs!"

Down came the last scraps of sail, leaving *Alacrity* drifting to the west, at the mercy of Cross Bay's sandy bottom. Should the anchors fail to hold, she would be wafted onto coral a couple of miles astern before they could get a way on her again!

She snubbed! The best bower anchor, weighted with thirty feet of fist-thick chain and a two-pounder brass boat-gun to ease the jerking which might dislodge the flukes had held! And a moment later, so did the second bower, similarly weighted on its rode.

"Mister Harkin, pay out half a cable on each hawser and even the scopes!" Lewrie called, then turned to Ballard. "You wanted delegated action at Conch Bar, Mister Ballard? Now you have it! Off you go! Make it quick before the storm's really upon us!"

"Aye, aye, sir!" Ballard replied, summoning his boat crews. They would row out the stream and kedge anchors from astern and set them down to match the angles from the bow cables. "Cony, Odrado, let's go!"

It took an hour of juggling and pulley-hauley to equalize scope on the cables. By then, as the hands fell exhausted from the capstans, the storm was upon them, and a curtain of furious rain sheeted over the decks, blanking out all vision beyond a couple of feet, blowing so hard it was nearly horizontal. Lightning forked and arced around them, one explosion striking the island, the next so close-aboard their hair went on end, and the thunderclaps were so loud and continuous it felt like *Alacrity* was being hulled by thirty-two-pounder fortress guns, making the deck tremble and leap as the rigging and masts wailed an unearthly, eldritch chorus of harpy's shrieks.

Lewrie was wet right through, the rain driving past tarred tarpaulin coat and hat like they were gauze, soaking breeches and shirt. Cool as the rain was in the winds, he was clammy and hot beneath, and stiff with blown salt water, cloth flogging painfully.

With the storm had come unnatural, eerie nightfall, a yellow-green dusk torn by lightning bursts on either hand. Trees ashore bent and tossed, sickly green. Palmetto fronds and leaves came slapping in the air to cling wetly for a moment, then be torn away to swirl aft.

Alacrity jerked, trembled and snubbed on bow cables, on stern cables, tossing her head like a colt being held to be saddled.

"What's astern should we drag?" Alan asked Fellows in one of the few partings of the rain in which they could take bearings.

"Little Bahama Bank, sir!" Fellows shouted back. "What the Dons called 'The Great Shallows'! Miles and miles of coral heads and reefs!"

Alacrity was whirled by a gust, drove forward, and snubbed on a stern cable hard enough to make them stumble before paying back to jerk on best bower, then second bower, making the cables groan on the bitts!

Hellish sunset became black night, blue black with lightning frying iron gray rain clouds that brushed the mast-trucks, with the winds moaning all about like a witches' coven. But it was not a cyclone, not a hurricane —just a terrifying winter storm, and it finally blew out by four bells of the evening watch. The rain drummed vertical and with less punishing force, thinned at last, then ceased. The clouds parted to the east, revealing a late moon and a few kindly stars, even though Cross Bay still tossed and churned, and *Alacrity* continued to quiver.

Soon, the winds eased to half a gale, with lulls between gusts. They could see the storm astern now, a spectral sea battle raging on the leeward horizon as it tore across the Gulf Stream and the Florida Channel, a wall of blackness supported by a thousand legs of flaring lightning strokes, like blue fires on dark velvet.

"Not a millpond yet, sir," Ballard commented, grunting with a weariness brought on by tension and fear. "But it's over, praise God."

"Calm enough to suit me, Arthur," Lewrie muttered. "You turn in and get some rest. Set regular anchor watches and a harbour watch. I think our people have earned some sleep at last."

"And you, sir?" Ballard inquired.

"Dry clothes, and a boat cloak, and I'll doss down in my deck chair. I'll take the middle watch," Lewrie offered, aching though he was with exhaustion, and the blessed release of being spared disaster.

"No, sir, you turn in," Ballard objected almost truculently. "I normally stand the middle."

"Damme, Arthur, you're silly enough to offer, I'll give you no arguments," Lewrie smiled for the first time since midday. "Call me at eight bells, my 'normal' time, then."

"Aye, aye, Alan. Our normal routine," Ballard said shyly.

"And damned glad of it!" Lewrie commented as he went below.

Chapter 6

There were, for once, lashings of fresh water aboard, sluiced into barrels from all the rain, and Lewrie, after waking from gummy-eyed sleep, was enjoying the pleasure of a bath from a lavish five-gallon bucket, when he heard a lookout cry that a ship was entering harbour.

He dressed quickly in clean clothing and dashed to the deck.

"Warship, sir," Lieutenant Ballard informed him as he lowered his telescope. "A sloop of war. *Whippet*, I do avow."

Lewrie borrowed the telescope to eye her himself. Yes, it was Commander Benjamin Rodgers's *Whippet*, of the bright red gunwales and a lower-steeved jib boom than the older sloop of war on station. A recognition signal flag flew from her main yard.

"Mister Mayhew, hoist this month's private signal in reply," Lewrie ordered. He gave Ballard his telescope back and scratched his chin, which still wanted shaving. "Cony, we'll breakfast Commander Rodgers, more'n like. And where's my coffee?"

" 'Tis a'comin' this minute, sir," Cony assured him.

" 'Nother hoist, sir!" Mayhew piped from the bulwarks, clinging to the starboard stays. "She's flying 'Make Sail', sir. And here is a third, sir! 'Take Station on Me'!"

"Then we won't have breakfast ourselves," Lewrie spat. "Mister Ballard, pipe 'All Hands' and prepare to single up to the best bower. Mister Mayhew? Hoist 'Anchor,' then numeral Four, and hope he gets our sense."

Whippet prowled north and south off the coast, with 'Make Haste' flying continually, until *Alacrity* had taken in all her anchors, made sail, and joined her. Once out of harbor, *Whippet* hoisted 'Captain Repair On Board' and left it flying until Lewrie was in his gig, and being rowed across to her.

"Took you long enough," Rodgers commented sourly, so unlike his usual merry style.

"Your pardons, sir, but I had four anchors to get up after we took refuge from the storm last night. I trust our signals . . ."

"What, you no-sailor, you!" Rodgers laughed suddenly, becoming his charming self again. "Runnin' into a hurricane hole at the first half-gale? What's the Navy comin' to, I ask you?"

"You rode it out, I see, sir," Lewrie said, peering about the deck at the sailmaker and his crew who were stitching madly, at the hands aloft still reeving new stays and halyards.

"Had to lay-to with a single trys'l jib, a Spanish-reefed main tops'l, and the spanker at three reefs," Rodgers boasted. "Put out a sea anchor, and I was just about ready to spill ev'ry drop of oil we had before the storm passed. Nasty one. Had I been closer inshore, I'd have been tempted. Damaged, are you?"

"No, sir. Small stuff, mostly, easily set right."

"Good!" Rodgers exulted, cracking his palms together. "Damned good! There's work afoot, Lewrie! More bloody pirates!"

"Didn't know there was winter traffic enough to prey on, sir."

"Ran across a Spanish three-master yesterday off Great Isaac at the mouth of the Providence Channel. Thought it suspicious that she was makin' nor-nor'east closehauled, as if she were goin' to put in for Grand Bahama, when there's not much here. Smugglers or banned traders, I thought at first. But when we got her hull-up, we saw a schooner with her, and then she flies up in-irons and all-aback, and the schooner scoots off north fast as her little legs'd carry her. She'd been pirated, by God! Chased them until the storm came up, and then it was 'save y'rself'!"

"Might have gone down in the storm, sir," Lewrie suggested.

"Only port on their course was here by Settlement Point, where they could strip their prize in private," Rodgers went on. "That's why I peeked in here, t'see if they'd sheltered an' hadn't cleared harbour yet. You saw no other vessel at all?"

"Once we got the anchors set, I couldn't see farther than the end of my arm for all the rain, sir," Lewrie had to admit. "No."

"Damn!" Rodgers spat, all but stamping his foot on the deck in frustration. "Damn!" he reiterated. "She was too small to ride out a storm like that. Smaller'n your little *Alacrity*. I was so sure . . ."

"Might have sheltered 'round north of us, sir, nearer the Bank, and we'd never have known it," Lewrie commiserated. "By Indian Cay."

Damme, all this folderol for nothing, then, he griped to himself? And I still haven't had me breakfast! Hmm . . . still . . . !

"Ah, sir," Lewrie added. "You took their prize back, and they were running here."

"The storm, dammit!" Rodgers groused.

"Not in the morning, sir," Lewrie said slyly. "And once they were aware a storm was building, they *still* ran for a lee shore during the afternoon? Doesn't make sense. Unless they had someplace specific in mind. Some hidey-hole. An uninhabited cay somewhere in the Little Bahama Bank where they felt snug. And a place to ride out a storm."

"Damme, but you're a knacky 'un, Lewrie! Of course!" Rodgers realized with a grin. "Where they thought *Whippet* couldn't follow 'em! You were right about Doyle's hideout, you may be right in this. Now look you here, sir."

"Aye, sir?"

"I draw twelve feet forrud, so I dasn't risk the Banks, but I could cruise offshore. You draw . . . ?"

"Eight and a half, sir," Lewrie replied, getting a sudden onset of nerves. Damme, here we go again, tiptoeing through coral!

"North of Memory Rock yonder, there's a ten-fathom pass," Commander Rodgers schemed, oblivious to the harm *Alacrity* might suffer on this mission. "Mister Cargyle! Chart!" he shouted over his shoulder to summon his sailing master the way one would shout for a slow-coach waiter. "Ah, here! We *both* could enter. I'll take the deeper water between Middle Shoal and the Lily Sand Bank, nor'east across the Bank to just north of Matanilla Reef. *Alacrity* will go inshore of me to exit through the Walker's Cay Channel farther south and east, and we meet up there. Then we'll both have a peek at Walker's Cay. 'Tis a famous pirate's lair of old. Mayhap these buggers're usin' it again!"

"Aye, aye, sir," Lewrie answered, knowing what Lieutenant Coltrop down in the Turks had felt like at last.

"Don't get too close to Walker's Cay, don't spook 'em out too soon, Captain Lewrie," Rodgers warned him. "If they're there."

"Should I be so fortunate as to get across the Bank in a whole vessel, I'll not, sir," Lewrie commented wryly.

"Still have that Trinity House sailing master Gatacre aboard?"

"No, sir," Lewrie sighed. "Commodore Garvey promoted his first officer off *Royal Arthur* into the schooner I took, and sent 'Dread-Nought' away to survey the east coast of Andros."

"So Lieutenant Garvey is now third in *Royal Arthur!*" Rodgers grunted.

"Rising like a spring tide, his career does, sir."

"Gawd, old 'Horry' must bloody love *you* these days!" Rodgers laughed. "Right, then! Off you get. Trinity House pilot or no."

"Aye, aye, sir."

Lewrie scrambled over the side into the stern sheets of his gig for a lumpy ride back to *Alacrity* after the salute had been paid to him. The sea was still fractious in the wake of the storm, and he held on for dear life.

At last, he thought, though; I'll get my coffee, my shave, and my bloody breakfast!

Chapter 7

As the crow flies, it was only forty miles sailing from the deep-water entrance on the western side of the Little Bahama Bank, roughly eight miles north of Memory Rock, to deep water on the east side, in the middle of Walker's Cay Channel.

In the wake of the storm, though, the winds had gone lunatic. One hour they might have nor'easterlies, the next hour they'd clock around from the north or the nor'west. The morning's watch had been sailed roughly closehauled to weather, but in the afternoon, they even had winds up the stern from the west.

It took *Alacrity* all that first day to navigate her way eastward to the

Lily Bank in waters than ran from twenty-seven to thirty feet deep, but
near sunset, they encountered shallows not fifteen feet deep, and there
was no pass through the Lily Bank and its myriad sand bars which lay
bare or awash, with thousands of sea birds crying and wheeling over
them as they fed on tiny reef fish or mollusks.

They anchored at true dark at about 78°32′ west and 27°10′ north at
the Lily Bank's southeast extremity, having covered only a heartbreak-
ing thirty-two miles, eight tantalizing miles short of Walker's Cay.

Just a bit before sunrise the next morning, they found depth enough
and open water to the northeast, except for one quick fright when it
shoaled around a circular submerged outcropping from eighteen feet
deep to a bare ten. Then, within musket-shot of the northern side of
Walker's Cay Channel, they'd shaved the topaz shallows of Matanilla
Reef's southernmost tip to give the island a wide enough berth so any
pirates in harbour would not be alerted, but giving *Alacrity*'s lookouts a
chance to spy out the anchorages.

They then headed out to sea to meet *Whippet* and report.

"Your schooner is there, sir!" Lewrie told Rodgers in his cabin, which
Lewrie had to admit was even fancier than his own. "May not be your
pirate schooner, but a schooner. And a three-masted ship, too."

"How near did you go?" Rodgers fretted. "Think they saw you?"

"No, sir," Lewrie grinned. "We struck our topmasts and reefed the gaff
courses and jibs low to the deck, then kept off seven miles, with only our
lower masts and fighting tops showing. They showed no sign of alarm,
long as we had 'em in sight."

"Damned good, Lewrie!" Rodgers nodded in relief. "They must think
we're still huntin' 'em off Grand Bahama, or goin' all the way north-
about outside the Little Bahama Banks. Where exactly?"

Lewrie spun the chart around on the table, so everyone could have a
good view; he and Rodgers, the sailing masters Fellows and Cargyle, and
the first officers.

"They're in this long tongue-shaped inlet north and west of the island
proper, sir," Lewrie sketched out. "They've rocks and shoals to their
nor'west on the east side of Walker's Cay Channel, coral and exposed
rocks north, and shallows on the east to Seal Cay. But there is a chain of
tiny islets running nor'west from the western tip of the island. They're
anchored here, half a mile or less off the beach by the last one west.
They must have fifteen to eighteen feet depth in there, sir."

"Sand bars on the south side of Walker's Cay, too, sir," John Fellows stuck in. "They trail off south then east all the way to this Grand Cay. And there's reputed to be a one-fathom shoal sou'west of the island. About here, perhaps. Making one entrance channel into their sheltered inlet off those islets, sir."

Lewrie thought it odd that Cargyle said nothing at all, but he put that down to the man having been daunted by Rodgers's aggressive personality in the past. He thought it an unproductive relationship.

"They're in a cul-de-sac!" Rodgers elated. "If that shoal you suspect does lie to the sou'west, Mister Fellows, then there are only two escape routes. They come to deep water in Walker's Cay Channel and run out that way, or they take the eastern side of your shoal back down south over the Little Bahama Bank again. How big is it?"

"No one knows, sir, sorry to say," Fellows fidgeted nervously. "But . . . from the south end of *this* shoal nor'west of the island, one could reasonably expect a channel into the anchorage, and this long tongue inlet where they are moored of perhaps . . . mile and a half?"

"And were *Whippet* to be in the middle of that channel north of your mysterious shoal at dawn, her guns could cover anything that moved!" Rodgers sighed with pleasure. "And here is where I wish your *Alacrity* on the morrow, Captain Lewrie!"

Oh, bloody suffering Hell, Alan thought as he saw where Commander Rodgers was jabbing at the chart.

"You enter Walker's Cay Channel ahead of us, go south and east until you get 'round the six-foot shoal that forms the two channels, and block the southern one. Your guns have as much reach as mine, so we have them between us to squeeze! If they can anchor a proper ship that far up this tongue of deep water, then we can sail right up and give 'em broadsides at pistol-shot range from two directions."

"I see, sir," Lewrie nodded.

"Feel game for one more quadrille 'cross this bloody little pond, sir?" Rodgers demanded, much amused.

"Of course, sir!" Lewrie replied with false ardor. To get to the desired position by sunrise, and sunrise would be best if Rodgers wished tactical surprise, he would have to take *Alacrity* back through the three-mile span of Walker's Cay Channel *in the dark*, grope about like a blind man with a cane tapping against the curbs and cobbles, avoid a shoal no one knew the extent of, then round it and feel his way into artillery range in that southern channel which could not be a mile wide at best!

Now I know why Lieutenant Coltrop turned so pale, Alan thought! This is going to be trickier than falling downriver from Chatham from one stream anchor's grapple to the next! At least *sane* people try that in broad daylight!"

"That's my lad, Captain Lewrie!" Rodgers praised. "I knew you had the bottom for it!"

"Long as I have a bottom under me by tomorrow noon, sir," he rejoined with a wry expression.

"And a half, two!" the leadsman cried mournfully, telling his depth marks by feel on the lead line. *Alacrity* showed but one light on the quarter-deck, the lantern in the compass binnacle, and even it was shielded by a tent of canvas.

"Bloody wonderful," Lewrie complained softly. "Wind's right up our arse. The current's running dead-set against us. And the chip log's no clue to our speed, 'less we take time to anchor and measure the flow. And to top it off, 'tis darker than a cow's gut tonight!"

"Who'd be a seaman, hey, sir?" Arthur Ballard chuckled back.

Ballard had the sometimes infuriating capacity to take a great deal of joy in having his seamanship tested to the ultimate by what a reasonable man would have thought a stomach-churning horror. Lewrie would have put it down as insanity, or sublime ignorance of the consequences had he not seen Ballard's keen intellect at work, judging to a nicety his own, and the ship's, limits. Infuriating he might be, but Alan was beginning to find Arthur Ballard a calming influence for his own "windier" moments. As long as Arthur Ballard was composed, he could assume there wasn't much to get panicked about!

"We should be southerly 'nough now, sir," Fellows muttered from the darkness. "Walker's Cay should be nor'east of us, and astern."

"Very well, Mister Fellows," Lewrie allowed. "Mister Ballard, time to alter course. Lay us abeam the wind, course due east."

"Aye, aye, sir," Ballard replied, sounding game for anything. "Bosun, no pipes. Hand to the sheets and braces. Off belays and haul taut, ready to come about."

"Two fathom!" the leadsman called out forward.

"Helm alee, Mister Neill," Ballard commanded. "Course due east. Nothing to weather. Ease sheets and braces, Mister Harkin!"

Alacrity came about slowly, with care, her rehoisted tops'l yards creaking, her courses rustling and mewing as the wooden balls of the hanks that bound sails' luffs and boom throats to the lower mast shifted to a new angle. Blocks squealed aloft as the tops'l lift lines were run to level the upper yards level to the sea for a more efficient use of the night-wind's power. Gaffs and booms gave out croaks as they bound for a moment as they tilted.

They'd been running before a northerly wind, sailing no faster than it could blow. Now, with wind-abeam, they could feel the night's close, balmy tropic damp turn just the slightest bit chill as the wind soughed across the deck. *Alacrity* began to pick up a little speed as well, her bow rising and dipping.

And then it dipped, rose . . . and stayed there!

"*One* fathom, Christ!" the leadsman wailed.

Well, shit, we've run her aground! Lewrie groaned silently. He had been filled with so much tension, so much dread of ripping her hull open on coral, that a soft, almost unfelt grounding on mud and sand was a relief, and he found himself almost shivering with humor.

"B'lieve we found that *shoal* for you, Mister Fellows," he said with a lazy drawl, loud enough for everyone aft to hear, and the deck exploded with nervous laughter.

"Ahem," Fellows grunted in the dark. "Shit!"

"Grounded gentle enough, though," Lewrie said, going to the side to peer over to leeward. Dark as the night was, he could see, or only imagined he could see, a faint, rippling line of disturbance, lit with eery phosphorescence that ran south and east from *Alacrity*'s bows as the northward-set current brushed the shoal and folded back under and over itself. He walked back toward his staff's shadows.

"Mister Ballard, let go course sheets, so she won't drive forrud. Flat-in the jibs. The wind will push the bows south, and this current may be strong enough to walk the stern north to ease us off."

"Aye, aye, sir. Fo'c's'le captain, flat-in yer sheets!"

"Mister Parham, what's the chip log doing?" Lewrie asked.

"Streaming abeam to weather, sir," the midshipman answered from the taffrail at the very stern.

"Long as we're not *going* anywhere for a few minutes, take a cast of the log, Mister Parham, and determine the current," Lewrie said calmly, grinning widely.

Damme, I must be getting right good at this nautical humbug, he told himself; I haven't cursed or yelped yet!

With her fore-topmast stays'l run up and flatted-in with the inner and outer flying jibs for leverage, *Alacrity* began to shuffle, to slowly pivot about on her bows, with the current shoving against her side.

"Helm up hard aweather," Lewrie ordered to assist the current.

"Knot and a quarter, near as I can make it, sir," Parham told him a few minutes later.

"Thankee, Mister Parham. That'll require we steer a point, or point and a half to loo'rd to make due east, Mister Neill."

"Aye, aye, sir," the senior quartermaster responded stolidly.

There was a shudder, a faint groan, and a rushing noise over the side as the bows came off at last, and *Alacrity* began to sail to the south once more, leaving behind a swirling eddy of mud and sand.

"Due south, nothing to larboard for now. Sheet home courses for a run, Mister Ballard. Mister Fellows, do you think we should let her have her head for at least a mile before we try that again?"

"Aye, sir," Fellows replied. "And sou'east at first, sir, not due east. Just in case."

"Very good, Mister Fellows. Carry on, Mister Ballard," Lewrie replied. "Oh, one more thing, Mister Ballard."

"Sir?"

"Damned odd, but it's so dark tonight, I thought I could see a trail of blue or green fire in the water, where the shoal was, right along the edge. As our wake appears in tropic waters sometimes. Do you see it out there, sir?"

"Uhm . . . not really, sir."

"Who among the hands has remarkable eyesight?"

"Mister Early, the quartermaster's mate, sir," Ballard replied, shivering with a touch of awe.

"Post him amidships on the larboard gangway to windward, facing the shoal out yonder. Have him sing out should we have to bear away if it gets too near. Summon him, and I'll point it out to him."

"Aye, aye, sir!" Ballard gulped. He'd heard tales of such feats, the uncanny lore of the truly great old seamen, had thought he had some touch of the gifts sometimes, such as in almost being able to feel the return scend against the hull of waves rebounding from unseen land.

But he never thought to see them in such a casual captain as their idle, devil-may-care "Ram-Cat" Lewrie!

"Damme, but we got away with one that time, did we not, sirs?" Lewrie chuckled, breezy with relief and filled with good humor still.

"Aye, sir."

"Hellish good fun, for a time, too, damme if it wasn't!"

"Oh, aye, sir," Mr. Fellows groaned. "Fun!"

Chapter 8

"Hands is eat, sir. Galley fire's doused overside. An' it lacks a quarter-hour to proper sunrise at six bells, sir," the bosun Harkin reported.

"Very well, and thank you, Mister Harkin," Lewrie replied as he hitched his sword's slim baldric into a more comfortable position under his coat. "Mister Ballard, hands to stations to hoist anchor and get under way."

"Aye, aye, sir."

Alacrity had been anchored with her bows pointed north toward Walker's Cay, three miles south of the island, a mile short of where the southern channel narrowed. They hauled her up to her bower with muscle power on the capstan and the help of the current, letting out the stream hawser as they went. Sails were hoisted and sheeted home, and as she strained to begin sailing, they buoyed the bitter-end of the stream cable, let it slip, and were under way in a twinkling.

The winds were more nor'westerly that morning, which would be a "dead muzzler" for any ship attempting to flee out the channel that led west from the anchorage and into Walker's Cay Channel. To short-tack in such a narrow gut would be an invitation to disaster, so one escape route was effectively blocked already, and *Whippet* would have the winds large on her larboard quarter when she drove down the passage with her nine-pounder carriage guns run out and loaded.

"Mister Ballard, beat to quarters," Lewrie snapped. His men were ready, knowing what the morning would hold. They were blooded by one success, and trained by constant practice to a high level of proficiency. They were almost cheerful as they cast off the lashings of the artillery, rolled them back to loading positions inboard and prepared their pieces for firing.

"Wind's backed a piece," Fellows commented, eyeing the commissioning pendant aloft as it swung to stream more abeam. "And holding. Might have westerlies once the sun's up and hot."

"Better that than heading us and short-tacking up this damned channel," Lewrie agreed, smiling in anticipation. He felt there was something most agreeable about having Rodgers in command, with none of the awesome burden of decision upon his shoulders this once, and a clear and subordinate role to play. After his independent cruise in the Caicos, this was as easy as sailing with a full squadron.

"*Whippet!*" the lookout shouted from aloft. "Four points off the larboard bows, 'bout three mile off, sir! Enterin' the pass!"

"Got 'em, by Jesus!" Fellows cheered.

"That puts us about . . . four miles south of their anchorage?" Lewrie guessed. "Speed, Mister Mayhew?"

"Uhm . . . !" the midshipman stalled as he cast the chip log in haste. "Six knots, sir!"

"Half an hour to close broadsides, then," Lewrie calculated in his head. "A quarter-hour if they get under way and try to fight their way out. Aloft, there! What's happening in the anchorage?"

"They be makin' sail, sir! Both ships!"

"Pity there ain't no prize money for captured pirate ships," Fellows sighed. "A full-rigged ship of theirs'd bring a pretty penny."

"Shoals to starboard! Five cables!"

"One point to windward, quartermaster," Lewrie said with a nod. "Keep her in deep water, well as you may."

"Aye, aye, sir!"

"Shoals to larboard, five cables! Clear water ahead!"

"Center of the channel, then, quartermaster," Lewrie beamed.

Whippet came gliding east down her channel, flags flying and under all plain sail, a marvelous sight against the dawn. The suspect vessels were now underway, having cut their cables and hoisted courses and jibs, not trying to free any tops'ls. Perhaps short-handed, Alan wondered, with half their crews ashore for some reason? The larger ship could find no escape over the southern route into the Little Bahama Banks. According to the charts, south of Walker's Cay there were Triangle Rocks, Double Breaster Bars, and the Barracouta Banks, where the depths shoaled to ten feet or less.

"Damned fool!" Lewrie spat as he used his spyglass from his perch on the after shroud lines, halfway up to the fighting top. The full-rigged ship was turning west to challenge *Whippet!* And a moment later, he could espy ruddy blooms of gunfire from her! "Idiot!"

Whippet veered northerly, wearing ship to bare her starboard battery. Before the dull bangs of the strange ship's artillery had even reached them, *Whippet's* side lit up orange and red in a gush of powder smoke, the broadside tolling steady as a gun salute from bows to stern. The unidentified ship quivered and pulsed in the round ocular of his telescope as she was hulled. Her main yard leapt free of all restraints and came crashing down in silence, her lower mizzenmast jerked and splintered, sheering off the upper masts to fall like a sawn tree and drape over her stern and leeward side. She bore off to the south to seek refuge.

"She'll be on our shoal if she shaves the southern bank of the channel that close!" Fellows was hooting in derision.

"She'll hope to get past before *Whippet* can come about," Alan heard Ballard state calmly.

But *Whippet* wore once more, this time pointing her bows toward *Alacrity*, heeling over with the press of wind as she gave her foe one more timed broadside. The range could not have been half a mile, and Alan could see pieces of timber, bulwarks and decking flying in puffs of dust and smoke. The ship bore away even steeper, looking as if her master was trying to tack across the wind, even as *Whippet* bore down on her for another broadside.

"Schooner dead ahead, fine on the bows, sir!" a lookout called.

Lewrie swiveled about and saw their particular foe about a mile away and closing. Down-sun as *Alacrity* was, and with their attention drawn to the battle, they might not yet have spotted *Alacrity* as she came up from the lee of sunrise, dark against the last of the night's horizon.

"Mister Ballard, broadsides to either beam!" Lewrie shouted as he jumped down to his quarter-deck. "We'll wear across the channel to block it. Mister Fowles, your gunners'll have to hop lively for me!"

"They will, sir!"

"Helm up to windward to open the larboard battery."

Alacrity turned nor'east, almost running with the wind. Her gun ports flew open with a crash, and the hands tailed on the run-out tackles 'til the carriages butted home against the bulwarks.

"As you bear . . . fire!"

Seven cables range; three-quarters of a nautical mile, and cold iron barrels tore the morning apart as the six-pounders barked and came thundering inboard to snub on the thick breeching-ropes! Shot struck fantastic plumes of spray short of the schooner in a ragged line before her bows.

"Shoals ahead, three cables, deep water to larboard!"

"Helm alee, Mister Neill. Wear ship closehauled, Mister Ballard!" Lewrie ordered. "Stand by the starboard battery!"

Gun captains transferred to the starboard side while loaders and rammermen, tacklemen and powder monkeys remained to larboard to complete swabbing out and reloading the expended guns. To carry the full complement of five men per gun deemed necessary to serve their six-pounders would have taken fifty men out of the sixty-five adults aboard, so it was standard drill to work both sides short-handed in preparation for moments such as this, and required only thirty.

"Open yer gun ports!" Fowles was droning on. "Done, larboard? Come run out starboard. Gun captains, point! Cock yer locks!"

"Fire as you bear, sir!" Lewrie shouted.

The schooner had turned away to the west, almost in-irons into the teeth of the wind, and, if she held that course, would end up on that uncharted shoal of theirs.

"Fire!" Fowles called as the deck rose up level and hung still for a moment. "Ah, *yes* by Christ! Oh, well shot, my *bully* lads!"

They'd fired individually, but on the uproll, which forced them to hurry in tugging the lanyards on the flintlock strikers, so it was more a planned broadside. This time they hit her and she shook like a piece of meat taken by a shark, and paid off the wind in disarray to point her bows at *Alacrity* again!

"Hands wear ship, ready the larboard battery!"

Lewrie was zigzagging up the channel, blocking any hope of escape, and going wide enough off the wind to present all his guns.

"Fight me, you poltroon!" Lewrie screamed across the waters. "Got no stomach for a *real* foe, you murderin' bastards?"

The schooner fell away to run sou'east, dangerously close to the sand bars south of Walker's Cay, trying to shave a passage down the channel. *Alacrity* served her another broadside, then wore once again to run due east to block that side of the narrow passage even as the gunners got off another broadside from the larboard guns.

"Shoals ahead, two cables!" some lookout screeched on the bow.

He could not hold this course a minute longer, Alan realized! The schooner's master was praying that he'd have to bear away soon, whilst he could continue to run south and perhaps get astern of the gun ketch that was tearing his little command to bits.

" 'Vast, there!" Lewrie shouted. He was out of syncopation in his turnings with the schooner. "Mister Ballard, lay us closehauled to weather on the larboard tack. Then once you have way 'nough, tack us and wear about sou'east, to keep us ahead of them!"

"Aye, aye, sir!" Ballard grinned, nodding with understanding. "Hands to the sheets and braces, hands wear ship aweather! Mister Harkin, prepare for stays!"

Alacrity swung away from the schooner, almost showing her her stern,

but kept on turning, crossing the eye of the wind and heeling over with
the wind on the starboard side, pointing sou'west.

The schooner's captain took the opportunity to run south, and steer
wide of the threatening bars and shoals.

Then *Alacrity* wore, falling off the wind in a small circle to race back
across that narrow channel on her best point of sail with a bone of foam
in her teeth, and her larboard battery ready once more.

There would be no escape.

"As you bear . . . fire!" Fowles cried.

The schooner was smothered in spray as even the two-pounder boat-
guns got into the act from fo'c's'le and quarter-deck at a bare two-cables'
range. She staggered under the impact of solid round-shot, and swung up
toward the wind as if to cut across *Alacrity*'s stern.

"Shoals ahead, one cable!"

"Helm down, Mister Ballard. Beat sou'west and keep ahead of her.
And be ready to haul your wind should she duck back toward the shoals
on the east side of the channel."

"She's in-irons!" a lookout called as most of the crew and the officers
were busy with the maneuver and the reloading. "They're all aback!
Takin' t'the boats, sir!"

The schooner was being abandoned. One small launch was being led
around from astern, another was already filled with men and was being
rowed east toward the shoals, the oars worked like hummingbirds' wings.

"Wear about to the sou'east!" Lewrie demanded. "Get the guns on
them before they escape!"

But before they could fire more than two broadsides, they had to turn
once more to keep off the shoals themselves, and their route was almost
blocked by the abandoned schooner, listing and drifting toward the
shoals. The boats with their two-foot draft got over the shoals and bars,
and into deeper water off Grand Cay.

"Cease fire!" Lewrie shouted, fuming. Once more, pirates had outsmarted him and escaped him. "Mister Ballard, secure the people from
quarters. Send Mister Odrado, with my coxun Cony, over to take charge
of the schooner before she takes the ground. Mister Harkin, we'll fetch-
to! I'll see to this, Arthur. You carry on."

"Very well, sir."

"Helm alee, lay us closehauled on the larboard tack, Mister Neill.
Stations for stays, Mister Harkin! Fo'c's'le captain, we'll leave the jibs on
larboard tack! Brace-tenders, prepare to back the main tops'l! Ready
about? Helm alee!"

Alacrity rounded up as if she would cross the wind's eye, but stalled in-irons, her gaff sails trying to drive her forward on the starboard tack, but her backed jibs counteracting their force like brakes, so she cocked up into the wind and came to a halt, slowly drifting north on the current and making a tiny leeway.

"A neat morning's work, sir," Fellows congratulated, swiping his thinning ginger hair and looking more like a harried clerk. "The schooner took, *Whippet* with her foe aground in the north channel, and another pirate band with their business stopped."

"Ummph!" Lewrie commented.

"Damme, the way we handled her, sir, sweet an' fleet as some pleasure yacht! My word, sir . . . 'twas hellish fun, that."

"They got away, though," Lewrie glowered.

"Can't have it all, sir," Fellows chuckled.

"Why the devil not, Mister Fellows? Just why the devil not?"

Chapter 9

"It's a regular treasure-trove ashore, sir," Lieutenant Ballard reported to Lewrie and Rodgers. "Arms and powder, of course; money and plate. But there's heaps of cargo, covered with sailcloth and palmettos. A ship's chandlery and fancy-goods shop in one. An ocean of drink, too, sirs. Fancy wines, brandies, rums . . . I've put a guard over that so the hands don't get at it."

"Yet who shall guard the guardians?" Rodgers mused.

"Loot, from a dozen ships, more like," Lewrie commented.

"And that ship out yonder, the *Guineaman*, bung-full to her deckheads with general cargo, too," Rodgers grinned, a very happy man. "No manifest, goods from Cuba, from New York an' Baltimore an' Charleston aboard, goods from Europe . . . yet, gentlemen, *yet* . . . no recent voyages in her log t' any o' those places! Like Lewrie here says, it's loot, bought from the pirates that took it."

"Well, sir . . ." Ballard pouted, "there's a civilian merchant ashore in charge of the cache, a Mister Runyon, who *claims* the goods are warehoused here, that they're held until the prices go up in the winter when . . ."

"Aye, just like this Captain Malone of *Guineaman* claims that he was taken by buccaneers!" Rodgers hooted in derision. "Oh, he's wily, he is! Yet when I demanded he produce the pirates who sailed her out an' fired into a King's Ship, he cannot. Swears they went over the side an' escaped in a ship's boat, an' he an' his crew got free too late t' save her from groundin' on the shoals. Not from where I was watchin', they didn't! And do you know who *Guineaman* belongs to, eh? A Bay Street merchant name o' John Finney. 'Calico Jack' Finney, as he's better known in these parts."

"Finney!" Lewrie exclaimed, startled out of his skin, but glad the next moment. "Merciful God, that's wondrous! I mean, I've met the man. *Thought* he wasn't straight, from the very first. Heard he was cherry-merry with cutthroats and such. And that pirate band I did for was led by a friend of his. A so-called former friend! Why, he must be in league with 'em!"

"Well, o' *course* he's in league with 'em!" Rodgers chortled. "Always has been, always will be, far's I know! Ran an 'all-nations' an' a buttock-shop for 'em, got rich off their trade, made loans for 'em, traded this for that since he set foot in Nassau. He . . ."

"Excuse me, Commander Rodgers," Ballard said with a cough. "I did learn that this Runyon fellow ashore is one of Finney's agents!"

"Well, there you are, then," Rodgers exulted triumphantly. "We have proof positive against him, even if our pirates did escape us."

"Well, sir, this Runyon claims, as I said a moment ago, that the goods are cached here secretly, without having to pay duties or bonded-warehouse fees in Nassau, until hurricane season ends and the shipping trade across the Atlantic or down from America ceases until spring. Then they're loaded aboard his ships and sold at the peak of their scarcity, when their value is highest. All over, sir."

"He just came out an' admitted it?" Rodgers said, going bug-eyed. "Well, damme, the fellow's just convicted himself, an' his master with him! That's confession o' smugglin'!"

"Not exactly, sir," Ballard objected. "In a court of law, he could make it sound a plausible defense. If pirates discovered his secret cache, they would be tempted to raid it. He might even try to prove that a consortium of other Bay Street merchants put them up to it, to eliminate the competition!"

"Ah, rot!" Rodgers snorted. "Now here's the way I see this was done, sirs. Finney does nought of the dirty work, see? But his old mates pirate inbound ships, and some passin' near enough. They have to have a method of profitin', and Finney's their middle man, their shore agent, if you will. They'll keep the money, jewels and plate, but the dry goods and such, the foodstuffs . . . Finney's agents meet 'em in just such a hidey-hole as this 'un. There's a deal o' lonely cays in the Bahamas with decent harbours, safe from pryin' eyes. A swap is made. Give 'em a quarter o' what it's worth—half-crown to the pound, perhaps less. They keep what takes their fancy, vessels they deem faster and better armed, and play the upright tradin' men in public anywhere they please between voyages."

"And they scuttle the poor ships far out at sea, along with their crews and passengers," Lewrie stuck in. "Once they've had fun with some of them. Damn their blood."

"Or resell some o' the ships down in the West Indies or over in America for even more profit, aye," Rodgers grimaced. "A European oak-built ship'd be worth two Yankee ships made o' their poor excuse for ship wood. Might even create new documents for 'em to ease the sales. But aye, it's wholesale murder for the victims. Then, here's the part where Finney makes his money back. He ships the pirated goods to New Providence, Eleuthera, Great Exuma, over to the Abacos, down to Long or Cat Island and sells 'em as clean goods!"

"Would he not have to pay duty on them, sir?" Ballard asked. "Land them in-bond first?"

"Even so, what's the cost to him?" Rodgers scoffed. "Were he to send ships across the Atlantic out of season, pay an honest price for a cargo an' pay duty, it's a losin' proposition, or a damn' thin one, what with insurance and all. But, to get a cargo for a fourth its worth, sell it dear as salvation when no one else has the fancy stuff . . . well, what's a few shillings per hundredweight matter?"

"And once landed and reshipped, they're legal," Lewrie grasped. "With Bahamian authorities, on Hispaniola or Cuba . . . anywhere!"

"And sky's the limit on what he could reap!" Rodgers laughed. "Oh, we see his vessels settin' out for England, for the Continent, for America . . . and we see 'em come back months later. But do they ever really *go* anywhere, I ask you?"

"Some must, sir," Ballard pointed out, ever the keen one.

"Aye, some must, granted," Rodgers allowed. "But enough come to lairs like this 'un, especially in winter. Only his most trusted masters and crews. He probably has captains and hands who never see this part o' his trade."

"So he might undercut the other merchants only slightly," Lewrie exclaimed. "Whilst the others do business at ten or fifteen percent profit, Lord . . . Finney must earn fifty or seventy percent!"

"Exactly!" Rodgers said.

"But why, sir?" Lewrie asked, perplexed. "Damme, the risk of being found out sooner or later . . . he made over 200,000 pounds from the war, I'm told. Owns a dozen fine ships, a planting and that big house in town . . . a hero and all . . ."

"And partnership in a bank," Rodgers added. "Heard tell he put 60,000 up as his share to launch it proper. Far's we know, he plays banker and ship's husband for his pirates, too! And loans to these new arrivals . . ."

"That's just it, sir," Lewrie insisted. "Mind you, I dislike him as much as cold boiled mutton. But why, once one has that sort of 'blunt', that sort of respectability, would one risk it all just to make more, if an honest profit atop his bank and his pickings from the war would buy him a small country in Europe? It doesn't make sense."

"Because he's a semiilliterate dog who hasn't the sense t' not feed like a starvin' wolf 'til he spews!" Rodgers sneered.

"Captain Lewrie has a point, sir," Ballard interjected. "He's not a stupid man, for all his lack of public-school letters. Look at how far he rose, and what native intelligence it required."

"Aye, he could have been as dense as his mate Doyle, once he'd gotten a purse full of 'chink', sir," Lewrie countered. "Risen, then fallen in a fortnight. But he didn't, sir."

"Revenge," Ballard commented slyly, his sober countenance, and his slightly sad-but-observant eyes crinkling with secret mirth.

"Oh, rot!" Rodgers snorted with disdain.

"Vengeful amusement," Lewrie added, sharing a smile with his first officer.

"Against who, pray tell?" Rodgers demanded.

"Why, against just about anyone and everyone, I'd expect, sir," Ballard intoned with a quirky cock of one brow.

"Rot, I tell you," Rodgers reiterated. "'Tis of no matter why. What does matter is gatherin' evidence. Among all this cargo, there must be some sign it came off foreign ships, that it wasn't ever his."

"How do you come by that, sir? Why foreign ships?" Alan asked.

"Even he'd not be so foolish as to loot a British ship," Commander Rodgers chuckled. "They'd be missed! But foreign ships, which compete with British merchantmen, and undercut every New Providence merchant, well, they're fair game, as long as they aren't carryin' a Bay Street shopkeeper's cargo! Those fellows'd turn a blind eye an' like as not stand the pirates a round o' drinks, if it's piracy keeps their prices high. Cuts down on Finney's competition, and lines his purse at the same time, too! We have no way of knowin' how many foreign-flagged ships set out, or when, whether they were comin' to the Bahamas, or just passin' by. How long would it be before some Boston ship's husband sends a letter to inquire about a missin' ship? And, with just the one overworked American consul, it might take years to answer, if answered at all, an' the bulk of 'em put down as 'lost at sea, cause unknown', with their home port so far off."

"Bristol, Plymouth and Liverpool are just as far off, sir," Ballard stuck in, unable to stop himself.

"There's papers to look through," Rodgers said, disgruntled at having his logic questioned. "There's that pirate schooner to search from keel to truck. You strike me as a slyboots, Lieutenant Ballard. Why not turn your hand to delvin' me some answers, then? And listin' what we seized. I'll salvage *Guineaman*. I'll be too busy."

"Aye, aye, sir," Ballard intoned.

"We'll get to the bottom of it, sir," Lewrie promised, vowing to help Ballard in any way he could. Besides, he thought, there was more than one person in the Bahamas who could relish revenge. And, when it came to vengeful amusements, even he would be the first to admit to being "buck-of-the-first-head" at it!

Chapter 10

"God Almighty," Lieutenant Ballard sighed wearily, as he and Lewrie pored over the lists they'd made. He rubbed his eyes with the heels of his hands and peered about the dimly lit dining coach of Lewrie's cabins to see if the coffeepot was still simmering atop a lamp-base warmer on the sideboard. "Cony, is there any of that left?"

"Aye, Mister Ballard, sir. Polish yer brass with it by now, ya could, though, sir. I could roust cook out an' fetch fresh."

"Trot that lot out, Cony," Ballard yawned. "The blacker the better. May it be strong enough to melt a pewter spoon, then it may also dissolve the dam in my poor wits."

"Don't see as how we're getting anywhere," Lewrie carped, deep in a brown study. He had looked forward to harpooning John Finney in a court of law, even though paper-work drudgery was never his strong suit.

Had the records they'd seized, the inventories of booty they'd recorded, shown any promise, he might still have felt enthusiastic to continue delving. But so far, they could find nothing truly damning, and Alan envied Commander Rodgers, who was being all nautical and tar-handed at salving *Guineaman.*

"We shall, sir," Arthur Ballard assured him.

"It's all circumstantial, Arthur," Alan muttered. "Half of the goods are bulk cargoes. Rice, flour, dried beans and such in sacks or barrels. We know it comes from the Americas, but that's all. No sign or markings of seller, shipper or buyer! Same for the iron tools and farm implements, cloth and all. It could be his, legally."

"Yet none marked as consigned or bought by John Finney, sir," Ballard pointed out hopefully. "There're fancy goods from Spain, France and Portugal, with the producers' names for proof. There's sign they cleared foreign customs, there's sign export duties were paid."

"But no marks of who bought it or shipped it," Lewrie protested. "Could be construed as looted goods from a dago merchant. Or could be Finney's, after all."

"Aye, sir, but no proof *positive* of his ownership. *Ergo,* 'tis not his, and *prima facie* evidence it could be booty."

"I take no joy in that argument," Alan complained. "He could claim ownership, and produce all the sham records he wished. Or, he could say he purchased the fancy goods in Havana or Santo Domingo, or a dozen other ports from others and brought 'em here."

"And been skinned by the original importers, sir?" Ballard said with a grin. "No one on a court would ever believe that tale, not if they were any sort of merchant or shopkeeper!"

"What we need is some sign that part of the trove ashore belongs to other Bay Street merchants."

"We'll never get that, sir," Ballard sighed. "If they imported wares in foreign bottoms, they violate our Navigation Acts. Naturally, they would not wish their cargoes marked for a customs official to see."

"Finney could say the same."

"The other merchants do not possess a fleet of trading ships to do their carrying, sir."

"And if all goods in one of his ships are his, then who's to gainsay him when he claims they needed no markings?" Alan countered.

"Granted," Ballard shrugged as Cony set a pewter mug before him. "Then, there're the odds and ends the pirates left behind, sir. No written records of their gatherings, though."

"With three out of four sailors illiterate in the Fleet, 'tis only to be expected," Lewrie frowned. "Uhm . . . Arthur, excuse me . . . but, you're really going to drink that?"

"Sir . . ." Ballard whispered back with a tiny grin. "Alan, do you allow me to be prodigal with your personal stores, I shall take it with four sugars. And all evident avidity!"

"Yoosh!" Alan commented with a sour-mouthed shudder.

"Ditto that opinion," Ballard said once he'd tasted it and set it aside. "There're weapons, watches, navigational instruments, clocks and such that bear the inscriptions of unknown men. And some unknown vessels, sir. Far too valuable, the most of it, for common seamen."

"But we didn't capture a single pirate, they all escaped us," Lewrie sighed. "And to track down the goods' original owners, to find the ships mentioned . . . even if we had captured a few, they could say they bought them half a world away as used. Got 'em as gifts! How does one track down 'Cock Robin' off the good ship *Barnacle* outa New York? All that's left of her is anonymous bosun's stores, nails and a pocket watch, if she was pirated. Probably sunk, and seaman 'Cock Robin' murdered and gone down with her! Now were we to find goodies from old *Barnacle* aboard the pirate schooner, and ashore, *and* aboard *Guineaman*, we have your *prima facie* case to lay."

Lewrie leaned back in his chair and gazed through half-shut eyelids at the overhead beams as Ballard could be heard shuffling his stacks of papers over again, between sips of his vile coffee.

"That might not do it, even then," Lewrie muttered. "Say someone aboard *Guineaman*, one of the mates, had a packet of used goods in his sea chest. The pirates could have rifled the chest when they took *Guineaman* . . . if they ever did . . . and it could have ended up ashore or in a pirate's sea bag when they went shares of their spoils, so . . ."

"There is a fine box of Manton pistols, with an inscription on the case as belonging to a Captain Henry Beard, sir, that were found aboard the schooner, in her master's cabins," Ballard informed him. "The inscription tells us Beard was master of the *Matilda*. Then, we have several hundred pounds of chain and ankle bands and wrist locks ashore. The sort of restraints used to arrange slaves into coffles, sir. Rusty, abandoned for some time I'd say. But they bear Liverpool markings, with the name *Matilda* scratched into them on the bands. There was something . . ." He urgently riffled through his papers.

"A Liverpool ship?" Lewrie asked, tipping his chair forward to take more interest. "Damme, a British vessel?"

"Ah!" Ballard said, "An especially fine spyglass with a brass plaque bearing the name Nathaniel Marriyat. Presented to him by his family upon becoming first mate of . . . the *Matilda!* And, damme!"

It was rare for Ballard to swear.

"That was found aboard *Guineaman,* in the ready-use rack by the compass binnacle and the traverse board, sir!" Ballard almost shouted with joy. "Three items from the same vessel, linking together. This *Matilda* must, from this scant evidence, be a Liverpool slaver. Rusty as the chains and fetters are, she must have been taken at least one year ago. The pistols, *and* the chains, that proves the pirates were here at Walker's Cay before this incident. The spyglass proves that *Guineaman* had met them *before* yesterday. Wait! Wait, I . . . ! Yes!" Ballard giggled, losing all his soberness as he sorted more papers. "Boxed set of navigational instruments. Brass ruler, dividers, compass . . . and a sextant! *Guineaman's* second mate had them! But they were engraved originally as this missing Captain Beard's, sir! When we questioned *Guineaman's* crew, he claimed he'd bought 'em in Liverpool, a year or more past!"

"*Matilda,*" Lewrie pondered. "*Matilda.* Now where have I heard that name? Seems I have . . . damme, I'm sure I have."

"A Liverpool 'black-birder' could sell a cargo of slaves here in the Bahamas, sir. Do the Middle Passage, Dahomey to Nassau, with the demand for slaves increasing here now that . . ."

"Wait, Arthur! Ssshh!" Alan demanded, raising a hand. "Let me think."

It was recent; he was certain of that much. Since arriving in the Bahamas? He tried to remember ships which might have lain nearby *Alacrity* at anchor. Portsmouth—no. On the voyage out? Again, no. Slavers stank to high heaven. They crammed three or four hundred men and women into hard wooden racks, forced them to lie back-to-belly as tight as cordwood and fettered for months. Fed them in those racks, half the time, if the weather was bad. Puking sick, incontinent from rotten hog-swill victuals, they fouled their own sleeping spaces and had to lie in excrement like beasts. One remembered slavers close by!

Slavers were fast ships, frigate-built, or like a "razeed" 3rd Rate, cut down to two decks from three. Were they slow, the rates of mortality cut their profits to nothing. The faster the ship, the more slaves arrived alive for sale, though twenty-five percent attrition was the norm for even the most considerate and "gentle" captains.

Where had he seen such a fine, frigate-built ship, a vessel a seaman would envy, foul as that line of work was? In the Caicos, in some harbour . . . Nassau Harbour . . . Cat Island . . .

"Christ!" Lewrie gasped. He got to his feet and crossed over to the chart-space to grope through his bookshelves. "Cony, fetch a light!"

William Pitt hissed at him from the dark. He had been sleeping like a tawny, orange-colored plum duff on the high outboard shelf by the chart table between the chronometer and the sextant case, and did not like his nap interrupted.

"Oh, bugger y'rself!" Lewrie griped. "Ah, thankee, Cony!"

He found the gold-lettered spine of the book he was seeking, *Les Liaisons Dangereuses*, and flipped through it to see if his memory was correct.

"Eureka, Arthur! Bloody hell! Read that dedication!"

"My God," Arthur Ballard said with a bemused expression when he had completed it. "How the devil did you come by this, sir?"

"Bought it used for six shillings," Lewrie crowed. "Look at the date. March of 1785. It's accounted so bawdy there was an Order In Council to ban its publication in England, but some printer . . . a *Liverpool* printer, mind . . . ran up a few hundred on speculation, 'stead of the usual subscription. *Matilda* was at short-stays, ready for a new slaving voyage, with Nathaniel Marriyat just promoted first mate into her. Time enough for your chains to rust?"

"But *where* did you get it, sir?"

"At Finney's on Bay Street, Arthur!"

"Aha!"

"At bloody 'Calico Jack' Finney's, not two months' past, damn his eyes! Arthur, they pissed in the font! They did the unspeakable! They took a *British* ship! A ship we can ask about among the slaver captains who frequent Nassau, among the slave dealers who dealt with her in the past. We can document one of the victims, show that goods off her were aboard *Guineaman*, the schooner, and piled with other loot ashore long enough ago to confirm *when* they took her. There'll be a brace or two of 'black-birders' in port soon with the first slaves of the summer. They'll have seen *Matilda* in Africa, they'll know of her people, and whether she went missing. And this book proves that Jack Finney has bought pirated goods. We've *got* the bastard! Even if he doesn't do a hemp hornpipe on the gallows, he's finished in these islands, or I'm a Turk in a turban!"

Book VI

HERCVLES

"*Licent tonantis profuga condaris sinu,*
petet undecumque temet haec dextra et feret."

"Though you run and hide in the Thunderer's bosom,
everwhence shall this hand seek you and hale
you forth."

Hercules Furens 1010–1012
SENECA

Chapter 1

"But he's as guilty as home-brewed sin, sir," Commander Benjamin Rodgers blurted out. "*Matilda*, all our evidence . . . no one's seen her for over a year. Due here about July of '85, and . . ."

"That's as may be, Commander Rodgers," Commodore Garvey shot back, pacing angrily behind his desk. "The court said he is not!"

"But she *was* pirated, sir," Lewrie ventured to interject. "I find the idea that her people sold off their most prized possessions ludicrous. Why would Captain Beard pawn his navigation instruments just before embarking on a voyage? Why would this Nathaniel Marriyat pawn his brand-new spyglass and his books?"

"Gambling debts," Garvey dismissed with a savage chop of his hand. "To raise money for buying blacks of his own for sale in the West Indies. We don't know, and we will never know. *Matilda* could have gone down in a storm. It *happens*, don't ya know, Lewrie. The few items of your flimsy evidence were accounted for by documents of sale, and your case confounded."

"Forgeries, sir!" Rodgers exclaimed. "They had over a month to concoct what was wanting."

"I warned you when you laid this before me, your supposition was weak. I did everything in my power to dissuade you from pursuing this fantasy," Garvey sneered. "The prosecutor . . ."

"Was a brainless arse, sir," Rodgers retorted. "He didn't like it. He was afraid of prosecuting a powerful man, so he did his least, and that, badly!"

"He told you beforehand it wouldn't hold water, and it didn't. Finney was absolved faster than any court I've ever seen," Garvey said. "Listen to the mob out there, sirs. Listen, you fools! Now Finney's being chaired through the streets like a sitting member of Parliament on his hustings, and King's Justice has been made a mockery. The Navy has been made to look stupid, sirs, the Bahamas Squadron, and me with it! Our new governor Lord Dunmore is *most* exercised over this. Bade me over to ask me what sort of idiots I had under my command, and were there any *more* of 'em out there, running roughshod! What could you have been thinking, Rodgers? There're untold tens of thousands owing Finney now.

You shot *Guineaman* to rags, wounded some of her people, put her on a shoal . . . you deliberately torched every stick of goods on Walker's Cay, and sank everything that wouldn't burn in the bay! He'll demand recompense, and even should the Crown uphold you, I expect it'll take the entire budget for governing these islands for the next year, sir! The next year entire!"

"She fired into me first, sir, and if pirates *really* held her as Finney and Captain Malone claim, then nothing is owed, sir. God damme, sir, I salved her afterwards, didn't I? Set her . . ."

"You'll not blaspheme in my presence, Commander Rodgers, do you hear me, you simple dullard?" Garvey bellowed. "You could have put a guard over the cache of goods . . ."

"We could not carry it off, sir, and there was too much drink to guard," Lewrie said. "We'd have had to torch that, or tip it into the harbour, anyway, or we'd have lost the crew left behind as guards."

"You do not interrupt me, Lewrie! You do so at your peril! I hold you responsible for this. You're just as culpable, and liable in this affair, as Rodgers!"

"He was following my orders, sir," Rodgers stated.

"Finney's agent Runyon *told* you it was private property, saved for later sale in the off-season, yet you persisted!"

"It was not *marked* as his property, sir," Lewrie rebutted. "We did bring off the coins, plate and all, and those items we could identify as Finney's. The rest could have been pirate booty, so we . . ."

"So you set fire to it, with fiendish, childish delight, just to see it burn, you pyromanic! You hen-headed simpleton!"

"Sir, we . . ." Lewrie attempted.

"Both of you! Going off at half-cock quick as a brace of two-shilling muskets! Wasn't one band of pirates enough for you, eh, Lewrie? Did you get a taste for acclaim and glory? Had to go out to win more, hey? And you, Rodgers. You *were* sure to be made post your next commission. What need had you to gild your laurels with this . . . this act of complete lunacy? Envy Lewrie his crowd of backslappers? Feel left out or ignored, did you, you vaunting coxcomb? Ha? Did you?"

"Sir, I did my duty as best I saw it," Rodgers growled deep in his chest, with his chin tucked back hard against his neck-stock. "I saved a Spanish merchantman and gave chase to the pirates who had taken her. I tracked them down to Walker's Cay and I engaged them. I saw no pirates fleeing *Guineaman*, and I was fired upon by her, so I opened fire into her, aye, sir. I discovered evidence which led me to believe that the goods on the island were booty, and this Finney neck-deep in the support of criminals, sir. I . . ."

"What pirates, Rodgers?" Garvey roared. "You let 'em escape! You did not arrest one person who *should* have been in the dock! You had no captives to interrogate to determine whether it was booty or not! And out of spite, out of frustration that you'd been bested, you saw what you wanted to see, learned only what you wished to hear, abused the master, mates and crew of *Guineaman,* brought scandal upon their good names, invented a circumstantial fairy tale, then laid a case against one of Nassau's most illustrious merchants, just so you had something to show for your swaggering antics!"

"Sir, I take deep, grievous exception to your characterization of my actions, sir," Rodgers said, almost strangling.

"You failed, sir! Hear me? You failed! Failed to capture a single pirate. *Failed!"* Garvey almost howled. "You could have left a guard over the goods, brought *Guineaman* back here, and discovered the truth quietly. Finney and the other merchants would be cheering *you* for saving his ship and his goods, but no! You demean honest men in a court of law, and . . ."

"Honest men," Lewrie muttered with scorn.

"What? Did you speak, sir?" Garvey ranted, turning on him. "A court says he's honest. A court just said he's completely innocent! He was shrewd enough to import extra and cache it until the price was high enough. Know who's cheering Finney, Lewrie? The same people he will skin when they buy his off-season imports. They call him knacky to be the only one with their fancy goods they cannot do without, and will pay his prices gladly. If he undercuts the other Bay Streeters, yet cheats *them,* that's just the nuts to them, the fools!"

"Being shrewd doesn't mean he isn't guilty, sir," Lewrie said. "The book, sir. How did he come by that, if . . ."

"Be quiet, you silly clown! 'Twas you and your first officer who brewed this case out of thin air, then laid it at this fool's feet and convinced him he was onto something. And all for jealousy, sir! Because you were jealous, I ask you!"

"Sir!" Lewrie goggled.

"The whole town knows Finney was spooning 'round your little 'batter-pudding', Lewrie," Garvey scoffed. "And you didn't like it, did you?" Garvey accused, dropping into a nursery-room singsong. "You didn't have the nutmegs to warn him off as a man should, so you plotted a way to confound a rival in your wife's affections by naming him a confederate of pirates. Was he simply *too* handsome for your peace of mind, sir? Too fearsome an opponent to confront man to man, hey? Too fierce a foe to call out? Or would his hanging on false charges make you feel more sanguine about your wife while you were at sea, sir?"

"Damme, sir, that is *patently* unfair!" Alan exploded. "And you cast foul aspersions upon my wife's good name and morals for no good reason, sir! If you do have any allegations about her, I demand you say them straight out now, or never, sir! You may be my superior officer, but that doesn't give you the right to demean her, sir!"

"Oh, Christ," Alan heard Rodgers grunt under his breath.

"I *am* your commanding officer, you insubordinate dog!" Garvey howled, jowls flapping. "You do not shout at me, sir, nor will you use foul language in any address to me! And I'll cast any aspersion I please! An officer junior as you has no business marrying in the first instance, nor in fetching his mort out to a foreign station for his comfort and pleasure in the second. She has affected your skills as a sea officer, prejudiced your administering of King's Justice, so unwitted you that you laid false charges against a man for revenge for some slight. Perhaps it might be best if you resign your command and commission, and take both her and you home. Failing that, put her on a ship, leaving you to concentrate on the salvation of what is left of your career."

"Sir, that goes beyond what a commanding officer may order any subordinate to do," Rodgers protested at once. "An officer's personal life does not fall under your regulation, sir. And I cannot believe that I have heard a superior officer use his office to slander a fine and blameless young lady in such a callous fashion."

Alan could not speak, and thanked God for Rodgers's courage. There was a humming in his ears, a red mist before his eyes, and the room swam about him. He had never been so angry, nor so impotent to act. Should he speak for himself, he would explode, and damn every consequence. Should he even move, his first action would be to draw his hanger and run Garvey through!

"Believe what you will, Rodgers," Garvey barked. "What, Lewrie? No fine words? Cat got your tongue at last, hey?"

"I have no doubts at all concerning my wife, sir, and I bitterly resent *your* words about her, sir," Alan managed to drag out between clenched jaws. "Finney traffics in stolen goods, sir. We had a case. Not the tightest case, it turns out. But the truth was told, sir. I stand by my allegations. I stand by my wife, and I resent . . . ."

"Truth! My God . . . ." Garvey hooted, checking himself as he almost blasphemed himself. "You make me want to spew, the two of you! There'll be a Court of Inquiry into your actions, sirs. There'll be civil charges laid by Finney to recoup lost goods and incomes. Your truth is a pack of fabulist slanders, and he'll most likely sue you both for that, too! Until any or all of those courts convene, you're to make yourselves scarce as hen's teeth. Out of my sight so I am not tempted to relieve you of your commands and break you!"

"And will you schedule the Court of Inquiry preceding the civil suits, sir?" Rodgers demanded. "Would that not be prejudicial should I be found . . . ?"

"Should have considered the consequences before you acted, sir," Garvey almost snickered. "You serve, and you will now wait, pending *my* pleasure and convenience. Commander Rodgers, 'tis coming up on whale season, did you know that?"

"Sir?"

"And saltraking will soon commence with hotter sunshine down south. You will sail this evening, sir, making the best of your way, and relieve *Aemilia* as station-ship in the Turks."

"Sir, I draw two fathoms," Rodgers protested. "I couldn't sail a tenth of my patrol area down yonder!"

"Purchase a lugger or two from the fishermen, then, to act as tenders to *Whippet*," Garvey shrugged, sitting down at last in a fine leather desk chair. "Perhaps Lieutenant Coltrop has one already."

"Out of Admiralty funds, sir?" Rodgers asked, suspiciously.

"Your stupidity *leaves* me with no Admiralty funds, Rodgers. I leave it to you to deal with out of your own purse if you wish to perform your duties . . . 'as best you see it'."

"Aye, aye, sir."

"And you, Lewrie," Garvey simpered. "You're going south, too. Long Island, Cat, Rum Cay, Conception and Watling's will be your area. Should I even hear a *rumor* of your tops'ls being seen north of Flamingo Point on Cat Island until I send for you, I'll have you cashiered for mutiny and desertion, sir."

"Aye, aye, sir," Alan nodded, too numb to grasp.

"Now, my fine turd-barge captains," Garvey glowered, "get out of my sight. Get out of my harbor, and stay out! And, should I get word you've done something else so abysmally chuckleheaded again, I promise I will have no mercy upon you. Go. Go!" Garvey concluded, shooing them away with a languid wave of his hand as if flitting off flies.

* * *

"Mine arse on a bandbox!" Alan fumed once they had reached the streets. "How *dare* he!" he hissed, close to tears of impotent rage. "He had no right! No right at all!"

"No, he doesn't," Rodgers groaned as they plodded heavily downhill towards Bay Street. "And if Caroline sails, will *his* wife, his daughter, or his sister and her dominee husband sail with her, hey?"

"Can he force her to leave?" Alan asked fearfully.

"No, he cannot, and he knows it, Damme, what a bloody mess! Damn the court, damn the panel, damn our timid mouse of a prosecutor . . . damn the very law! We *know* Finney's guilty, but he's got clean away with it. And he'll keep on gettin' away with it, now. He ought to be swingin' in a noose, but he's a hero all over again, damn his blood!"

"And the next time, it'll be one of Garvey's anointed who let him get away with murder. Damn the man! Damn him to hell! I never knew a senior officer so . . . !" Lewrie raged. "The bastard!"

"He was wrong, wasn't he?" Rodgers was forced to ask after a long minute or two of silence as they plodded along despondently. "What Garvey said about you dislikin' Finney so much you might have . . . about you bein' nettled by his attentions towards your wife?"

"He'd sent invitations to his functions. Acted overly familiar in public at 'dos' they attended separately," Alan replied, as calmly as he could. "It was being handled, quietly. The man's dense, and a boor. But I was a long way from fronting him, or calling him out about it, sir," Lewrie lied.

"And your dislike didn't prejudice you when you . . . ?"

"Not at all, sir. Oh, I admit to being *most* pleasantly surprised to see him implicated, but we had real evidence. I invented not one whit of it, sir. Arthur Ballard came up with most of it, and he's unaware of the situation, so he was as objective as anyone would wish. He's damned clever, sir, and would have dissuaded us if he didn't deem our case plausible. Look at the consequences, sir! I knew them going in, and the court warned us, too. No matter how much I might detest a man, I'd not risk all we face now to vent my spleen. Even *I'm* not that stupid, sir! I still don't understand it. If the prosecutor thought it was too weak to present, and he feared losing so much, then why did he end up taking it to court? Why are we not being sued right now for damages, instead? I mean to say . . . the charges against Finney should have been dropped, and then he'd have turned around and sued us over his losses, if he had a mind to."

"I don't know," Rodgers sighed. "And I wish to God I'd never heard of 'Calico Jack,' or *Guineaman*, or Walker's Cay. Damme, he'll have my last ha'penny 'fore he's through with me."

"Mine, too," Lewrie commiserated.

"No, you acted under my orders, Lewrie. It's my burden to bear from now on. At my Court of Inquiry they'll call you as a witness, no more. And thankfully, none of Commodore Garvey's vile assertions about our motives will see the light of day."

"Damn him, if he starts slandering her in society, I'll call him out, damme if I won't, the Articles of War bedamned!" Lewrie vowed.

They passed in front of a popular tavern as they turned the corner to Bay Street. Several boos and catcalls from within followed them, along with a few gnawed rib bones, as the patrons jeered them.

"Damme, I'm a King's Officer, how dare they?" Rodgers erupted.

"Captain Tom of the Mob, sir," Lewrie said, restraining him. "I fear we'll have to put up with it for awhile. Bad as any sauceboxes in London when it comes to putting down their betters when they're caught out. Best we ignore 'em before they summon a real mob and we end up 'de-Witted' like that Dutchman got torn apart in 1672."

"They wouldn't dare!" Rodgers huffed, but allowed himself to be put back in motion, and led at a slightly quicker pace away from their detractors.

"The mob, sir? They'd dare anything, until the garrison has to be called out and the Riot Act read to 'em. And we don't want that."

"S'pose not," Rodgers allowed. "Well, if I'm to sail this evening, I'd best go aboard ship now."

"You will not dine with me and Caroline, sir? Bring Betty along for a last supper?"

"Uhm, Betty . . . hmm," Rodgers blushed. "Tell ya the truth now, Lewrie, I'm not the marryin' sort, like yourself. And your Caroline's corrupted Betty Mustin somethin' awful lately. Put ideas in her pate 'bout wedded bliss an' vine-covered cottages such as yours, ah . . ."

"Should I give her your respects, at least, then, sir?"

"Hmm. Best not," Rodgers frowned. "I've sent her a note. And I'm off for the Turks for a long spell, it seems, so this might be the best thing, in the long run, don't ya know."

"I see, sir," Alan nodded sadly.

"Ah, Mister Chatsworth. Mistress Chatsworth," Rodgers said as he doffed his cocked hat to salute a couple of his acquaintance, and Alan did the same, recognizing them from several salons. "Delight . . ."

"Hmmph!" that worthy said as he turned his head away to deliver the "cut-direct." His wife, made of sterner stuff, actually turned her gaze heavenward and out to sea, the "cut-sublime," and nudged her man in the ribs to steer them to the opposite side of the street!

"Well, shit!" Rodgers spat in bruised wonder.

"Only to be expected, sir," Lewrie sighed heavily.

Damme, that irks, he thought!

"Shopping at Finney's are you, Mister Chatsworth?" Lewrie could not help calling after them. "Mixing your wine with the blood of poor murdered sailormen, are you? They've a fine special on cutlasses and pistols. Just the thing for carving your Sunday roast, madam! Or for making Mister Chatsworth walk the plank!"

"Lewrie, for God's sake!" Rodgers flushed, half outraged, yet more than half amused. "Does nothing repress you, sir?"

"I'm minded of your earlier statement, sir, about this being a funny world, but no one laughs about it. Thought I'd try humor on, just to see what happens, 'cause I can't imagine things getting worse. Shall I see you to the dock and into your boat, sir?"

"Thankee, Captain Lewrie, I'd admire that. Might consider you row out with me, then over to *Alacrity*. Then take your own gig t'land on that beach just b'fore your house, 'stead o' takin' the road home. Never know what our *fine* citizens hereabouts might think up."

"Aye, sir, I'll do that very thing," Lewrie agreed.

"Share a bottle o' champagne with me, 'fore you go?"

"I'd best not, sir," Lewrie decided. "Caroline'll be worried."

"Pity, 'tis a damn' good year," Rodgers chuckled. "I've twenty dozen stored in my lazarette. Ought to hold me for four months, do I ration m'self close. An' they'll be an absolute delight t'drink, for they came from Finney's stash on Walker's Cay, don't ya know."

"Damned *good*, sir. Take joy of them!" Alan brightened.

"He *is* a pirate, Lewrie," Rodgers spat, sobering. "And someday we'll prove it proper. Garvey's wrong, ya know. The Crown won't make good his losses. They were unbonded, undutied goods. Just the same as smuggled! The mob may think it was knacky, but the Court'll think it just shy o' criminal. And I surely can't. And won't! Should the judgment go against me, I'd abscond to Havana 'fore he gets a single farthin'. We hurt him where it hurts him the most, Lewrie! Thousands and thousands o' pounds o' goods, gone up in smoke! Might stretch him sore. Make him desperate. And should one o' his ships cross my hawse, why then I'll hurt him all over again!"

Chapter 2

"Darling, I'm so very sorry things turned out as they have," Caroline attempted to console him. For a final evening before sailing, it was a horrible occasion. Betty Mustin had gotten Rodgers's note which severed their relationship and ended his financial support, so she'd run to Caroline's for comfort, and was weeping disconsolately on one of their settees, a noisy, unlooked for intruder.

"You're not the only one, my love," Alan grimaced as he packed his shoregoing bags. "Damn, it's so unfair. Finney's guilty, we know it. Proving it's another matter. Now even the imps in the road are spitting at us. Got bones and horse dung flung at me before I got into a boat at the docks."

"I know, love," Caroline nodded, as near to tears as he was at this sudden separation. "I sponged your coat best I could."

He left off his packing to cross the room to her and hold her.

"Caroline love, I fear the mob's anger with me will happen to you," he told her. "Best let Wyonnie and Daniel do the shopping for a few weeks, 'til things quiet down." She nodded her agreement against his neck. "And, from what little I saw this afternoon, there're sure to be some snubs from people we thought liked us," he confessed. "I fear your popularity in society's to suffer. Sorry. My fault."

"Damn my social life, Alan!" she said fiercely. "And damn them who regard Finney above you, or me! We'll discover who are faithless and fickle, and who are our true friends. Then, no matter how high a body be, should they snub me now, then they couldn't have been worth much to begin with."

"God, how much I cherish you, Caroline," Alan muttered, lifting her off her feet to embrace her snugly. "You're so sensible, so good for me when I'm not. Which I fear is often. My treasure!"

"I won't have much need for society, anyway, Alan," Caroline whispered in his ear. "Not for the next seven months, anyway."

"Why? Afraid of running into Finney?"

"I'd meant to tell you properly, darling," she whispered, and leaned back a little, took one of his hands and directed it down to her belly. "Now is my last chance, so . . ." She wore an impish smile.

"Well, surely this'll all blow over by . . . WHAT?"

"And you will be back in port for the birth of our first child," she said, and he could feel her smile against his shoulder, even if he could not see it. He let her down to her feet and stood back from her, his expression about as betwattled as it had ever been and saw the happy, and so pleased-with-herself confirmation in her fond gaze. "You look *shot*, Alan! Does it not please you, darling?"

"Oh . . . my . . . God!" he yelped in cold confusion.

Sure, try humor on, why don't I, he thought! Try to imagine things getting worse, why don't you! *Now*, of all times, when I can't be here! Thankee, Jesus! Thankee very much! S'not like we haven't gone at it like stoats so much it hadn't happened earlier! Do, Jesus, a baby! Now!

"Alan?" She whispered, losing her confident smile. "You look so pale, you think you'd seen a spook! Do you not . . . *want* . . ."

"Oh, God, no, Caroline, don't think that, don't ever think that!" he tried to reassure her. "Christ, *me* a father! Who'd a thought it?"

Not like I ain't been damn' fortunate so far, he told himself; and thank God for Mother Green's best condoms all these years!

"Surprised, more like, Caroline," he babbled on. "Damme, taken all-aback! In-irons! Lord, God, me a father! I mean, you a mother! I adore it!"

Scares me so bad I wouldn't trust mine arse with a fart!

"You truly do, you do!" she grinned.

"God, leaving you anytime is hard enough, but now, Caroline!" he sighed, pulling her to him again to hold her safe for what little time he was allowed. "That's what nigh put my lights out. *Damn* the Navy! I should be here with you! I love you so much, and now there is so much to worry about. Write me daily! I love you so much, and I could lose you so easy. I do love it! I do! I'm that proud of you, m'girl. But, had they physicians on Long Island . . . hell's teeth, just *one*, I'd take you there so I could keep an eye on you 'til . . . no, there're better physicians here in Nassau. Oh, Christ!"

"I'm healthy as a colt, Alan. My entire family is," Caroline assured him. "I'll look after myself. The Boudreaus have the finest physician in mind for me, and Betty will move in with me to share my confinement. Until August."

"That's good," he agreed. "For you, and her, consid'rin'."

"Wyonnie and her husband Daniel'll be here for my heavy chores, and I . . ." She planned, then broke off and began to weep. "God, I'm going to miss you so bad! I *do* want you here, but I know you can't. No idea when . . . ?"

"A few months, I think. When Commodore Garvey sends for me. Exile until then. Look, m'girl, he's that angry with me. Suggested I chuck my command and commission, and . . ."

Damme if I'll worry her with that bastard's slanders; no!

"We could sail home to England, love," he concluded.

"We'll do no such thing, Alan," she decided firmly. "It's too late for that, and sea voyages aren't safe for pregnant women, I've been told, so I'm better off here. As for his sorry treatment of you, he'll come to regret it. Once this has settled, he'll see your merit again. Once the truth about Finney comes out, you'll be able to hold your head up high as anyone! You won't quit now, Alan. You've too much pride to slink away. Too stubborn, too, if the truth be known. Part of what I absolutely adore, darling. Part of the father of our child I cherish and respect. And wish for our children to possess."

It took everything he had not to weep with gratitude for her boundless confidence in him, or for the joy he felt, brief as it now could be, at being so unconditionally loved. This joy he was losing as the sun sank away his final hours ashore with her.

"Thank God for you, Caroline," he muttered, his eyes hot and moist, be-dewing her sweet-smelling hair. "Remember how much I love you! And God knows, as I'll remember whilst I'm gone!"

Slink away, he did, though, as *Alacrity* cupped the last of the twilight Trades, soft-parting slack harbour waters as she steered her way through the throng of shipping in the port at sunset.

The sun declined in almost gaudy grandeur, blood red as hothouse roses, as amber gold as dancing candle flames, with the clouds regular wavy mottles and swirls like angels' tresses. Lanterns were being lit ashore, on the docks, on the many moored vessels as twilight gathered, and *Alacrity*'s fo'c's'le belfry, helm and taffrails glowed warm yellow as well.

"Put your helm down two points, quartermaster," Lieutenant Ballard instructed softly. "Lay her head nor-nor'west for the main channel."

"Aye, aye, sir, nor-nor'west," Mr. Neill echoed.

"Ready for the gun salute to the flag, Mister Ballard?" Lewrie asked, sunk deep in the "Blue Devils" and gazing astern to see if he could espy a light on the porch of a particular house above Potter's Cay, on the beach road.

"Aye, sir."

"Wonder why yon ship is dressed all over, sir?" Midshipman Parham said, pointing ahead to a fine three-masted lugger profuse with flags and bunting. Her decks were afire with lanterns in profligate array all down her gangways, and about her quarter-deck railings.

"Shut yer mouth, Mister Parham!" Lewrie heard Ballard whisper in a harsh tone as he recognized the house flag atop her mainmast.

"Sorry, sir," Parham grunted, blushing as he saw it, too.

Lewrie came to the nettings over the waist and raised his spyglass to look her over. "She's a new 'un. Oh. One of Finney's. They seem to have something to *celebrate* yonder this evening."

The faint sounds of a band could be heard tootling merry tunes as the many guests danced or sang with rowdy good cheer.

"Goddamme!" Lewrie shuddered as he read the name on the transom plate of the new ship. "Goddamn him!"

"What is it, sir?" Ballard asked.

"Here, see for yourself, Mister Ballard!" Alan said, shivering with dread, and strongly reconsidering an immediate resignation.

"Why, the bastard!" Ballard yelped in outrage.

There, in ornate, serifed letters, bright with gold leaf, was the new ship's name: *Caroline!*

"How dare he presume, sir!" Ballard growled, repulsed by such a boorish, flaunting deed, his prim sense of decorum scandalized!

"Put your helm aweather, Mister Neill," Lewrie decided quickly. "New course due west. Steer up yon lugger's transom, but be ready to come about again to due north for the channel when I call."

"Sir?" Ballard queried, coming to his side.

"Helm's aweather, sir. Comin' about t' due west, sir."

"You'll be using the larboard battery for the salute, Mister Fowles?" Lewrie called down to his master gunner in the waist below.

"Aye, sir. Ready any time you want, sir."

"Oh, sir," Lieutenant Ballard objected, but not too forcefully, as he got his quizzical, bemused look. "Surely *not!*" he tried to pout.

On their new course, they would ram *Caroline* in her very stern, or pass down her starboard side at close pistol-shot at best!

"Open your ports, Mister Fowles. Ready with the salute."

At half a cable's distance from a collision, Lewrie turned to the quartermaster. "Helm alee, Mister Neill. Nor'west."

Alacrity bore away upwind of the anchored *Caroline*, crossing her starboard quarter at a forty-five degree angle at one hundred yards!

"Fire your salute, Mister Fowles," Lewrie grinned.

BOOM! "If I weren't a gunner, I wouldn't be here. Number Two gun
. . . fire!" Fowles paced out the stately measure, walking aft with the
guns. *BOOM!* "I've left me wife, me home, and all that's dear. Number
Three gun . . . fire!" *BOOM!*

Guests aboard the *Caroline*, and her mates, had cringed when they
saw *Alacrity* bearing down on them. They'd laughed at Finney's japes
against the Navy as he celebrated his victory. Then, here was the Navy
bearing down upon them as if to ram and board her! Civilians dashed
about in sudden terror as the first cannon fired its reduced powder
charge. Women screamed, and the band came to a sudden gurgling halt!
Crewmen ran for weapons, sure they were being fired at, or took themselves below for safety, as their mates bellowed for order on the quarter-
deck. Hot powder smoke, rank with rotten-egg and hell-fires' stench,
wafted over them as *Alacrity* cruised slowly by across their quarter like
vengeance.

"Ah, there's our host," Lewrie chuckled.

John Finney came clawing his way through his terrified, darting guests
to the rails, to stand head-taller than the rest, gaudy in pale silks and
satins, with a white-powdered tie-wig askew on his head, as he shook his
fist at them and mouthed curses lost in the shouting, the screams, and
the deafening gunfire.

"Helm down, Mister Neill. North for the channel," Lewrie said as the
last shot of the salute belched forth and echoed off *Caroline*'s hull. "Haul
taut, forrud! Brace up, sheet home! Give us a tune, you men!"

The ship's idlers who played fiddle and fifes lurched into life, playing a
gay pulley-hauley chantey, "Portsmouth Lass", the only one allowed in
the Fleet, as *Alacrity* turned her stern to *Caroline* and steered away for
the sea, her flags flying and her commissioning pendant streaming as
saucily as some teasing, taunting coquette.

"Salute's done, sir," Fowles said after carefully counting his shots.

"I should certainly say it is, Mister Fowles!" Alan laughed.

Finney could be seen tearing the tie-wig from his head to throw it
after them, screaming imprecations that were only thin howls under the
chantey-tune, the hull's creaking and the wake's bustling swash.

"He may play the hoary seaman, but he's a shopkeeper, Mister Ballard," Lewrie said loud enough for the afterguard to hear. "Just a jumped-
up *purser*, and a 'Nip-Cheese' 'un, at that! Take that, you bastard! We'll
have you yet!"

For a final fillip, Alan raised his right hand and presented an upright
middle finger to Finney, a *very* English gesture of long usage.

To Alan's amazement, Lieutenant Arthur Ballard stepped to his side at the rails and did the same, as did the midshipmen, and Mister Fellows the sailing master!

The last Finney saw of *Alacrity*, as all but her lights faded into the rosy dusk, was her entire crew standing to attention as taut as Sunday Divisions, hands raised in scornful "salute"!

Chapter 3

"Damme, Mister Keyhoe, there *must* be some correspondence!" he barked at his round little purser.

"Only pay vouchers, I fear, captain," Keyhoe sighed, shrinking into his dark blue coat to escape Lewrie's wrath. "The paperwork that comes with Admiralty stores shipped down from Nassau in the packet."

"Did they at least send money for the hands, then?" Alan asked.

"Uh . . . nossir. The usual certificates, and those six months in arrears, as usual," Keyhoe had to confess.

"So the jobbers ashore'll buy 'em up, and the hands'll have a quarter to a half their true pay, aye," Lewrie almost kicked furniture in his anger.

"Hardly any pay, sir, once they settle their previous debts," Keyhoe muttered on. "Half of it pledged to me for slop goods, tobacco and sundries. The rest with brothels and taverns ashore on every island hereabouts."

"Damme, this goes beyond punishment," Alan fussed. "This now begins to sound very much like vindictiveness! Bosun's stores?"

"None, sir," Keyhoe confessed.

"Powder and shot?"

"Again, none, sir. Just rum, wine, small beer, biscuit and salt meat, captain. Enough for another two months at full rations."

"And what about officers' pay, Mister Keyhoe?" Lieutenant Ballard inquired. "Certificates, too?"

"Aye, sir," Keyhoe huffed. "Had I a way to communicate with my agent in Nassau, I could offer two-thirds value on the certificates, so those vultures ashore don't skin 'em so bad, but I've no coin."

So you're the king-vulture and pocket it all when the ship pays off in 1789, Lewrie thought sourly. There was only one ship's purser he'd ever liked, Mr. Cheatham aboard the *Desperate* frigate during the war. And he'd kept a chary eye on *him* too!

"Well, there'll be drink enough to keep our ship's people easy and groggy," Lewrie stated with a sadly bemused snort. "They'll not starve, but it's issue rations, and nothing fresh, 'less we continue to purchase for 'em when we buy wardroom stores. Damn Garvey!"

"Aye, sir," Ballard said. "But none of us . . ."

"I know, Mister Ballard, we're 'skint', too!" Lewrie nodded in total frustration. "Very well. Working party, Mister Ballard. Warp the packet brig alongside and transfer cargo."

"Aye, aye, sir."

"And call away my gig. I'm going ashore," Lewrie decided of a sudden, feeling imprisoned on his own decks.

Alacrity had been in her new patrol area for six months. Long Island, Rum Cay, Conception and Watling's were sparsely settled, if at all, and the principal settlements were on Cat Island. In that remote corner of the southeast Bahamas, packet ships came irregularly, most often quarterly. For *Alacrity*, they brought provisions and vouchers, but no mail, and no replies to Lewrie's letters to the Bahamas Squadron. As indolent and hand-to-mouth as life was in these islands, it sometimes felt as if the rest of the world had somehow ceased to be since they had attained them, as if all civilization had fallen.

There had been no summons to a Court of Inquiry into Walker's Cay. There had been no notice of a civil trial for damages laid by John Finney. And no answer to Lewrie's urgent requests for powder and shot, sailcloth, rope, tar, paint and nails with which to keep *Alacrity* in fighting trim and able to keep the sea. Live-firings to maintain the gunners' accuracy were a thing of the past, as was drill at small arms beyond swords and pikes, since dry-firing shattered the flints in their muskets and firelocks on the carriage guns.

There didn't seem to be much point in patrolling the area, either. There was very little sea traffic except for fishing boats and the rare interisland packet. There was no foe to fight, no trade worth the name to protect, and hence, no piracy to defend against. It was rare to see a deep-draught seagoing ship pass by, since most of the trade headed for Nassau, Eleuthera or the Exumas up north, or down south to the salt isles of the Turks and Caicos in season.

Alacrity made a nuisance of herself by stopping every ship she could catch to inspect cargoes and manifests to enforce the Navigation Acts. And plead for their personal letters to be forwarded to Nassau, should a ship be going there.

Yet, most mystifyingly, there had not been one article of mail from the outside world received in the entire six months. And with the lack of personal correspondence, the hands had gone sullen and slack, as had the warrants and officers. Try as they might to keep the men active with hydrographic work, with the erection of night-beacons and day-marks to aid navigation, it was a half-hearted endeavor as weeks wore by with little pay, few amusements and dulling drudgery to face with no hope of novelty, or relief.

With no Admiralty funds with which to purchase fresh meat and vegetables, Lewrie had resorted to many refreshing shore expeditions. They would land and hunt wild goats, pigs or iguanas. They would lay at anchor for a day or two and let the hands fish, or gather conch from the shallows, then stage "maroons" with music, singing, dancing and drink enough to at least mellow the men as their food cooked by nighttime beach campfires. By day, they'd extemporize the means to play village games like football or cricket, endless "best-of-seven" tournaments of watch against watch. Even that had palled, lately.

Turtle races, cockroach races, ratcatching . . . they'd tried it all on. They'd allowed the hands to keep parrots they caught ashore, wild kittens and puppies. They tried to capture wild pigs and temper them to abide being penned in the manger forward by the break of the forecastle for later consumption. Lately, only William Pitt was fond of the menagerie, licking his chops in drooling expectation over the fractious shoats, and attempting to creep up on unsuspecting parrots.

On almost uninhabited Rum Cay, Lewrie had rented a small piece of white land, and had hired an older man to watch it for them, with hopes of fresh vegetables and melons, buying the seeds out of his own pocket, as he had several other small lots of supplies. But now, he was down to his last thirty pounds, and was practically living on the ship's rations himself most of the time, with no replies from Nassau requesting funds from his personal accounts. Every officer or warrant with a shore agent was similarly cut off!

And, he had no idea if he was now a father.

Or a widower.

There had been no letters from Caroline; not one!

Childbearing, the ordeal of childbirth, was the scourge of women, no matter how healthy. "Childbed Fever" they called it and even back home in civilized London, the annual bills of mortality bore thousands and thousands of victims. What could be expected in such a rude climate as the Bahamas with so few skilled physicians he could not force himself to contemplate any longer.

And half of those hopeless drunkards, he thought miserably!

He threw himself into anything, if only so he could cease his frantic brooding for a few hours. Swordplay until he frothed with sweat. Practice upon the flageolet until he could carry a tune from start to finish at a regular meter. Hunting and fishing. Amusing William Pitt with a cork on a piece of string for hours.

And sulking. And morose imaginings of Caroline dead, until his lack of news for good or ill, his hours of staring raptly at her portrait, his fretful sleep and vivid, nightmarish dreams, had sunk him into a deep despondency, a surreal resignation.

Clarence Town on Long Island was a dreadfully boresome place, worse than Anglesgreen on Sunday, and this was a market day. He took a table in the shade of a veranda at the one inn the settlement could boast and ordered rum, lime juice, sugar and water for a cold punch. He put his feet up in a rickety chair, removed his hat, undid his neck-stock, and settled in for an afternoon of drinking, an activity which was beginning to figure more prominently in his life lately.

There was a London paper nine months old to read, what was left of it, after being pawed over by countless other patrons, so he was in for the day, if he read all eight pages slowly.

"Ho dere, Navy mon," a fetching black girl said from the railing overlooking the sandy street. "Got no-thin' bettah t'do on ya run asho', now, an' you a hon'some young feller, Lord."

Did I bring my condom with me, he asked himself? No, I'll not! There's Caroline, now. Well, would it hurt to sit and at least *talk* with a woman? Six months, it's been.

"Cat got ya tongue, fine sah?" she teased. She wasn't as dark as most, tarted up in a decent sack gown she'd altered so it fell low off her strong shoulders, and bared a darkly shadowed cleft between heavy breasts that swelled her bodice far beyond the original owner's design. She sported a wide-brimmed straw hat, tied beneath her chin with a yellow ribbon, and to keep off the August sun, a small parasol which she twirled fetchingly.

Damned handsome wench, Lewrie appraised silently. More coffee-milk than black. Huge brown eyes, that pouty mouth, and . . . Christ!

"Just taking my ease for the day," he said at last.

"Dot rum punch be bettah wit' de pineopple in it, sah. Ya let me show ya how, sah, an' do I get a glass, I be obliged," she teased. "De son, he be hot t'day, cap'um sah."

Oh, Christ, I'd best . . . ! He squirmed inside.

"Take a seat with me," he said instead. "Indeed, it is a hot day. I'd not see a lady suffer. And it's a very old paper. And who might you be?"

"M'name's Wyannie, sah. Wyannie Slocum," she smiled in victory.

Hot, sweaty couplings they had, in a rented room of the tavern. Bodies sheened with perspiration as they plunged away at each other in total, wanton abandon. Her legs were strong and muscular, and Wyannie bucked and thrust back at him with equal vigor, enfolding him with all her limbs, writhing and shoving to meet him hard enough to lift him in the air off the crackling straw mattress and creaking bedropes. She squalled and grunted, panted and lowed like a cow, cursed and groaned and shuddered, then ended each time in hissing screams.

There was more rum punch between bouts, mutual spongedowns with a pitcher of water and a mildewed handcloth, which renewed their heat. She'd roll a firm thigh across him to ride St. George as he squeezed those heavy breasts, or teased large, dark rock-hard nipples with his thumbs. Once she romped atop him facing away toward his feet, which led to her bent forward, kneeling on the side of the rickety, low cot and him standing behind her with a death grip on her madly rocking hips as he thrust deep into her as frantic as a hound, sweat rolling off his chest and belly, off her solidly firm buttocks, to mingle with their juices. They'd bellowed like bulls and had fallen almost senseless in an exhausted swoon after that one, Alan's mind areel with her cheap perfume, a woman's odors, and her exotic, musky aroma.

"You come t'Clarence Town agin, Alan?" she breathed lazy as a cat as she lolled open and idle beside him. She picked up a top-silver palmetto-frond fan and began to cool him. "Got me a nice shack down t'the beach. We c'n go dere nex' time, luvah-mon. Save ya money an' not need t'rent a room heah."

"We never did discuss your fee," Alan sighed. "We were a touch too . . . eager, for tawdry business talk."

"Ah ain't no who'," she chuckled as she rolled over to kiss and fondle him. "Jus' walk inta town t'market, an' sell m'melons an' veg'tables. Jus' comin' heah t'buy m'rum, an' dere ya wuz, a'lookin' *fine!* Hod me a mon, but he drown las' year fishin', an' nobody else since. Nobody 'roun' heah wort' messin' wit'!" she snorted in contempt. "Some as tried. An' I ain't sayin' de lonely don' pester me s'hard I didn' sport wit a mon a time'r

two. I be a who', Lord, I en' up payin' you, darlin'! No, I got me a patch
o' white lan', I got de nets, an' goats an' chick'ns, so I c'n keep m'self
right good most de time. Ya don' owe me nottin', luv."

"Well, stap me!" Alan purred, pleased as punch at the news.

"I know ya ship come heah once de mont'," she said, sitting up on one
elbow and leaning over so her breasts spilled over his chest. "Ya come
t'me, hey? I be yer wo-m'n when yer ashore. Ya sport wit' me good's ya
do t'day, Wyannie don' need dese no-'count Clarence Town bo-eys.
None o' 'um's ram-goat as you, cap'um Alan!"

"You make a tempting offer, Wyannie," he told her. "A damned
handsome offer!"

"Shack needs t'fix up some. An' I may need a few t'ings, so I c'n look
pritty fo' ya," she allowed. "Ya know wot dey say, shillin' he be good's de
poun', in Clarence Town. Mebbe ya gimme two, t'ree shillin' t'tide me
ovah 'til ya get bock t'me an' I c'n luv ya agin, hey, darlin' mon? Den I
be ya wo-m'n, an' ya have me all t'y'self."

Right, and I'm Prince Henry the Navigator, Alan thought wryly; I
thought it sounded a little too good to be true! Still . . .

"Wot ya say, luv?" she cooed, drawing him over to her, lifting a breast
to his face to be suckled and licked, trailing her lips over his neck and
shoulders. She reached down to dandle his waking member.

There came a sudden rapping on the flimsy door.

"Damn my eyes," he muttered under his breath. "Who is it?"

"Lieutenant Ballard, sir."

"Oh, shit," Alan started. "Uhm. A moment! Get dressed, girl."

He got to his feet, fuddled with rum punch and weak-kneed from past
exertions and staggered into stockings, breeches and shirt, gave up a
search for his shoes, and went to open the door. He tried to step out into
the rude hall and close the door behind him so Ballard would not see his
companion, but Wyannie had walked into plain sight to bend over and
retrieve her shift, and stood there, splendidly, provocatively nude.

Arthur Ballard's brows lifted, his wary eyes flew open, and for a fleeting moment of shock, he lost his usual calm composure. His jaw sagged,
until he swallowed and shut his mouth into a prim set, his lower lip even
more pouted than usual.

"What is it, Mister Ballard? Something amiss aboard?"

"Ah, no, sir," Ballard replied, still flustered, and blushing like a
schoolboy. "But there's a note come aboard, sir, from the local magistrate. Said there's a letter in his possession for us from Cat Island. Been
held by him for a month or more, sir."

"Hallelujah!" Alan whooped with joy. After six months of silence, any missive at all was nothing short of miraculous! "Give me a moment to dress, and I'll be right with you."

"Aye, sir. I'll wait on the veranda," Ballard blushed again.

"Do me buttons up, luvah-mon?" she asked him, dressed but for the back of her gown.

"Sorry we were interrupted. I have to go back aboard."

"Dot's fine," she smiled as she turned around to face him. "I gotta be gettin' back t'my place, anyways. Lef' m'chillun wit' m'ma t'watch. Don' ya worry 'bout de kids nex' time ya come, cap'um Alan. I shoo 'um off fo' de night ovah t'momma's."

"Of course," he said, cringing inside.

Christ on a crutch, she has children, he thought! Here I've been bulling her all over the shop, and Caroline . . . what of my child? Damme, but I can be such a bloody *fool!*

"Here, Wyannie," he said, pressing a crown into her palm.

"Lord o' mercy, Alan, ya don' need t'gimme dot much!" Wyannie protested. "I tol' ya, I ain't a who'! Two shillin' keep me fine 'til ya get back. An' ya don' *need* t'gimme ev'n dot, luv."

"Five shillings keeps you better," he said gallantly, smiling in spite of his sudden chagrin, and knowing he'd never see her again in this life, if he had any willpower left. "Dresses you prettier, and takes care of those sprouts of yours the better, hey? Widowhood is hard any place you are. And you're much too young and pretty to be a widow in need."

"Ya sweet," she warmed to him, and accepted the coin. She gave him one last fervid embrace, one last series of open-mouthed and moist kisses. "Walk me t'de road, like a gen'mun, hey, cap'um?"

He saw her down the hall, onto the veranda, where she retrieved her straw baskets and produce bags, doffed his hat and gave her a bow which made her smile so widely that she dimpled as she curtsied to him, and watched her stroll away loose-hipped and proud with a profound sense of relief, yet a smile of pleasant reverie on his face. Even if Arthur Ballard was watching his antics.

"Well, shall we stroll over to the magistrate's, Arthur?"

"Aye, sir."

They set off down the single street Clarence Town could boast, the afternoon swelter of a late August day only slightly tempered by the sea's breeze, kicking up small clouds of sandy dust with each step.

"Uhm, Alan," Arthur said at last. "Sir, I . . . uhm."

"Yes, Arthur?" Alan asked, certain that this was not to be an official matter.

"Damme, sir," Ballard cursed for the second time in Alan's recollection. "I know it's not my place. Or my concern, how you conduct your personal affairs, sir."

"No, it isn't, Arthur," Alan replied. "Yet . . . ?"

"I mean to say, though, sir. Well, there're . . . you are married, sir. There're vows and such," Ballard strangled out. "And to such a *fine* young lady as your dear Caroline, sir. Were the . . . uhm . . . had you been with a white woman, sir . . . dash it all, Alan, it seems such an incomprehensible slip for you to make, sir, with Caroline waiting for you in Nassau. With child! And to lay with a Cuffy slattern . . ."

"A handsome young widow, Arthur, with children of her own," Lewrie stated calmly.

Damme, but he's a priggish young swine, he thought!

"Not a year over twenty, she is. Proud, free and independent. For your information, she did it for free, Arthur. And she was damn' good, let me tell you," Lewrie said, his perverse streak standing up on both hind legs and baying the moon down. "She's a lonely widow, and I am a weak and foolish man. We crossed hawses once, and like as not, we'll never come bulwark-to-bulwark again."

"I understand your loneliness, Alan," Ballard stuttered. "How worried you've been without news from . . . from Nassau."

"Don't you ever get lonely, Arthur?" Alan inquired. "Doesn't a craving for abandon come over you so powerful of a sudden that any old drab doxy'd do you? Don't you ache to put the leg over?"

"I hope to set my aim a bit higher than mere rutting, sir," Lieutenant Ballard rejoined primly. "I'd wish someday for . . . well, sir, for some bright and lovely young lady as fine as your wife, sir."

"Yet you turned your nose up at Elizabeth Mustin."

"A bit too frippish and . . . flibbertigibbet for my lights, sir. I hope you do not take that the wrong way, seeing as how you and your wife set such store by her company, sir, but . . ." He shrugged.

"I don't know why I care for you as much as I do, Arthur," Alan chuckled, clapping him on the back. "You're shy as a spanked puppy in women's company. You'd lie like a butcher's dog next to a handsome bit of quim as yon Wyannie and never sniff the beef! You don't drink but a bottle a day, bad days or good! And you're as stiff-arsed as a parson in a poor parish."

"True, sir," Ballard grimaced, rueful at the truth.

"But you've wit, and you've sense, and damme if you're not right about most things," Alan allowed, laughing out loud. "I use mine for jollities. And I'd go dashing off on a tear without your advice half the time. Begrudge me my faults, Arthur. Mind you, I'm not asking you for forgiveness, Reverend Ballard. That's between me and Our Lords Commissioners for the Execution of the Office of Lord High Admiral of this world, and the next. Takes all kinds. I am most often one of the sorry kind, and when it comes to Caroline, damned fortunate. Made me feel good, Wyannie did. She and this mysterious note of yours have put me in a fettle such as I've not felt in months, sir! As my old Captain Lilycrop would say, feagued me so well as a lump o' ginger up a prad's rump! Ought to *issue* girls like her. Good for morale."

"I see, sir."

"No, you don't, you're only making noises like you do," Lewrie cajoled him. "Wish to God you did. Damme, but you take life serious, Arthur! God knows sailors don't mean much by their sins, when they do get the opportunity. Precarious as we get Life, we're a pack o' hymn-singin' *castrati* compared to landsmen. Try putting a foot wrong, now and again, Arthur. Go on a tear, why don't you?"

"Takes all kinds, as you say, sir," Ballard replied, grinning shyly in spite of himself. "I'll not meddle again, sir. Sorry."

"The devil you won't," Alan chortled. "And I may bark to pin your ears back, but remember I mean nothing by it. And if you care enough about me to warn me when I'm about to do something lunatic, then that's what friends are for. As oddly matched as they sometimes are."

"Aye, aye, sir," Ballard nodded. "Now, pray God we've good news at last!"

Chapter 4

The letter was from Col. Andrew Deveaux, one of the major planters on Cat Island, informing them that he held mail for them at his mansion near Port Howe on the southern coast, mail sent directly to him from Nassau by his old friend from South Carolina, Mr. Peyton Boudreau.

Upon that elating news, *Alacrity* was up-anchor and out of the harbour at Clarence Town by dawn the next morning, beating into the nor'east Trades for Port Howe.

*   *   *

There was one narrow break in the coral reefs surrounding Port Howe, with breakers lazily spuming on either hand, and behind the reef was a shallow port ill suited for anything much larger than *Alacrity*.

"They ought to drop the 'E'," Lewrie commented once they were come to anchor, with the courses handed and being lashed secure.

"Sir?" Ballard smiled.

"Call Port Howe H-O-W," Alan grimaced. *"How* the devil a ship may enter without wrecking herself is beyond me. And where are the day-marks, and the warning beacon we erected in May, I ask you?"

"I have no idea, sir."

"Carry on, Mister Ballard. I'm going *ashore!"*

He was rowed to the town's one long pier, debarked onto a lower land-ing stage atop a catamaran work platform, and almost ran down the pier for the tiny village. A man on horseback waited for him at the shore end, with another mount held by a groom near at hand.

"Lieutenant Alan Lewrie?" the man asked. "That is the *Alacrity* yon-der, sir?"

"She is, and I am, sir. And you are?"

"Andrew Deveaux, sir. Delighted to make your acquaintance," he said, springing down from his saddle lithe as a cavalryman. Deveaux was a rather small and lean fellow, shorter than Alan. His face was fox-lean, with a pointy patrician nose, almost a woman's soft mouth, large, liquid brown eyes, and a smallish, tapering ball of a chin. He wore two-tone black and tan top boots, white sailcloth breeches, and a loosely flowing silk shirt, his face shaded by a very wide-brimmed woven straw hat. They shook hands, muttering the expected "your servant, sir", and that's when Alan discovered the steel in the man, for his grip was stronger than a fencing master's.

"Didn't think you'd come to Port Howe," Deveaux commented. "I was prepared to ride to The Bight on the western coast, if necessary."

"Alacrity is shallow-draught enough to enter, sir, so I thought this would save time. You've been watching for me?"

"For nigh a month, sir. Here, sir, do you ride? My groom has a mount for you, and my coach can be fetched if you do not."

"I ride, sir. Thankee."

A black servant brought a fine gelding forward and held reins while Alan got aboard. They set off down a sandy track between thick clusters of sea-grape trees for his plantation house to the west. Alan was struck by how young Deveaux was, how unremarkable.

"This is quite an honor, Colonel Deveaux," Alan said. "To meet you, a hero of the Revolution, and the man who recaptured Nassau from the Dons." Another of those frail but game scrappers? he wondered.

"Neck-or-nothing," Deveaux shrugged. "But bloodless. People do make much more of it than it really was. I am quite honored to meet you, sir. I heard in the Nassau paper of your feats at Conch Bar, and Walker's Cay."

"Well, Walker's Cay, sir . . ." Alan grumbled sadly, then sat up and looked back toward the harbour. "Sir, we put up day-marks and some warning beacons earlier. They're gone now. Do you have any . . . ?"

"Oh, those!" Deveaux hooted, throwing his head back in delight. "Damme, sir, do you not know that before the war, a third of Bahamian revenues came from shipwrecking and salvage? Blackbeard, Henry Morgan . . . Port Howe was one of their old haunts, so the locals tore down your marks the minute you were out of sight and moved 'em ashore for lures, to make the town look bigger at night. Needed the timber for buildings, too. They light the place up like a major city, put lights in the harbour so it appears deep-draught ships are anchored in Port Howe, in hopes of luring the foolhardy onto the reefs, so they may strip the wreck. You got off easy, sir. I'm told a Navy officer formerly in these islands was almost lynched for even *suggesting* he'd erect a lighthouse on Great Exuma!"

"Worse than Cornishmen, I do declare," Lewrie smiled, surprised all over again in spite of his supposed worldliness.

"Indeed. We get so little news here on Cat Island. What about Walker's Cay, sir? Peyton writes that all talk of suits and such have been dropped long ago. Did you . . . ?"

"Dropped?" Alan cried. "I had no idea, sir. I've not had even a single word from Nassau in six months!"

"Not even from your wife?" Deveaux frowned. "Pardon me, but he also wrote that she was most greatly upset that she had not heard from you, Lieutenant Lewrie."

"She is well, Colonel Deveaux?" Alan demanded with alarm. "Did he say more? She's with child, and I've been beside myself with fear!"

"He did state she was expecting, and that he and his wife were perturbed that her worries about your silence would affect her health. But she is well, Lieutenant Lewrie, he did assure me of that. She had begged him to discover what had happened to you, and why you hadn't responded to her letters."

"Damme, sir, I *got* no letters! Nothing!" Alan shouted. "No one aboard *Alacrity*'s had a single thing, except for our purser, and only inventories of supplies sent out to sustain us, which do not require an answer. I've sent request after request to my squadron commander, and dozens of letters to Caroline, and it's like dropping a stone down a wellshaft and never hearing even a splash. I feared . . . you cannot *imagine* what I have feared, sir!"

"Well, rest easy," Deveaux assured him. "There's a small bag of correspondence for you and your ship, sir. And a thick packet of letters from your wife. Peyton could not believe you would ignore her so callously. He stated in his note to me that he suspects your superiors are withholding your mail to and fro."

"I know Commodore Garvey was wroth with me over Walker's Cay and John Finney's trial. He sent us down here out of anger. But I never thought he'd be *that* vindictive to me!"

"You've written him often, then?" Deveaux demanded.

"Weekly, sir. We're running out of all manner of stores except for food and drink. Sir, if this goes on, my ship'll be crippled for lack of new spars, rope and sailcloth. Yet, without specific orders, I am barred from returning to the Navy dockyard at Nassau."

"And I trust you've saved a fair copy of your every plea, sir?" Deveaux hinted slyly. "As a precaution for the future?"

"Aye, sir, that's customary. And in black ink, too," Alan had to grin as he said it. "But why would he interrupt my mail? How can a man be so spiteful?"

"We'll discuss that later," Colonel Deveaux told him. "Once we get to my house, you read your letters. And fill yourself in on what has been happening in Nassau in your absence. Then we'll talk more."

Caroline was alive! And well!

He went to her letters first, reading the one with the most recent date to assure himself of her existence and her safety. She wrote that she was blooming big as a mare about to foal, the baby was kicking lustily, and that she carried low, which the physician and midwife she had engaged considered signs of a man-child. Except for the usual complaints and pains, the clumsiness and heaviness, she reassured him that her confinement was not too hard, although she missed the pleasures of riding, gardening, and doing her own cooking; yet, between Betty Mustin and Wyonnie (Lewrie flushed with remorse as that similar name appeared) she had no difficulties.

After that joyous news, though, there was a plaint that brought tears to his eyes as he read of her tightly denied fears; that he and *Alacrity* had been sunk or wrecked; that he had died of some fever; that he'd fallen out of love with her and now spurned her; that he did not really desire children, and had turned his back on her, as a rich man might discard an inconveniently pregnant mistress who was no longer as attractive or slim.

> . . . I try and try to imagine you being so involved in some stern Duty that even our Love must be relegated a poor second for the nonce, but dearest Alan, it has been *so long* since you sailed away, and not one word from you have I received, nor any hearsay as to . . .

"Oh, Caroline, Christ!" he whispered through a throat constricted by his weeping. "Goddamme, no, it's not like that!"

He would sail at once to Nassau, he vowed. Damn the threats, or the consequences! Let them court-martial him for anything they damned well pleased, just so long as he could see her one more time, and tell her that her fears had no substance!

"And Goddamn the bastard who did this to me!" he raged. "Cruel, malicious *bastard!* How could anyone . . . ? Dozens and dozens of letters and they've kept 'em all. Damme, do they read 'em? Do they gloat over her pain? By Christ, I'll have their *heart's blood for this!*"

On the patio, Andrew Deveaux and his wife sat in the shade, and winced as they heard the strangled howl from within their drawing room.

"That poor young man," Mrs. Deveaux shuddered. "And his terrified young wife, Andrew! Do you truly believe that his commodore keeps his letters deliberately, dear?"

"I do," Deveaux scowled, running his hands through his thick and unruly long blond hair. "That, and a lot worse. Oh, it's foul, I . . ."

"You're dead, swear to Jesus, you're a dead man!" Lewrie wailed.

"I'd not wish to walk on Lieutenant Lewrie's bad side, dear," Mrs. Deveaux frowned. "Not even were I the King of France!"

It took an hour for Lewrie to collect himself enough to join them on the patio for tea, though he was still fretful and jerking at inability to be in action that instant. He could not keep his hands still, and one crossed leg juddered upon the other as he rocked irately on his chair.

"I trust your wife is well, Lieutenant Lewrie," Deveaux asked.

"Aye, sir," Alan said, trying to be as gracious as his hosts. "The physician and midwife are confident the child's due late this month. A boy, they believe. Why, I could be a father now, even as we speak!"

"And your other letters are reassuring as well?"

"From my shore agent, Coutts & Co., my bank back home, my grandmother in Devon. Even one from my father in India. Caroline had saved them, no longer . . ." he gulped down a threatening spasm of raw emotion, "no longer believing I could, or would, respond to her until I returned to Nassau."

Sore as he hurt, he had to grin slightly, remembering what his father Sir Hugo had penned. It had begun "You silly, rantipoling dog, sir! Have I not drummed into you one should rent, not purchase, quim?" That smile, however, was just as quickly gone.

"God, it's so petty. So base! So cruel to her!"

"It's Jack Finney," Deveaux declared bluntly. "Sugar?"

"Finney? How could he get at Fleet mail, sir?" Alan gaped.

"Not Finney directly," Deveaux allowed. "I doubt he has interests in your personal letters. But you did anger him when you caught his ship trading in pirated goods, and you stung him upon his sorest spot when you burned the cache and hauled him into court. He has powerful friends, sir. And money enough to buy anyone he desires."

"So even you believe he's a pirate, sir?" Alan hoped aloud.

"I'm certain of it," Deveaux stated firmly.

"So he's bought himself a clerk in the Commodore's office, then. That way, he'd know where our patrols would be, so he might tell his piratical confederates," Alan realized. "And he never sued us because he would have been exposed as a smuggler at the least! Those goods we burned were never landed or bonded. And all this time Rodgers and I were fearing he'd end up making us jump through his lawyers' hoops!"

"I expect it cost him considerable to stay out of court on any smuggling charges, to boot," Deveaux smiled thinly. "The assembly in which I sit, sir, the courts, the Governor's Council . . . see here, sir, Nassau is an offal-ditch, an open sewer, a cesspit of corruption, and *all* is for sale! When I was awarded my grant of land for what little I did to retake New Providence, I was more than happy to settle on Cat Island. Did you know even this salubrious isle was named long ago for an Arthur Catt, a pirate? And does that not *tell* you something about the Bahamas, sir? Most of the year, I am quite content to avoid Nassau with all its backstabbing, money-grubbing squalor, and limit my visits to Assembly sessions. Even so, this far happily removed, we still get a whiff of its corruption, like an ill wind from an abbatoir. I have heard rumors. Peyton did not speak of them in his letter to you?"

"Some vague hints, sir. But I took them to involve my letters. And my exile. He wasn't sure what had happened to me, either. He had written before, demanding me to answer him, to answer Caroline, or tell him why I would not. But how could I? I never got those, either!"

"And thought to use me as intermediary after he no longer could trust the Navy to forward mail. Or trust the Navy at all, sir," Colonel Deveaux said grimly. "He's begun to suspect something foul in our government, and said to me he'd also begun to nose about, to make discreet inquiries. I only pray to God they are discreet. There're thousands at stake in this, and the men involved are not above murder to keep their doings quiet. And to ask about John Finney's doings . . . though a power of talk about him is common coin. People love to gossip about 'Calico Jack.' He's the sort who gets talked about. And loves it."

"Do you know him well, sir?" Alan inquired.

"Well enough, only as an acquaintance, mind," Deveaux smirked. "He's not the sort one has for a firm or trustworthy friend."

"I hear a lot of people say the same, Colonel Deveaux."

"Nodding acquaintances before the Dons landed, and allies when I mustered the volunteers. He helped arm them, you see, and brought his battleworthy bully bucks along," Deveaux chuckled. "In such need as we were, beggars can't be choosers. Back to those suspicions, and the rumors, though. Drunk sailors will brag, and the brag in taverns on the docks, and in Over-The-Hill, is that some of Finney's old hands were up to their old games, once their wartime prize money ran out, as you and Commander Rodgers believed. Too smart to take British ships, but assured that no one'd cry over foreign vessels if they got taken. Not only was Finney profiting from the cargoes he bought up cheap, but he was selling arms and powder to support them out of his chandlery, and brokering the best ships they took after they were repainted and renamed, and all marks of their former identity erased. Just as you thought in the beginning."

"And I wish we'd caught just one of 'em who could have been made to swear to that at his trial, sir!" Alan growled.

"Faint hopes of that, Lieutenant Lewrie," Deveaux smiled. "Look at how quietly Doyle's men went to the gallows. I suspect Finney was no longer dealing with Doyle. Just too untrustworthy and wild! But he'd done so in the past, and they could have exposed it all to save their lives, were it not for the certain knowledge of what Finney would have done to their wives, sweethearts and parents. Their children."

"I find it hard to remember that murderous buccaneers have such, sir," Alan responded.

"Now who stands to profit most from their depredations?" Deveaux prodded. "Who gains? Who loses if it ends?"

"Finney, of course, sir," Alan said quickly. "He's reaping a bumper harvest from it, and undercutting the other Bay Street traders something sinful. I'm surprised they haven't done for him long ago."

"Ah, but he only undercuts them by a few pence overall, so as long as their prices stay high, they have no complaints," Deveaux said with a crafty glint in his eyes. "British ships are not bothered, so their insurance rates stay low. Foreign traders are . . . discouraged, also keeping cheaper goods off the market to compete with theirs, most of the time, at least. Now, who else might profit by this?"

"Well, the ships' husbands in England, the shipowners here in the Bahamas," Alan pondered. "Insurance companies and mercantile interests in England. Stap me, I s'pose that pleases Parliament, too, if they own commercial interests. Or members who are owned by merchants!"

"Parliament is pleased, brokers and bankers in the City," Colonel Deveaux chanted, "the Privy Council is pleased, and so, do I assume, is His Majesty King George. Revenues are up, insurance is low, trade flows freely . . . and piracy is a minor inconvenience for foreign competitors only, just the thing for Dons, Frogs and crude rebel Yankees. And not so much piracy that anyone has to really *do* anything about it! Until you came along, that is, and quashed Doyle's band like so many noxious bugs. You even made our Royal Governor look good!"

"Surely not the governor, sir?" Alan frowned. "You cannot mean that Finney could purchase a Royal Governor. Were the Bahamas still owned by the old proprietors, but we're a Crown Colony now, and . . ."

"Oh, not Maxwell!" Deveaux barked in sour humor. "Our previous governor was decent enough. And certainly not this new clown, our third Earl of Dunmore! He's too rich to bribe, and so arrogant, he'd be insulted if one tried! Lord Dunmore was Royal Governor of Virginia before the Revolution, you know. And I do think he *started* it, all by himself! Had he not been such a venal, greedy, lofty, pustulant *toad* as to set off Patrick Henry and Thomas Jefferson, we . . ." Deveaux had to sip his tea to calm down. "No, Lewrie, Lord Dunmore was born without a jot of brains, and he's lost ground as he's aged. While he may be grasping and greedy, he'd never scruple piracy. I was thinking of someone a trifle lower down. Someone . . . nautical, perhaps."

"You can't mean . . . !" Lewrie almost choked on his tea. "Damme, but . . . your pardons, Mistress Deveaux . . . Commodore Garvey, sir? What possible motive could he have?"

"Beyond money?" Deveaux snorted. "Think! How does one enforce the Navigation Acts? How does one succeed in command of a foreign squadron? And prosper?"

"Suppressing piracy'd suit," Lewrie said, rankled by Deveaux's impatient tone. "Keep down smuggling, keep the sea lanes safe. Seize ships and goods not British, and . . . oh! And avoid getting sued to his hairline for false arrest! Christ! Pardons again, ma'am. As long as Finney and his crowd pillage only foreign ships, he's every Bay Street merchant's darling. The competition is frightened off, so he doesn't have an armada of interlopers to deal with, so our weak squadron isn't overrun. And if Finney does Garvey's dirty work, the Navy isn't sued so often. And money, of course."

"And money, of course," Deveaux echoed. "And how is it done?"

"We're too few already, sir, to really patrol the Bahamas," Alan said, shutting his eyes in thought for a moment. "Finney would be told which areas are unpatrolled. Maybe Finney asks him to keep warships away from certain cays. Or, he could send our worst officers, knowing which ones are just too bone-lazy, stupid, or fearful to intervene, to certain areas."

"In like manner, once you and Commander Rodgers are perceived as energetic officers, you are sent very far away," Deveaux added. "To isolate you from this year's playing field. So there will not be any Court of Inquiry at which any dangerous discoveries might appear that would harm either Garvey, or Finney. And your evidence from Walker's Cay is lost forever. Peyton Boudreau has heard some whisperings about that. Some very guarded rumors, so far. One goes, 'we won't have no more trouble from those sods any longer—Calico Jack's stopped their business for us.' He overheard that one personally, Captain Lewrie, which set him to digging and suspecting."

"Well, I'm damned, sir!" Alan breathed. "Despise Garvey though I may . . . and you'd best believe I do! . . . still, he's a Commission Sea Officer, sir, and a senior one. A man sworn, and an English gentleman! To condone piracy for a price, that's . . . !" Lewrie spluttered. "I know you must consider me hopelessly naive, Colonel Deveaux, but condoning Finney's piracy is condoning wholesale murder!"

"Peyton Boudreau is a top-lofty, aristocratic cynic, Lieutenant Lewrie," Deveaux said with wistful amusement. "Or at least, he poses as one. A hard man to shock. Yet even he found it hard to dismiss after a time. There were too many rumors, too much muttered gossip to ignore.

There's a toast that's heard in Over-The-Hill that Finney's old mates and sailors enjoy. 'To our Navy—our own, and the one we *rent*,' d'ya see? He's learned enough to lay evidence with the solicitor-general, William Wylly. He's another Loyalist, not so long in these islands that he's been corrupted. Nor will ever be, if his repute is as good as I've heard. They were going to peek into Garvey's finances."

"Stap me, sir, should Finney get wind of it, though," Alan said.

"I know. Thank God he had enough sense to see Wylly, instead of proceeding further on his own. I fear for him. We like him very much, sir. And there's too much at stake for them to go gentle with him, if his investigation was exposed."

"As do I and Caroline, sir," Alan assured them. "Remote as you are here on Cat Island, how do you converse so easily with Nassau?"

"I've a small schooner. I know nothing of the sea myself, you know," Deveaux confessed with a small laugh. "But, with packet boats so rare or irregular, I thought to establish a mail-boat service for my own use, and the use of my neighbors. It breaks even, just."

"I *must* get a letter to Caroline!" Alan exclaimed. "And one to Mr. Boudreau, as well, warning him. Tell me your schooner is here!"

"Anchored in The Bight, due to sail two days hence," Deveaux was quick to assure him. "Your wife will be overjoyed to hear from you at last. Instruct her to send future letters here, addressed to me. Better yet, have her give them to Peyton, so she's not seen with my mail-boat captain, and we will have to pray no one will suspect him sending mail to me, an old friend from South Carolina. The fewer who know you're in communication with Nassau again, the better, for a lot of people."

"You don't think Finney or his mates might harm Caroline, do you, sir?" Alan paled.

"I told you there were thousands at stake in this, Captain Lewrie," Deveaux cautioned sternly. "There's no telling what they might do, to protect their reputations, and their profits. It might be best if she could give no sign to anyone that she had heard from you."

"I understand, sir. I'll tell her," Alan said, rising. "With your permission, Colonel Deveaux, I'll go back aboard *Alacrity*. With mail to cheer my people. And letters to write. Lord, thank you for everything, Colonel Deveaux! I cannot begin to express my gratitude. Even if my exile *was* mere spite, I'm forever in your debt for being able to exchange letters with my Caroline again."

He pumped Deveaux's hand energetically.

"Before I sail, though, sir," Alan added. "Could I have a fair copy of all that you and Mr. Boudreau suspect? Before, we had no way to prove

Finney guilty, none a court would accept. This time, we just might have a chance of having his head on a plate! And nailing Commodore Garvey's hide to my mainmast into the bargain!"

"You will have everything, Captain Lewrie," Deveaux promised. "But sail, sir? For where? Not Nassau, I beg you. It's too early to tip your hand, before Mr. Wylly finishes his secret investigation."

"Nay, sir, 'tis far too late, I'm thinking," Alan countered in a fever to be on his way. "But not Nassau. Good Lord, sir, I'm banned from going there, am I not? But," he concluded with a crafty smile, "I don't recall Commodore Garvey saying a blessed thing to keep me from sailing south!"

"South, sir?" Deveaux was forced to query with a frown.

"To put my wits together with Commander Rodgers, sir," Lewrie told him gaily. "And after that, why . . . one never knows, sir!"

Chapter 5

Abeam the Trades, on a soldier's wind, *Alacrity* flew like some mythical courier, threading between Rum Cay and Watling's, and out to deep ocean, taking the outside passage nor'east of Samana Cay, a day's run of 160 nautical miles from one noon to the next. When they "shot" the sun, they'd gained 72°40′ west and 23°30′ north.

"Another day's run'll put us in Turks Passage, sir," Lieutenant Ballard nodded happily as he stowed his sextant away after taking noon sights.

"Wish to God we'd done this months ago." Lewrie paced, restless and impatient. "Garvey might have relented. *Whippet* may no longer be in the Caicos."

"He hadn't relented against us, sir, so why should he spare her before *Alacrity*," Ballard shrugged. "I still can't absorb the fact our Commodore is up to his neck in collusion with Finney and his pirates!"

"Money!" Lewrie snapped, scanning his masts to see if there was one more place where stuns'ls or stays'ls could be deployed that wasn't already being used. "It all boils down to money. What happens to the crews of the pirated ships, he never sees, and it's no concern of his. Even if he did sometimes wonder 'bout it, then money is a great salve to one's conscience."

God knows when I stole that French Commissary gold in '81, it did a power o' good for *mine*, Alan confessed to himself with a rueful grin.

"Sails ho!" the mainmast lookout called from the cross-trees of the upper mast. "Deck, there! Two ships beatin' nor'west, fine on the bows!"

"What's showing?" Ballard hallooed back in that deep, carrying voice which was a surprise for most to hear coming from such a small man.

"Tops'ls 'bove the horizon, sir! Courses, a corner! Under all plain sail!" the answer came wailing back.

"No one's running from pirates, then. They'd have their royals and t'gallants flying, else," Lewrie speculated. "Damme, as much as I hate to, we'll have to close 'em and speak 'em. They might be Yankee interlopers."

"Shall we board them if they are, sir?" Ballard queried.

Alan tried to imagine how long a delay that would be—hours, a whole day, if they had to inspect cargoes and manifests, fetched-to!

"No, Mister Ballard, we'll close 'em, and see if they frighten off with a stern warning," he announced. "We can't spare the time!"

"Sir!" the lookout said after skinning down a stay to the deck. "Capt'n, sir! I seen those ships afore. One's *Whippet*, sir. And the other's that Yankee merchantman we saved last year, the *Sarah and Jane*."

"*Whippet*, by God!" Lewrie whooped with sudden delight. "Thankee, Lord, thankee kindly! Mister Ballard, did you hear, sir? Wear us hard on the wind, get us up to windward of 'em so we may take station on 'em as they fetch us. And get my gig down and ready."

"Aye, aye, sir!"

It was *Whippet*, shepherding the dowdy *Sarah and Jane* of the year before off West Caicos. As they came hull-up over the horizon and the distance between them shrank, Lewrie could make out a Yankee flag flying beneath the Red Ensign aboard *Sarah and Jane* as a prize. *Alacrity* reduced sail, and as they came abeam, hauled her wind to leeward, and rounded up a quarter-mile off *Whippet*'s starboard side. All three vessels then fetched up into the winds, and Lewrie was in his gig and off toward *Whippet* before Rodgers could hoist 'Captain Repair On Board.'

*   *   *

"Damn my eyes, what the devil're you doin' down here, Lewrie?" Rodgers shouted, pumping his hand energetically after the salutes were done. "You'd not be poachin' in my own game park, would ya now?"

"There's been wondrous news from Nassau, sir, so I . . ."

"News from Nassau?" Rodgers gawped, getting keener. "Then you're leagues ahead o' me, Lewrie. I haven't gotten letter one from anybody since I fetched Turks Island! Thank God I stumbled over this Yankee clown, buyin' an' sellin', bold as brass, in Hawk's Nest Harbour, which gives me a legitimate excuse t'sail back to New Providence."

"Aye, sir, but . . ." Lewrie tried to interject, but Rodgers was on one of his "tears".

"Damme, sir, *Whippet*'s ready t'drop her quick-work, same as the *Royal George*, an' sink at her moorin's," Rodgers ranted on. "Copperin' or no, she leaks like a sieve, there's a forest o' weed on her, and I suspect I'm teredo-wormed! Thank Christ, here comes an interloper for me to arrest an' take back to Admiralty Court, so I may get her into a dockyard 'fore we keel over an' go under."

"Sir, if you would but listen to me . . ."

"Well, if it ain't young Captain Lewrie!" *Sarah and Jane*'s captain said, coming on deck to join them. "Now you're here, young sir, I trust you'll tell Commander Rodgers how I aided the Royal Navy, and let me go 'bout me innocent occasions, as you did last year, sir. I've already give him enough threats 'bout false arrest and all. But will he heed me, sir? He will not!"

"I've noticed," Alan snapped in exasperation. "Captain Grant, I recall. Delighted to make your acquaintance again, sir. I did warn you, did I not, sir, that you should not return to Bahamian waters?"

"I'm but a poor merchant skipper, sir, and . . ."

"Later, perhaps, sir," Lewrie cut him off. "Commander Rodgers, I've abandoned my patrol area. There's news from Nassau, and we have to talk. It's urgent, sir!"

"Signal Ballard to get underway," Rodgers nodded. "And let us go below. Mister Cargyle? Get sail on her and resume our course!"

"Good Christ!" Rodgers sighed when Lewrie had finished. He had cut his hair much shorter for summer, close to the scalp as an urchin infested with lice and fleas, and he rubbed his stubble with two hands. "The bastard! The son of a bitch! No, more'n a bastard, he's a bastardly gullion! In league with Finney an' his pirates? I always wondered how he could afford that *palacio* of his. Damn' near good as the Governor's mansion, an' filled with fine plate an' furnishin's. A Commodore won't draw more a year'n a post-captain of a 1st Rate, an' £350 or so won't cover half his expenses, high's he's been livin'. Him an' that chick-a-biddy wife o' his, that semi-ugly daughter, an' good Chaplain Townsley an' his lawful blanket're sure to be expensive to keep as well. What'd ya wager, Lewrie, he banks with Finney's private merchant bank, an' there'll be no way your Mr. Boudreau and Solicitor-General Wylly'd ever smoke him out?"

"I hadn't thought of that, sir," Lewrie deflated as he poured them more claret from Rodgers's much-depleted final stock. "Surely, though, there must be something we can do, if the investigation can't convict them."

"I'm tempted t'sail into Nassau Harbour, all guns blazin', myself," Rodgers gloomed, knocking back half a glass. "'Nother reason for action. Damme, but I'm outa champagne! Wish we knew which ships were patrolling where. That might give us a clue as to where to go."

"Banned though we are from going north," Lewrie commented with a sneer.

"We've this interloper Grant as a fine excuse," Rodgers perked up, leaning his elbows on the table they shared. "He has t'face the Admiralty Court for violatin' the Navigation Acts."

"Not both of us, sir," Lewrie counseled. "You and *Whippet*, for certain. And the Governor's Council and the Bahamian Assembly were kicking 'round the idea of turning Nassau into a free port. If they vote that in, Finney's undutied goods are safe as houses from here on out. Might as well void the Navigation Acts, too, I suppose."

"Did you really let him off last year?" Rodgers grinned.

"Needed his testimony hellish bad, sir," Lewrie blushed. "Only way I knew to have evidence the pirates were caught in the act. But I thought he was smart enough to take my warning to heart. What was Captain Grant up to?"

"Sellin' bricks an' timber, buyin' salt, so the Yankee fisheries can preserve their stock-fish for export," Rodgers sniffed. "Hell, *name* a good he wasn't sellin'!"

"So he's bung to his deckheads in salt now, sir?" Lewrie asked.

"Aye. Takin' it north as evidence against him."

"Hmm, sir," Lewrie grinned.

"What, sir?" Rodgers grinned in reply, expectantly.

"I was thinking, sir, that bagged salt is just as good as dirt-filled gabions to absorb round-shot and musketry," Lewrie mused.

"Whatever are ya drivin' at?" Rodgers asked, sitting up.

"Bait, sir," Lewrie explained. "Were we to find where pirates are operating, we could trail *Sarah and Jane* under Yankee colours as a tempting bit of bait with a Navy crew, armed and ready for anything."

"And just where'd we do the trailin', Lewrie?" Rodgers demanded. "We haven't more of a clue than we did last year. Walker's Cay was a fluke o' fortune." He winced. "Of a *rough* sort, mind."

"My Lieutenant Ballard suggested that one of us put into Harbour Island or Spanish Wells on Eleuthera," Lewrie went on quickly. "They're major ports, and a man o' war from the squadron should be in the area, or at anchor. They could inform us where our ships are operating, sir. Now we know Finney's a pirate for certain, now we *almost* have it as Gospel our commodore's involved, where our ships are would point the way. Or, more to the point, where our ships are *not!*"

"Or where fools such as your Lieutenant Courtney 'Cow-Flop' hangs his hat?" Rodgers grinned briefly, then scowled. "Lieutenant Ballard. God! He's the one got us banished, when you get right down to it. All that talk o' his 'bout irrefutable evidence, and that missin' slaver, *Matilda.*"

"Damme, sir, but wasn't he right?" Lewrie pointed out. "*Matilda* was pirated, and her people slaughtered. There's a knacky wit churning in that head of his, sir, 'click-clack' like some German clockwork. I know he's right about this, too, sir."

Pray God Peyton Boudreau was wrong for once, Lewrie cautioned his eagerness; don't let him be a slender reed one couldn't count on!

And, Alan also warned himself; keep your bloody mouth quiet for once! I can't urge him any harder, or he'll balk like a hunter at the high fence! We either pull this off successfully or we get cashiered at the easiest—or hanged for mutineers!

Rodgers twisted and turned for many long minutes like a corpse on the gibbet, shifting restless and frightened on his chair, trying to decide what to do that wouldn't ruin his career if they failed.

"There's Captain Childs in *Guardian*," Rodgers said at last. "I think he should be informed, Lewrie. About the commodore, that is."

Shit! Lewrie thought.

"The more who know, the more who talk, sir, and word gets back to Garvey and Finney, and then we'll have abandoned our patrol areas for nought," Alan shrugged, taking the softest approach he could.

"If Coltrop's in an Eleutheran port, word'll get back to them, you can wager a *rouleau* o' guineas on't," Rodgers spat, lips pursed in a sour pucker. "Dammit t'hell. Dammit t'hell, though . . . if they get away a second time! If we end up with nothing to show for it!"

"Not if they take the bait, sir," Lewrie promised.

"Hmm," Rodgers stalled. He slapped the table top hard with the flat of one hand. "Damme, let's do it, then! This Yankee-Doodle Captain Grant . . . I s'pose I'll have t'let him off, same as you did, once we find our pirates?"

"I fear so, sir," Lewrie nodded, all but turning St. Catherine wheels with barely repressed glee. "A small price to pay, after all."

"Best it be *Whippet* stands into port. To water, let's say," Commander Rodgers schemed. "You take over escort for *Sarah and Jane*, make what arrangements you will aboard her, and stand off-and-on tops'l down over the horizon t'the east'rd. Pray God Childs an' *Guardian*'ll be the ship in port. Not that Lieutenant 'Cow-Flop'!"

"He may be as out of touch with Nassau as we were, sir," Lewrie hoped out loud. "And that somnolent arse wouldn't stir up his bones to see the Second Coming."

"Somnolent, sir?" Rodgers laughed, rising and fetching his hat. "Damme, but you've been readin' again, ain't ya? After I told ya it was bad for ya, for shame."

"Well, it was only the one book, sir," Lewrie chuckled, getting to his feet to drain his glass. "And a damn' thin 'un, at that."

"Let's go on deck, then, and beard our Captain Grant, sir. And then, lay a course for Eleuthera!"

Chapter 6

Sewallis Alan Lewrie lay sleeping in his cradle, at last, after a noisy afternoon of colic and wailing that had quite worn his young mother to a frazzle. Caroline sat at the side of the cradle, formed in the shape of a miniature dory, that a New England Loyalist joiner had made for her months before, feeling vaguely disloyal.

Women were supposed to adore children, she thought wearily. It was a given that all a young woman could wish for in this life was a brood of offspring to tend. But so far, one was more than enough to deal with, and after six weeks of maternal devotion following the boy's birth, she wasn't so sure she cared to experience the terror and pain again. The physician had rated her labor easy, a mere nine hours! To hold her firstborn like a tightly swaddled roast at the end of it, to peer into those grave little eyes, had not seemed worthy enough reward.

Then had come the interrupted nights, at the mercy of his cries, the shambling sham of wakefulness between precious naps, to brave his supping at her breasts with the frantic lustiness of his absent father, almost dreading the aching, until Heloise and Betty had suggested a wet nurse to spare her, to let Wyonnie tend him for a few hours.

Her body felt destroyed. Where was the lissome figure she'd had, she wondered when she bathed? There was still a heaviness, a gravid and palpable puffiness that only now was departing as she began to take rides and putter in her gardens, her kitchen and pantry. And the stretch marks which traversed her formerly alabaster flesh like fault lines, or desert tributaries of a failed river. Would Alan be repulsed by the sight of her when he returned? She could no longer claim to feel like the lithe girl she'd been—and she had yet to feel comfortable accepting a role of young matron; it was surreal.

Yet . . . She looked down at the puffy little face screwed up with a puckered repose. And had to fight the urge to pick him up to hold him close to her, to carry him out to the dog-run and croon to him as she sat and rocked in the clean air, instead of the humid stuffiness of the bedroom, permeated with the smells of incontinent infancy.

Sewallis Alan Lewrie had been powdered and changed, and she bent down, fearful of waking him, to inhale the aroma of his skin, and of the milky, corn-silks smells he bore like a Hungary Water. She kissed him lightly, brushed his little tuft of hair, and sat back in her straight-backed chair with a fond smile, in spite of all.

Yes, he was a darling baby (most of the time) with his father's gray blue eyes, but with her nose, her paler hair. And her mouth. It felt more than odd to feel his tiny, demanding lips at her nipples, yet it was her mouth, not Alan's.

"You take a rest, missus," Wyonnie offered, entering the room. "I watch 'im fo' awhile. Po' chile cry hisse'f right out. But, he be bettah when 'e wakes. Dot *obeah*-mon's yarbs get rid de colic, jus' as I tole ya. Un de corn-meal fo' dot rash'll ease 'im."

"And I expect he'll wake up hungry," Caroline grinned with a wry lift to a brow. "God save womankind, Wyonnie, from men's . . . needs!"

"All de mo' reason ya naps a spell, missus," Wyonnie chuckled in reply as she sat down opposite Caroline and began to fan him.

"I will, and thank you, Wyonnie," Caroline said. She left the room on tiptoe. Darling or not, Sewallis Lewrie showed signs of a light sleeper, and she felt she'd more than earned this brief respite.

She paused in the parlor to open her stationery box and take out her letter from Alan before going to the dog-run. Even though she had devoured it fifty times at least in the week since it had arrived, it was forever new and reassuring. Hugging it to her bosom, she went out onto the dog-run terrace where a fair wind was blowing, and the air was so much cooler and fresher. She took a seat in her rocker, put up her feet on an embroidered, padded footstool, and began to read it all over again between small sips from a glass of Rhenish.

All over again, she savored his protestations of love, his fear for her and the baby's life, his anguish at being separated so long, and his inability to communicate with her. Once again, Caroline seethed with outrage at the injustice, of their mail being cut off, by how base Commodore Garvey could be. She blushed as she read Alan's curses called down on Finney and Garvey, knowing that she had used similar curses directed at him in the bleakest moments of her despair during his hellish silence. Or what she'd called him during her labor, she snickered!

"Two months I fretted," she whispered. "Damn Peyton and Heloise. I know they didn't want me worried, but they could have told me of their suspicions to ease me!"

But all was right again. Alan still loved her. And, with her harshest memories of pain and fear subsiding, she was once more as much in love with him as the first moment she saw him. And surely he would come back soon. Do something about Finney and Garvey. Hold her again. And there would be no more cause for longing and dread.

The late afternoon heat was ebbing, and a cool wind rushed into the dog-run; Alan's nor'east Trades, which might waft him home at last. She finished her wine, folded up the letter and slipped it onto the table under the wine glass, then put her head back on the small lashed-on pad to take Wyonnie's advice about a nap. She eased the ache of her neck and shoulders with a shrug and a stretch, closed her eyes, took a deep breath, and, with a wistful smile, fell asleep.

She woke in the twilight of another spectacular sundown, rummy with barely eased exhaustion, rocking forward with a start, and listening close for her baby's waking cry, which was what she thought had stirred her. But it was a carriage.

Bay Street, a narrow sandy track, ran in front of their house, and a second, narrower sand and shell lane forked off southeast from the coast road, parallel to the front porch for awhile before winding south along the garden to the great house. A coach had turned in at the gate, and now stood in the lane, half hidden behind the tops of her palmetto hedge. A man was walking toward her through the gate in the "tabby" wall, and up the crushed-shell path to the front porch.

Caroline stood and peered to see who it was. The hat was laced with gold, and for a fleeting moment, she thought it was Alan returned.

"Hello, the house," a voice called. "Anyone to home, be they?"

"Good God!" she whispered in alarm, putting a hand to her mouth. It was John Finney!

"Ah, there you be, Mistress Lewrie," Finney said, stepping upon the deep front porch and coming to her in the mouth of the dog-run. "A very good evenin' to you, Mistress." He took off his cocked hat, laid it upon his chest, and performed a deep, formal bow, one leg extended.

"Mister Finney," she replied, trembling a little with fear that he'd dare appear so boldly. "And to what do I owe this unasked visit?"

"Why, 'tis concern, good lady," Finney replied, stepping closer, and making Caroline wish to shy back, though she stood her ground. "We heard you'd birthed a fine man-child, spittin' image of his beautiful mother, so 'tis said in the town, yet never hide nor hair t'be seen of him, nor yourself since."

Finney had a smile playing at the corners of his mouth, and his eyes sparkled with secret merriment.

"Call it curiosity, Mistress Caroline," Finney went on. "Worry about how ye fare. I'm that fond o' children, ya know, and I wished t'satisfy meself that you were recovered an' all. And t'gain a peek at the little lad, if I be so bold, now."

"He is sleeping, and it's best he's not disturbed," Caroline rejoined, losing her fear as her outrage took over, and the crease in her forehead deepened. "He is quite well, as am I, sir. But I am not yet receiving callers, Mister Finney. It's not seemly for you to be here."

"I'm not so polished as most, I'll tell ya, Mistress Caroline," Finney shrugged with a fetching smile. "'Tis my lack o' manners I most regret, ma'am. I but meant to assure meself o' your good health. And yer contentment. I brought a few things for the little lad, d'ya see. Gewgaws from me stores. Toys and pretties. Hope ya won't bedrudge a feller bein' so bold as to be offerin' a fine young lady such as yer sweet self a few trifles t'start the lad in life. 'Tis rough I come up, Mistress Caroline, an' ne'er a pretty'd I have fer my amusement. I'd not care t'see yer wee one deprived as me."

"I thank you for the sentiment, sir," Caroline allowed. "But I do not think that my son will lack for ought. I could not accept any gift from you, Mister Finney."

"Been a hot one t'day, Mistress," Finney said, fanning himself with his cocked hat and stepping even closer to her. He picked up the wine bottle, peered at the label, and poured himself a glass of Rhenish, spilling a few drops on Alan's letter which was still on the table. "A glass o' somethin' cool'd be appreciated. With yer permission?"

"Ya got comp'ny, missus?" Wyonnie said, coming from the parlor side door onto the dog-run. "Oh."

"Company, aye," Finney said, taking a seat in one of the wooden chairs as if he owned the place. "P'raps Mistress Caroline'd be needin' another glass, woman. Fetch it."

"I will not be needing another glass, Wyonnie. And Mister Finney will be leaving," Caroline snapped. "Really, sir!"

Her eyes went to the letter, and she almost gasped aloud at the idea of Finney knowing that she'd heard from Alan. Of knowing what the Boudreaus suspected, and were investigating on the sly! Did he already know, she wondered? Was *that* why he'd come?

"Oh, I'll be on me way, quick as a wink," Finney promised, taking a tiny sip of the wine. "Soon's I've finished me drink. I know how it is, ma'am. I'm the great bogeyman ye've heard s'much bad about, an' you're a proper lady. But I do wish t'talk to ye, Mistress Caroline. An' seemly or no, I did bring presents fer the lit'l'un. Wot you from the Carolinas'd call an Injun's pipe o' peace. Do sit an' be mannerly, just fer a bit."

"Very well, Mister Finney," Caroline nodded, sitting down in her rocker once more, and reaching out for the letter to fold it up and put it deep in a side-pocket of her child-tending apron.

"A letter from home, is it?" Finney asked with a twinkle. "An' do yer parents know o' the blessed event yet, ma'am?"

"I have written them, sir, but my post will not reach them for at least three months more," Caroline said, relieved he'd not seen it.

"Most tasty wine ya have, Mistress Caroline," Finney said. "One o' me best imports, I declare. And does yer husband know? Sure, an' it's that proud he must be, t'be the father of a fine boy! Ye'll not have a glass with me?"

"No, thank you, Mister Finney," Caroline replied coolly, raging though she was as Finney played his cruel game with her, like a cat at a house lizard. "I must keep my wits about me."

Damme if I don't! she thought with fear.

"My son will awaken soon, and want his supper. And I must begin my own. Speaking of . . . Wyonnie, do go up to the Boudreaus and inform

Miss Mustin we'll dine in one hour, will you? Should Sewallis wake up, I can go in to him."

"Yes, missus," Wyonnie replied, and spun about to depart.

"Sewallis. That'd be yer own father's name, now?" Finney said.

"How do you know that, sir?" Caroline frowned, a terror growing.

"Ah, call it me curiosity again, wot killed the cat. Soon's I saw you, Mistress Caroline, I've been that curious, I have, about you. Wot yer poets call 'worshippin' from afar.' Such a fine an' handsome lady, so refined an' all, here in our scruffy little islands, like a goddess fell from heaven. Fergive me, but I've asked about. 'Twas easy, after all, ye bein' so well received at parties an' such, an' so many people as impressed as I, gossipin' about ya, an' praisin' ya to the skies."

"And did that involve . . . ?" Caroline began to blurt in accusation about her intercepted letters! ". . . did that force you to name your new ship after me, sir? That was most rude and overassuming on your part. I would never have given you that license, Mister Finney." She caught herself quickly, and picked another complaint, instead.

"Ships is . . . ships are lovely creations, Caroline," Finney said with an almost mawkish rapture. "I but thought to name the handsomest o' my vessels for the handsomest, and finest, lady o' my acquaintance. I know I shoulda asked, but like I said, I'm new-come t'fine manners o' the quality. I was tryin' to honor you, thet's all."

"I wish you would change her name, then, sir," Caroline replied, turning to see if Wyonnie had fetched Peyton Boudreau from the great house to aid her yet. "People assume I did give my permission, and I will brook no loose talk. Naturally, I'm sure it is an honor, but it was not one of my choosing."

"Ya don't choose honors, Mistress Caroline, they just come to ya," Finney laughed softly. "An' 'tis the devil's own bad cess t'name a ship, then change it. Think of it as a foolish gesture from a man o' deep respeck . . . respect for you. I thought t'cheer you, abandoned as you've been. A young wife with a child t'care for, all alone in a hard world, so far from home an' all."

"I am hardly abandoned, sir," Caroline retorted, getting to her feet. "If you've quite finished, I must insist you leave, sir. And I do not think it proper to take any presents from you."

She almost screamed as he seized her hands and held them harshly in rough but be-ringed bear-paw fists. "Tell ya the truth now, Caroline," he said, losing his teasing, bantering tone, and looking up at her in part triumph, part gruff shyness, "first night I saw ya, dinin' yer first night ashore, I thought I'd seen an angel from heaven. But, there ya were, with yer *man*, such as 'e is! A fine an' proper young lady, o' the most refined ways, wasted on a rantipolin' rogue. Know what his nickname is, Caroline? People call 'im the 'Ram-Cat'! Now he's sailed off an' left ya joyless, with a newborn babe t'care for, an' spurned ya fer another. There's talk he won't even answer ya, now ya've had his child. Oh, I seen . . . I've seen you traipsin' back from town so forlorn, achin' fer news o' him, an' niver a letter did ya get. More people gossiped, the more me heart went out t'ya."

Dear Jesus, is that why you did this to us? Caroline wanted to shout in his face. You *read* them! So you'd know best how to play on my fears! So you could *have* me? It was all she could do to keep her face composed, for fear of revealing too much.

" 'Tis a hard world, it is, with men like that in it, Caroline," he went on with what she thought a well-rehearsed oration. "Ye're now a widow, as much as if he died, and good riddance t'bad rubbish! Yer best shed o' thet caterwauler. But yer alone now. Now, I know 'tis maybe a bad time t'mention it, an' I niver was good with words like a proper feller o' yer upbringin'. But I worship the ground ya walk on, an' thet's the Gospel truth! Caroline, I'm a man with a whole heart, an' it's yours t'command, with thoughts for none but you, these many months past. I've means t'care for ya, t'keep ya in style an' ease! An' you can trim my rough edges as ya get t'know me better. As ya may come t'love me as much as I love you, lass. I mean t'make ya happy, me girl. I mean t'do right by ya, Caroline, as none other can."

Terrified as she was, held prisoner with easy force no matter her attempts to pull away, his words held her pinioned like a rabbit might be hypnotized by a rattlesnake's weavings. Yet, Finney's plaint of love, presented in such a clumsy, lugubrious and teary-eyed way was amusing to her, as if she were watching an incredibly poor player in a French farce hawking up high-flown sentiment. She could not stifle a giggle escaping her lips, nor a smile of cruel humour.

"Ah, she's smilin', she is!" Finney cajoled, misinterpreting. "S'prised ya may be, bein' spooned s'soon, by a rough 'un such as me. But yer thinkin' on it, aren't ya now? Now yer babe's born, yer able t'get out an' about more, we could spend time with each other, let ya get accustomed t'the idea. Accustomed t'me, dearest Caroline, an' . . ."

"Let go of me, sir," she hissed back, pronouncing each word in arch contempt. "Let go of me and leave this house and never come here again!" Even as she said it, she knew she should have played along to delude him until Alan could come back, until Mr. Boudreau could gather enough evidence to hang this rogue. But her grievance against

Finney was too great, and her utter revulsion too quick to contain longer.

"There's fine things I could buy ya, things I wish t'lay at yer feet. Me town house, where ya'd be the finest lady . . ." he pleaded.

"Never!" she shouted back, struggling against his grip. "I am a married woman, most happily married, sir! Your suit is not only rude and unseemly, it's odious to me! Let me go, sir! Now!"

She was amazed that he did, in shock perhaps, release her hands to sit back in stupefied hurt, all his hopes confounded. She turned and sprinted for the side door to the parlor, slamming it shut behind her and dropping the latchbar. She rushed to her bedroom, scything herself for being a fool, for not being able to play him along until he was ruined. She massaged her wrists where he'd held her, and felt soiled. She heard a noise and froze.

Dear God, the latchstring, she cringed! It wasn't pulled, and he could get in! The key-lock she hadn't thought to turn . . . !

She opened her chifforobe and took out a large walnut box, and set it on the bed. Peyton Boudreau had wished to give her some pistols the week before, after Alan's letter had come, and she had accepted, never thinking things would become so desperate. This pair were twin-barreled, heavy as fireplace andirons, but already loaded.

"Dear God, save us!" she whispered as she heard the latchbar rise and fall with a creak, heard the squeak of door hinges. "Where's Wyonnie? Why haven't they come?" In desperation, she picked up the first pistol and drew back both hammers to full-cock, then did the same with the second. She took a deep breath to steady herself, thinking of earlier times in North Carolina, and flipped up the frissons on the pans to check her primings, as her brothers had shown her.

"Caroline," Finney said, no longer mocking, no longer pleading. She whirled, the pistols hidden behind her skirts, behind her thighs, and came to the door of the bedroom, to deny him entrance, taking one moment to assure herself that her son was still safe.

"No further, Mister Finney!" she warned him. "There're people . . ."

"Me coachman Liam's got yer nigger wench, so we got all the time in the world, girl," Finney smirked. "An' I know fer a fact yer Betty Mustin's off t'dine with others, so that won't wash, either. Listen t'me good, now, an' heed me," he said, advancing on her slowly. "Yer fine man left ya t'founder, you an' the babe, Caroline. An' he ain't niver comin' back t'ya. His sort don't. They takes their pleasure, then when things get 'inconvenient' for 'em, why divil a care do they have fer the poor, sad objeck o' their lusts. Twenty pound, an' out o' the parish, girl, 'fore the magistrate sics 'is hounds on ya! I had me a sister. She went thet way. All starry-eyed over a feller. Thought he'd do right by her, that rich man's boy, but back she come, half dead from havin' his get, and rooned fer life, an' us too poor t'help her, d'ya see. Now, wot ya want with a life like that, when I kin offer ya . . ." he crooned, slowly advancing upon her.

"No closer!" Caroline swore, raising the first pistol. "Out of my house, now!"

Finney checked for one brief moment of open-mouthed surprise, then put his hands on his hips, flaring out the skirts of his coat and rocked on the balls of his feet.

"Oh, 'tis a crackin' great barker ya got there, miss," Finney chuckled. "Girl as delicate an' refined as yer sweet self has no business messin' with such brutes. That's a man's thing, girl. Put that down, now, an' let's be easy with each other."

Sewallis Alan Lewrie took that moment to wake up and begin to fret and wail.

"See there, Caroline?" Finney japed. "Even yer babe knows yer doin' wrong. Put that down, girl. Tend yer babe. I'll pour us some wine, an' we'll sit an' get acquainted."

"I said get out, Mister Finney!" Caroline shouted.

"Caroline, darlin' girl," Finney cooed, stepping closer with no sign of fear, arms out as though to cosset her out of a pet. "My . . ."

She pulled the trigger of the right-hand barrel, and the heavy pistol leaped and bucked in her hand near enough to tear away from her!

"Jaysis!" Finney yelped, and backpedaled quickly six paces to the door. There was a fresh hole in the left breast of his coat, level with his heart, having passed through front and back as it had been held out away from his body!

"That was *not* a lucky shot, Mister Finney," Caroline glowered as she took aim with the gun, going for his groin with one eye shut. "My brothers Burgess and Governour taught me to shoot before they went off with their Volunteer Regiment to fight for their King."

"You . . . you bitch!" he fumed. He started to rush forward, but she fired the left-hand barrel, and he stopped short, turning pale as a corpse's belly as the lead ball stung the flesh between his thighs, inches below his genitals! And before he could rise or even speak, Caroline brought up the second pistol in her left hand.

"No more teasing, sir! The next one's for your black heart!" she shouted over her baby's screams. "Get out of here, you Beau-Nasty bog-trotter! Run, you son of a whore! Buy yourself a fetching drab in town

and pledge your love to her. Go roll in the muck like the Irish hog you
are, sir. But I warn you, if you do not leave my house this instant, you'll
be a *dead* bogtrotter, as God is my judge!"

Teeth almost chattering in her head, hand sweaty and slick on the
curved butt of the pistol, and her vision tunneling, she was just about at
the end of her tether. But the twin barrels never wavered. And then,
thankfully, there came the sound of running feet thudding through her
garden and onto the stone of the dog-run, drawn by her shots!

"What the devil?" Peyton Boudreau shouted, dashing inside with a
smallsword in one hand, and a bell-mouthed coachman's shotgun in the
other. His freedman black major-domo was behind him with a musket,
and Daniel, Wyonnie's husband backed them up with a cutlass. "You
dog, sir! I'll have the baillifs on you, damme'f I won't, sir!"

"For visiting a lady o' my acquaintance, Boudreau?" Finney attempted
to bluster.

"For frightenin' a lady enough to have her shoot you," Peyton sneered
in reply, something at which he was awfully good. "Trying to rape a
married lady, were you, you scurrilous ill-bred scum? Damme, that'll
make a merry tune for the town criers tomorrow! That'll be a fine topic
for a broadside sheet to be handed about in every tavern! 'Calico Jack,'
not only spurned, but nigh debollocked by a woman defending herself
with a pistol, haw haw! Get out of here!"

"You wouldn't dare!" Finney shot back.

"I would," Caroline vowed. "I will, I promise you."

"Ephraim, take his sword. Pat him down for a knife or pistol,"
Boudreau instructed his major-domo, pressing the muzzle of the shotgun
to Finney's breast. "Tell your brute outside to let go Daniel's wife, or I'll
have your heart's blood. Do it, or it's your life, sir, and not worth more to
me than gnat's piss at this moment, I most heartily assure you, haw!
Come near my house again, come near Mrs. Lewrie one more time,
anywhere on New Providence, and you're a dead man. Do you even dare
to ride past my property, I'll shoot you dead in the road as I would a
rabid cur, sir! That all of it, Ephraim? Good. Now begone! Hear me?
Begone, you son of a bitch, haw haw!"

With Finney disarmed, Caroline at last lowered the pistol and carefully rode the hammers forward one at a time, almost blind to the task
through tears of relief, her hands now trembling like sparrows' wings.
Now that the threat was ended, she was in horror of what she had
almost done. She'd never aimed at anything but stationary gourds or
bottles in her life, and here she'd almost taken a man's life!

She wanted to throw up, to scream, to fall to the floor and let her shuddering wails loose at last. But, now that Finney was being herded out the door and off the property, she went instead to her baby to pick him up and try to comfort him as he squalled in terror. She held him snug to her chest and shoulder, patting his back and stroking him, dandling him up and down as she paced the bedroom in a small circle, and commanding herself not to faint as long as he needed her, much as she wished for a ladylike spell of the vapors.

"There, there, little man," she wept, trying to smile for him. "There, there. It's all over. Bad man's gone, and won't be coming to hurt you. Momma's here, and she won't ever let anyone scare you ever again, Sewallis! Swear to God, baby, swear to God! And your daddy'll be home soon. Your daddy's coming, and he'll make everything better, you'll see!"

And pray God, make it soon, she thought as she paced.

Chapter 7

"It's Walker's Cay, sir," Lewrie said at last.

"Again?" Commander Rodgers scoffed. "They wouldn't dare!"

"Oh, they'd dare, sir," Lewrie replied grimly. "And think it a knacky jest. It's perfect as a hideout, as we already know. And why would anyone ever suspect them to return to it, after we scoured it so well before, sir? Added to that, there's no Navy patrol stationed in the Abacos except for a visit now and then by a cutter, and never to the north of Pelican Harbour, Marsh Harbour, or Carleton Settlement."

"Finally, sir, there's that Portuguese master you spoke to," Lieutenant Ballard stuck in, a hopeful note in his voice. "On his passage south past Walker's Cay, he reported seeing masts, and lights ashore as it grew dark. There should be no one there, sir."

"He wasn't chased," Rodgers muttered. "He saw no pirates."

"They didn't see him at twilight, sir, to the east'rd of the island," Lewrie suggested. "He got lucky."

"God, I wish you'd never talked me into this," Commander Rodgers sighed heavily, rubbing his face in puzzlement. "God Almighty, I've half a mind to . . ."

"Could be Finney's *Guineaman*, sir," Lewrie added. "Still caching undutied goods there, still smuggling. We could burn him out, hurt him sore as we did the last time, and then be off for Nassau, with evidence enough this time to prosecute him for smuggling, if nothing else."

Come on, you dithering twit, Lewrie thought; don't whiffle out on us now!

"There is that," Rodgers allowed, grudgingly.

"*Sarah and Jane*'s ready, sir," Alan pressed. "Do you transfer your Marines into her, Lieutenant Ballard can be off Walker's Cay by dawn to see what's what. If no pirates come out to pursue him, he could sail in, anyway, and how would they know he wasn't there to deliver goods, sir? I'll give up thirty hands to help, and take Captain Grant and his crew aboard *Alacrity* to guard 'em, whilst you keep *Whippet* fully manned."

And if it's Arthur doin' it, there's less involvement for you to fear, you hen-hearted dog, Alan thought; upon my head be it!

"Oh, very well, then," Rodgers said at last, permission to go wrung from him like a dishclout in a mangle.

"Right, sir!" Ballard said quickly. "I'll go aboard *Sarah and Jane* at once, with your leave, sir. With your Marines, we'll soon make hash of 'em!"

"If you will excuse me, sir, I'll see Mister Ballard over the side, and transfer my spare hands over to the merchantman," Alan said, rising to gather his hat and sword. And they left the great-cabins before Commander Rodgers could change his mind.

"Christ, I thought he was going to back out," Lewrie complained in a soft voice as the sideparty mustered to see them off.

"He is a damned good seaman, though," Ballard assayed with a wry expression. "If not . . ." he shrugged in conclusion.

"Well, here you are, then, Arthur," Lewrie said, clasping him by the shoulders at arm's length. "An independent action of your very own at last. Take joy of it."

"Thank you for getting it for me, sir."

"Think he'd want *his* first lieutenant that involved?" Alan japed in a whisper. "If it all goes bust, then it's less risk for him. And, Lord, I owe you after Conch Bar, don't I? Should have given you charge of the landing, and I could have gone into *Aemilia* to put some bottom in 'fool' Coltrop. Hindsight's better than no sight at all, I guess! But I know you'll do us proud. Just, take care of yourself, mind? As stiff as you are, me lad, I'd miss you should anything happen. Be your knacky self. But not too bold, Arthur."

"Coming from you, Alan, that's a wry 'un," Ballard snorted. "Do but listen to yourself, gainsaying 'bold.' Sir."

"God speed, then, Arthur," Lewrie smiled, stepping back to doff his hat to him. "Mister Ballard. Now go catch me some pirates for my breakfast!"

Sarah and Jane stood westnor'west, loafing along under all plain sail, the striped flag of the United States flying from her mizzenmast truck. Marine Lieutenant Pomeroy's thirty-five privates, one corporal and sergeant were sprawled on the deck in what shade they could find, dressed in their usual slop clothing for working parties, though with their Brown Bess muskets, hangers and bayonets close by.

Ballard was showing only ten seamen on deck or aloft, what would be expected of a skinflint Yankee shipmaster, with the others napping below, or resting beside the great-guns. *Sarah and Jane* mounted only twelve six-pounders, little better than *Alacrity's* batteries, with two of those disposed in the mates' wardroom below facing aft, or up on the forecastle for chase guns. The rest were spaced out to either beam at every second gun port, so that *Sarah and Jane,* designed for a stronger armament, sailed *en flûte,* like a piccolo with "open holes."

Huge bags of "white gold" had been hauled up from her holds to line either beam between the guns, piled up three deep to make breastworks on the gun deck, on the sail-tending gangways above, to absorb the expected musketry, and the impact of a pirate-ship's guns. There was a low breastwork around the quarter-deck and fo'c's'le as well, with a final redoubt of bagged salt around the double wheel and binnacle to shelter the helmsmen.

"Dawn for fair, sir," Midshipman Parham said, looking at his pocket watch. "And my watch is accurate for once, there's a wonder."

"Reefs an' breakers t'larboard!" the masthead lookout sang out. "On the 'orizon, sir!"

"That should be about six miles to leeward," Ballard told them, muttering half to himself. "Close enough to prance past Walker's Cay and see what comes out, but not so close that they think we're stupid. Mister Parham, go aloft. You've seen these isles before from the sea. Tell me which we're closest to, Walker's Cay, Grand Cay or Romer's."

"Aye, aye, sir."

"Schooner to loo'rd, sir!" the lookout called suddenly. "Hull down an' bows on! Two points off the larboard bows!"

"Belay, Mister Parham," Ballard said, with only a slight twitch of his mouth to indicate any excitment, or notice. "It no longer matters." He paced aft to the taffrails, savoring the windward side which was a captain's by right, then back to the railings overlooking *Sarah and Jane's* waist and gun deck. Hands clasped on his rump, fingers not even twining upon each other, as much as he wished to do so. Arthur Ballard had a firm grip on his emotions, as a man who aspired to the status of gen-tleman should, as a taciturn, self-controlled Navy man should. He en-vied Lewrie his boyish lack of control, his ability to enthuse or show anger, sorrow, or frustration so easily, and Lewrie's ability to command and keep the hands' respect even if he did "let go." But it was not his style; it was not for him.

So Ballard paced, and the sun rose in the sky as the schooner stood out from the islands, seeming as if to pass ahead of the trading ship in all innocence, and *Sarah and Jane* kept her course, and her somnolent lack of notice.

"Schooner's crossin' ahead, fine on the bows, an' two mile off!"

"He'll haul his wind, keeping the wind gauge, and fall down upon our starboard side," Ballard announced as he paused in his pacing near the wheel. "See, he tacks, as if he's cleared ahead of us."

"Soon, sir?" Parham inquired, all but wriggling like a puppy on his first hunt in excitement. "Time for Quarters, sir?"

"Calmly, Mister Parham, calmly. You are never to show fear or excite-ment to the people," Ballard instructed. "They're steadier for your being steady."

"Aye, aye, sir," Parham grimaced, as if his bladder was full, and Ballard was detaining him from dashing forrud to the "head."

"Hmm," Arthur Ballard sighed, peering at the schooner, which was then a point or two off their starboard bows, sailing off sou'easterly, closehauled. "I should think now, Mister Parham. Beat to Quarters. But keep them down and out of sight. Lieutenant Pomeroy? Your men To Arms, if you please! On the gun deck, still. Stay away from the gangways until they're close-aboard!"

"Bearin' up, sir!" the lookout announced. "He's tackin' 'cross the wind to the starboard tack!"

"About three-quarters of a mile off the starboard bows," Ballard mut-tered. "Very nicely done! Even better than wearing off the wind to fall down on us and round up alongside on the same course. Saves sparing hands on the sheets and braces to continually adjust on a rounding course to come close-aboard us, do you see, Mister Parham? That means more men free to serve his guns, and make up a boarding party."

"I see, sir."

"And all settled down and ready for it when it comes," Ballard went on with his praise. "One may learn a lesson or two, even from a pirate."

Once tacked to a parallel course with *Sarah and Jane,* the schooner hauled her wind almost at once and began to fall down on them fast, giving them little warning, and pinning their ship between threatened gunfire and the jagged teeth of the coral reefs to south and west. If they chose to loose sail and run, they could not find sea room enough for an escape, nor could they tack and flee sou'east as long as their foe lay off their starboard bows.

"Panic party, Mister Odrado!" Ballard shouted. Designated men ran to the shrouds to scale them, as if going aloft to cast off reefs and make sail. Others rushed to the gangways for the braces to their squaresails to adjust their angle for a new course, and more speed.

"Hands at quarters, sir," Early, the quartermaster's mate said. "Guns run out to the portsills, an' port lashings cast off. Swivels loaded, tompions out, an' manned. Larboard gun crews shifted to starboard, an' that Lieutenant Pomeroy is ready to mount his men on the starboard gangway."

"Very well, Mister Early," Ballard nodded quickly, then smirked just a trifle. "I wonder, Mister Early. Do you think they will run up the 'Jolly Roger?' Or is such a convention out of date these days?"

"Well, I don' know, sir, it . . ." Early began, then paused. "Ah, that's a little joke, isn't it, Mister Ballard, sir?"

"Aye, Mister Early," Ballard said with a sober face. "But a feeble joke. Away with you, now, and stand ready."

The schooner was sidling up to them quickly, closing the range to about a cable. She was as gaudy as a Spanish royal galley, tricked out with gold leaf on bow and stern, down her upper bulwark rails, and around her entry ports. There had to be at least seventy men in her crew, making Ballard wonder how they got out of each other's way when working the ship. He could espy a larboard battery of five nine-pounder cannon, and at least half a dozen swivel guns on either beam.

"Let's not look too easy," Ballard called. "Mister Woods? Do you fire the forrud chase guns! Make it look clumsy!"

One six-pounder fired, raising a splash near the enemy's bows. A moment later, the schooner fired in reply.

"Everybody, down!" Ballard called, though he kept his feet, and his calm composure as the heavy balls droned in. *Sarah and Jane* leaped and cried in protest as round-shot tore through her thin scantlings and bulged the bulwarks inwards. Bagged salt thumped and tumbled, and some bags burst apart, spilling white crystals about like snow.

"Ahoy, there!" came a call from across the narrowing channel between them. "Strike yer colours, cut yer braces an' sheets, and let fly all, or I'll let ya have another broadside! Gimme no resistance, and you'll still be alive when this is over! Show me fight, though . . ."

"Let fly all, Mister Odrado!" Ballard shouted, putting a panicky edge to his voice, then turned to shout to the pirate schooner with his brass speaking trumpet. "Hold your fire, for God's sake! We'll strike to you! Mercy, in the name of God! Hold your fire!"

The American flag came tumbling down to trail astern as its halyard was cut, and the sails began to luff and thunder in disarray.

"Now, sir?" Parham insisted.

"Not yet, Mister Parham," Ballard said. "Calmly, now, remember? We'll do it the way our captain said he served a French privateer during the late war. Close enough to smell 'em, first! But do you extend to Lieutenant Pomeroy my compliments, and tell him it's time he posted his men on the starboard gangway, below the bulwarks, and be ready to volley at close range."

"Aye, aye, sir!" Parham replied, dashing off in haste, in spite of Ballard's cautions.

The schooner was now a quarter-cable off, not fifty yards away, and almost at decent musket-shot. Her boarding party was already up on the bulwarks, with lift lines and parrel lines dangling so they could swing over to board once they got hull to hull. Others poised at bow and stern with grappling irons.

And she fired another, lying, broadside!

Sarah and Jane was shaken hard. Ballard could hear her timbers wail as they were shattered below, hear scantlings and bulwarks starred open with ragged holes as round-shot ripped into her. But the bags of salt kept deadly wood splinters from flying to scythe her crew down.

"Close pistol-shot," Ballard muttered, smiling thinly at last. "Open your ports! As you bear, *fire!*"

Double-shotted guns erupted in smoke and flames! Chain-shot to take rigging down, the halves of the balls flying apart as they left the muzzles and whining through the short space between them, linked with chain that made them whirl like birds' wings. Canister on top of that, bags crammed with musket balls that spread out like gigantic shotgun pellets in a cloud of deadly lead. All aimed at the upper bulwarks, all designed to take down people, instead of rigging.

"Marines!" Ballard screamed as the smoke ragged away enough to see what was what. "Swivels!"

The panic parties that had gone aloft fired swivels down into the schooner's decks; more canister-shot to erase the pirates about the wheel, on the schooner's quarter-deck, forecastle, and rails.

"Cock your locks!" Pomeroy shouted. "Level! By volley, *fire!*"

The schooner's decks were about six feet below *Sarah and Jane*, so pirates trying to find a hiding place anywhere but close up to the larboard bulwarks were wide-open to the shattering volley of musketry. There was a concerted groan of terror at the sight of those muskets, then screams as the volley rattled out like a short roll on a drum.

"Grapnels away!" Ballard shouted, drawing his sword. "Boarders! Remember, we want prisoners! Away, boarders!"

Seamen and Marines went over the side as the hulls crashed into each other. Grapnels flew and lodged deep in wood as both vessels rebounded and threatened to part. Upwind as she was, though, the schooner could not slip away, pressed to *Sarah and Jane* by the Trades. The boarding party surged over the schooner's decks, meeting light resistance, and beating that aside quickly. These pirates were used to having their own way by dint of terror and confusion. Few of them were used to a hard fight against disciplined opponents, so the survivors threw up their hands and dropped their weapons, while their comrades lay bloody and still, or shrieking with pain.

"Not much to 'em, hey, sir?" Pomeroy sniffed, disgusted that he hadn't even had a chance to bloody his sword. "My lads didn't even get up a good sweat!"

"Make sure they've no hidden weapons, and herd them forrud, if you please, Lieutenant Pomeroy," Ballard said, sheathing his own blade. "And I'll have those survivors from the afterguard brought here."

"Aye, sir."

Half a dozen men were brought to him by the Marines at bayonet or cutlass point, and were forced to kneel, hands already bound behind their backs.

"Now, who is captain of this vessel?" Ballard inquired. "Well, speak up! Where's the dog in charge of you?"

"'E's dead, zur," a surly little fellow replied in a grunt.

"How convenient," Ballard simpered. "What was his name?"

"Anastatio Ruiz," another volunteered, in a painful whimper.

"And the mates?"

"Oh, they be dead, too, zur," the little fellow added, speaking from a mouth almost devoid of teeth. He had the gall to smirk.

"Dear God," Ballard said, drawing a pistol. He had been simply appalled by what Lewrie had done at Conch Bar. But he had to admit it had been effective. "Tell you men what I'm going to do. I am going to start shooting you, one at a time, until I get some answers. For your information, I am from His Majesty's Sloop *Alacrity*. Does that name ring a bell, hey? The same as did for Billy 'Bones' Doyle, down in the Caicos last year."

"Ye cain't be, she's s'posed t'be posted t'Cat Island," one of the younger survivors exploded, almost indignantly. "She ain't got no Marines, so . . ."

He shut his mouth and gulped as Ballard cocked the pistol, and laid it against his temple.

"The Marines are from *Whippet*," Ballard said coldly. "Remember *Whippet*, from Walker's Cay? And no, we are *not* supposed to be here! But we are, by God, and if one of you doesn't start talking this very instant, then God save you!"

"Oh God, sweet Jesus, holy Saviour!" the threatened sailor wept, all but fouling himself in sudden terror. "Don't, sir, please! Don't shoot me like yer cap'n done Ramirez! I know ya, sir, yer that Ballard feller! They say yer meek an' mild, a true Christian, sir, an' a true Christian'd *not*, sir!"

"Stop yer snivelin'!" the surly one warned. "Die game, damn ye!"

"At the count of three, lad, I send you to Hell for your sins," Ballard assured him. "Want to die game for *this* bastard? One . . . two . . ."

"Jesus, no, don't do it, I'll tell ya, I'll tell ya!" the young man screamed as he fell to the deck to writhe and wriggle away from his compatriots. "'E's Laidlaw, 'e's first mate, 'e knows! Christ, I wuz just aboard a year, sir, I don't know much, please don't shoot me when I tells ya I don't know somethin', please!"

"The man who tells me all will live to see the sunset," Ballard promised them. "And, if he testifies in court, he doesn't hang. The ones who don't cooperate with me . . ." Ballard paused dramatically as the thought came to him, and he smiled as he concluded, "the ones who don't tell me the truth, who don't lay it all out for us, I'll give to my captain, 'Ram-Cat' Lewrie. He doesn't like pirates much, ya know."

Several of them turned quite pale at that threat. Throats went dry, and they gulped saliva to ease themselves, before they began to bay a chorus of expostulation in noisy competition with each other.

Guineaman and another of Finney's ships waiting at Walker's Cay; his agent Runyon ashore, serving up free rum to all to keep them hot; Nassau whores at bargain prices for those with money; cargoes piled up waiting to be smuggled into ports all across the Caribbean; Finney, yes, it was Finney, it was always 'Calico Jack' Finney!

"Mister Parham, Mister Early, Mister Woods," Ballard beckoned to his more literate fellows who had good handwriting skills. "Dry work for us, I fear. We'll separate those that sound eager to talk, and get it all down on paper, with their signatures or marks made against their confessions, before we rejoin *Alacrity*. Mister Odrado? Do you go into *Sarah and Jane* and get her underway, out to sea. Soon as we have this vessel squared away, we'll follow you."

And, to the amazement of all who were familiar with the taciturn first officer, Arthur Ballard actually cackled out loud with glee!

Chapter 8

Whippet and *Alacrity* fell upon the anchorage just at the break of dawn the next morning. Sou'west down Walker's Cay Channel, east through the upper passage above the shoal; *Whippet* taking position to block the southern pass this time, much closer to the island, and *Alacrity* given the task of scouring the moored vessels, after she had landed Lieutenant Pomeroy and his Marines in the twenty-one-foot-deep oval tongue of water to the east between Walker's Cay and Grand Cay. With most of the ships' boats used, they landed on the eastern tip in the dark, after a two-mile row in from the hasty anchorage, and a slow march down the three-quarter mile length of the isle to take the camp unawares from an unexpected quarter.

"There's *Guineaman*," Lewrie spat. "Anyone know the other ship?"

"By those white upper bulwarks, I'd say she must be the *Dublin Lass*, sir," Sailing Master Fellows opined. "Seen her in Nassau. One of Finney's ships, for certain, sir. I know that house flag."

"Better and better, Mister Fellows!" Lewrie exulted, rubbing his hands together. "No schooners present which might escape us into shoal water this time, we did for her yesterday. And most of their boats on the beach, not gathered 'round the anchored ships."

"Bulk of their crews ashore, most like, still roistering, sir," Ballard commented. "Or sleeping it off."

"Well, here's a rough awakening, then," Lewrie grinned. "Mister Fowles, we'll close yon farthest ship, the *Guineaman*. Ready the starboard battery!"

"Hullo, they're up and awake, some of them, sir," Ballard warned. "On *Dublin Lass*. There's a gun port opening!"

"Mister Fowles, stand ready! We'll rake this one in passing!"

"Ready, sir!" Fowles shouted back, after fussing over his gun-captain's aim, with a tug or two at the quoin blocks to suit himself about the proper elevation.

"As you bear, fire!"

The range was half a cable—100 yards—as they grazed past the anchored, and sleeping, ship. The threatening gun port was open, but all they could see poised over the grim black muzzle of a cannon behind the port was the white face of some poor wretch who had opened it so he could spew his load of rum and supper over the side, who took one look in his misery, made his mouth a perfect O, and went parchment pale as the artillery blasted him away.

Dublin Lass shuddered as a six-pounder ball ripped into her, punching clear through her thin planking, shattering timbers and deck beams, making her leap and froth a hull-shaped, spreading ripple around her as she rose and dropped back into the still waters of the harbour.

"Serve her another, Mister Fowles! In the guts, this time!" Alan demanded. "Sink her!"

As *Alacrity* cruised by *Dublin Lass*, her guns rapped out again, quoin blocks inserted and barrels aimed low, to riven her waterline, and the trim little three-masted ship heeled over with each crashing round-shot, rocking as ragged gashes were shot through her scantlings, then rolling back to starboard so those holes could suck and froth with sea water. The few crewmen left aboard as an anchor party came running up from below, where they'd been napping, to find their ship sinking beneath their feet!

"I can see the Marines ashore, sir!" Midshipman Mayhew shouted. "There're red coats among the sheds on the far side of the camp!"

"Angle's gone, sir! Guns won't bear in the ports!" Fowles reported at last.

"Cease fire, Mister Fowles. Wait for the *Guineaman*," Lewrie ordered. "Mark that, gentlemen. *Dublin Lass* opened her gun ports to fire into a King's Ship, to take arms against the Royal Navy. Think you that's another compelling proof of piracy?" He smiled.

"Well, more like to puke on us, sir," Ballard whispered at his side. "Compelling, none the less, I suppose. If contempt counts."

"It'll sound good in testimony," Lewrie scowled. "And damme if I'll give Finney and his captains one chance to wriggle out this time!"

Once clear of the *Dublin Lass*, *Alacrity* faced the open waters between the two anchored ships for a minute or two, so they could see what was happening on the beach. Pirates and merchant crews were all running in terror from the dripping bayonets of the Marines, some few trying to make a fight of it with muskets and pistols.

The morning erupted in heavy gunfire once more as *Whippet* came even with the tortured *Dublin Lass* astern of them, and gave her broadsides with her nine-pounders. Rigging and spars, upper masts and yards, came tumbling down in ruin to churn the water alongside, and *Dublin Lass* canted over even farther until her starboard railings were in the sea. She bubbled and groaned as she filled and began to go down.

"Chase gun forrud, Mister Fowles!" Lewrie shouted. "Wake those buggers up yonder!"

The starboard chase gun on the forecastle, one of the portable two-pounders, barked as sharp as a terrier. Its light ball hit *Guineaman* astern, shattering the ladder from quarter-deck to poop, barely making her judder. Men could be seen, though, running up from below, waking from their swaying hammocks on the upper decks where it was cooler, to the waist of the ship.

"By God, I think they're going to man their guns!" Fellows gaped. "That Captain Malone must be desperate as hell, sir!"

"He mounts twelve-pounders, sir," Ballard intoned. "If you recall."

"Warm work in the next few minutes, then," Lewrie sighed as he steeled himself for a slaughter on his own decks. "Mister Fellows, is there depth enough on *Guineaman's* larboard side for us?"

"God only knows, sir," Fellows muttered, eyeing the ship which was anchored bows-on to them. "I doubt he'd be anchored that close up to shoals, though. Anyone see a kedge anchor from her stern? If she were swinging on just her best bower to wind and tide . . ."

"Ready on the gun deck, sir," Fowles reported from the waist.

"Mister Fowles, we'll bear off and give her starboard, then be ready with your larboard battery, quick as you can, at close range."

"Aye, aye, sir," Fowles replied quizzically, taking off his hat to scratch his grizzled head so hard his "tarry" queue of hair which hung as low as his waist twitched at his mercurial captain's orders.

"Helm alee, Mister Neill," Lewrie said. "Steer three points to larboard. Mister Ballard, prepare the hands to wear ship so we cross *Guineaman's* bows once we've fired, and fall onto her disengaged side."

"Aye, aye, sir!" Ballard replied, crisp and efficient.

"Guns bear, sir!" Fowles warned.

"Fire, Mister Fowles!"

As the first limb of the rising sun peeked over the horizon at last, the artillery came to life, tolling rage down the starboard side from bow to stern. *Guineaman* screamed as she was hulled; like a steer might bellow and jerk, shivering with terror and anger, as it was bound for the approach of the butcher with the poleaxe.

"Helm up, hard up, Mister Neill! Wear ship!" Lewrie cried as the last gun went off. *Alacrity* came wheeling about in her own dense pall of gunsmoke as it was blown down onto *Guineaman*. Sailors dashed to sheets and braces in the confusion, as gunners below them abandoned starboard guns to run out the larboard cannon and open the ports. Ballard kept yelling orders into the bedlam, and, drilled and trained to boresome perfection as the crew was, order was never lost, not one second was lost.

Artillery could be heard ahead and to port as *Alacrity* sailed off nor'east for the beach; *Guineaman* firing at last, at where they thought her to be. *Alacrity* trembled with a sharp slam, a shuffling judder of her stern, as she was struck aft. Mr. Burke on the tiller with his mate Neill gave a soft curse as he fell to his knees in a welter of blood, a long, jagged splinter of bulwark driven through his midsection. Midshipman Mayhew was lifted off his feet and flung halfway across the quarter-deck to the starboard side by a chunk of red-hot round-shot as the twelve-pounder ball shattered. He skidded on his back to fetch up against the after mooring bitts, his left arm and shoulder almost gone, awash in his own gore, and gasping hard.

Alacrity almost felt as if she'd tripped over something, her forward progress arrested, the deck canting over to starboard.

"Her anchor cable!" Ballard intuited.

"Helm up, Mister Neill! Steer due north!" Lewrie called.

"Aye, aye, sir," Neill replied, stepping over the body of his dying friend, his tears almost blinding him, to put the tiller over.

"Surgeon's mate!" Ballard snapped. "Mr. MacIntyre! Loblolly boys aft!"

The smoke wafted nor'east on the dying winds, clearing the view at last, as *Alacrity* rumbled and slithered down the anchor cable that scrubbed her larboard underbody. And there was *Guineaman*, not twenty yards off, her larboard gun ports closed.

"Ready grapnels, Mister Ballard. Mister Harkin, Mister Warwick, we'll be boarding her after the broadside," Lewrie instructed. "Starboard your helm, Mister Neill, and lay us hull to hull."

"Aye, aye, sir."

"Ready!" Lewrie shouted to his gunners as *Guineaman* came abeam. "On the up-roll . . . *fire!*"

Guineaman heeled over to starboard under the weight of the iron hailstorm, her bulwarks turning into kindling and whirling in the air thick as an uprooted pine forest in a hurricane. Gun ports and thin planking caved in, and a portion of the larboard sail-tending gangway went flying in one long, ladderlike piece.

"Grapple to her, Mister Ballard," Lewrie said in a normal tone, once the echoes had ceased. "And away boarders."

"Aye, aye, sir!" Ballard snapped, sounding almost enthusiastic.

Lewrie jumped to the top of the bulwarks, drew pistol and sword, and leaped for *Guineaman*'s forechain platform to scramble alongside his men to the forward gangway.

"Christ!" he shuddered, seeing the devastation that his cannon had wrought. The waist was filled with dying men, half lost in scraps of wood, in a maze of broken timbers. Several of the larboard cannon had come loose from the shattered bulwarks and had rolled down on the men serving the starboard battery, crushing them like millwheels.

Those who could were already raising their hands in surrender, the urge to fight shot out of them. Lewrie went over to the starboard side to make his way aft to the quarter-deck, where some of *Guineaman*'s mates stood or sat around the butt of the mizzenmast.

"You!" Captain Malone growled, half in shock at the ruin of his ship. He brought up the tip of his sword while the others got out of their way, ostentatiously empty-handed as *Alacrity*'s boarding party came to back Lewrie up. "What are you doin' here? We thought . . ."

"Maybe 'Calico Jack' couldn't afford to bribe Commodore Garvey any longer, Malone," Lewrie offered, thinking fast, and hoping for a confirmation. "Now we've a new Royal Governor, the price went up too high. You and Finney are on your own."

Lewrie reached out with the tip of his hanger to ring steel on steel; one beats, two beats tip to tip on Malone's sword. Malone went backwards, crouched over more like a knifefighter, body square-on.

"Either drop that sword, or do something real with it, Malone," Lewrie snarled. "Fight me, you coward! Got the nutmegs for it, hey?"

Malone allowed the next beat to slap his blade low and away as he let go the hilt and dropped it on the deck. "Oh, no, ya don't! Ya've put yer foot in it this time for fair, Lewrie. Aye, I'll strike to ya, but soon as we're in Nassau Harbour, it'll be you up on charges again, an' this time yer really finished. Firin' on peaceful merchantmen . . ."

"John Laidlaw of the *Fortune* schooner says different," Lewrie told him with a laugh, a laugh which was reinforced by the shock that Malone displayed, as if he'd just seen his own corpse swaying from the gibbet. Lewrie stepped forward and put the tip of his sword to Malone's throat.

"Jesus, easy, sir!" Cony gulped from behind him. "Don't!"

"John Laidlaw tells me *Guineaman* branched out on her own, did a little piracy on her way here to the rendezvous in '85. Was Finney upset with you, Malone, when you took the *Matilda*? Remember her, the Liverpool slaver? Laidlaw tells my lieutenant that if we dig in the right spot, we'll find the bones of her officers and crew here on the island. And the bones of over an hundred sick slaves you slaughtered 'cause you didn't want the time or trouble to heal 'em up before you tried to sell 'em off. Men *and* women slaves, Malone! Care if I and my hands do some digging, do you?"

"Now, look here, mebbe we kin deal, sir, if . . ." Malone gasped.

"Still have the stuff from *Matilda*, do you?" Lewrie sneered at him, pressing a little deeper with the point. "Sure, you do! You're the sort that keeps his mementoes of good times. And that's more than enough to hang you for piracy and murder this time. You're done for, Malone, you *and* Finney, damn your eyes!"

"You'll never get 'Calico Jack,' ya bugger," Malone attempted to swagger.

"Think not?" Lewrie laughed again. "Cold comfort to you the moment the hangman turns you off. But, I promise you, he'll have a noose right next to yours."

Lewrie stepped back and sheathed his sword.

"John Canoe!" he shouted for the huge escaped slave.

"Aye, cap'm, sah."

"He's yours to guard, special," Lewrie grinned.

"Aye, sah," Canoe growled deep in his throat, taking Malone by the upper arm and hauling the heavy-set man into his custody as easily as lifting a child.

"Captain Malone, you're under arrest," Lewrie called in a loud voice, turning to face the other disarmed pirates. "All of you damned hounds! I arrest you . . . in the King's Name!"

"Damme, sir, look what ya've done with me poor ship," Captain Grant bemoaned as Lewrie came aboard after funeral services for Burke and Midshipman Mayhew. "Scantlin's shot through, bulwarks all chewed up. It'll use most of me spare timber patchin' hull shots, and what, I ask ye, will the Royal Navy do to compensate me?"

"Let you go free, sir," Lewrie told him, in no mood for dealing with the shifty merchantman. "Go sing 'Oh, Be Thankful,' for all that I care.

Last of your crew's coming aboard now. I'd set a course for home, were I you, and get out of Bahamian jurisdiction before we change our minds."

"She rides light," Grant commented as *Sarah and Jane* bobbed and rolled beneath him. "How mucha me cargo did ye use for breastworks?"

"Rather a lot, I fear, Captain Grant," Lewrie told him. "We've dumped that over the side. You'll find enough salt left to keep you ballasted and trimmed proper on your voyage. Might even be enough to pay for your repairs and break even, once you pay off your crew back in your Philadelphia."

"No profit, sir?" Grant wheezed. "Damme, sir, a whole sailing season, a whole voyage wasted?"

"That's the risks you take for money," Lewrie shrugged, then turned to leave, to go back to his *Alacrity* and escort their prizes, and their captives, home. "Stay out of our seas, Captain Grant."

"I'll write the consul," Grant warned, following him to the entry port. "I'll complain to Congress, to the President if I have to. And I will be back, ye know. Ye pass that Free Port Act, and I'll be more'n welcome in the Bahamas again. Me and every American ship."

"Captain Grant," Lewrie said, turning to face him, "I've no more time to play this sly little game with you. Aye, they may pass Free Port Acts; aye, you may be welcome someday in the future, and you may cock your nose at me all you wish. Just remember, though, that a very good mariner, and a promising young midshipman died this day making it safe for you and your ship to sail Bahamian waters. Don't make me dislike you. There's no future in it. Ask those pirates."

"Point taken, sir," Grant replied, leaning back a little from the intensity of Lieutenant Lewrie's grim expression. "Point taken, indeed," he reiterated, as he doffed his hat to him as Lewrie descended to his gig.

Chapter 9

John Finney was having a rather bad evening. He had stayed in that night, ostensibly to go over his books; but mostly to avoid the sneers he'd been getting on the streets since the mocking broadside sheet had appeared days before. *Tale of The De-Bollocked Bumpkin*, it was titled in large block letters. There was an engraving, a satirical cartoon below that which featured a slim young woman holding both baby and pistols, shooting at an overdressed, lump-faced churl in a hugely unfashionable wig, tiny hat and flaring coat, like a "Macaroni" of a previous decade, the suiting portrayed as checkered calico, and the male figure leaping legs widespread like some damned "Molly" in an Italian toe-dance company to avoid losing his wedding tackle. A long, stringy caption above the female read: "In his abfence, my dear hufband's piftols shall defend mine honour, cur!"

Whilst over the leaping male figure, a caption read: "Oy means ter have yer, niver a care have oy fer any damnd marriage vow—Oicks!"

There was printed below a short narration, a titillating story of caution to all lusting bachelors who pursued happily married women too hotly. No names were named—but then, none were necessary, as it stated ". . . as one here in Nassau did quite lately!"

"I'll murder Augustus," Finney swore, tearing the sheet into tiny bits. It was only the fourth he'd gotten in anonymous mail so far. He was certain Augustus Hedley was the artist, Peyton Boudreau the author and sponsor, and Caroline . . . "Thet bitch! Oh, thet bitch! I'll make her sorry she wuz iver born, I will! Wipe thet sneer off 'er face, take 'er an' have me way with 'er, make 'er beg fer it!"

He instead took another full glass of claret in two gulps, and filled his crystal stem with more. For the moment, he had more pressing worries. He returned to his ledgers, both the legitimate ones his clerk prepared, and the illicit ones kept in his own scrawls, which he himself had trouble reading a month later. It was not a good year.

After Conch Bar, and the wholesale hangings which had followed, half the old lads had gone off for easier pickings; deeper in the Caribbean, or up to the American coast, where Congress was too cheap to keep a navy, or a coast guard worth the name. Walker's Cay had run more away to waters less well patrolled. Finney had had to increase the import of legitimate goods as stolen wares reduced in quantity, so his profit margin had fallen to only a little better than his Bay Street competitors.

He'd lost huge sums, too, in all the goods that Rodgers, and that damned Lieutenant Lewrie, had burned at Walker's Cay, the pirated, and the hoarded true imports. Those staples, those delicacies, all gone up in flames, depriving him of his expected large markups. And there had been the import duties the cynical, greedy Searcher of Customs had imposed on goods he'd *never* be able to land and sell, and the bribes demanded to keep him out of court on smuggling charges to boot!

There wasn't much better news from his grandiose plantings on Eleuthera. His overseer had written that both white lands, and red lands farther inland, were failing. Bahamian soil was like a lying whore; rich and fertile to start with, but too thin to turn under and hope it would revive after a fallow year, its nutrients sucked out of it. And with so few animals in the Bahamas, and lack of grazing land for big herds, costly to manure and fertilize. Unless he shipped in tons of manure, his overseer wasn't confident. Cotton, sisal, hemp, sugar cane, even indigo and aloes —none of it prospered. And, the overseer had ended on a dismal note, the Georgia Tidewater and Sea Isle cotton nurslings *might* be infected with the dreaded Chenille Bug!

He'd be forced to sell, before the fine plantation house could be completed, as fine a mansion as any in the Bahamas, grander than the one Col. Andrew Deveaux had erected on Cat Island. The only value he'd get back from the sale would be the slaves, the ones he'd gotten for so little from Malone (the foolish, greedy bastard!) after he'd taken the *Matilda!*

Finney took another sip of claret and made a face. Try as hard as he might, he'd never developed a palate for it. Petulantly, it went into the fireplace to shatter in a shower of wine across the imported Turkey carpet!

"Fireplace!" he gloomed at that extravagance, a gaudy, useless showpiece in a climate that never got close to freezing. He went over to his sideboard to pour himself a cut-crystal glass of Demerara rum.

"Excuse me, Captain Finney, sir," his butler said, opening the wide double doors to the entry hall.

"Clean it up," Finney snorted, putting his feet on his desk.

"I will, Captain, sir," the butler agreed, secretly amused by his plebeian employer, and his demand to be addressed with a title he never really had—Captain. "In the meantime, sir, this letter came for you. From Commodore Garvey, sir."

"Fetch it here, then, damn yer eyes," Finney sulked, finding no joy this evening in the obsequiousness of his hired help. Finney tore the wax seal off and unfolded the letter. "Damn 'is blood!"

Another of the broadside sheets! Finney wondered just how much he had to pay the bastard to at least be civil to him. They acted as strangers in public, no matter their agreement, or the sums he shoved into Garvey's accounts by the side door at the bank. Now he was down, Garvey'd shoved the knife in, sarcastic and sneering, as was his way. Finney dreaded Garvey might demand even more than the princely three hundred pounds a month he already cost him. "Shit! Shit!"

My dear sir;

Have you seen one of these? I was not aware your interest in interrupting *Alacrity*'s mail had an Intimate *Raison d'Être*.

was the inscription penned in the left margin.

The enfolding, larger folio-sized sheet of paper had a hastily written note which quite took his mind from the curses he was about to hurl at the uppity cur, who'd sprinkle his notes with Latin, French or even Greek, just to (Finney swore) gall him over his lack of schooling.

Lt. Coltrop's *Aemilia* cutter is just returned from Spanish Wells in some haste. He informs me that *Whippet* put into port there four days past, inquired of Lt. Blair of the *Barracouta* sloop as to the nature of my patrol Assignments, and was last seen heading North towards Great Abaco! A ketch-rigged Warship and a merchant ship were seen to be in company with her by a fishing lugger who put into Spanish Wells.

Aware of my stringent Requirements for *Whippet* and *Alacrity* to stay far South, Lt. Coltrop came to me at once, sure that Rodgers and Lewrie may be staging some immense Mutiny against me, sir. The only cause for hope they may have to redeem themselves would be, as you know, a sudden Revelation about a certain Matter. Do what you think best, as shall I, from this moment forward.

"Jesus an' Mary," Finney shivered. "It's all up, ain't it?"

"Sir?" his butler inquired distantly.

"Get out. I said, get out! Leave it!" Finney shouted as he got to his feet. He shoved the broadside sheet and the letter into one of his private ledgers, tucked them under his arm, and began to pace his palatial parlor and receiving rooms. He took inventory of his fineries as if seeing them for the first time, a visitor to his town house. The inventory took him through the dining room, into the large salon on the other side of the entrance hall, through stillrooms and butler's pantries, through wine cellar and library, up the stairs to peek into all four huge bedrooms, marveling again how well furnished they were. Sumptuous, some said. Bordello "Flash," others cruelly whispered behind his back—*after* they'd had his meats, wines and music, after they'd fawned to his face and simpered at his japes!

"It's all up," he told himself again, halfway between tears and rage. "Don't *want* me t'have nothin', won't *let* me have nothin', niver in this life, the bastards! Build all this, they find a way t'take it from me, they do. Wisht t'God I'da had time t'kill Boudreau . . . an' do fer that uppity bitch an' her rogue! Ah, well. Me curses on 'em, 'tis the best ye'll do, Jack, me lad. It's all up. Ye had a good run, did ya not?"

Not only would he lose the plantation, but he'd lose the slaves, this house and all its lovely "pretties," the best that money could buy. His stores, his ships, his chandlery, his . . . "Ah, shame of it, now!"

But, there was money in the house, and money in his stores. And in the bank. Enough to start over somewhere else. And he still had a fine little ship in the harbour, ready to take him anywhere in the wide world he wished. He ripped open the chifforobe in his own bedroom, took out a leather traveling case, and set the ledgers inside it, then began to pack both it and an ornate sea chest, his mind already calculating the best of the tide.

Chapter 10

"Damme, what a rotten business," Lord Dunmore grunted after he had read the confessions. "All this happenin' right under my predecessor Maxwell's nose, and him ignorant as sheep, ha ha! That'll make int'restin' readin' in London! But, it's over now. We've bagged the miscreants, and they'll hang in tar and chains until their bones fall apart, damme if they won't."

"Finney did escape us, milord," Solicitor-General William Wylly informed him. Wylly had not known Lord Dunmore but a few months, but he had already developed a blazing dislike for the new governor, and had been heard to call him "obstinate and violent by nature," with a "capacity below mediocrity, little cultivated by education, ignorant of the constitution of England . . . the lordly despot of a petty clan."

"Best rid of him, then," Lord Dunmore shrugged as he poured a round of brandy for them all; those he had to cultivate, at least. Lewrie, Rodgers and some other minor officials were not included in that category, while Wylly, Garvey and Peyton Boudreau were. "Once he's proved guilty in court, all his goods'll be liable to seizure. Bound to be a pretty penny in all that, hey? Might even help defray the cost of me new fortifications I'd planned for the western side of the town. Fort Charlotte, I think to name it, for our Queen."

"There is the matter of the bank, milord," Chief Justice Matson put in. "Finney and several . . . ahum . . . of the finer and wealthier of the colony had formed a private merchant bank. There were hundreds of depositors, milord. It's been looted, I fear, and gone with Finney to God knows where. Many of your Privy Council had their accounts there, milord. *I* did, more to the point."

"Well, send a ship after him and get it back!" Lord Dunmore told them with an impatient arrogance. "That'd be easy enough, hey? What we have the Royal Navy for, if you can't go seize a ship when you wish to, what? How long's he been gone? Two hours, three? Garvey?"

"There is the problem of *where* he's gone, milord," the commodore muttered, looking most unwell since he'd seen *Whippet* and *Alacrity* come into port with *Guineaman* and *Fortune* as captures that morning. "I have three ships in harbour at the moment, but they'll not be enough. And *Whippet*, the sloop of war, is wormed and weeded. She would not be swift enough to catch him, even if we did know his direction."

"Excuse me, milord," Lewrie spoke up.

"Who the devil are you, sir?" Lord Dunmore scowled at him.

"Lieutenant Lewrie, of the *Alacrity*, milord. Finney did not use the nor'east Providence Channel, else he'd of had to sail past us to get out to sea. He'd be going west or south, milord. South down Tongue of The Ocean to the east'rd of Andros, to Cuba. Or he went up the nor'west Providence Channel to pick up the Gulf Stream and sail north. That would be the fastest escape, sir."

"Wherever those are," Lord Dunmore laughed, his round, fleshy moon of a face broken only by a huge overhanging beak of a nose wobbling with incomprehending humour.

"I'll send Lieutenant Coltrop and *Aemilia* north, then, milord," Garvey decided. "And Lewrie down Tongue of The Ocean."

"Excuse me again, milord, but if the swiftest, and most logical, course he'd steer would be north, then *Alacrity* has a longer hull, more sail area, and more and heavier guns," Lewrie countered. "I stand the better chance to catch him, and bring him to book."

"That make the slightest bit o' sense to you, Matson?" Dunmore japed at his chief justice. "Sounds like Greek to me. Tarpaulins!"

"And only if Lieutenant Lewrie is ordered to sail at once, milord," Rodgers added quickly. "And, with your permission, Commodore Garvey, I will turn *Whippet* over to my first officer so she may get her . . . long-delayed . . . docking and breaming." He could not resist the urge to put his own knife in. "And sail with Lewrie, sir."

"That sounds, and you will pardon the play on words, milord, I trust—

like the best *course*, haw haw," Peyton Boudreau said with a lazy, aristo-cratic air, as if it was 'just between you and me of the better sort' to Lord Dunmore, who was already under Boudreau's lofty spell. "Rodgers and Lewrie are, to my limited knowledge, two of the most energetic officers in the Bahamas Squadron, as I am certain that Commodore Garvey will agree. Damn my soul, have they not proved that today, milord? Best let 'em be in for the kill."

"Bless me, d'ya think so, Mister Boudreau?" Lord Dunmore asked with a wry cock of his head.

"Should they seize Finney and recover the funds, there's sure to be Finney's money as well, liable to condemnation as Droits of The Crown, I trust. More funds to support the construction of your Fort Charlotte. And to support the administration of the Bahamas Colony, milord," Boudreau concluded with a broad wink.

"Zounds! Damme if that don't sound right to me, Mister Boudreau!" the governor agreed heartily, his eyes piggish with greed. "Well, go be about it, you sea dogs. Go get him! Sic 'im, boys, sic 'im, hey? I say, Commodore, you're lookin' a touch peaked. Not coming down with something . . . tropical, are you?"

"Got out on the first of the rising tide this morning," Lewrie speculated as they left the Governor's mansion and began to trot down to the quays. "Four hours, just about. Damme, that's a hellish long lead. And that three-masted lugger of his is bound to be fast."

Lewrie could not bear to name Finney's ship, the *Caroline*.

"There's a chance," Rodgers puffed, trying to keep up with him. "He's no longer on the waterline than your *Alacrity*. And he couldn't have known we're only hours behind his sailin'. I'd wager he'll take deep water up the nor'west Providence Channel. With your shoal depth, we might try cuttin' closer to the Berry Islands, and gain the current of the Gulf Stream afore him."

"Gentlemen, please!" Peyton Boudreau insisted, blowing with the ef-fort to maintain their pace. The refined gentlemen or ladies *never* went faster than an idle strolling pace; the richer and more refined they were, the more languid! "This haste is unseemly! Lewrie, I must speak to you before you sail. About Caroline!"

"What about her?" Lewrie snapped, coming to an abrupt stop.

"I'll go on," Rodgers decided. "Join me soon as you're able."

"Aye, aye, sir," Lewrie responded perfunctorily before wheeling on Boudreau again. "Is anything wrong with her, or the baby?"

"They're fine," Boudreau assured him. "I meant but to show you this. Finney came to your home. He attempted to woo her with a tale of you abandoning her."

"So it was not Commodore Garvey interrupting my mails?"

"It was, but at Finney's behest," Boudreau said. "I believe he took your letters back and forth, so he might discover what would work best upon her insecurities when the time was right. Last week, before you arrived at Spanish Wells, I should think, he made his move."

"The bastard!" Lewrie screeched, clutching the hilt of his sword.

"This was the result, sir," Boudreau said proudly, producing a copy of the broadside sheet. "This was what 'Calico Jack' received as reward for his scheme."

"Well, damme!" Lewrie exulted as he took in the title and the engraved scene. "Good Lord, but she's got bottom!"

"I told you to trust her loyalty, and her good sense," Peyton praised her. "Enough to put a bumptious clown such as Finney to shame, even in what passes for Bahamian society, haw haw!"

"He went into our house, though?" Lewrie frowned suddenly.

"When he saw his plans had gone for nought, he did, and she . . ."

"He persisted?" Lewrie shouted. "He attempted force, after she spurned him? Force enough for her to shoot at him?"

"I fear he did. I ran him off at gun-point."

"I'll have his heart's blood, swear to God!" Lewrie said, with a sincerity that gave the pacific and elegant Peyton Boudreau chills. "Let's go, Mister Boudreau. I have to sail. There's not a single minute to waste, now!" he said, setting off at a faster trot once more.

But there was. For at the foot of the hill, at the landing quay on Bay Street by the Vendue House, sat a carriage which contained Mrs. Heloise Boudreau, and Caroline.

She alit from the equipage and ran to him, holding up her long skirts with one hand, hair flying behind her beneath a sunbonnet. He turned his course and met her, shouting her name as he lifted her into his arms and twirled her around as she collided with him, so fierce was her greeting. Snickering watchers bedamned, he kissed her in public; she returned his kisses just as ardently.

"Oh, God, at last!" she breathed against his cheek.

"Damned right!" he growled, laughing as he trembled with relief to see her well. Not only well, but as slim as he remembered her, just as lovely as before. And alive and hale! "Lord, you're beautiful! I missed you so much!"

"I love you so much," she echoed. "Alan, come see our son!"

He went to the carriage, where Heloise Boudreau held up a baby in swaddling clothes for him to see. Caroline took him and turned to show him off, cradled in her arms.

"Sewallis Alan Lewrie, this is your father," she said proudly.

Poor little *bastard*, Alan thought: what a horrid name! Well, he ain't rightly a bastard, is he? Not like I was. He has a father, and a mother. Godparents and grandparents, and all! Ugly, though, I must admit. S'pose all babies are.

"Hullo, little man," Alan crooned, putting out a hand to touch the child on the cheek, to stroke the incredibly soft flesh with one tentative finger. By God, this was reality, and a damned awesome one! He stroked the back of one tiny hand, and felt wee fingers grasp his. "Well, I'm damned!" Alan breathed out with awe as little Sewallis gave him a grave going over with his tiny eyes. He chucked him under the chubby chin. "Sewallis, I'm your father. What think you of that?"

Sewallis Alan Lewrie screwed up his face and began to wail.

Damned right, Lewrie thought: I would, too!

"Early days," Lewrie shrugged helplessly.

"Let's go home, this instant," Caroline invited.

"Dearest, I can't. We're off after Finney."

"Oh, God!" she gasped. "Alan, must you? I thought . . . !"

"I care to be no other place but with you, love, but we've been ordered to hunt him down, if we can. I have to sail at once. But, I will be back, I swear. Soon, darling."

"I'll take him, Caroline," Heloise offered, holding out her arms to receive the child. Arm in arm, Caroline strolled with him down to the quay, where a gig rocked on the tide.

"Peyton showed me the broadside, dear," Alan tried to cajole her. "You're the bravest, stoutest girl I know! That took courage, and I'm that proud of you for fending off his vile advances."

"You'll have to fight him," she shuddered, head buried against his shoulder. "There'll be a battle, I know there will. God, Alan, I have this fear, of a sudden! You're barely back at all, and gone!"

"I'll be back, Caroline," he insisted. "I love you! Now we've a real family, now I've a son to raise, I'll not do anything stupid, I swear. Once I'm back, we'll have all the time in the world together."

"Promise me you'll do nothing too rash, Alan? Please?"

"I'll do my duty, Caroline," he vowed. "And nothing rash. And, he's a good head start on us. We may not catch him up at all."

"You will, though," she sighed on the verge of tears. "I know you will." She looked up at him intently, as if trying to memorize his face for a final time to last her through the rest of a long life without him. "I love you, Alan. I will always love you."

"And I love you, Caroline," he replied, getting a fey feeling. He bent down and kissed her. "I'm sorry, but I have to go. Be brave for me, dearest girl. I'll fetch Finney back in chains, and we may add attempted rape to his crimes. Though we've enough to hang him a dozen times over already. Goodbye, love. Just for a week or two, a month on the outside, I promise."

"I'll be waiting," she told him, attempting to smile, holding back her tears as he stepped away from her. He walked to the dock and stepped into the stern-sheets of the gig. The bowman shoved off, and Cony snapped out his orders to backwater away from the pier.

Caroline watched as Alan was rowed out to his ship, stayed rigid on the dock as he mounted to the entry port to take his salute, stayed to wave to him as he doffed his hat to her. And stayed unmoving as *Alacrity*'s crew began to draw her up to short-stays to up-anchor, drumming round the capstan, though the gun ketch swam in her watery vision.

She could hear the canvas rustle, the sheaves shriek as she made sail even before the anchor was catted, as fiddles and fifes played a hauling chantey, gay but insistent.

She stayed on the dock until *Alacrity* cleared the harbour, and receded to hull-down over the horizon. Only then did she go back to the carriage, to stand inside to keep the ship in sight for a little longer.

"We should get home, Caroline," Heloise Boudreau offered at last. "Little Sewallis needs his sup soon. She's almost out of sight."

"I know, ma'am," Caroline nodded, wiping her eyes.

"He'll be back, you know. He will!"

"I pray so."

"We will all pray for his quick return, then."

"Let me have him," Caroline requested, and Heloise handed her her baby, who at last was napping, shaded from the tropic sun by the parasol Heloise held. "Once we're home, I have to talk to Wyonnie," Caroline added after she'd settled Sewallis in her arms. "There is something she must do for me."

"Home, driver," Heloise ordered the coachee. "And what is that, my dear?"

"I wish to see the *obeah*-man," Caroline replied.

"Oh, Caroline!" Heloise gasped. "Those are but fancy stories! I know his herbs helped Sewallis's colic, but . . ."

"We're both from the Carolinas, ma'am," Caroline intoned. "And we know what our 'mammies' told us growing up, about hexes. I wish to lay a hex," she said, looking straight ahead at the road, determined and grave. "Two. One of protection for Alan. And one a curse."

Chapter 11

Nor-nor'west for the Berrys, then north of west through the shallows of the Great Bahama Bank to Great Isaac, *Alacrity* bowled along off the wind. Stuns'ls rode at either end of the tops'l yards, doubling her sail area aloft, and a stays'l flew in the space between her masts on a jury-rigged jumper stay. Eight-and-a-quarter knots she made, eight and a half toward evening, racing for the Gulf Stream and its relentless northward currents. By five A.M. of the next morning, they had found the darker waters of the Gulf Stream, and bent north, riding the mighty river that added another four-and-a-half knots made good to their forward progress.

"No sign of him," Rodgers gloomed as he ate Lewrie's food and took liberal sips of Lewrie's dwindling wine supply, and had slept in Lewrie's double hanging-cot in Lewrie's stead.

"He stayed in the middle of the Providence Channel," Alan said. "We may even be slightly ahead of him to the Gulf Stream, if he sailed more north'rd of us, closer to the west end of Grand Bahama. Perhaps tomorrow's dawn will tell, sir."

"We're drivin' hard, I'll give us that," Rodgers shrugged. "Do you think she rides a mite bows-low? That'll make her crank for close maneuverin', light as she is aft."

"We're shifting supplies aft into the stern, sir," Alan replied.

"And it might not hurt to shift the Number One cannon from each battery aft as well, sirs," Ballard suggested. "*Alacrity* used to mount sixteen side guns as a bomb ketch, in addition to her deck mortars."

"Aye, there's ring bolts, side-tackle bolts, and gun ports being wasted," Lewrie agreed. "Two guns all the way aft, into the great-cabin here. Just forrud of the quarter-galleries. That's over eighteen hundredweight each, or more. Just enough to lift her bows . . . six inches?"

While Lewrie was a dab-hand navigator, physics was beyond him.

"About that, sir," Ballard said solemnly, furrowing his brows as he calculated the proposition in his head. "Perhaps an inch less."

"Run out the starboard battery, too, and draw the larboard close to her centerline," Lewrie plotted on. "Chock the trucks with old shot-garland rope to keep them steady. *Alacrity*'s flat-run on her bottom, and hard-chined aft. The more upright she sails, the faster she'll be."

"I'll attend to it, sir, soon as the forrudmost guns may be shifted," Ballard replied, jotting notes to himself about the order in which chores had best be performed.

"Four hours lead, though, sirs," Rodgers sighed sadly. "Even if Finney took a longer northern route . . . more like five, if ya count the time it took us to up-anchor an' clear harbour. He could be over on Andros, laid up 'til any pursuit'd passed him by. Damn him, but he's a clever 'un."

"Next dawn may tell, sir," Ballard offered hopefully.

"Dawn *will* tell, dammit all," Lewrie insisted, slapping at the table top. "Dawn *will* tell!"

The sun rose next morning, blood red and threatening, from an horizon of gunmetal gray. The Gulf Stream waters rolled and heaved to either beam, heaping high enough to smother *Alacrity* in the troughs between each long-set rolling wavecrest, and set her canvas luffing before she could rise up to clear air, and crack sails full of wind.

One hundred and sixty miles she'd made on her night passage up the American coast. Lewrie had not slept a single sea-mile of it, but had lain tossing in a chart-space berth, honing his anger.

Finney had violated his home, frightened his wife and son, and however he'd gotten word to flee—if he hadn't fled, Lewrie thought miserably, he'd have taken some revenge of Caroline for spurning him; he knew enough about the brute to not doubt that she might have been dead by then because of the broadside sheet, her and Peyton both!

He had taken the deck at eight bells of the Midwatch, at four of the clock in a chilly, dark morning, as the hands surged up to stow their hammocks in the nettings, wash down the decks, and stand to Dawn Quarters before their breakfast. To fret and pace as the stars paled from the gloomy skies, to see details in the clouds in the false-dawn, and watch the last of the moon sink below the horizon.

"Aloft, there!" he shouted to the lookouts.

"Nothin', sir! Clear 'orizons!"

"Damn!" he spat.

"Sir, it's . . ." Ballard attempted to console.

"Oh, the devil take you, Mister Ballard!" Alan snarled. He took a deep breath to calm himself, and paced off his disappointment, back to the taffrails before returning. "Very well, secure from quarters, and release the people to breakfast."

"Aye, aye, sir," Ballard replied, not in the slightest miffed by Lewrie's petulant outburst after a year and a half together.

"Sorry, Arthur," Lewrie muttered, smiling sheepishly.

"It's just your way, sir," Ballard smiled in return. "Soon as the galley's hot, I'll send Cony up with coffee for you. I assume you will keep the deck." That was not a question.

"Aye, I will, and thankee," Lewrie nodded. "More of my bloody . . . way!" Distressed as he was, Lewrie could not help smiling at himself.

Say Finney's lugger made seven-and-a-half knots, though, Alan calculated in moody silence; five hours lead to start with, and 160 sea-miles to The Stream . . . whilst we fetched it in 150 miles. God, we might have cut three hours off his lead. And we're a knot faster, say, all last night and all day today, with the current, now he thinks he's clear of pursuit. We'll make twenty-four more miles a day than he, so . . . if his original lead was only thirty-seven miles . . . Christ! What if he *did* put into Andros, the Berrys, inshore of the Gulf Stream down to Bimini to wait it out? Or, he could be flying everything aloft but his laundry, all this time . . . We'll never catch him up!

"Coffee, sir," Cony announced half an hour later.

"Hmmph?" Lewrie growled, startled from his musings.

"Yer coffee, sir," Cony offered. "An' wot'll ya 'ave fer yer breakfast, sir?"

"This'll do, Cony. This'll do for now," he grumped. "Thankee."

"Aye, aye, sir," Cony nodded sorrowfully.

Bounding, swooping, rolling at the top of a wave, *Alacrity* was driven on, her course due north. Foam creamed down her flanks to lay roiled astern, quarter-waves sucking low at her after hull as the sea made a perfect shallow S, horizontally from bow to stern, frothing in a millrace under her transom. Eight-and-three-quarter knots now, as enough cargo and artillery had been shifted aft to lift her bows. On steeper rollers she surfed forward, and sometimes defied the ocean a hold on her, the bow-wave breaking aft of her cutwater, and her whole hull lifting from the sea in her haste, as if she would take wings and fly in those moments when wind and sea conjoined, before falling away to snuffle deep and plow the water again with a disappointed soughing.

"Sail ho!" the lookout screamed at last from the cross-trees.

"Where away?" Commander Rodgers shouted back, wakened from his nap in Alan's sybaritic canvas sling chair.

"Two points off the larboard bows! A little inshore! Nought but tops'ls an' royals!"

"What's to loo'rd?" Lewrie asked, rubbing sleep from his own eyes, his skin tingling from too long in the sun in a restless nod.

"Almost due west by now, sir, 'tis Savannah," Fellows reported. "Nor'west is Charleston. Little over an hundred mile to either."

"And we're to windward of her, whoever she is," Lewrie crowed, fully awake. "She carries on north, she'll ram herself into the sand shoals off Wilmington, but she'll not weather the Outer Banks, not if I have a say in it! Mister Ballard, you have the deck, I am going to spy out our little mystery ship."

He slung a telescope over his shoulder, leaped for the shrouds and went aloft, aching to see for himself.

"There she be, sir," the lookout said, once he'd found a perch on the narrow slats of the cross-trees.

"Look like a lugger to you?" Alan demanded, extending the tube of his glass.

"Hard t'say from 'ere, sir. Jus' tops'ls, so far," the lookout opined. "Funny angle, though, cap'n, sir. Like Levanter lateens, or some'n ain't got 'er lift lines set proper to 'er royals."

Alacrity lifted on a swell as Lewrie laid the spyglass level on the tiny tan imperfections that marred the even horizon. Miles off, the other ship was lifted upward as well for a long breath or two, but dropped almost from view as *Alacrity* settled in a deep trough.

"I'd almost . . ." he sighed, lowering the heavy tube for awhile. He stood, precariously, on the cross-tree braces, wrapping one arm to the upper mast, inside taut halyards and lift lines. Braced securely, he raised the telescope again. The distant sails swam into focus.

"Three-masted," he grunted. "Aye, like lateeners, or . . . *Woooo!*" he whooped, loud enough to startle people on the decks below. "They're topmast stays'ls! She's a three-masted lugger!"

A lugger would mount small, oddly shaped sails between the tip of the upper masts and the gaff boom at the top of her mainsails, and that was what he had seen! It was a lugger, sure! But whose?

"Keep a sharp eye on her," he told his lookout. "Sing out, if she alters course or changes the slightest bit."

"Aye, aye, sir!"

Lewrie took a stay to the deck, tar and slush bedamned on his clothing, to join the curious on the quarter-deck.

"It's a lugger. Mister Neill, steer us a point free larboard. We'll close her, slow. I make her twelve miles off now. By the end of the first dogwatch, we'll have her at less than ten miles, so we may figure out if she's the *Car* . . . if she's Finney's."

"If she wishes to keep to the Gulf Stream, she's going to have to harden up and go closer-hauled, sir," Fellows suggested. "Allow me to suggest we stand on north, sir, we'll close her even so. Another two hours, and we'll lose the current ourselves inshore."

"And so will she, if she can't get to windward of us," Alan said. "And she won't."

"Chase is goin' closehauled, sir!" the lookout hallooed.

"Belay, Mister Neill. Mister Ballard, lay us hard on the wind."

"Aye, aye, sir."

Whatever she was, whoever the lugger belonged to, she was trying to flee, to get up to windward, and keep the advantage of the current of the Gulf Stream to weather Cape Hatteras and the Outer Banks. One more confirming sign that it most likely was Jack Finney, awakened to the fact of a pursuit.

No longer a mystery, Lewrie thought with satisfaction; now she was a chase!

The afternoon wore on, with both vessels clawing up to windward. *Alacrity* was already the possessor of the wind gauge. Weatherly as a lugger was, she could attain perhaps a full point closer to the winds, but *Alacrity* was just the slightest bit faster. Making leeway as she did, she still headreached her chase, and closed the range to eleven miles, to ten, to nine, bringing the lugger almost hull up, as *Alacrity* sailed the shorter closing angle.

"We're gaining on her, by Christ!" Rodgers chortled with glee.

"The *Caroline* was New Providence-built, sir," Lieutenant Ballard told him coolly, blushing a bit as he pronounced her name. "As flat-run and shoal-draught as *Alacrity*. Perhaps more so. But she makes just as much leeway as we do, with so little below the waterline for the sea to bite on. Long as we hold the weather gauge . . ."

"And damme if we might just be half a knot faster," Lewrie added with joy. "A full knot off the wind in the Gulf Stream. She'll be within range of random shot in six hours."

"He'll try to slip away once it's dark," Rodgers snorted. "No lights showin', they could tack an' pass astern."

"We've moon enough to see that, sir," Lewrie countered. "And to expect to beat against the Gulf Stream, no."

"Chase is 'aulin' 'er wind, there!" the lookout interrupted. "Turnin' west an' runnin' free, d'ye hear, there!"

"By God, here's another angle to cut short!" Lewrie laughed as he grabbed Ballard by the arm. "Arthur, haul our wind, now! We might gain a mile on him if we're quick enough! Come about to west-nor'west!"

"Aye, aye, sir. Mister Harkin, all hands! Ready to come about!"

Rodgers and Lewrie got out of Ballard's way, taking a corner of the quarter-deck free of tumult to inspect their chase with telescopes.

"Runnin' for Charleston, it appears, into neutral waters," Commander Rodgers decided. "Damn him."

"He has too much sail aloft," Lewrie stated. "Inshore, he'll pick up a land breeze later today. See how she heels, sir? That's too much heel for a flat-run hull, even off the wind as she is now. She's sailing on her shoulder, not her bottom. If he doesn't reef in those lateener topmast stays'ls, she's working too hard, bows-down."

"By God, he's no real sailor, is he, Lewrie?" Rodgers hooted. "Had you some champagne, I'd pop it now, to celebrate. We'll have him, by God, we'll have the bugger yet!"

"Many a slip, 'twixt the cup and the lip, sir," Lewrie smiled. "Aye, he may not be as tarry as he boasted. But he's running us one merry little chase. And, when it comes to it, he'll fight like some cornered rat. Now, to keep him out of American jurisdiction, we have to overtake him, take the lee position to block him."

"We'll have him," Rodgers insisted stubbornly. "We'll have him."

Chapter 12

By sunset, *Alacrity* left the Gulf Stream, inshore into waters that chopped instead of rolled. *Caroline* was still an hour ahead at the least, out of the Stream first, and making a more direct course, with less lee-

way, even as the land breeze found her. Try as they might to counter the
last of the powerful current, *Alacrity* ended up dead astern of the chase,
beating against the land breeze, lumping and booming against the chop
and the short rollers of the returning scend of waves breaking over the
horizon against the Carolina coast.

"She still makes too much heel," Lewrie decided after pondering the
dark spectre in his telescope. "So do we," he added, comparing the angle
of his decks against the chase's.

"Nighttime land breezes will be gentler, sir, not as strong," Ballard
speculated. "That'll ease her."

"Topmen of the watch aloft, Mister Ballard. We'll take first reef in the
fore-tops'l," Lewrie ordered.

"Are ya daft, Lewrie?" Rodgers hissed from the gloom of sunset by his
elbow. "I thought ya wanted t'catch the bastard?"

"I do, sir. But the fore-tops'l depresses the bows, and heels us too
much, even going closehauled as we are. Letting the fore-and-aft sails do
the work lets us pinch up to windward half a point."

"You are captain, sir, but I'm your superior," Rodgers grunted.

"Do but let me try it, sir," Lewrie begged. "Two hours. There's moon
enough to see her, and a sextant'll tell us if she's gaining, by the height
of her mast-trucks 'bove the horizon. We're even in speed for now,
perhaps a quarter-knot or half-knot faster, and that's not enough to
intercept her before she's in American waters."

"Two hours, then," Rodgers allowed at last. "But should we fall too far
behind, it'll be your fault, Lewrie. Your fault, hear me?"

"Aye, aye, sir."

Eased just the slightest bit, though, sailing more upright on her flatter
bottom, *Alacrity* closed the range. Six miles off, five and then four, with
more of Finney's *Caroline* visible above the horizon at each chiming of
the watch bells. Satisfied that his solution had worked, Lewrie slumped
down for a nap far aft on the signal flag lockers, muffled against the sea
wind's chill in a grogram boat cloak. With his head lolled against the
taffrail, he nodded off at last, his last waking sight the dark, creaming
wake alongside.

Cony came to wake him just before eight bells of the Middle, a few
minutes before four A.M., with a mug of black coffee. Alan took one sip
to sluice foul sleep from his mouth, spat it over the side, then drank deep

before handing the mug back to his servant. He walked forward for his telescope, and a view ahead, to assure himself that their chase was still there.

Caroline loomed even taller above the horizon of false-dawn, a slanted black semi-colon on the glittering silvery trough of the last of the moon astern. Using a sextant and a slate, Lewrie determined, assuming *Caroline's* masts stood seventy feet above her decks, that she was still being slowly overtaken, and was now a little less than three miles off, no matter how much sail she flew, which course she steered. And she was still heeled over too far!

"He said he'd made third mate," Lewrie muttered to himself as he stowed the sextant away in the binnacle cabinet. "Surely, he must know to ease her aloft."

"Sir?" Sailing Master Fellows queried his grunts.

"Two hours, I make it, to good practice for our guns, sir," he substituted.

"But by dead reckoning, captain, sir," Fellows countered wearily, "three hours to the Charleston Bar. And within range of the forts. We will be cutting it exceeding fine, sir. I doubt our rebellious cousins would appreciate us taking her right on their front stoop."

"I doubt the United States of America would shelter pirates. All the more reason to catch her up before we reach their waters."

"Aye, sir," Fellows nodded in agreement. "Excuse me, sir, but I do believe the sea wind is returning. A puff or two from the south'rd, so far, but it is veering, sir. We'll have stern winds in an hour, I believe, on our larboard quarter, from the sou'east."

"My respects to the first lieutenant, Mister Fellows, and . . ."

"I'm here, sir," Ballard announced from Lewrie's off-side, just at his elbow, which made Alan almost leap in surprise.

"Ah, good morning, Mister Ballard. Hands to the sheets and the braces, sir. And shake out that reef in the fore-tops'l."

"Aye, aye, sir."

"Land ho!" a bow lookout shouted aft. "Charleston Light, fine on the bows!"

"Less than three hours to the three-mile limit, then," Fellows sighed. "Sorry, sir, it seems my dead reckoning's off a mite."

"Time enough," Lewrie insisted. "Just barely. I hope."

True sunrise came, and with it, steady offshore winds out of the east-sou'east, laden with the smell of storm and rain later in the day; the

dawn a gray and gloomy beast that dingied the whitecaps and stained
the seas iron gray as spilled washwater and suds. Two miles astern of
Caroline they approached, relentlessly gaining; then only one mile, the
range of random shot for their six-pounders, even as the coast appeared
to the west, a thin dark green and blue thread, and the tall spire of St.
Michael's church rose skyward above The Beacon and the Charleston
Light. *Caroline* wore off the wind a little to the nor'west and *Alacrity*
surged directly up her wake, following the leads and the sea marks for
Five-Fathom Hole inside the Charleston Bar, south of the Ship Channel.

It would be cut exceedingly fine, as Mr. Fellows had predicted; half an
hour would spell the difference between Finney's escape or his ruin, of
being brought to battle or his gaining American waters.

"Seven cables, sir," Ballard estimated hopefully. "About fourteen
hundred yards. We could try shots from the bow chase guns."

"It's no good, Lewrie," Commander Rodgers griped, all but wringing
his hands. "To fetch him broadsides, we'll have to enter the three-mile
limit, in range of Fort Johnston an' Fort Moultrie. Damme if we ain't but
two miles off the Charleston Light now, sir."

"They do not have a battery to enforce their jurisdiction there, sir,"
Lewrie countered, drawn from dire musings about something aloft carrying away, of some structural failure which would rob them of the prize at
the last second. "We can chase her another two miles farther, out of
Five-Fathom Hole, right to the bar, sir. That's what their guns cover,
sir."

"He must bear off more northerly out of Five-Fathom Hole, sir," Ballard suggested slyly. "Might we not wear ship now and cut the angle to
close even more?"

"Splendid, Mister Ballard!" Lewrie grinned. "And begin firing with
the larboard battery. I'd admire did you Beat to Quarters, sir."

"Chase gun!" Midshipman Parham shouted, spotting a puff of gunsmoke on *Caroline*'s stern. The light ball moaned past the starboard side
to skip twice until it buried itself astern. "She has opened her fire upon
us, sir!"

"Mister Harkin, hands wear ship! Mister Neill, larboard your helm.
Steer nor-nor'west," Ballard called, as another ball soared by to strike
closer to the starboard side. *Alacrity* went tearing past a local fishing boat
busy with her nets, the Americans aboard shaking fists at them, and the
black slaves gaping wide-mouthed at the sight of a British warship with
all her colours flying. "Beat to Quarters!"

Alacrity's crew boiled into action, casting off the lashings of the great-guns, fetching handspikes and crows, removing tompions from the muzzles of both batteries, and opening the gun ports. Charges came up from the magazine, shot was selected and rammed home, flintlocks were primed and cocked.

"Ready for battle, sir," Ballard reported at last.

"We'll bear off a little more to starboard to give the gunners a better angle," Lewrie decided. "Oh. With your permission, Commander, of course."

"Ahum," Rodgers pondered heavily.

"Sir, we've come this far!" Lewrie groaned in a soft voice. "A half a mile more? With round-shot?"

"The repercussions, Lewrie!" Rodgers whispered. "We'll never hear the end of it from the damned Foreign Office, the Admiralty . . ."

"Please, sir. There's time enough!"

"You'll not violate the three-mile limit," Rodgers wheedled.

"Open fire, Mister Ballard," Lewrie snapped, before Rodgers had a chance to change his mind, interpreting that for a "yes."

"Larboard yer helm! Mister Fowles, as you bear, sir! Fire!" Ballard shouted at once.

The forward two-pounder chase guns rapped out first, followed by the deeper voices of the six-pounders, angled in the portsills as far forward as they might bear. The range was six cables, twelve-hundred yards, with *Caroline* stern-on to them, a difficult and narrow target. Shot tore the sea around her, close to her waterline, raising towering pillars of spray twice as high as her rails. Her mizzenmast jerked to a hit, and the aftermost lugsail folded in on itself as it was pierced by a ball, before ripping in twain from leech to luff! A ball struck her right on the stern, low on her transom near the rudder and made it twitch once like a dog's ear pestered by a fly.

"Chain-shot and bar-shot, Mister Fowles!" Lewrie shouted to his grizzled old gunner, who was pacing the gun deck bareheaded. "Play a Frog, and aim high to take his rigging down, sir!"

It was French practice to open fire at long range with expanding bar-shot, two halves of a round-shot connected by sliding lugs on iron bars, to tear rigging and sails and shatter yards and spars. Chain-shot was two lighter balls, connected by a stout length of links, designed to whirl end over end. British practice was to close beam to beam and aim "'twixt wind and water" to smash hulls, overturn guns, and shoot crews to rags; to slay, not cripple; to sink, not capture.

Caroline lengthened as she turned off north in the narrow and shoal-lined channel. Her gun ports flew open. Inexplicably, instead of running, Finney was going to fight it out!

"Eight side guns to our five, I make it, sir," Ballard pointed out after studying their foe with a spyglass. "Nine-pounders, no less."

"For what we're about to receive," Lewrie nodded, muttering the old saw, "may the good Lord make us grateful."

Caroline opened fire, her starboard side erupting in a gush of brownish gray powder smoke shot through with stabs of quick, hot flame. *Alacrity* seemed to shudder in fear to the rising moan of round-shot on the air before she was struck, and rose a little on the scend of the sea, as if holding her breath in dread anticipation. A nine-pounder ball struck forward near the larboard anchor cathead, turning part of the bulwarks to flying splinters. Another fell short but skipped over the water to thud home deep in her lower hull amidships, and the sea around her was flayed with close misses, crashing up spray like the breaching of whales.

"On the up-roll . . . fire!" Fowles screamed. The broadside roared out, and *Caroline*'s rigging jerked and twitched. Her foremast and jibs collapsed, broken off twenty feet above the deck, and she ploughed up a furrow of foam as she lost speed in the blink of an eye.

"Got him, dammit!" Lewrie hooted. "Solid shot, Mister Fowles!"

They were out of Five-Fathom Hole, running hard due north for the inner side of the Charleston Bar, with Charleston Light and The Beacon abeam and to leeward, Caroline just a little ahead of *Alacrity*, and not four cables' range—800 yards away, and in the best killing zone for six-pounders.

Caroline fired again, her second broadside more ragged than the first, unable to match the taut discipline of naval gunnery. *Alacrity* leaped under their feet as another shot hulled her, as a ball struck her forward on the gunwale. With shrieks, two more sailed overhead, close to the deck, stunning people with their shock waves.

"Hull her, Mister Fowles!" Lewrie shouted, feeling the lust for blood rising in his veins. "Serve her hot and fast, lads!"

God help me, but this is bloody marvelous, he thought; rejoicing in the hot, satanic reek of powder smoke, the ringing thunder of guns! I must be daft, but this is what I do truly love as much as life!

The broadside crashed out, round-shot hammering home into the soft Abaco pine of *Caroline*'s hull. Lighter and less forgiving than good Kentish oak, they punched great, ragged holes into her, her timbers and scantling planking screaming and winging away from each strike, even as she continued to fire, her guns lighting up throughout, her masts and remaining sails wiggling in pain above the smoke clouds.

Iron crashed into *Alacrity*, men screamed as they were plucked backwards by splinters of wood or broken metal. Seamen writhed about on the deck, suddenly legless, pierced by jagged arrows of oak, blood reeking in the morning like liquid copper. Loblolly boys tried to tend them, even as Fowles, Woods the gunner's mate, and the captains of each artillery piece thumped and lashed the lucky to keep firing, to keep swabbing out, to keep covering the vents while swabbing so the touchhole did not burn out, for the powder monkeys to keep arriving with their fireproof cylinders of powder bags, to keep ramming powder and shot down the hungry barrels, to stand it like men and strain on the tackles to run out, aim, and fire.

Back the guns leaped, carriages hopping like crippled toads in the air to stutter on their trucks, the decks shuddering with every cruel impact, the guns slewing at the extent of the breeching ropes. Belching explosions of powder gushed from the muzzles, and ears ached with so much noise, ears bled with so much torture; ears would sing for days afterward, and some hands would be deafened for life, yet think themselves lucky if that was all they suffered this day.

"Cover yer vents! Sponge out! Overhaul the run-out tackle!"

Caroline stood on north, with *Alacrity* directly abeam of her now as her rigging draped in tatters about her, almost lost in powder smoke rolling down onto her like a Channel fog. Shot howled in the air like witches, raised great feathers of spray alongside, thudded into her side. One passed just over the larboard bulwarks and flew out to sea, not touching a thing, a black streak at the corner of the eye, and two waisters on the gangway fell dead, their hearts stopped by the shock of its passage.

"Charge yer guns! Shot yer guns! Grape atop ball! Run out yer guns, and overhaul them tackles! Prime yer locks!"

"Keep pinching us up, Mister Neill," Lewrie told his helmsmen. "Keep closing the range."

"Aye, aye, sir," Neill replied, and shared a look with Mr. Early, the quartermaster's mate who had been promoted to replace Mr. Burke. Early took a look at the compass binnacle for the new course, then at the faint smudges on the deck where Burke had bled to death, which had yet to come up in two weeks' holystoning, and almost swallowed his cud of tobacco.

"Cock yer locks! 'Twixt wind an' water, lads! On the up-roll . . . fire!" Fowles howled, looking like an angry Moses come down with the tablets, his mouth open in a rictus of a smile.

The broadside exploded outward, long tongues of quick pink and amber flames and sparks following the smoke and the iron, and *Caroline* wailed in torment as the weight of round-shot ripped her vitals.

"We're almost on the Charleston Bar, sir!" Fellows shouted in Lewrie's ear. "We'll be aground, the very next minute!"

"So will she, Mister Fellows," Alan shouted back. "But are we yet within three miles of Fort Johnston, or Moultrie?"

"No way to say, sir, in all this smoke."

"Then maybe there's no way for their gunners to say if we are or not, either. For all this smoke," Lewrie grinned. "Wear ship to larboard. Steer due west to miss the bar. Mister Ballard, starboard battery. We'll bear off west and rake her."

Alacrity delivered one more smashing broadside at less than two cables' range, then spun about on her heels to sail away from danger, pointing her jib boom due west at Fort Johnston. Once in clear air, they could see the flags flying on the fort, and the thin trails of smoke from the furnaces, where shot was being heated for the heavy thirty-two- and forty-two-pounder artillery should they get within range.

"Well, damme, look at that!" Rodgers exclaimed, pointing at *Caroline*. "Just do look at that, the clever, lying *hound!*"

Upon *Caroline's* mizzen, nailed to the mast above the gaff as the halyards had been shot away, was the striped red and white banner with the starred blue canton of an American flag!

"As you bear . . . fire!" Fowles called to his starboard gunners, delirious and uncaring, drunk on the power of his artillery. *Alacrity* heeled over to the broadside. The range was a little over a cable, and *Caroline* came apart under the shock of their fire. Her elegantly oval transom caved in, the transom plate below her taffrails which bore her name was shattered to matchwood and gilt. The mizzenmast bearing the false flag was shot clean off just above the quarter-deck by shot, one which slew everyone on the tiller in passing. It stumped forward as it fell, off the quarter-deck and onto the lower deck, then cried over the larboard side. And a moment later, *Caroline* ran aground on Charleston Bar, her bows leaping upward like a dolphin, heeling over so far on her starboard side she put her gun ports in the water, and her last middlemast fracturing and falling forward and to starboard!

"Cease fire, Mister Fowles! Drop it, she's a dead 'un!" Lewrie called out. "Mister Ballard, put us about, quick as you can, back out to sea. Fetch-to soon as Mr. Fellows determines we're legally outside the three-mile limit. Mister Harkin? Ship's boats over the side. We will board the wreck. Mister Odrado and Warwick to lead the boarding party."

"Uhm, they both be dead, sir," Harkin had to report.

"Christ," Lewrie spat. "Damme, we'll miss 'em. Select whom you will, then, Mister Harkin."

"Aye, aye, sir."

Well, we'll miss Odrado, him and his guitar, Alan thought; ship's corporals were never loved—feared, damn' right, but never loved, and Warwick was half a brute. Kept good order, though.

"Sir!" Parham called, pointing over the side. "Sir, there's a cutter putting out for us from shore. From Fort Moultrie, sir. Flag of truce in the stern-sheets."

"Uhm, Commander Rodgers, as senior officer present, perhaps you might be best in dealing with the Yankee officials, sir?" Alan hinted. "I'll go aboard the wreck and arrest the survivors."

"Thankee, Lieutenant Lewrie," Rodgers sneered heavily, fiddling at his uniform and sword. "Now we've created an international incident, why thankee *most* kindly! Let me know what evidence ya find. We'll be needin' a power of it, an' that soon. Fetch me Finney, if he lives. Least we can have somethin' t'show for it."

"Aye, aye, sir."

"Ah go wit' ya, cap'm, sah," John Canoe insisted, shoving his way into the boat at the last minute by Cony in the stern of the gig.

"Boat's full, Canoe," Lewrie snapped.

"Dot boat full o' Chawlst'n men, sah," Canoe pleaded. "Ah don' wanna see 'um, sah."

"Whyever not?"

"Dis w'ar ah 'scape f'um, cap'm, sah. Mebbe one 'o dem 'spys me, dey take me bock, sah."

"You paddled from South Carolina?" Lewrie goggled.

"Down t' Flo'da, sah," Canoe grinned. "An' dem come lak a free mon wit' dot Colonel Deveaux. Oh, no, sah, even *ah* don't paddle canoe all de way t' de Bahamas, no sah!"

"You're a free black Ordinary Seaman in His Majesty's Royal Navy, Canoe," Lewrie promised. "No one's taking you anywhere. Oh, sit down. Cony, shove off!"

"Thankee, sah," Canoe grunted, taking a place on a midship seat between oarsmen. "Thankee."

Caroline was a total ruin. Rigging, sails, halyards and sheets lay in messy profusion on her decks, decks quilled with splinters and bulging upwards in star-shaped cavities where masts had spiraled out of the keel-wedges, where entering shot had ruptured her. Thin smoke rose from smouldering canvas where powder charges had burst or burned, where hot metal barrels had seared sails. Her artillery had been shot free to roll down to the starboard side, crushing gunners into pasty, broken mannequins splashed with gore so freely it looked as if some lunatic had run amok with barricoes of red lead paint. Bodies lay sprawled on every hand; broken, quilled, dismembered, disemboweled.

Wounded cried piteously, dragging themselves over the decks and leaving slug tracks of blood. Those hale were busy binding up those they could; or drinking with single-minded purpose from scuttled kegs of rum. Dozens of wine bottles rolled in the scuppers, already empty, and a buccaneer sat on the midships cargo hatchway gratings, shouting and weaving with a bottle in each hand, drunk as a lord, with the stump of his shattered leg sticking straight out in front of him.

"Where's Finney?" Lewrie asked.

"Woy, 'iz lordship's aft, admiral," the wounded buccaneer cackled and hawked up phlegm to spit. "An' bad cess t'the brainless bugger, oy sez! Haw! Aft in 'iz *great*-cabins!"

"Tend to that man," Lewrie ordered. "Let's go, Cony . . . Canoe."

He stepped down into the well which held the short ladder into the great-cabin hatchway. The door had been shot away by ball. Lewrie drew his sword, and Canoe and Cony backed him up with cutlasses and a pistol each.

Aft past the first mate's cabin, the chart-space, and into the master's cabins, pushing the door open with the tip of his blade, to peer inside, and gasp in awe.

Finney's cabins were lush beyond imagining; cream bulkheads all picked out with gold leaf, polished wooden deck almost completely covered with Turkey carpets, and the furnishings rich and gleaming. Or, they had been. Now the transom lay open to the wind and sea, and it had all been scattered like a rummage sale in a secondhand shop, the chairs, dining table and desk shattered and overturned in a sea of fine clothes, drapes and bedclothes.

Lewrie sucked in his breath as he espied a corpse buried in a pile of clothing and spilt sea-chest items. He used his sword tip to lift the cloth aside.

"Well, damme," he shuddered with disgust.

It was not Finney, but a woman! A tarted-up doxy with bright blonde hair, overdone with rouge and paints. One sightless blue eye was fixed on the rich carpet. The other, and half of the back of her skull, had been hacked away by grape-shot.

"I'm over here, ye bastard," Finney growled from the shadows by the starboard quarter-gallery, making Lewrie jump. "Thet wuz jus' Molly. Decent enough trull she wuz, fer a 'Over-The-Hill' dramshop whore."

"Dig him out," Lewrie ordered, and Cony and Canoe hefted a few crates and chests out of the way so he could face his foe at last. He could not help hissing in his breath again when Finney became visible, lumped up against the bulwarks like a broken doll, one arm shattered and bleeding his silk shirt red from wrist to collarbone, and another gory stain in the lap of his fine ecru silk breeches. A trickle of blood oozed from Finney's lips, and from his nose, making him hawk and cough to clear his throat to breathe.

"An, thankee," Finney smiled through his certain pain. "Thet last broadside done fer me, Lewrie. An' fer poor Molly. Figgered I could use a woman's comforts, so I fetched her along. She'd niver seen Charleston, an' had a hankerin' t'come away with me. An' niver will, now, by Christ! Weren't fer yer meddlin' Peyton Boudreau keepin' sich a wary watch, coulda been yer Caroline alayin' there dead, now, an' by her own dear husband's hand!"

"What the devil are you talking about?" Lewrie growled.

"Woulda took *her*, if I'd had a mite more time t' spare fer me . . . for my escape," Finney grinned, still trying to play the gentleman in his speech, knowing it would be his last. "Woulda been a devilish fine thing, t' spite ye, an' her. Had ye known I had her, ye mighta held yer fire, an' I'd be strollin' flash on the Battery this minute."

"Let's get him on deck," Lewrie decided. "This ship's going to break up, the way she's pounding." John Canoe pushed his way along the outer bulkhead over wreckage and trash to put his arms under the pirate, though Finney begged him not to touch him.

"No, don't, Jaysis, no!" Finney howled as Canoe began to lift. He gave out a shrill scream as terrifying as a rabbit in a fox's jaws. "Put me down, Jaysis, Joseph an' Mary, love o' God, put me down, will ye? Leave me be, man! Think me back's shot plumb in half. I cain't feel nothin' below me waist, but atop, aye . . . Jaysis! Let me die in peace, willya now. Me arm's broke t' flinders, think these chests o' mine stove in me ribs."

Lewrie's eyes lit up with pleasure as he saw that part of the cargo that had shifted and crushed Finney as *Caroline* ran aground were the chests of gold and silver coin looted from the bank, part of Jack Finney's personal hoard. Mixed among spilled coins were certificates of exchange and ledgers.

"Lookee here, Lewrie," Finney cajoled, once the worst of pain had subsided. "There's a bottle o' brandy yonder in my wine cabinet I see as hasn't been smashed. Been studyin' it somethin' fierce the last few minutes. Have a heart an' fetch it, willya, Lewrie? Let a sailin' man go to his Maker with a reason t' smile, hey? Lemme have one taste 'fore I pass over? Won't be long, fer either of us."

"Cony, fetch the devil his brandy," Lewrie frowned, pacing up the steep slant of the deck to larboard. He could feel the *Caroline* dying, could feel her shift and shamble as the morning tide and the current played with her, as waves made her pound on the Charleston Bar. Timbers groaned deep within, planks sprung with sharp cries, and now and again, something in her hold thumped and drummed, or gave way with a sharp crack.

Won't be long before she breaks up, Lewrie thought; we'll have to get all this stolen loot aboard *Alacrity* before then.

"John Canoe," he said. "Fetch Mister Woods the gunner's mate, and a working party to pack up this loot and get it aboard our ship."

"Aye, aye, sah."

"Now tell me about Commodore Garvey, Finney," Lewrie demanded once Canoe was gone.

"Right tasty, this," Finney replied, leering back at him between deep gulps from the neck of the bottle. "One o' me . . . one of my finest imports, I do declare, sir."

"We don't have much time, Finney," Lewrie pressed, coming down to starboard again.

"You do, don't ye, now!" Finney snapped, then cried out with the vehemence of his accusation that had caused fresh waves of agony. "Ah, Jaysis, 'tis a hard life I've had. But a few good years in the Bahamas, an' now ye've ruined it all. Doesn't seem fair, it don't, you to go on livin', with a wife handsome as yer Caroline, a boy-baby an' all, an' I t' be dyin', ruint an' broke."

"My God, you . . . !" Lewrie spluttered in amazement, thinking of all of Jack Finney's victims. "Seems *damned* fair, to me, after causing all that misery and murder. Now what about Commodore Garvey? I want to know for certain. Tell me how he helped you. And how much he cost you."

"Ye don't get it, do ye, Lewrie?" Finney laughed softly. "God, how much I hate ye, Lewrie! Iver since thet night in the inn, when ye turned yer nose up at me invitation . . . looked me over like a muddy pig an' . . . spite me, willya? Sneer at me, willya? Well, 'tis only fair I get a last chance t'spite ye back. Garvey's an English bastard, same as ye. Much as he deserves it . . . I'll give ye nothin' to make any more fortune on. Thet way, I goes t'me death with somethin' ye want, so in a way, I beat ye, after all, Lewrie. Now, why don't ye shit in yer fine hat there, clap it on yer head, an' call it a brown tie-wig?"

Woods's men arrived and began to fetch out the crates and chests, scooping up loose coins to cram back into the boxes, and, Lewrie knew, their own pockets if someone didn't look sharp after them. There would be no prize money, no head bounty, and all that they recovered would be Droits of The Crown instead of Droits of The Admiralty, so his men would have nothing to show for death or wounds. Lewrie decided to ignore the little they could get away with this time; they'd earned it.

"Take all o' this, sir?" Woods inquired, waving about the cabin.

"Aye, all of it. There may be some evidence hidden away in the odd chest or bag," Lewrie nodded. "Leave the bastard nothing."

"We be leavin' him, sir?" Woods asked. "Beg pardon for me to be suggestin', captain, but the seas're gettin' up. We'd best be quick about it, sir. Mister Ballard's sent our other boats over."

"Aye, we will be," Lewrie nodded, scuffing about the cabins in frustration over Finney's hateful, mocking silence about Garvey.

"Uhm, you'll be wantin' us to take this, too, sir?" Woods said, gesturing to the shadowed forward bulkhead where the dining space had been. "This pitcher, sir?"

"Christ!" Alan rasped in shock. On the bulkhead hung a portrait, now askew and gnawed in a lower corner by grape-shot in canvas and the frame. It was a copy of his own portrait of Caroline! Not an oval, as was his, but rectangular; copied closer about her face to eliminate the gardens and East Bay. Augustus Hedley had done it himself, for in the lower right corner was his florid signature.

"Wot a bastard," Woods grunted. "Namin' this lugger o' his after your good lady, sir, an' now this! Take it to the boat, sir?"

"Aye, Mister Woods. I'll not have her go down with him, or give him any comfort to look upon. Thankee, Mister Woods."

"Aye, aye, sir."

"Finney, you miserable shit!" Lewrie shouted, wheeling about to walk back to the man, flexing his hand on his sword's hilt, pondering hard on whether to kill him that instant, or let him groan in agony and drown as the best, and most painful, death for him.

"Many's the nights I wuz inspired t' gaze upon her, Lewrie," Finney boasted. "Rattlin' a whore, an' lookin' at her, an' wishin'. Almost had her, damme'f I didn't, though."

"Don't, sir!" Cony said, stepping between to block Lewrie from drawing his sword. "E's agoadin' ya, sir, so 'e kin die quick. God o' mercy, sir, let 'im drown! E's aspittin' up blood arready. Drown in gore'r sea water, sir. Ev'ry rock o' this wreck's apainin' 'im good as the fires o' Hell, sir. 'Tis best 'e suffers so, Mister Lewrie!"

Lewrie panted hard, affronted to be held in check.

"And lookee this, sir," Cony whispered, pointing with his chin to a cylindrical traveling bag on the deck. From beneath a pile of hastily crammed in silk shirts and neck-stocks, peeked a stack of old ledgers. "Lookee this 'un, sir. In 'is own 'and, sir."

Lewrie fought down his rage and opened the ledger Cony offered him. It was in Finney's near-illegible scrawl; not so much an account of debits and credits, but a log such as a mate would keep, more like a diary. There were entries of ships taken, by whom, how many shares the crew got, who had died and would require settlements for wives or girls, expenditures of powder and shot, values of goods taken, of how much pirated ships sold for in Havana or Cartagena. Along with such dry accountings of mayhem and murder, Finney made his comments about his illegal business, wrote his screeds about the high cost of bribing government officials, listed . . . !

"Oh, my God!" Lewrie smiled suddenly. "Bless you, Will Cony!"

"Thankee, sir," Cony grinned shyly.

"Ah, 'twas a lovely brandy," Finney groaned blissfully, tossing the empty bottle aside. "Given enough warnin', 'tis right a man gets a chance t' die dead drunk."

Lewrie took the ledger with him as he walked down the deck to Finney for the last time.

"Me curses 'pon ye, Lewrie," Finney beamed, coughing on blood in his mouth, trying to spit some at Lewrie, who stood just a little too far away to hit. "Bad cess t' ye, yer handsome bitch, yer brat, an' all yer kin! Bad cess fer the rest o' yer lives!"

Lewrie held up the book. Opened it so Finney could see, and recognize his own hand, and know it for what it was.

"Ah, no!" Finney groaned, screwing up his ruggedly handsome face like a petulant child. *Caroline* was swept by a breaking wave, making her thump and pound on the Bar harder than before, and shift with the sound of sliding sands. Wood croaked and screamed.

"I'd tell you to go to the devil, 'Calico Jack,' but then, we both know that's where you're bound, don't we?" Lewrie chuckled as he put the ledger under his arm. "How did it go? 'Calico, calico, who will buy my calico? 'Tis Jack, Jack, the Calico Man'?"

"Oh, ye brute! Oh, ya bastard!" Finney raved, as water began to seep into the cabins, to froth in through loosened plankings.

"Know how to swim, 'Calico Jack'?" Lewrie taunted. "That might keep you alive a minute longer. It'll hurt like Hell, of course."

"Youuu!" Finney screamed.

"Let's go, Cony. We have what we came for."

Epilogue

"Any nation that won't support a navy to protect its interests can't have much objection to make now, can they?" Captain Childs said with a guffaw as he dined Rodgers and Lewrie in, in the great-cabins of his frigate *Guardian*.

"The point was made, sir," Rodgers snickered back. "Diplomatic, though. Not quite so pointed as you couch it. An' after they learned Finney was a British master, in a British-flagged ship, that shut them up."

"Well, 'tis all settled now," Childs went on happily. "Finney's dead, his enterprises foundered, and his pirates all scattered Hell to Hutters-field. Bank funds recovered, all of Finney's ill-gotten gains property of the Crown. A neat bit o' business, in the end."

"What about his commercial interests, sir?" Lewrie was forced to ask. "His legitimate interests, that is? And surely, sir, I found many names in his ledgers of civilians who turned a blind eye, or did his bidding, for a price. Government officials . . ."

"Ahem," Childs sobered. "The, uhm . . . our Royal Governor is now in possession of those ledgers, Lieutenant Lewrie. I would imagine that some investigation is proceeding. And that someday, they will be brought to book. Civilian doings. No matter to the Fleet."

"Finney's stores're already taken over by the other Bay Street mer-chants, lock, stock, and barrel," Commander Rodgers added, reaching for the wine bottle on the sideboard. "Stock bought up at pence to a pound at auction. Though devil a hope we have o' lower prices in our lifetimes."

"Amen to that, sir," Childs chimed in, eyeing Rodger's liberality with his wine. "Might pass that down, once you're done, sir."

"And the Commodore, sir?" Lewrie presumed to question.

"Ah, well," Childs scowled. "Hmm. Pity 'bout that tropical ague that took him of a sudden. Didn't look that sick for so long, as they say he was. No, 'tis best he's off home, to recover in milder climes."

"With nothing but his Navy pay, in the end," Rodgers laughed as he passed the bottle down. "And that in arrears for all his high living."

"The Admiralty'll probably send someone else out next spring to command the Bahamas Squadron," Childs sighed. "Can't have a mere frigate captain such as myself in charge for long, with so many senior men with impeccable connections sitting around on half pay."

"But copies of the allegations did go to the Admiralty, sir?" Lewrie pressed harder. "After all, I would assume Commodore Garvey had impeccable connections that could . . . well, preserve his career."

"Aye, I sent 'em, Lewrie, if that's what you're wondering, sir," Childs glowered at him. "All we may do is but hope that Our Lords Commissioners will take them into account for next time."

"Hope he makes bloody Admiral," Rodgers snorted, well into his cups at their very private supper. "Sir, gentlemen, allow me to propose a toast. To Commodore Horace Garvey . . . may he attain the rank of rear admiral in His Majesty King's George the Third's Royal Navy . . ."

"Bloody hell," Lewrie muttered, but forced to raise his glass.

". . . of the permanently retired 'Yellow' Squadron!" Commander Rodgers concluded with a bark of a laugh, and tipped his glass up to drain it right down to 'heel-taps.'

"There's the fine little fellow," Lewrie cooed to his son, who had at last warmed to his presence, and didn't bawl when he saw him any longer. Lewrie sat rocking on the dog-run terrace, young Sewallis a tightly swaddled bundle in the crook of one arm, entertaining him as he would William Pitt the cat, with a length of smallstuff tied in a bowline dangled for tiny fingers to grasp. Every time he succeeded in getting hold of the loop in the line, he gurgled his pleasure and lit up his features with a radiant, cockeyed smile. Lewrie rewarded him with a dandle on his knee, which made Sewallis even more ecstatic.

"Lucky fellow you are, Sewallis," Alan assured him. "First son, bound for the law. Oxford or Cambridge. You'll never have to go to sea like your daddy does. 'Tis a miserable bloody life."

"Don't teach him bad words, Alan," Caroline said, coming out to sit by him, and deliver two glasses of wine. "He'll learn them soon enough. Yes 'e *will*, pretty baby! Ooh, li'l man Sewallis, yes! Your *daddy!* Like to have daddy play with oo, yes oo *do,* mommy *knows* oo do!"

"Mommy *can* speak the King's English, Sewallis," Alan snickered. "Daddy *knows* she can. And someday, oo will, too! Ain't that a bloo . . . won't that be a wonder?"

He turned to look at Caroline, she looked at him, and they both laughed at themselves for a fond moment. Until Alan wriggled his nose and looked down at his lap. Young Sewallis had become so delighted he had fouled himself, and quickly soaked through his swaddlings to turn Lewrie's breeches both wet and pale brown. "Oh, bugger!"

"I'll take him, sah," Wyonnie offered, coming out to the dog-run. "Time fo' his nap 'fo suppah, anyhow, sah."

"Thankee, Wyonnie," Lewrie said. "Thank God it's my worst and oldest breeches."

"I fetch ya a towel, sah."

Fatherhood, Lewrie thought; hmmm! It *must* get better as they become continent! Surely!

"How long will *Alacrity* be in dock?" Caroline asked, sipping her wine, putting her feet up on her hassock and enjoying the sunset.

"About a week to ten days," Alan replied, taking his own wine in hand. "Little more than a year in Bahamian waters, and her bottom is foul as the Forest of Dean, copper or no! Least she wasn't eaten with teredo worms like *Whippet* was. 'Tis a miracle to me we made the speed we did, catching Finney, with that much growth on the bottom. Or him being foolish enough to break off his flight to fight us, just within sight of safety. Carrying too much sail. Loafing along . . ."

"Perhaps a higher power aided you, dear," Caroline said with a secret smile. "A higher power with a strong sense of justice."

"I would suppose so," Alan allowed.

"So we have two blessed weeks to look forward to, then," she said. "You at home every evening." She scooted her chair over closer to his so they could lean together and put their arms about each other's shoulders companionably. "Sleep in the same bed each night . . ."

"Wake together so close and snug," Alan suggested.

"Alan," she said, after a meaningful purring noise. He looked for the tiny vertical line between her brows; and found it.

Oh, shit, he thought with trepidation; what now?

"When Finney was here that evening . . ."

"The bastard!"

"Yes, but . . ." Caroline agreed, taking a sip of wine and gazing out toward Potter's Cay. "Among his blandishments to win me, he told me . . . or he strongly *suggested*, that is . . . that you were known in the Navy by a nickname. That you were awfully young to have gained one, but that in the Fleet, you were known as . . . the 'Ram-Cat.' He as much as said right out that it alluded to . . . faithless . . . amorous . . . Where did he come by that, dear?" she concluded, looking at him closely.

"Oh, God," Alan smiled, hiding his panic damned well, even if he did say so himself. He threw in a tiny chuckle. "Caroline, love. I suppose it came aboard the *Shrike* brig, under old Lieutenant Lilycrop. I ended up with William Pitt, and half a dozen other cats. He'd make me a present of one from every litter, and we had so many litters we were ankle-deep in kittens! Fobbed 'em off on every passing ship we spoke, and it was me that had to make the offers, half the time. And, well . . . Navy blue coats and cat hair don't mix, don't ya know. Every time I reported somewhere, I was constantly brushing myself down. And having William Pitt in London with me. I believe Admiral Hood named me that in jest, before I went out to the Far East with Burgess. When I reported to him, Pitt had been at my coat. I expect that's where it comes from, darling."

"You went to Sir Samuel Hood's with cat hair on your coat?" she giggled.

"And the smell of his 'blessings' on me, too, most like," Alan tried to giggle back.

"Oh, God, what a picture! No wonder he called you 'Ram-Cat'! He could smell it on you! And see it! Darling, it's a wonder at all he gave you an active commission!" she laughed out loud.

"Better than herding swine on half pay, and facing him in straw and pig shit!" Lewrie agreed. "Promise you'll never tell that on me."

"Oh, I'll not, ever!" she told him, leaning closer to hug and kiss him. "But I can't help thinking about it, just between us."

"It'll make a fine tale to tell Sewallis when he's older."

"Yes, it will," Caroline agreed. "And, it's not a bad sobriquet for you to have. You'll always go after your foe like William Pitt, like an angry 'Ram-Cat.' "

"That I will," he said.

And thank bloody Christ she bought that, he thought gratefully.

Afterword

John Murray, Fourth Earl of Dunmore, Royal Governor to the Bahamas from 1787 to 1796, was just about as bad as I portrayed him, and as the estimable William Wylly cited further writes, nor was "the immorality of his private life any less reprehensible than the defects of his private character." Fort Charlotte, familiar to all visitors to Nassau, was started at an estimate of £4,000, and ended up costing the government £32,267. He was more interested in his own mansion, and a magnificent estate and house at Harbour Island, which is officially named Dunmore Town, but never by the long-suffering inhabitants who ever had anything to do with him, or pay his exorbitant rents. His administration was as corrupt as they come, his appointments termed by another writer "bankrupts, beggars, blackguards and the husbands of his whores"; for one his Searcher of Customs, whose wife bore him a child during his tenure. For anyone interested in delving further into the history of the Bahamas, let me recommend A History of the Bahamas by Michael Craton.

Did Caroline's *obeah*-man cause Jack Finney's downfall? To get to him at long range after he sailed, she would have needed the power of an expensive witch, far beyond the powers of an average "white-magic" *obeah* practitioner. An *obeah* doctor would need a "snake-witch," an animal that could swim long distances to "fix" people far away. Witch in this instance is the curse itself, as in what an oldtimer in the islands would say when he or she threatens "to work witch on ya."

There's a good chapter on *obeah* in Insight Guides: Bahamas, 3rd Edition, available in most tour-guide sections in your local bookstore, or Dr. Timothy McCartney's book Ten Ten, The Bible Ten—Obeah In The Bahamas. Should you visit Nassau, take a side-trip to Fox Hill, and ask around—respectfully.

Lastly, I hope the citizens of the Bahamas will forgive me for making John Canoe, even briefly, a seaman in the Royal Navy. He was reputed to be an escaped slave, a mythic figure of hope to those still in slavery, a strong, proud man who stole a boat and paddled away from chains and whips, still honored every year in the Bahamas, whether he was a real man, or a hoped-for hero of cleverness and power who could surmount contemporary problems, like Anglo-Saxon "Jack" tales, or the stories about "Brer Rabbit" who always won indirectly by wits.

Besides, doesn't it make a better story than the Yoruba word of the Egungun cult *gensinconnu,* meaning "wearers of masks," to name the annual festival Junkanoo for John Canoe?

Finally, what further lies in store for Alan Lewrie? The peaceful end of an active commission in the Bahamas, of course, which takes him to 1789. But just a few years later, there was war with France, a naval war which dragged on until 1815, the highest fruition of sailing ships and square-rigger warfare—The Great Age of Sail.

Would the Admiralty not consider themselves fortunate to have the services of such a splendid (on paper, at least) sea dog? Or, in this case, ram-cat?

Will he ever live that sobriquet down? Will Caroline ever suspect its true origin? Will Arthur Ballard influence Alan Lewrie, or, will Lewrie corrupt Ballard, when next they cross each others' hawse?

As we used to say down in Memphis to tease the 10 P.M. report on "Action News-5" . . . stay tuned.